A LAND OF MYTH AND MAGIC

Emma Bradley

For every reader
who dreams of forever home,
you're welcome in mine.

ISBN: 978-1-915909-32-9

Avenia's Forest
Dragnar
New Kirenia
Eadil Tree
East Wood
Rikler Mines
Jakiris
Apexlonia
Forlaith
Orlain
Harvest Grounds
Mik's
Spice Mines
Carahdyl
Sanctuary
Lake Isles
Morlan
Hamlin's
Blancastel
Great Tree
Tydlwood
Branphalia
Sepora
Kirelonia
Adretia

CHAPTER ONE

The suns rose above strange white-trunked trees, both orbs glowing brighter until they cast the swathes of forest in a steady heat.

Wedged into a small gap between an enormous white tree trunk and a scratchy bush with tiny purple leaves, Neri faced a new day with the urge to panic rising in her chest and clawing at her throat.

After the firebird appeared to her in the cursed forest and beckoned her into a whirl of ash and flame, its sorcery had transported her to another land entirely. The dark trees of the cursed forest had disappeared and given way to the towering spectres of the forest that surrounded her, but while Niall had been beside when she walked into the flame, he was nowhere to be seen on the other side of it.

Glancing around to ensure she was definitely alone, Neri wiped a hand over her face and seethed through her teeth. The skin on her palm was marked shiny pink, but although it prickled when touched, it was surprisingly pain-free when left to the mercies of the fresh air. Flexing her fingers around the stiffness, she eased her way out of her hiding pace.

A sweet, fragrant breeze filled her lungs and she dropped her head back as she breathed it in deep.

If I really have somehow passed through the cursed wood from the east to the westlands, then everything the Governance were hunting me for is true.

Scuffles echoed in nearby bushes, with the odd swoop

of a bird rustling above or the whining buzz of some insect, but in terms of other folk she was still utterly alone.

As she stood and surveyed the forest around her, self-preservation flickered.

I survived nineteen winterspans without Niall, even after Mamma and Gramma died. I can survive the rest without him too.

The breeze turned fierce and whipped her brown hair around her face. Despite the heat from the suns bearing down, the weather seemed to have swift moods, so her short trousers and almost sleeveless shirt didn't fare well against it. With a steadying breath and a weary shiver, Neri started to walk.

Unlike the cursed forest, or any other woodland she'd ever been through, the ground wasn't a mass of undergrowth and briars. Springy moss in hues of dusky pink and faded green softened each step, but she couldn't see any sign of settlements or dwellings, no footprints or signs of tamed animals passing through.

She'd called to Niall for ages after the flames turned to ash and burst away in the wind, but not a single echo of him answered her. She had nothing useful to trade in her pack either besides a blade, which she would need to keep for safety, a blanket and a few half-burned down candles. She had Hamlin's book and watch along with his letter, the only mementos she had of the mentor who had taught her candle making and died giving her time to run. She had Emelyn's book, a gift she wouldn't dare part with.

Her stomach growled as she walked, the swoop of hunger sickness forcing a dizzying flush across her cheeks. Niall had carried their food and now she regretted not being more sensible.

The pale forest with its springy ground stretched in

every direction, but the sound of bubbling water echoed nearby. She rounded a crop of rock and found a stream cutting through the trees.

Crouched at the bank, she dipped a fingertip in the water. It was clear, free of sediment and debris, and it smelled of nothing. She licked the liquid from her finger tentatively and huffed in quiet relief when she found it was water.

She spooned handfuls to her lips before turning her attention to some bushes nearby, thick with rich brown leaves and some questionable pink berries.

She picked one and held it up in front of her face.

"Don't eat those."

The masculine voice was little more than a breathy rumble, but she recognized it all the same. She spun around and searched between the trees but saw nothing and nobody.

"Niall?" She called out. "Where are you?"

Silence and the distant call of a bird answered her. She considered the possibility that she was turning addle-headed, but it didn't help her with the immediate issue of being stuck in an unfamiliar forest, possibly in an unfamiliar land entirely.

"I'm here." Niall's voice echoed stronger. "I thought I'd have time to explain but there was none."

Relief spilled over into frustration. Neri's chest tightened and tears burned her eyes. She let the berry drop from her fingers and clenched her fists at her sides instead.

"I thought we'd been separated or you got stuck behind. Where are you?"

Rustling came from nearby but still Niall didn't appear.

"If I come out it might be a bit of a shock," he said. "Finn warned you about me, remember? He said there were things you didn't know that might change your mind. I didn't get the chance to tell you."

The low, bittersweet tone only added to her frenzied worry. Thoughts swelled and raced, the idea of the past few days being part of a joke or some dream still resonating.

"What do you mean? Tell me what? Will you at least talk to me face to face?"

Niall didn't answer so she started walking along the edge of the bank beside the stream. After a few mere paces her senses swirled with the overpowering scent him, like cake-spice. Her eyelids fluttered closed before she could stop them, the smell somehow more potent than she'd ever known before.

"If I show you what I am now will you at least try to stay calm?"

She whirled around but saw nothing except shadow amongst the trees. In her panic-fuelled frustration she hadn't considered that Niall might be hurt.

"I'm anything but calm so you might as well stop mucking about. If you're hurt I can help you."

She stared as a shape formed beside a nearby tree, the dark wisp of shadow that made up a man's form stark against the white of the trunk.

Neri's mouth dropped open and Niall sighed.

"This is what I am."

Where skin and fine dark hairs should have been forming his arm, there was only shadow. The imprint of features hung in darkness, mere swirls and lines of spectral being.

Neri reached out to touch the outline of his forearm but he pulled away from her too fast.

"What is this?" The words came out as a hiss.

Niall took a step back to put more distance between

them, but Neri could read the tormented expression from the harsh lines on his shadowed face.

She raised a hand to her forehead and looked up into the black of Niall's pupils, only shown by the spectral pale hue of the outsides. His irises, sometimes brown and often going dark in his angry moods, were now non-existent.

"They call us shades, shadow-folk," he said. "You teased me about it before, remember? Turns out you were right. We're not as welcome as some but I can usually survive on my own. It changes a lot."

Niall's bitterness brought a swell of anxiety back to Neri's chest. She sighed and pushed her good hand out on instinct, her fingers sliding into shadow as she attempted to curl them around his arm. Warmth tingled with such ferocity that she almost believed her skin was burning. The sensation numbed after a second to a satisfying throb and she looked up into Niall's eyes, which were angled away from her.

"It changes a good many things," she admitted. "Probably all stuff I don't understand. But it doesn't change how I feel."

Her voice wavered and Niall snorted in disbelief, the sound rippling past her on the whistle of the wind.

"I do know where we've come out at least," he said. "I'll take you to a safe place for now where you can rest and I can figure out what to do. I thought… it wasn't meant to happen this way. It was a mistake to bring you here."

Neri latched her fingers into his wrist and tried to curb the return of the warm connection stroking her skin.

"Well you did bring me here. I'm not going to run off screaming to the hills because you've lost, I don't know, a bit of body matter or whatever."

She took the echo of his low chuckle for the simple

blessing it was.

"A bit of body matter, that's how you see it? You'll soon change your mind. We need to walk a fair way yet so we should get moving."

He moved his 'matter' away from her and Neri felt the loss of it, not only the disappearance of the warmth but what it represented. Folding her arms across her chest, she gave him the best withering look she could muster when she was shivering against the freezing wind. She eyed his shadow, unable to see any sense of clothing but no shivering either.

He gave her one final once over and set off without another word.

All too fast the warmth of the day beamed down, the heat strong despite the increasingly vicious wind. Neri's clothing gave no protection against the elements as she followed Niall with her teeth chattering and her bones shaking from exhaustion.

Despite the fierce weather and the darkness of Niall's shadowed form some paces in front, something about the surroundings lifted her heart with an unfamiliar sense of freedom.

She finally had no Governance chasing her, and Niall clearly knew where he was going. He would be able to find them food most likely and her stomach growled in agreement.

Left alone with her chaotic thoughts, she remembered the day they first met and the night Hamlin had died. Niall had been striding through woodland back then too without once looking back, exactly like he was doing now.

She distracted herself from fears by avoiding stones, briars and roots in her path, until Niall stopped up ahead a long while later. So focused on her footing, she nearly missed the ground dropping away in front of her. She stumbled to a halt and stared down into a massive ravine below. She inched away from the cliff edge and slumped her back against the trunk of the nearest tree.

In the full light of day without the shade of the trees, Niall's shadow was an almost solid shape, his facial features and the lines of his body vague outlines beneath the surface.

"Are you okay to continue on?" he asked.

Her stomach was threatening mutiny and she couldn't stop shivering from the cold, but she took a deep breath, pushed all her aches and grumbles down deep, and nodded.

The silence continued as they left the trees behind and walked down a steep path that wound along the edge of the ravine. Neri focused all her attention and effort on her footing, the path little more than a groove in the rock.

By the time they arrived at the short widening of the rock that acted as a resting place, her head swam with dizziness. She stopped beside Niall to stare at a sheer drop that continued on down a short way to a glistening lake below.

"I don't believe in prophecies like most folk here," Niall said.

Neri lifted her head in surprise. He hadn't said a word to her the whole way and now he was talking about prophecies.

He stared off toward the skies and she took the chance to sneak a good look at him. His rugged face was fuzzy beneath the imprint of darkness but somehow the lack of bulk or angles made him look more ethereal.

Realising she hadn't said anything, Neri then knew she couldn't think of anything to respond with anyway.

"I'm bringing you with me because I want to send you

back to a proper life," he added. "You should have stayed behind. The sanctuary would have kept you safe enough and I shouldn't have dragged you into any of this."

Neri guessed his words weren't supposed to sound cruel or accusing but she couldn't help the ire that sparked inside her.

"Stayed behind with the Governance?" she asked, her tone icy. "Spent a life waiting for them to round me up like they did to Emelyn, or until they sent more traitors like Eva in to root us out? Sitting on my own making candles while wondering where you were, if you were safe or dead, playing house with Ma and games with Emelyn forever? The Governance were after me. They wanted me. That path through the cursed forest only opened because of the feather I had."

She drew in a sharp breath, willing herself to calm down before she continued.

"I don't know how much of this is down to you. Perhaps if I'd not come with you, the Governance would never have found me. But the firebird did. If that was all real, it would have found me with or without you."

She folded her arms as his shade form darkened and he turned his head away from her.

"Besides, *you're* the one that asked me to come with you," she insisted. "Then when it doesn't go the way you want, you think you can blame your cooling feelings on me not wanting to hang around. Just throw me back into the Governance's clutches instead, really thoughtful of you."

Fury cascaded off her tongue before she recognised the signs of him baiting her. His attempts to push her away were working.

With a heavy sigh, she pressed the heels of both hands

to her eyes. Peeking through her fingers a moment later, she watched as Niall opened his pack.

He had no answer for her. No comfort.

She wanted to shake him and rattle his bones, assuming he still had any in his shadow form, until he gave her some kind of emotion, anything to show he still cared.

He didn't look at her as he extracted a clawed spike from his pack and a long length of rope, digging the spike into the dirt and curling the rope around a tree root protruding out of the ground.

"Do you want to go first?" he asked. "It's a fair way down. Have you ever rope-scaled before?"

She stared at the rope, then at the drop. The rope wasn't anywhere near long enough to go all the way down, and a jolt of hysteria made her laugh.

"No, not many sheer drops where I come from."

Niall might have grimaced but she couldn't be sure if the flicker of movement was expression or just the natural curling of shadow.

"I can take you if you can bear to be close to me."

He took a firm hold of the rope with one hand and wrapped his arm around the end as he turned to face her.

Neri noticed the flicker in his black eyes, a shiver of emotion that disappeared as fast as it had appeared. Her intention to be angry with him melted in that instant and she stepped forward. Curling her arms about his neck took all her resolve. The warmth that zinged from his being to her skin teased at her senses and she wondered if she should ask how her touch felt to him in his new form.

The worry that she would sail straight through him raced in her mind as, in one agile move, Niall hooked his free arm around her waist and took a step back. The heat of his spectral form solidified around her, his embrace becoming weighty.

Before she could protest the cliff edge rushed past her eyes in a swirl of breath-stealing wind. Every time she tried to inhale she got a nose full of choking cold air, and her gut lurched as the ground rushed up to meet them.

Niall circled his arm in one swift movement to dislodge the rope and the spike. He bent his knees on impact, landing on the ground light footed and upright. Neri crumpled as her feet hit the ground and rolled over, clutching at her leg.

She sat up and sucked the air through her teeth in big gasps, half from breathlessness and half due to pain. With tentative fingers she inspected the skin on her knee and found a wound split open with blood oozing out. Queasy at the sight, she looked to Niall as he lassoed the end of the rope, curling it in the air with grace as it fell into a neat coil on the ground. He stowed it back in his pack and turned to where she sat.

She recognised the flicker in his eyes, the hint of his mouth curving in worry beneath the shadow, but dampness from the grass was seeping through the seat of her short trousers distracted her.

"Does it hurt?" Niall asked, pointing to her knee.

She wasn't sure whether to laugh it off or to burst into tears.

"It'll be alright in a moment. Could be worse, I could have broken it, or both."

She lifted her head and glanced away from the source of the pain. A large crescent of dark brown-grey rocks surrounded them in rising escarpments, the lake in front of them shadowed until it turned to shimmering silver under the rising suns. She struggled to her feet and limped to the edge of it, sitting on the edge to dunk her legs in. The water swilled up to her thighs and soothed some of the pain in her knee. She stared at her reflection, her brown eyes dull and lidded with weariness, her face still streaked with dirt.

"How can the rope extend like that?" she asked.

She hoped her curiosity might draw Niall into some kind of interaction, anything to draw her mind away until the pain dulled fully.

"You wouldn't believe it if I told you."

Neri rolled her eyes and tilted forward to peer at her knee through the water ripples.

"Humour me."

Niall's silence resonated ever louder. When she pulled her legs out of the water, Niall knelt down with a pot of light blue gunk and began to apply it to the cut. His shadowy fingers wisped over her leg with gentle precision, that warmth that zinged when he touched her making her insides flutter. Even with his moodiness, she welcomed the contact.

"We should set off," he said. "We can't afford to lose any time and it'll be dark soon."

The moment she was on her feet with her pack shouldered, Niall led the way around the edge of the lake toward a gap in the cliffs.

Neri wanted to ask questions, about the world, about his new form, but she couldn't think of a single way to phrase it that might get her an answer.

The crescent of cliffs soon lay behind them and a slope led down to vast flat plains of green. Low-hanging trees grew with spindled dark trunks and pearlescent petals in varying pale shades of red, blue, green, purple, more colours than Neri could count in such dazzling sunlight. Tiny yellow flowers sprung from the earth and low-lying, gnarled branches snaked through the grass without leaves or a visible trunk.

"We can make the edge of Forlaith forest before nightfall," Niall said. "Folk rarely go that close so it should give us some safety to rest."

That appeared to be it for conversation when he turned and set off around the edge of the lake. Neri sighed and limped after him.

They stopped briefly here and there but she couldn't judge how long they had been walking for, and the vast landscape didn't change the further they walked. With her head down to forge on against the growing pains, she only saw the carousel of fertile green grass underfoot. Being alone with her thoughts didn't give her much comfort and doubt began to creep in over whether they'd survive to wherever they were supposed to be going.

They saw the odd wanderer or group but Niall noticed them in the far distance every time and kept a large gap between them and others.

Neri wished she could ask him the inevitable questions, like how much he actually knew about the west, how far their destination was and what dangers she might need to watch out for.

The thought of actually having reached the fabled westlands she'd grown up hearing far-fetched tales about kept her mind dancing with enough worry to while away the endless steps she had to take. Niall slowed his pace to accommodate but always stayed a few steps in front of her.

When he finally spoke she almost missed it.

"The rope is made from *Madil* venom. Think of it like an elasticated web."

The suns were already beginning to dim, their glare not so dazzling any longer, but that meant it getting ever colder, and she didn't want to add elasticated webs to her list of worries.

"Oh."

She refrained from asking what a *Madil* was because the mention of venom didn't sound positive. She was sure nobody had ever mentioned any creature by that name to her before, another suggestion she was somewhere entirely 'other'.

By the time the suns disappeared and turned the sky to dusky purple, Neri noticed the edge of a forest on the horizon. Niall seemed to be making a beeline for it and she rubbed her eyes in tired amazement as thousands of tiny lights began to glow between the trees. One moment the darkness loomed and the shadows crept, then suddenly uncountable glowing orbs cast a pale blue echo of light over them.

"We'll stop here." Niall dropped his pack on the ground. "No getting any closer. You need to sleep."

Neri stopped beside him, noting the constant, uneasy glances he cast toward the forest and its ethereal glow. His unwillingness to move nearer to the edge of the trees made her even more curious about what dwelt inside.

"Why can't we get closer?" she asked.

She didn't expect an answer but he surprised her.

"There are things in there that stop folk from coming out again."

Fear clenched in her chest but she couldn't find the energy to focus on it, too busy struggling to get her body down to the ground. Her limbs buzzed with soreness and her knee had swollen past the point of fully bending it. She hit the ground with a thud and hissed at the pain.

Niall flicked a look at her then at her knee, but on seeing no fresh blood he returned to watching the forest again.

"What causes the lights?" she asked.

"Some say it's *aerie* light, but rumour is there are flowers in there that cause the glow."

Neri pulled her blanket from her pack and shuffled to sit on top of it. Niall disappeared toward a cluster of tall rocks without a word, but she could see him gathering something from the branches of a tree growing there. When he returned, he dropped several round fruits bigger than her palm on her lap, the waxy skin smooth, shining and dark blue.

"Here, it's not much but it'll stave off the hunger," he said. "Peel them and eat the insides only, not the skin or the rind."

Before she could offer to help, Niall had some gathered wood in a pile and a flint-stick in hand. Moments later, a flame ignited and Neri flinched.

Echoes of the Governance screaming behind her and the hot brush of air from the firebird's flames filled her mind, the memories clutching around her. She closed her eyes tight and breathed, in and out, slow and steady, the way her gramma had taught her.

"Eat."

Niall's voice brought her eyes open again, the stern command anchoring her to the present. She pulled one of the fruits toward her and dug her nails into the skin. The insides were a lighter blue than the outside, or at least that's what they looked like in the flickering amber light of the fire now gaining strength.

After eating, Neri piled up the peel leftover from her dinner and curled up on the blanket with her bad knee jutting out to stop it catching on the fabric.

Niall lay on a blanket of his own with his back to her, a clear sign he didn't want to talk. In a way, she couldn't blame him. In another way, this was all his idea in the first place.

When sleep refused to come despite her exhaustion, she watched the mass of stars in a desperate attempt to avoid her thoughts, but they circled her mind all the same. Her knee throbbed and any movement on the hard ground sent screaming pain through every inch of her, but she didn't once make a sound. She closed her eyes as her mind flirted with sleep, dreams of things wisping over her arms filling her head, until a gentle tinkling sound echoed through the otherwise silent night.

Lie on the hard ground in pain, or distract myself by having the quickest of looks a bit closer to the forest.

She managed to get herself balanced on her hands and her good knee, rocking back and forth to ease the rigid stiffness of her muscles. Sheer determination coordinated her balance as she clambered to her feet and tiptoed across to Niall's still form.

He snuffled as she limped nearer, but his deep breathing suggested he was asleep. She would take the quickest of looks, a tiny stroll to ease her limbs a little. She would keep him in sight the whole time to ensure he wasn't left unguarded.

Neri crept toward the forest, bemused when the stretch of grass seemed to shrink to beckon her in. She reached the edge of the trees and paused with her hand settling onto the trunk of the one nearest.

Niall had told her not to go near the forest yet here she was on the border of it.

Did I really walk that far that quickly?

She wanted to look back and check on Niall, but the forest drew her attention with its eerie glows and enticing music.

Dusky turquoise lights glimmered around the edges of

spectral grey trunks, highlighting a carpet of flowers on the ground. She took a few tentative steps, determined to stepping on any, then bent low from the hips to avoid irritating her knee.

The pale blooms curled up to meet her touch as she brushed her fingertips through the air above them. Shimmering bluebells seemed to be chiming and sprigs of *liliam* climbed up the nearest trees with big fragrant flowers.

She picked a bluebell and a spring of *liliam*, knowing that if all else failed and she woke in her bed in the sanctuary, or somewhere other entirely, she would at least have a souvenir to prove whether her journey there was real or not.

With a hazy thought for Niall, she glanced over her shoulder.

The edge of the forest and the grass beyond were now very far away. Her eyelids hung heavy after a day of excruciating walking, and the bluebells chimed a lullaby that sounded so soothing. Her body sagged, the memory of knee pain hazy until she felt a tug on her wrist. In a daze she stumbled over the blooms to follow the pressure.

The sweet, oppressive fragrance filling her nose lifted in one swift moment and left her gulping fresh breaths.

She opened her eyes wearily.

Strange, I don't ever remember closing them.

CHAPTER TWO

Neri blinked away the dregs of unnatural slumber as Niall untied a rope from her wrist. She had no idea how it got there or when but hazarded a guess that Niall trusted her less than she'd assumed. Memories swilled of dreams that things were sliding over her arms and she clutched the delicate blooms in her hands.

The whites of Niall's eyes had almost disappeared amid his shadow form, the shape of him only visible because of the dying fire behind him. Neri glanced back to find the forest now deceptively far in the distance, as if she'd not walked more than a few steps from the fire at all.

The moment the rope was back in his pack, Niall sat on his blanket with his arms around his knees and faced away from her.

Neri slipped the blooms into the small pouch at the front of her pack, her heart sinking. If he was determined to push her away before, he would be furious with her now. Not just for disobeying him and putting herself in danger, but for making things more difficult. She didn't dare say a word to him as she lay down on her blanket with her back to him.

The fears of him leaving her behind swelled, but she stayed in place until light started to dawn on the horizon.

She got to her feet with great effort and eyed her stiff, swollen knee. The scab had crusted over again but without constant cleansing it would soon get infected. Niall gave knee one look as he kicked aside the remnants of their fire, and her none at all. As she packed her blanket, she made a decision.

They would reach civilisation at some point. He would either cool off after the worry was over, or he would continue pushing her away. If he wanted to get back to some kind of life there without her, then she would either find a way to make one of her own, or find a way home. The Governance would still be hunting for her, but she could get back to the sanctuary and hide, or get far away from England.

Niall set off and skirted around the edge of the forest, keeping his pace slow as she limped behind. It took all her effort not to seethe through her teeth when she stepped on a stone or uneven ground, but he never once looked back. The day passed in a rising blaze of heat and a fast waning of it, until Neri was sure she'd either get badly sunburnt or feverish from cold. She kept her blanket around her shoulders, but it flapped and fluttered in the wind until it played havoc with her already unsteady balance and she had to remove it again.

By the time they reached a wide track packed with dirt, she'd already shed a handful of silent tears. Each time she wiped them away, determined not to let Niall see them.

The track looked like it served as a main road, the earth rutted with thin wheel lines and hoofprints, but Neri only gritted her teeth and soldiered on. The hard played on her joints and soon the desolate crushing reality of the situation swamped around her.

They passed the odd few folk, some with pale skin tinged with an under-hue like moonlight and others with bronzed skin and shimmering hair of varying burnished shades. Niall didn't pay them any heed but the day waned into evening and Neri wondered if she dared ask how long it was to their destination.

Niall slowed his pace to allow her to keep up but now the pain took precedence enough for her not to notice him. All her thoughts focused on taking the next agonising step and then the one after that in case he decided to leave her behind.

"We'll stop here." Niall slowed to a halt. "We've made good progress and should reach the settlement tomorrow."

She managed to lift her swimming head. The path they followed dipped through a forest on top of a hill and overlooked a settlement some miles away full of little brown huts.

As Niall laid out his blanket, Neri found the nearest tree and used it to inch down onto her own blanket some metres away from him.

She watched him but he didn't move to start a fire, standing with his gaze trained on the track. She wondered what could have him so tense, the set of his shoulders visible even in the waning daylight.

Until he vanished.

One moment he was there, then gone. She tried to sit up and squeaked in pain. He'd left her. She could barely stand again, and he'd left her.

The moment she heard approaching footsteps, she sagged against the tree. So many times she'd been running, from the men who'd come to search her grandmother's flat. From Amis and his men that killed Hamlin. From the Governance for the past few weeks. She was so, so tired of running.

Two figures approached, but she barely had the willing to lift her head.

"That's some wound." A woman's voice reached her.

She forced her head up and shrugged as two women, both dressed in sturdy boots and thick cloaks, stopped a few metres away.

"I'm unlucky," she said.

The women exchanged a look and Neri eyed them both, curiosity sparking. The woman closest held a long, thin blade in one hand, purple curls tumbling loose over her shoulders. Her yellow-haired companion also held a blade, but her eyes narrowed a moment before both women whirled around.

"Been a while," Niall said. "I take it I'm still welcome among you?"

The astonishment that he hadn't left her, that he'd apparently been hiding himself in the shadows to see who approached them, filled Neri with relief.

Moments before the yellow-haired woman sheathed her blade at her hip and ran across the grass to throw her arms around Niall's neck.

Neri stared, her insides twisting as Niall hesitated. Then he returned the woman's embrace. Neri's pulse began to thud, her anxiety swilling as she realised that the purple-haired woman was turning back to look down at her.

Was this who Niall wanted to get back here for? Was I only meant to be a way through for him?

She couldn't stay. With no idea where she was going to go on her injured leg or what dangers might be out there, she wriggled onto her good side and clawed at the tree trunk until she was swaying on her feet.

"You're not going to get far on that knee," the purple-haired woman said, a knowing smile quirking on her lips. "We've been following you since sunsdown and you're about to drop. I'm Cori, and that's my sister Hareili. We're… friends of Niall's."

Neri held onto the tree for dear life, knowing she had to find some way of getting her balance so she could walk away. Niall might not even bother to stop her. It might take some yelling, but he'd soon agree she wasn't worth the trouble of guiding. Not now he clearly had what he wanted.

All eyes were on her now though, and she couldn't find enough strength or spirit to begin walking unaided.

"I'll fix your leg if you like," Cori offered. "That's an awful heal, no offense to whoever patched it."

Niall snorted at the insult. "What's the trade? We don't have much."

"No trade. Don't be strange."

Hareili beamed up at him. "You know we never have trades between us, never have done. It's a beautiful sight to see you back again."

Getting no answer from Neri, Cori brought a small wooden pot out of the pack slung over her back and crouched down.

"This will sting but it'll help." She glanced up, the salve already on her fingertips. "You don't look to clear-eyed either."

"She went into Forlaith and didn't think to bring anything other than what she's standing in," Niall said.

Even though she didn't know the girls, and being here had clearly flipped Niall's cruelty lever, Neri hoped they couldn't see her cheeks turning red. Hareili gave a similar noise of derision to Niall's earlier snort, and Neri knew in that moment she had a rival. Although given Niall's recent behaviour, she clearly had no claim on him after all.

She ignored the urge to cry and let her head drop back against the tree. As Cori slathered gunk onto her wound and a needling burn began, Neri focused on that pain instead of the crushing heartache inside. The sound of Hareili talking to Niall filled her ears, girlish excitement being replied to with amusement, familiarity and maybe even fondness.

"Niall always was crud with healing," Cori muttered.

Neri looked down. "So you know each other well then?"

Cori grimaced, glancing over her shoulder. Niall and Hareili didn't look like they'd notice a meteor hitting.

"I didn't," Cori admitted. "But Hareili used to. Then he disappeared. She thought he'd… you know what, not my place. The salve will help the wound but you should get proper rest. You look like you haven't eaten or slept properly in days."

Neri couldn't stem the wave of nausea washing through her chest. She watched Cori binding her knee with a clean line of fabric, but kept flicking looks up to see Hareili standing close to Niall, a hand on his arm or a more-than-friendly touch to his shoulder.

"I'll build the fire," Cori called over her shoulder to the others, then smiled down at Neri. "Want to give me a hand?"

Neri nodded. She'd lit fires in the vats many times back at Hamlin's and often went out for the firewood. Her knee ached but the stinging was gone thanks to Cori's salve, so she gathered enough firewood to take back with Cori and slumped awkwardly beside the pile. Cori held out a flint-stick to her and cast a critical eye over Neri's shivering limbs.

"Here, I've a spare cloak. How you've not frozen to a block I don't know. Light the fire and I'll fetch it."

Neri took the flint-stick and peered at it. The two rocks were pierced and tied together with a bit of rope. Inspecting the sides which were scored with strike marks, she looked up in time to see Hareili whisper something into Niall's ear.

He wasn't tense either with her, his body not a rigid column of shadow like it had been the last day or so.

This was what it was all about? Getting back here to her?

Cori had been on the edge of saying something telling and backed off, perhaps guessing that Niall had been keeping Neri sweet. Perhaps he'd even known she had some kind of affinity with the firebird and decided she was his only chance to get back to Hareili.

Warmth tingled in her fingertips. Before she could take up the flint stick in both hands, the one resting on the kindling sparked. She flinched away but the spark had caught the kindling and taken flame.

Neri stared at the unused flint-stick and shook her head. She must have shaken them without realizing.

"That was quick." Cori's impressed voice sounded beside her. "Is that your *ai-tan*?"

Neri shook her head. "My what?"

"Your gift, your element. We all have some small gift from our element don't we, some that can wield a bit of water or dry it, those who can move earth or sweep a gust of air for cleaning away the leaves. Is fire yours?"

Again Neri shook her head. She was sure that she hadn't done anything special, but none of this was anything normal. Even Niall's behaviour was unlike him. Unable to think of a long-term plan or any sense of safety, she gave Cori the honest answer.

"I don't know."

Cori eyed her for a moment, then clapped her hands loudly.

"Come and sit you two," she demanded. "It's rude to whisper in company."

Neri didn't want Niall and Hareili to sit with them. She

wanted to be alone. Niall had made it clear he had no intention of continuing their relationship despite the fancy promises he'd made before. He'd also mentioned that bringing her was a mistake.

Maybe he never truly thought I'd get here, or maybe he realised he needed me to get through the cursed forest.

Hareili hovered until Niall took his seat at the fire, then she settled right next to him. Neri focused on the fire. She wouldn't let him see he'd affected her as badly as he had. Cori at least seemed nice, enough to commandeer the conversation.

"So, what's changed since you've been away?" she asked, frowning. "The Lord of the Borderlands took Mindelan a winter after you disappeared, what was that eight winters ago now?"

Niall nodded to show he'd heard but didn't reply. Neri bit her lip. She didn't want to take any interest in this strange land because of him, but the tiny sliver of her that could push through the heartbreak was dying to ask questions. She'd never heard of any place called Mindelan, or the borderlands.

Cori rolled her eyes at Niall's moodiness and turned to Neri next.

"I won't ask any questions in case you don't want to answer them," she said with a grin. "So I shall tell you all about me instead. Not often I get to talk about myself. My little brother, Gyphur, does all the talking for an entire settlement combined."

Neri managed a small smile. "That suits me fine. Tell me all about you, where you're from, what you do, everything."

So Cori did. She talked about her family in the Morlan mountains, the underground dwelling she grew up in, the forests she roamed as a child, which Neri realised sounded exactly like the forest the firebird's magic had spat her out in. Cori seemed to somehow sense that Neri wasn't one of them, or at least sheltered and a long way from home, so she explained things as anecdotes without actually having to explain them outright. Warmed by the gesture, Neri repaid her in tiny smiles and thoughtful questions, to the point she managed to forget Niall's existence for a while.

"My biggest goal *was* to join the border guard," Cori groaned. "Then the Lord of the Borderlands took over and we're hearing bad things. So it will need to be the Jakirian guard instead."

"Which you should have wanted to join from the start," Hareili grumbled.

Cori rolled her eyes. "My sister is convinced my choice was treachery, but they have the best training techniques over there. Have you ever been to the borderlands?"

"No." Neri shook her head. "Can't say I have."

"Well it's meant to be imposing and cold, or the castle is at least, but I have to see it. Now, I think we should probably take turns to rest. Neri and I can take the first watch."

Neri nodded, although her heart sank. As much as Cori was saving her from a silent night of awkwardness with Niall for company, or worse Hareili, she was also throwing the two of them together.

Niall's made his feelings clear. She straightened her back despite the fact it was aching up a storm. *I'm sure whenever we get where we're going, there'll be time for a private cry before I find a way home.*

Assuming she could get home. With the others spending lifetimes searching for a way through the cursed forest, there was no guarantee a way back even existed.

She shuddered and pulled Cori's borrowed cloak tighter around her.

Hareili seemed to be hovering until Niall pulled out blankets and lay down with his back to them and the fire. Neri flinched as Hareili shot her a venomous look and copied him a metre or so away.

"She's always liked him." Cori veered close to whisper in Neri's ear. "Take no notice."

The words were barely there, no doubt to avoid being heard. Neri shrugged and leaned close enough to whisper back.

"Not my problem."

"You and him…?"

She shook her head. "We were briefly. He's made it clear it's a no since we got here."

Cori frowned, her amber eyes sparking in the firelight. Neri looked down at her knee, the throbbing increasing as she tried to get comfortable.

"He's an odd one," Cori said. "But I like you. Keep the cloak, no trade. We'll be off in the morning on our own errand but I wish you well."

Neri sighed. "Thanks. You're not so bad yourself."

A quiet chuckle later, they fell silent. After a while Neri tipped her head back and watched the stars dance across the dark skies, wondering about home.

Emelyn would be writing somewhere, assuming it was also night there. Ma would be knitting. Moonshine would be meditating most probably or trying to sort the cupboards while Ma wasn't looking. She didn't know them very well after so short a time with them, but she knew they were good folk.

And Finn, she hoped he was okay too, despite being a pain. He hadn't trusted her or been particularly kind, but he'd helped them in the end where it mattered.

Helped me so I ended up in this land with a man who no longer wants me now I'm not useful anymore.

When Cori stood and walked around the dying fire to wake the others for their turn, Neri refused to look their way. She settled on the hard, cold ground, wrapped Cori's cloak around her as best she could and closed her eyes.

If there was a way home, she'd take it. Or spend her life looking for it. But if Niall really was deserting her now he had what he wanted, then he didn't deserve her tears.

Silent and turned away from the others, Neri shed them anyway. She didn't sleep, forcing herself to go over potential plans instead. The moment soft daylight broke over them, she had made up her mind.

She would get to wherever Niall was taking her and find a way to rest and heal. Once she was strong again, she'd speak to folk and figure out a way to earn her keep. She'd learn all about them, their histories and their lore in the hope of finding another route home. Then she would go and find Emelyn, Ma and the others and insist they leave Governance territory for good.

She winced at the pain in her legs and hips, the cold of the night having settled into her bones despite Cori's cloak. The fire was out already and Cori and Hareili were gone. That left her alone with Niall again, but she didn't want to acknowledge him and stared around instead.

The night before they'd stopped after dark, but the morning light illuminated a small lake in a glade beneath the towering trees. The other side of the lake was the hill overlooking a small settlement of huts, and Neri soaked in the calming sound of water lapping. Her gaze zipped back and forth to watch the colourful birds swooping, and she eventually levered herself onto one elbow with an awkward grumble to see better.

A bird the size of a large cat with deep purple plumage took a nose-dive into the water and disappeared. Neri stared for several moments, but when the bird didn't surface she started to get to her feet.

"They're watellows, water birds." Niall's voice made her jump. "If you watch long enough he'll pop up again."

He nodded to the water but didn't look her way. Neri guessed he wanted to draw her attention away from him and any related discussions that might prove emotional or troublesome. Like why Hareili had left when she was so obviously obsessed with him.

She'd overheard most of their hushed whispers while lying awake and couldn't say for certain that Niall was as smitten as Hareili obviously was, but he had entertained her conversation after pushing Neri away.

A watellow bird resurfaced, whether the first she'd seen or another she couldn't tell, but lingering around wouldn't get her away from him and on the hunt for a way home.

She managed to sit up properly but grimaced to see her knee had swollen overnight. Using the tree to haul herself up, she wiped a hand across her clammy face. No way of telling if the damp warmth was leftover drizzle and dew from the night or sweat from a fever, but she could feel the rest of her body overheating from bone to blood.

She had to hold back the first few squeaks of agony as she attempted to put weight on her leg, but she shouldered her pack and limped forward.

Niall fell into step with her, walking slow to keep pace. He didn't tell her she should eat something and she didn't want to suggest they stop again, even though the hunger rumbled.

Each step sent jagged pain shooting up her body as the

morning passed into day, but Niall said nothing, not even when her stomach growled loud enough to frighten away any nearby beasts.

By the time she lifted her head to admit defeat and ask for a short rest, they were approaching another settlement, a large one cut into the edge of a towering cliff-line and surrounded by tall wooden walls.

Neri squinted, able to make out hints of green everywhere inside the settlement boundary, and a narrow, winding path of brown. It led right down to the gates from an enormous dwelling with shining white walls that glimmered in the sunslight, towering over all.

So focused on the sight in front of her, Neri stumbled and fell forward, only managing to keep her knee from hitting the ground by twisting and wrenching one of her arms badly as she landed.

The all-over pain had grown so strong it forced everything into a blur. She thought she could hear hooves approaching but didn't bother to get up.

Niall didn't want her. He was doing this out of guilt, he'd made that clear.

"Finn warned you about me, remember?"

His words danced in her head until a haze of shining white filled her vision, radiating warmth and an aura of calm. Strong hands grasped her waist and someone rearranged her legs around that glowing warmth, as if lifting her onto a glowing horse.

Reaching forward with uncoordinated fingers, Neri felt silken strands of mane.

Definitely a horse.

The horse's coat touched against her bare legs with unbelievable softness, similar to downy rabbit fur, and shone as an iridescent moon in the dark world that made up Neri's half-conscious mind.

Unfamiliar voices echoed around her and then the blurriness focused a little as they passed through the settlement gates. Rambling dwellings of wood and stone swept past, and a round of flaming torches that mingled into one disorientating carousel. She blinked hard and lifted her head.

Thick vines crept along the ground and up the sides of the dwellings with large, colourful flowers bursting in bloom. An overwhelming scent of *liliam* wafted around her and Neri couldn't stem the overflow of nostalgia.

She wished to be back in the sanctuary with the garden downstairs and Dog by her side to comfort her. The thought of Dog hurt her chest more than the injuries hurt her legs but the choked cry she let out could have been real or imaginary.

The horse came to a stop and Neri gave it a dull pat as somebody helped her off. She assumed the same someone carried her, strong arms conveying her along until they set her down on something soft.

She murmured vague mutterings of gratitude, even though she wasn't sure if anyone was around her anymore. She tried to focus on the sounds around her but they echoed without any discernible form. Then the memory of Niall distancing himself from her filled her head and she let herself drop down into the blissful dark of unconsciousness.

CHAPTER THREE

Neri's mind danced and swirled in and out of consciousness. Now and then someone would touch her with a point of warmth or a slight prickle, and she burbled the odd thank you while swilling in unjointed sensations, until her full consciousness emerged.

She opened her eyes and huffed out a breath. Wriggling slowly to test her aches and pains, she managed to sit up. Her knee ached but the swelling and the fabric binding were both gone, and so was the haziness of whatever fever she'd succumbed to. Bewildered by the cascade of memories she couldn't quite piece together, she stared at the large room spread out around her. Wooden beamed ceilings towered above, and the greystone floor was broken by a square bathing pool sunk into the centre of the room. She smoothed her hands over the bedding of softest muted green and eyed an open archway in the far wall. It led to an outdoor deck made of white stone that shimmered in the sunslight.

"How is your knee?"

Neri turned at the soft voice. A willowy woman sat on a small wooden stool in the far corner of the room. Much like the stone outside, the woman had an iridescent glow around her, serene yet confident, long white hair left loose around her an ageless face and wise eyes.

Neri looked down at her knee again. The swelling was gone and now only an ugly scab and a large patch of blackish bruising remained. She moved the leg back and

forth with caution and bent it.

"Much better, thank you."

"We have good healers," the lady said. "You are in Jakirian palace and the settlement of the Jakiris. You are guest of the Jakida and staying in her home. I am Zel, her advisor. Your guide is also currently resting here."

Jakiris. Her memory flickered.

Niall had told her he was from Jakiris before they travelled through the cursed forest.

Zel stood up and came to stand by the bed, clasping her hands in front of her as Neri leaned forward.

"Where's Niall?"

Zel smiled and settled in one fluid motion to sit on the bed like they were the oldest of friends.

"He's here, resting and safe. He carried you and sat with you until the healers were sure you would heal."

Neri turned her face to the door, almost expecting it to open or for Niall to have snuck in with his silent steps while she was distracted.

No Niall.

She sighed and allowed her forehead to fall into her palms.

"What an absolute mess."

Her mumbling carried through her fingers and she raised her head when Zel chuckled.

"Shades are much misunderstood," she said.

"Shades? So that's really what he is?"

Zel nodded. "They come to be from men who wish away their emotions, although some can be born. They're said to feel nothing, often making ideal mercenaries."

Neri bit her lip as the burn of tears gathered at the corners of her eyelids.

Niall couldn't help who he was, he'd admitted that

much. Clearly his body on the other side of the cursed forest had emotions and he'd lived them to the full, but here he didn't seem to have any remaining. In that one moment of crossing through she'd become a burden he had acquired in a thrall of emotion that he could no longer feel.

She wiped away the tears that started trails down her cheeks as Zel continued.

"Niall's *ama,* or mamma you might call it in other parts of the land, she wasn't a shade. She gave birth and left him with a guardian in the faraway parts of the westlands. For a long while, nobody knew what had happened to him until he turned up with you yesterday."

The see-saw of emotions zigzagged and Neri groaned.

Hareili knew him though, and Cori. Possibly more than I ever will.

Grappling with all the new information, she hooked onto the only thing she felt safe in asking.

"How do you know all this?"

Zel's smile softened and she leaned forward to pat Neri's hand. Neri forced herself not to pull away despite not wanting contact with this woman. Zel knew so much and while she wanted answers, she couldn't tell whether they would be the truth.

"I know a great many things. For now, let me reassure you that you are safe here. I am well versed in what goes on around here and I make it my duty to see to the good of the folk."

The Westlands. Neri's insides twisted. *It's all true.*

She sat up straighter and swung her healing leg over the edge of the bed. She needed to eat and figure out where exactly to start looking for a way home. These folk weren't her friends or her family, and Niall clearly didn't want her around any longer. Her only option was to find a way back through to the east then get to Emelyn and the others.

"I can't explain your destiny or Niall's," Zel added. "I only know what I have foreseen as prophecy and this land has existed a long time, but the great bloodlines that were once charged to care for it have started a war. The two halves of the land are split down the middle by the cursed forest, and the bridges have long since broken, both physical and social."

Neri huffed. "Of course there's a war. There's always a war, anywhere I go."

Zel stayed silent a moment, watching Neri test her knee. Then she sighed.

"You may well be right. But I long ago foresaw that one would come who could re-join the two halves. We do not yet know who this will be, but there is something untold about you. For all we know you may yet play a part."

Neri shook her head as Zel stood and walked toward the door.

"I doubt that. Niall's made his standpoint clear, so now I need to find a way home and get back to my folk."

Zel turned back when she reached the door.

"You will find your knee good enough to walk on but perhaps no over-exertion for a few days. We had your clothing removed and cleaned, but you'll find something more fitting for the time being hanging over there."

Zel's nose wrinkled ever so slightly at the mention of Neri's clothing as she pointed to something hanging by the stone deck.

Neri waited for a few moments after Zel closed the door, then eased to her feet. Although her knee was still stiff, it didn't hurt any longer and she took great pleasure in pulling on a dress made from fabric that felt like soft fur fitted at the chest and floating to her knees. She couldn't remember the last time she'd had any need to wear a dress, but it would have to do.

Someone had cleaned various cuts and scrapes on her hands too, and she inspected the handiwork while thinking of Cori. Perhaps Niall had already gone to seek out Hareili instead.

Pushing aside the stab in her chest at the thought, she went out onto the deck and lifted her face to the wind. The side of the palace overlooked a steep, rocky hill that fell down into the green of the valley below, but the wind seemed to reach just about everywhere in the west.

I'll have to be careful here. Be friendly but make no promises. Offer nothing.

Her self-preservation surfaced and the thought of her pack drove her inside. She found it next to the bed, and a quick sort through proved that all the contents were still intact. They'd even left the collection of magic flowers she'd taken from Forlaith forest nestled on the top that wafted scents and sounds. She palmed the sprig of *liliam* and held it to her nose, allowing the comforting scent to surround her.

She stood there until her stomach rumbled loud enough to draw her attention, along with an overwhelming wave of hunger gnawing at her insides.

Time to find the kitchens.

She considered taking her pack with her, but if they wanted to take her things they would have done so already, and she liked being free of it weighing down her shoulders. After a quick search, she found a small gap between the wooden headboard of the bed and the wall where she could hide everything. As she settled her pack in its new place, she took one of the tiny flowers from Forlaith forest in her hand, the delicate scent curling through the air as she left her room.

The hallway outside was long and lit with flickering firelight on the walls. She walked slowly, counting doors so she could find her way back and admiring the scenery through the open archways as the fresh air danced through. She hadn't thought to pull her boots on and quickened her step as her feet scuffed over the cold stone floor.

A door opened as she passed it and a woman hurried out. Dressed in deep red fabric and pale gold, the lady gasped as they almost collided. Neri eyed the woman's fiery red hair, unnerved to see the strands twisting and curling on their own.

The woman huffed and Neri uttered a meek apology before rushing on her way. She rounded a corner and came to a halt as they scuffed through warm, dry fluff instead of the cold, hard stone. She stared down at the embroidered runner beneath her feet and wriggled her toes against the russet threads.

A loud clanging noise bounced along the hallway, the sound of something kitchen-related and heavy rolling over and over with a mischievous *bong-bong-bong*.

Halfway through turning to go toward the sound, her gaze swept over the vast doorway leading out of the palace, and to a solitary figure standing near the bottom of white stone steps. The steps led to a wide, tree-lined lane tumbling down toward the settlement gates. Several dwellings occupied the lane, with hints of other lanes branching off visible between the trees, but beyond that her attention was fixed on the man in front of her.

Niall stood against a nearby tree trunk, his shadow form flickering as he smoked a pipe that emitted strange swirls of blue and purple. She hadn't seen him smoke before, not that she could remember.

More proof that I don't know him at all.

She scuffed her feet on the steps as she walked down in case he hadn't noticed her approaching, and he turned his head in her direction as she drew close, the white dots of his eyes darkening as they roved over her. She wondered if he was checking whether she was okay, but he didn't ask or give any sign that her health had worried him.

She forced herself to smile, although she felt more like punching him.

"Thank you for bringing me here safe."

Niall shrugged a shoulder and took another pull of the pipe.

"Have they told you more about what's supposed to happen next?" he asked.

Neri shook her head. "Vague hints about prophecies and stuff I didn't understand."

When he didn't respond, choosing instead to inspect his pipe, she tried again to force a reaction.

"It feels like I'm dreaming, like none of this is really happening."

When he didn't reply, Neri opened her hand. The sprig of *liliam* she'd carried all the way from her room filled the air with a gentle fragrance and she held it out to him, one last ditch attempt.

"I don't have anything of value, but take this. When I smell it I'm reminded of good things."

Niall stared at it.

Okay, now I'm just embarrassing myself.

She started to pull her hand back but he held his out. The flowers were stark and fragile against his shadowed palm, but he threaded the stem around the region of his chest. Against the hazy swirl of him, the flower seemed to shine.

"Thank you," he muttered.

No emotion, no response beyond the necessary. No sign of the Niall she'd known.

She turned away and walked back up the steps without another word, refusing to let him see her cry. He didn't want her but he'd shown Hareili enough enthusiasm when they reunited, so it was possible for him in his shade form.

The smell of *liliam* lingered on her fingers as she picked up her pace and forced herself to focus on navigating the halls back to her room.

Frustrated and lost, she started toward a set of double doors, wondering why the enormous dwelling didn't seem to have a single soul in it.

"Wait there." A strident female voice echoed behind her.

She turned away from the doors and found the woman she'd nearly bumped into earlier gliding toward her. Given the finery the woman was dressed in, swathes of rich red and gold, and the sheer aura of 'you will do what I say' emanating from her eyes, she wasn't someone to be refused. The woman came to a halt a few metres away, a wary frown dipping over her brow.

"I understand Zel spoke with you," she said.

Neri nodded. "Not with much I understood, but she did."

"I am the Jakida. You are most welcome in my settlement."

Neri bowed her head immediately. The action came to her on instinct and she remembered Zel mentioning that title as the person who ruled the settlement.

The Jakida moved forward in one fluid motion and put a soft hand under Neri's chin.

"Let me get a look at you. Zel seems to think there is

something untold inside you."

Neri refrained from asking what this 'untold' quality was, unnerved to have someone so close to her. The Jakida was a head taller and held herself with all the grace of entitlement, but something about her, the reflexes and speed of her movements maybe, suggested this was someone who knew how to hold their own in a fight.

Neri freed her face from the woman's grasp as respectfully as she could manage, but her stomach growled so loudly that the whole palace probably heard it. She pressed a hand over her belly, her cheeks burning.

"We have a harsh time before us and the path will not be easy," the Jakida added. "Still, there will be time to discuss that. If you come with me I'll show you to the dining hall."

She issued it as a command rather than an invitation, but Neri ignored the natural urge to stand her ground and followed the Jakida back along the corridor.

They didn't say a word to each other as they walked, Neri a couple of paces behind, but when they entered a vast hall of high ceilings and vibrant red furnishings lined with gold, Neri froze.

Niall sat at one end of the enormous table and looked up as they came in. She wondered if there was another route he could have taken, or if his shadow allowed him to sneak past when the Jakida stopped her.

"Join me, please," the Jakida insisted, ignoring Niall completely.

Just keep agreeing until you get the food. Then excuse yourself and go looking for some answers.

Neri sat to the Jakida's right at the table and folded her hands neatly in her lap, flinching when the Jakida hollered an ear-shattering command and maids appeared with trays of food.

Whole legs of dried meat were served on platters with some kind of purple and green cucumber-shaped vegetable that Neri had never seen before. It fizzled a weird, savoury tang on her tongue, but she was so hungry she ate two helpings.

By the time the Jakida cleared her throat and fixed Neri with a penetrating stare, Neri had eaten enough to turn her usually wary mind sleepy.

"I would like you to enjoy your time here," the Jakida said. "I can furnish you with a good horse and you can explore our grounds, but I must ask that you don't leave the walls of the settlement until the time is right. We also have plenty of volumes in the library you may find endearing."

I can't ask her why she's being so nice to me, but there will be a reason.

Neri took a deep breath.

"This is all very new to me still," she said, fighting to keep her voice gentle. "It'll take me a while to adjust but thank you for allowing me to stay."

The Jakida nodded and rose from her chair. Without another look or word she left the room, the tension in the air lessening several notches.

Neri glanced at Niall. Now would be the perfect time for them to share an awkward smile, or perhaps for him to say one of his usual sarcastic remarks.

But he still wouldn't acknowledge her. Frustration boiled into anger.

"So that's it?" she asked. "You won't even talk to me now, despite everything you've said before about us not being just a bit of fun? I expected better of you to be honest."

Niall's eyes darkened, the white almost engulfed by shadow. It usually meant he was furious, but now Neri couldn't tell.

She couldn't read him at all.

When he still didn't answer, she pushed her chair back and limped out of the room. She hurried as fast as her knee would let her toward the front of the dwelling, down the steps and along the lane.

Why do I keep trying? He's made himself more than clear.

Her plan was made, yet she kept hoping for even a crumb from him, some sign that he wasn't discarding her simply because he didn't really care.

Red-cheeked from the wind and unable to go far without getting lost, Neri saw the settlement for the first time. The lane sloped down to the main gates, but there were the many lanes and tracks running off on either side. Some lanes had huts made of wood and straw, others of stone. Most of the buildings had plants and flowers growing haphazardly either out of the roof or up the wall as bursts of colour amid the brown and grey.

Something about the close density of the trees that rambled in between the dwellings made her feel secure. It wouldn't be such a bad place to spend a few days, or even a few weeks. She sighed, turning to limp back up toward the dwelling.

A while spent here wouldn't be so awful until I can find a way home.

Fighting against the wind, she retraced her path back up to the palace and found Niall sitting at the top of the steps. His shadows were angled to the side, but given his stillness she guessed he'd been watching her arrive. She stopped a few steps below him, unsure of whether to speak to him or whether to sail straight past.

"How is it strange?" he asked.

She frowned. "What?"

"You said earlier this place was strange. How?"

She climbed the final few steps with far too much hope thudding in her chest and dropped to sit awkwardly beside him.

"The tree trunks are white and the ground in the woods is springy. There are birds here I don't recognise, and a whole vast land that I've never even really known of. I'm in a palace being spoken to like I'm someone even remotely important."

She wallowed in the moments of silence that followed and braced her hands on the step. His question was likely a pity one, and although she would struggle to stand up with any grace, sitting around with him not speaking to her hurt too much.

"I always wanted to be a painter," he murmured. "I loved to draw and dreamt of having my paintings hanging in the dwellings of lords and ladies. Artwork lasts longer than folk and you can have complete control with colours."

She hovered beside him as the shadowed lines of his face curved up with unexpected enthusiasm. Laughter lines began to show as quivering lighter outlines around his mouth and his eyes seemed to glow bright, lights amidst the fog of shadow.

She let herself settle beside him again.

"This is definitely the kind of place you could imagine hanging in fancy dwellings," she agreed.

When she turned her head in his direction, she saw his own hand sliding down away from a lump over his own chest.

"You're still wearing the wax charm I gave you?" she

asked.

His shadows clouded, the ghost of his lips twisting into a wry grimace.

"It became a part of me. I can feel it like a glow inside and there's no way I can get it off. You must be more magic than you think."

The slight tease lifted Neri's spirits. He might be feeling sorry for himself but at least his sarcasm seemed to be returning. She turned fully in time to see his face swirl back into a brooding frown as he caught her gaze and whipped his eyes away from hers.

"I'll have to speak in front of these folk later." He jabbed his thumb over his shoulder toward the dwelling. "They need to be convinced to find a hidden route through from this side of the cursed forest. We need to give everyone a chance to decide if they want to escape what the Governance is doing to your land."

Neri winced to hear him speak of his home and hers with such unattached separation.

He doesn't even see it as home. Perhaps he never truly has.

Somehow through the short time they'd known each other, she hadn't properly considered the possibility that during their time in 'her' world, he might have always planned to return to his own. Until they arrived and he'd made it abundantly clear.

"*My* land. So much for togetherness."

It served as enough of a retort to bring Niall to his feet. Neri watched the remnants of shadow that he had become walking away from her, his shoulders down and his head hung low. She couldn't dredge up enough regret to call after him.

What would be the point?

She sighed and thumped back on the step behind her, balancing her weight on her elbows.

"That's a mighty sigh. Are you ill?"

A girlish voice bounced above her head, and she sat up to find a young woman hovering over her. The woman wore deep purple robes that left her arms bare but her legs completely hidden, reminiscent of those that the Jakida wore. But the posture and general aura of exuberance however were anything but regal.

"I'm fine, thank you," Neri lied.

She waved her hand in a vague attempt to indicate her messy emotions, then flinched as the woman slid in one fluid move to sit beside her.

The blonde hair, yellow more than blonde but still shining with sunny light, bore a resemblance to Emelyn and Neri's heart ached with homesickness.

"I should think so too! the woman exclaimed. "Dragged into a whole different existence with a boy who then turns out to be something else and almost torn to rags in the process. It's exciting!"

Neri hesitated. "I wouldn't exactly say exciting but what's done is done."

"Hmm, true. I'm Livia, a lady and of absolutely no importance since my brother was born first. He'll rule and I'll end up being married off and I still haven't found a way out of this settlement to escape."

Neri blinked, startled by the rapid pace, but the openness was refreshing and she couldn't help but smile.

"I could help you escape if you're sure they wouldn't cut of my head or anything," she offered.

Livia laughed and put her hands around her own throat.

"They'd certainly imprison you in the tower. We don't have a tower but *Ama* keeps threatening to build one if I try to sneak out again. I want to see the realm and I want to fight in the war, but she won't even let me flirt with the guards."

Neri shook her head as the sudden urge to laugh bubbled inside her throat.

"We should go along to the meeting." Livia groaned. "It's all very serious stuff and probably nothing to do with either of us, but it's something to do."

She got to her feet with all the grace of a royal and held her hand out. Neri hesitated, unsure if she'd have guards running her down for touching what was probably a noble hand. When she grasped the offered hand, Livia hauled her to her feet by with surprising strength and quickly linked arms with her.

Bewildered by so much easy contact, Neri allowed herself to be dragged down the corridor and into the hall where she'd eaten before.

Folk were already assembled around the table and Livia propelled Neri down into a seat at her side. Niall sat across from her but she bent her head to listen to Livia's hushed whispers instead of acknowledging him.

"You've met *Ama* already and Zel over there. The man sitting next to *Ama* is chief of the royal guard. On her other side is my brother, Viljo, the grand and powerful Jakid in training."

Neri cast her eyes quickly over the assembled group. The chief of the royal guard had glanced at her with a quick flick of dismissive regard when she entered with Livia, through layers of beard and shaggy silver hair that somewhat covered the scarred remains of previous battle.

The Jakid in training glanced at her and she quickly turned her attention back to Livia in case he caught her looking. His dark green hair was trimmed short which accentuated a broad face, and she could imagine his burly shoulders and stiff-backed form residing over empires.

The Jakida cleared her throat and silence fell.

"We will hear the shade now."

Neri glanced at Niall. If the Jakida calling him by his kind rather than his name hurt, he didn't let it show.

Not that I can tell anyway with him like that.

He stood, his gaze trained on the Jakida as she sank against the back of her chair.

"You need locate a way through the cursed forest," he said. "Lots of our folk are suffering at the hands of the Governance there. They're growing beyond control. Neri also needs to get back where she belongs."

He paused long enough for a short bark of laughter from Viljo, who met his irritated glare with all the courage of a challenger.

"You can hardly claim them as 'our folk'. Why do you assume we can waste resources when our own land is on the brink of war, to find what has long since been lost? The way through the cursed forest is a myth. Nobody has seen or heard tell of it happening in living memory."

Invisible sparks of hostility crackled across the table between them. The Jakida glanced at Zel with a frown, the calmer woman's smile never faltering. Livia watched the men glowering at each other with an impish grin on her lips.

Then the shadowed lines of Niall's mouth curled into a smile.

"Do you also believe then that the three brothers are a myth?" he asked. "There's always some truth in myth I've found, and how else do you think we got here if not through the cursed forest?"

Silence swept the room as the Jakida stood to have her

say.

"There are those that believe the stories of origin are none but that, stories. Do you have some form of proof to suggest they exist more than mere shimmers?"

She stared at Niall as Viljo's hands clenched into fists on the table, but he remained silent. With something similar to victory glowing in his eyes, Niall nodded.

"Does the name Hamlin sound familiar?"

Neri sat up at the mention of Hamlin. The memory of smoke and burning filled her nostrils and she clenched her teeth to shake it off. His death and his kind treatment of her had started her on this mad path of discovery. Without Hamlin she'd never have found Niall, felt at home in the sanctuary with the residents and Dog as her family.

Even Livia leaned forward, intrigue scrawled across her face. Uncertainty drifted across Viljo's features and he cast a glance at the Jakida, who made no movement besides the gentle inclining of her head for Niall to continue.

"Hamlin trusted me with some information," he said. "Then he died. I believe he gave Neri something too, and with those we should be able to find a way through."

Neri gripped the edge of the table as all eyes turned on her. She floundered between being honest about what how much information Hamlin had entrusted her with, which was basically nothing, and her instinct to preserve some kind of leverage for protection.

Niall kicked back his chair and rounded the table, each step measured and even. Neri sucked in a startled breath the moment his fingers ghosted over her wrist.

She stumbled as her toes hooked around the chair leg but Niall's hold kept her upright as he dragged her to his side.

"We'll give you time to decide," he announced. "I

wouldn't take too long though if I were you."

Neri had no choice but to keep her dignity as he led the way through the double doors and into the corridor. It was either that or start fighting him in front of everyone.

As soon as they'd rounded a corner, his grip disappeared he stepped away from her. She clasped her fingers around her wrist, still tingling from his touch, and faced him.

"I don't know why you had to tell them that. Hamlin never gave me any information."

She turned away from him and moved to the open gap in the wall that overlooked a large waterfall. It cascaded down into a rockpool surrounded by a grassy bank and the sight of it tugged at her memory. Neri couldn't hold back the quiet gasp of awe as she remembered their brief visit to Niall's friend Mik shortly before disappearing through the firebird's portal. Hanging on the wall of the bedroom she'd shared there with Niall had been a painting of this very settlement.

The reality of everything she'd endured and refused to fully believe crashed around her.

It's all real. The forest, the west. The firebird too, wherever it ended up. Niall's shade self. All of it.

Which meant what Niall had said about finding a way back was a possibility too, unless he was lying for some reason she couldn't see yet.

But if Hamlin had intended to leave some information with her, he hadn't managed it. All she had from him was a hollowed out book, a pocket watch and an affectionate letter insisting Niall would look after her.

Niall, who clearly had no intention of replying to her. Hamlin's trust in him clearly had as much misguided hope within it as hers had.

Before she could walk away in the swelling awkwardness of silence, pattering footsteps echoed on the steps behind them.

CHAPTER FOUR

Livia hurried toward them and turned a mischievous grin on Niall before fixing her attentions on Neri, her eyes dancing with determination.

"I should show you our settlement," she said. "When you see Zel again later she will tell you all sorts of weird and wonderful things. I want to show you the good bits first."

Neri bit her lip. The thought of her life becoming even more immersed in weird and wonderful seemed both inevitable and ridiculous at the same time. Remembering Livia's previous admission about wanting to escape the dwelling, she dredged up a smile.

"You want me to help you dig tunnels, don't you?" she asked.

Livia beamed in delight. "Would you? I'm so glad. Come along, there's lots to see. Well, not *lots*. But things."

Neri allowed Livia to entwine their arms and followed her toward the lane without a single glance back. As Livia leaned her head close to whisper, Neri forced herself to remain still and not veer away.

"I enjoy a good upheaval and things get so boring here. Are you and Niall together?"

She caught the intrigue in Livia's dark grey eyes, but unlike Hareili, she guessed Livia was simply nosy rather than nurturing any secret crushes.

"We were. It seems now that he's back here he wants nothing more to do with me. I think I'm still in denial."

She sucked in a sharp breath.

He's a man. I've survived my whole life without him, and I can do it again.

She didn't want to believe his behaviour in the east had been an act, but now his actions were fairly clear and she had to let his actions tell her where she stood.

Livia's arm tightened around hers in a sympathetic squeeze and Neri forced herself to focus on their surroundings.

The packed dirt of the lane was springy underfoot and she wondered if Livia would agree to postpone their outing so Neri could go back and get her boots. But even with the cold, the ability to walk barefoot had a strangely liberating feel to it, so she ambled along without a word. When she snuck a look at Livia's skirts, she noticed bare toes peeking out from beneath them.

The incline of the hill brought trees to lean against buildings, vines weaving over the outsides and sometimes disappearing through cracks in the façades. Neri eyed plants she didn't recognise, a lot of the trees bearing large purple and blue fruit the size of oranges.

Folk bowed their heads low as Livia passed and their eyes turned to Neri with open curiosity.

"We'll avoid the market square for today," Livia suggested. "We have an inn there which serves food and a few indoor shops as well as our stalls, but folk will want to stop me to talk and they'll want to meet you and it's all very tiring."

Neri caught a glimpse of the large open courtyard when Livia turned her around again. Awnings of varying colours fluttered in the wind and the throngs of folk provided a hive of activity and noise.

"Viljo mentioned a war," she said. "Is this the sort of

place where folk go out and fight in combat?"

The thought of an impending battle didn't fit with the idyllic settlement but Livia's sad smile only confirmed her fears.

"It's a long story. The two sides of our land split long ago with the cursed forest parting the east from the westlands. But now here in the west, the Lord who governs the borderlands has threatened to try and take us by force. He won't win though. We're trained and ready for when the time comes."

Livia stopped and dropped Neri's arm. She took Neri's hands instead, the excitable gleam back.

"Perhaps I should train you to fight if you're to be here for a while? Can you fight?"

Neri tried to imagine the elegant lady in some kind of combat and failed. She nodded with a gentle smile, guessing Livia would forget or find them something else to do instead, and they resumed their walk.

"What is the east like?" Livia asked. "Is it much different to here? I've heard stories from times past, and I know some travel through on a shimmer and we learn their ways, but I've never spoken to one of you before."

Neri snickered. "One of me? You make it sound like I'm a myth. The east is similar to here in that there are rocks and hills, two suns and a sky. The water is clear too. But there are plants here that I don't recognise and your trees have white trunks. You don't seem to have many Governance patrols either."

Livia nodded, her face grave. "I see. What is a Governance? Also, what do you mean by patrols?"

"I…" Neri rubbed a hand over her mouth. "This is going to take a while."

Livia grinned. "I have many whiles."

That covered that, and Neri couldn't exactly excuse herself without being rude.

"The Governance, well it's a group who are like your Lord of the Borderlands. The enemy. They tear apart the land for its gifts and take folk away in wagons if they disagree."

"Ah. We would not tolerate that here. You should stay here with me where it's safe!"

Desperate to avoid having to explain anything more, or to promise anything she knew she couldn't stick to, Neri leapt into the pause with questions of her own as they walked along the lane.

"What is this place called?" she asked.

"Jakiris, this settlement we're in, is the seat of the crown of the westlands, and the westlands are in the wider realm of Kirelonia. We thrive as much as we can on the elements around us, and in turn the land gives us our gifts."

"Gifts?" Neri frowned.

"Yes, our *ai-tan*. That is the essence that allows us to wield certain skills. There are those who can make water dance, or air carry objects without a touch, or folk who can make the earth dance."

Neri stopped dead. "Wait, you're saying folk can control the elements? Like water magic or something?"

"Of course. I've heard of a few that aren't blessed with *ai-tan*, but they're all but a legend now. Wait, are you saying your folk don't have gifts?"

"Well, some folk are particularly skilled at various things, and there are legends of those with land gifts. But most don't tend to go around magically lighting fires or making water out of wind, if that's what you mean."

Livia wrinkled her elegant nose. "That sounds intolerable. So, you don't have any *ai-tan*?"

Neri shook her head as the regal dwelling came into view. She had no special gifts, and now she had no Niall. No Ma and Emelyn, no Dog, no Moonshine. No Hamlin. No mother or grandmother. No way home.

She couldn't keep the misery off her face and folded her arms around her middle.

Livia frowned and glanced upward. Neri copied her, guessing that given her recent luck she'd likely get plucked out of the sky by a dragon or some kind of harpy.

The suns were covered by a faint white haze, but Neri caught sight of a large droplet moments before it splatted on her cheek.

After the long, harsh summer in the east with no rain in sight for a long while, Neri's sorrowful heart lifted in innocent joy.

Holding her arms out wide she rotated with her beaming face upturned until the drops pattered on her skin. The rain turned to torrents in an instant and she revelled in it. Her hair slicked to her cheeks and only the thought that her clothes might become transparent when wet sent her up the steps.

Livia stood at the top already under the roof of the entrance, mostly dry and laughing.

"You should change into dry clothing," Livia insisted, a broad grin on her face. "If you leave your room and walk to the end, turn left and keep going until you reach two large doors on your right, you'll find the library. I'll wait for you in there."

Neri nodded as she swept her sodden hair from her face.

"Okay. This was the only dress I had so I'm not sure what folk will think of my actual clothes, but it'll have to do."

Livia was already on her way along one of the corridors

and waved an airy hand over her shoulder without looking back.

"Oh, I had them sort a selection for you, don't worry."

Neri grimaced and set off toward the hall she hoped led to her room. Livia's kindness was likely genuine, but she didn't want to risk owing anyone anything.

This is still a completely unknown place. They're being nice to me because they think Hamlin left me some kind of information.

Her heart sank at the thought of Hamlin. He would have made himself at home anywhere, even here, but Neri never had his unerring sense of confidence.

Shutting herself in her room, she noted the new cluster of dresses hanging near the balcony, way more than she'd ever end up bothering to wear.

Linen folded by the bed seemed to be solely for drying skin like smooth towels, so she sank into the bathing pool and washed the grime and grit away. The blisters on her burnt hand still smarted with a change in temperature but the pain had become dull and she could bear it.

As she soaked, her thoughts turned back to Niall. Whether she wanted him to or not, he was determined to push her away. She didn't dare hope that it was some kind of gallantry because of who he was, not after how friendly he'd been with Hareili.

And Cori hinted there was something between them. Neri sat on the edge of the pool and dried her hair. *If he wants to leave me here, then let him. I don't need him.*

That fact didn't make her want him any less.

Once clad in another sleeveless floor-length dress in dark green, Neri followed Livia's directions until she found the double doors and pushed one open a crack. She peered in, her eyes widening as she stepped inside.

Wide arches in the opposite wall looked out over the valley to show the relentless stream of rain still driving down. The cold floor of light marble shone beneath her bare feet, and she hopped across it until she reached a thick green rug. Wooden-backed chairs stood beside chaises upholstered with the finest soft brown fabric and the most intricate embroidery. Her eyes glazed over these and then settled on the ceiling to floor bookcases that ran the entire three walls remaining.

Alone in the vast room, Neri walked along past each bookcase with her fingers trailing over the battered, warped curves of the shelves. She recognised some books, no doubt brought by explorers tripping into shimmers by mistake if what Livia said was true, although nothing remotely modern had made it.

Other volumes spoke of gryphons and dragons, unicorns and sprites as though they were entirely real.

She reached the end of one side and moved past the open archways, leaning out for a moment to catch rain on the palm of her hand.

A quiet noise echoed behind her, a soft whoosh like displaced air, and she turned to find Niall watching her. Remembering the days when they'd first known each other and his ability to creep up without a single sound had irritated her, she paused in her wandering.

"It's always been too much to expect you to announce yourself."

The words, only a gentle tease, brought a frown to his shadowed face and she knew she wouldn't get a better chance for the truth than now while they were alone and she was remotely calm.

"I need to know whether what we have, or had, is over or not. You're pushing me away so tell me if you're trying to be gallant because of what you are now, or if you really don't want this anymore."

She took a deep breath and waited, refusing to look away. If he intended to break her heart then he would see exactly what it did to her.

His eyes pooled and the darkness grew until the whites disappeared, his mouth twisting, in pain or anger she couldn't tell.

"What I am now is a disgrace, do you get that? I'm sure folk will tell you all about my kind and what we are, so please allow my experience to be the judge of that."

The drench of bitterness in his voice echoing with eerie resonance around the room brought a chill to her skin, but she wasn't going to let him frighten her off that easily.

"So how I feel regardless of that doesn't matter?" she asked. "You make the decision and throw me aside with no thought of even trying to work something out?"

Her chest heaved with the effort of fighting the shudders that rolled through her and still trying to keep her voice strong. She couldn't look at him any longer and turned away.

"Don't pretend," he hissed. "When my guardian sent me east in the first place, it was to get rid of this shadow and it worked. My shade side was finally gone."

"How did he get you through the cursed forest?" Neri asked, her insides plummeting.

"I can't even begin to guess. One moment we were talking, then I felt dizzy, like I was falling through rushing air. When I woke, I was in the east on the edge of the woods."

"Maybe he can do the same again then. Maybe-"

"No, he won't. I thought it would be safe to come back here, that was always the plan for me. You had the feather from the kyne so you had to come through with me, but now I can't get rid of this shadow at all. It's constant, and it never used to be. Your fire must have burned away whatever *ai-tan* protection my guardian put on me."

"Maybe we can-"

"Neri, stop! I refuse to hang around while you bash your head against a wall because you think you love me."

She heard the relentless snarl in his tone, frustration but not a single catch or note of doubt. He meant everything he said, and one thing circled around her mind louder than the rest.

He needed a way through the cursed forest, and for that he needed me.

The only thing keeping her from rushing out of the room was that he still stood in the doorway. Refusing to let him see the tears that spilled, she clenched her fists tight and walked. She focused on putting one foot in front of the other until the marble floor dropped away and she moved through the archway to stand toe-deep in grass and dirt.

Rain soaked her dress and threatened to drown her skin as it washed away her tears.

This isn't going to work. She huffed against the sobs that broke free. *I can't let him ruin me this badly. I'm not a girl who runs into a rainstorm because someone broke up with her.*

She couldn't lie to herself and pretend it wasn't breaking her heart, but that didn't mean she had to take it lying down either.

She walked on across the valley and up the steep incline of rocks beyond. Stones bit into her bare feet and she caught her calf on a jut of rock, until eventually she had to stop and rest. The whole of Jakiris lay beneath her, the firelight of the settlement dancing below as the stars danced above.

All around her, life went on.

If Niall really had played her for his own benefit, then she had two options. She could find a way back east alone, to the sanctuary and folk she now trusted, or she could stay in the settlement for a while. Neither of those options would happen if she rotted from hunger in a deluge of rain.

She started back down, arms out to keep her balance. By the time she reached the side of the dwelling again, she was too cold and tired to think of much at all except getting into the bathing pool and then her bed.

She hesitated at the edge of the dwelling, eying the open archways. She couldn't walk back into the library trailing mud all over the pristine floor, and Niall might still be there.

Instead of going all the way around the dwelling to the front steps, she walked along the length of the building until she found her deck and struggled over the stone railing.

She pulled the soaked dress off and stepped straight into the bathing pool. Warmth cuddled her skin and, surprised at the temperature, she looked around the edges to see a tiny stream that bubbled in through a hole in the tiles, providing the dwelling with nature's bounty through what had to be a series of pipes.

Neri forced herself to focus on the logistics instead of her emotions, wondering whether the waterfall fell powerfully enough to push water through heated pipes or if the dwelling had waterwheels to churn it into motion. The thought of Orin's kitchen and the fire pit entered her mind and she wondered if that somehow provided the hot water.

The warmth stole some of the cold from her skin and

she floated on her back for a long time, inclining her head back and forth to swirl her hair through the water. She almost didn't hear the knock on the door, rearing up when it sounded louder a second time. She hauled herself out of the pool and grabbed a robe that hung from a wooden stand near her bed, glad it reached to the floor and engulfed her in thick, downy soft fabric.

She opened the door and peeked around the gap. If Niall had come to apologise she would slam the door in his face.

A man stood there expectantly, hands clasped behind his back, but it wasn't Niall and it took Neri a moment to recognise him.

Viljo took in her attire through the slim gap and smiled with his eyes fixed firmly on her face and his hands clasped behind his back.

"Forgive me," he said. "My sister couldn't find you and she worries easily. I said I would call on you while she searched the grounds."

Neri nodded and bit her lip. Niall had chased her out of the library and she'd forgotten her plan to meet Livia there.

"I forgot something," she fibbed. "In truth I didn't expect anyone to miss me."

She monitored the slight tilt in Viljo's head, the torches behind him catching on the dark green tints in his hair. She stepped back, intending that to be the end of their conversation, then paused when Viljo made no move to leave. He glanced down the hall.

"I will ask her to come to you." He lowered his voice to a conspiratorial whisper. "You may have noticed she has a habit for dramatics."

Neri couldn't help smiling at that. "I did notice. Thank you."

She shuffled back into her room and closed the door,

not wanting to give him any more encouragement when he lingered. She ambled toward the bed, hoping for a few moments quiet to nurse her broken pride, but the door slammed open before she could even settle onto it.

"Lords, I'm so glad you're okay!" Livia hurried in without invitation. "I wondered what could have happened to send you dashing out into the rain and Niall too. Did he find you?"

Neri felt dizzy just to listening to her, but she caught the necessary information all the same.

"Niall's gone?" she asked.

The apprehensive frown marring Livia's face confirmed it.

"A servant said they heard raised voices in the library. By the time Viljo and I arrived, you were gone and Niall was staring out at the rain. Viljo and Niall had an almighty row, almost came to fighting, and Niall walked out muttering about leaving the settlement."

Neri's heart sank. Niall had left her, no doubt off on his own adventures or to meet up with his real friends. She sagged on the bed, her eyes burning with frustration.

"He'll come back," Livia insisted. "Which means you can stay here until he does. I've got so much left to show you!"

CHAPTER FIVE

Despite Livia's enthusiastic visit, Neri managed to sleep through the night, although she woke several times dreaming of shadows in dark corners of her room. Each time she remembered Niall and sadness crunched around her.

But sadness couldn't keep the irrepressible hunger at bay. After a luxurious wash, Neri clothed herself in another dress and wondered idly if she could work in the kitchens or the laundry to earn enough for some proper trousers.

She wandered along the corridor, hoping that her memory served her well enough to find the grand hall. The double doors loomed and she stepped inside the hall to find it empty. Food had been laid out already, possibly in preparation for any early risers such as herself.

She took one of the dark blue fruits and sniffed. The sweetness tanged at her senses and brought moisture to her tongue. With a gentle nibble, she deemed the skin edible and polished off two in swift succession. Then she took one of the ready-cut slices of moist bread and ate it without any accompaniment.

Livia would be checking on her at regular intervals, probably in the sole hope that Neri would get up and provide some entertainment, but there was one place she could hide out and be invisible a while.

Hunger sated, she tiptoed down corridors until she found the one she needed. Delicious scents wafted out as she approached a door at the farthest end, and an almost unbearable heat struck her the moment she pushed it open.

Steps led down from the doorway into a vast room, a busy hive part of the dwelling. A fire-pit ran the length of the far wall and threw out almost unbearable heat, surrounded by scurrying folk. A young woman, barely more than a girl, was on her knees scrabbling to pick up several small green balls covered in dirt. The girl scooped the offending vegetables into a bowl and hurried across the room toward the sound of a voice shouting.

The voice screamed dominance and discipline with every note, and Neri took a hesitant step downward. With her knee not flexing fully and the absence of a banister, she pressed a hand to the wall to keep her balance.

"Are you here to work?"

That voice boomed across the room, drawing Neri's attention. The whole kitchen halted, but despite the many pairs of eyes swivelling to stare at her, she singled out the owner of the voice.

A woman in the midst of the crowd, hands on hips and her eyes narrowed with impatience.

Neri shook her head. "No. At least I don't think so."

She doubted they'd force her to work, but she also had to remember she had no roots in this world, no friends to lean on. She also had no direction to aim for until she found out more about the possible ways home.

The woman stepped out of the cluster, a mother hen emerging from the group of clamouring chicks. An overwhelming temptation to look apologetic and unassuming welled up in Neri's mind.

"Well that's something." The woman eyed her up and down. "I doubt you can cook a bedino. Are you lost, or seeking a place to hide?"

The woman waved a hand at an archway in the far

corner of the room opposite the stairs. Furthest from the fire-pit, there was a small wooden table and a stool nestled against the wall. Neri followed the woman across the kitchen, doing her best to dodge the folk who hurried around with renewed intent.

The archway led outside, but the woman huffed as Neri headed toward it and pointed to the chair instead. After a fleeting glance at the grass of the valley outside, Neri sat down. With the woman frowning down at her, she wondered if she should run while she still could. She had nobody to miss her, and considering Niall's recent behaviour, she doubted even he would worry much.

The woman pulled a wooden cup from the table with no ceremony whatsoever and filled it from a nearby jug.

"Drink up," the woman said. "Rude to refuse a drink in your host's domain."

Neri leaned forward to take the cup and sniffed at the liquid. As the woman whirled away to chastise her minions, Neri dipped her little finger into the drink to test it. Sweetness hit her tongue and the fresh fruitiness began to tingle on the inside of her mouth, the taste morphing into a more subtle linger as the liquid evaporated.

Throwing caution out along with her worries, Neri took a proper sip and watched the kitchen. Each person operated as a unit, doing their part and linking with other human units to perform a chain of events that led to a long table full of prepared ingredients. Neri reigned in the temptation to go and sample the food.

The woman was still issuing terse orders and sending folk dashing in all directions, but as she passed the small girl who'd dropped the vegetables earlier, she reserved a soft smile and a quiet word.

Neri got the sense that she could either have a friend or

ally depending on her next few moves.

"You are the one from beyond the land, are you?" the woman asked.

Neri nodded. She guessed she should get up and make excuses about being in the way, but she didn't want to leave yet. The kitchen was warm and made her feel small. Her short interaction with Zel suggested they might start taking an interest in her, which was always worrying.

Gritting her teeth she forced herself to admit what she couldn't yet believe.

"I came from elsewhere, yes."

The woman nodded, apparently satisfied, and threw an ear-crushing directive over her shoulder.

"*Halera gi Talgk!*"

Neri didn't recognise the language but then she only knew one. Knowing mirth lit on the woman's face and she grabbed Neri's cup, taking a swig out of it before handing it back.

"You do not know *Ai-erie*?"

Neri shook her head. The woman shrugged one shoulder to indicate it wasn't of much consequence and raked her hands through her short dark hair tinted with orange hues. Recalling Cori's wild hair colour, Neri tried with unerring desperation to convince herself there must be some magic hair colourant around. Thoughts of her gramma grinding and brewing powders to make paints for her surfaced, but Neri couldn't remember anyone asking for potions to change their hair colour before.

"*Ai-erie* is our natural tongue, our language. If you are not here to work, why are you in the settlement? No, that's your business. More importantly, why are you in my kitchen?"

Neri sighed. "I came from far away because the man I

was travelling with brought me here. Doesn't want anything to do with me now though, conveniently enough. But there are folk back home who want me dead because I don't agree with them, and because I got dragged into their battle. I intend to go back somehow and make sure my folk are safe."

The pent-up bitterness closed around her throat. She took another sip of the drink and tensed as the woman chuckled.

"Folk end up in my care for running from their problems or chasing their loved ones to the Jakida's employ. There are all veins of story in Jakiris if you know where to look. I'm Orin."

Neri nodded and opened her mouth to give her name in return, but Orin heard something kitchen-related behind her and threw up her hands. She turned and let out a stream of what Neri guessed was their native language.

Neri braced her hands on her thighs and leaned forward to stand, but her gaze caught on a small child drifting out from some unknown corner.

Bedraggled and covered in dirt and ash, the girl was shaking as Orin stalked toward her.

The girl sucked at her fingers and clung onto a grimy blanket covered with holes, but in one swift move Orin had dropped onto one knee with her body language soft and relaxed.

Neri couldn't hear what she said to the little girl, but a woman scurried over at Orin's command. She took the little girl by the hand and hurried her past Neri up the stairs.

As Orin approached, Neri stood to follow them out. Then she caught the sad look in Orin's amber eyes.

"She says she has lost her parents and comes asking me for a living. You may have some sway with those above if you don't work?"

Neri shook her head, not even knowing anyone in the dwelling let alone having any influence over them.

"I'm just a stranger passing through," she admitted. "But I hope she finds somewhere safe."

Orin shrugged as a young man brought over two cups with more of the dark blue liquid inside.

"This world is unknown to you."

Neri settled into Orin's habit of querying by making statements. Something about the woman's confident calm gave Neri her own sense of control and she nodded.

"It's different in so many ways. You have no street signs, the nature is different and even your food has very little similarity to that I'm used to. Do you have transport at all? What do folk do for entertainment? How many folk live in this world?"

She bit her bottom lip to stop the unending stream of questions from continuing. Orin's gold eyes danced and her mouth curved up.

"Questions I can help you with, if you ask them right. We use horses for travel and wooden drays for moving cargo to the smaller settlements. When we finish with our duties we spend time with families, those of us that have them. Those that can read do or we visit companions and spend evenings in the settlement."

Orin took another swig of her drink, pausing to frown at something going on across the kitchen until the situation seemed to rectify itself.

"We have no number on how many live here," she added. "As the east is fast becoming torn, their folk seem to mass in numbers and fill the lands they inhabit, whereas the westlands still lie mostly untouched. Some say the battles coming will settle the balance but I don't believe prophecies. Give me hard earth and *calideh* any day."

Neri blinked. "*Calideh*?"

Orin went to the table running along the wall opposite the firepit. She picked up a round fruit, much like a misshapen lemon but with a dark purple shade on the skin. Orin dug her nails in and tore the fruit open before she held it out to Neri, who took it.

"The fruit nourishes the *plida*, the gut." She gave her stomach a hard tap. "If pressed and left it will create the drink you have in your cup and the skins when pressed onto a wound can provide protection against loss of *dhrito*. *dhrito* is blood."

Neri wished she could write it all down. Not only did it interest her, but local knowledge would be useful.

"So which came first?" she asked. "You all speak the common tongue but yet often use words in your own."

She settled back against the wall. From that position she could see the edge of the valley, and if she stepped out she'd be able to walk to the right and round the corner to the front of the palace and the lane leading down to the settlement.

"Your tongue came many winters ago, long before Jakiris fully stood. But before then we spoke *Ai-erie*. Many of the smaller settlements do still and some don't speak the common tongue at all. Favour for each one rises and falls with time and with new lines of folk, as is the nature of all things."

Neri allowed the information to sink in. It would benefit her to learn the basic language. Travelling through was one thing but she had no idea where to go and communication would be vital. Orin could perhaps teach her the basics but Neri sensed her time of self-pity had to end and her only option now was to go back up to find Livia.

She drained her drink and stood up. The mysterious girl was now on the steps slicing away at the weird vegetable. As she passed, Neri grabbed one of the vegetables from the nearby table. The girl looked up when Neri held her hand out and she handed over the blade.

Testing the skin with her thumbs and fingertips, Neri took the tip of the blade and scored into the vegetable. It sunk deep despite the skin's resistance fighting her pressure, but she persisted and started to whittle. A while later, she ended up with a crude, but identifiable horse and passed it back to the girl, along with the blade.

"Thank you."

The sound, almost indistinguishable amid the clatter and hubbub of the kitchen, kindled a kernel of warmth in Neri's chest entirely unrelated to the fire-pit.

She turned back to the girl and smiled.

"You might want to try that on Orin from time to time," she whispered. "She's not as scary as she looks."

She left the kitchen and wandered down the hallway with no real notion of where her feet were carrying her. On reaching the palace steps outside the entrance, she sucked in a lungful of the cold, sharp air.

Dew glimmered on the ground, creating tiny sparkles as the suns' rays peeked over the tips of the cliffs that rose up above the hills. Neri contemplated going back to the library but a steady thud of footsteps attracted her attention.

She cast her gaze back to the lane and caught sight of Viljo walking toward her with his head bowed low and his expression sunk in deep thought. Before she could tiptoe back into the dwelling, he looked up and raised his hand in silent greeting. She copied the motion automatically and wondered if she could slip away before he tried to engage her in conversation.

Livia's words about him almost coming to blows with Niall were still stuck in her mind and she couldn't risk viewing Livia's brother as the final straw that chased Niall away, even though the idea was ridiculous.

"Livia's lost you again I see."

He stopped beside her, his deep voice was loud in the otherwise silent lane.

"I don't need minding." She shrugged. "What I do need is to ask whether anyone will be helping to find this way through to the east so I can go back home."

Viljo tilted his head to the side. Having only seen him on three occasions, the first of which he acted like a firecracker facing Niall down in the main hall, an odd sense of familiarity tugged at the back of her mind. With his gaze fixed on her face, Neri tried to push aside the sense of discomfort at his intense scrutiny.

"The shade confided his information to my sister before he left," he said. "With your part we will most likely be able to find it, if it exists. *Ama* has agreed that any searches will be made by those we can trust, so if there is a journey to find it, we will be accompanying you."

Neri grimaced. She'd forgotten that they all assumed she had some kind of secret knowledge passed to her by Hamlin. It might even be the reason that Livia and Viljo were both humouring her, although she couldn't believe that Livia would be that callous.

Then again, I trusted Niall before.

Even now Viljo's blue eyes were searching her face for some sign of secrets. Her discomfort under his perusal grew, but he refused to look away even when she did.

"Thank gods you're up! I've been dying of boredom."

Livia's voice filled the air like a blessing, filling the doorway with her broad smile full of cheek and mischief.

Neri heard Viljo's gentle chuckle behind her but didn't turn back around in case she once again became the object of his attention.

"Don't exaggerate, Livia. I've told Neri we're going to help her find the way east if we can."

Neri tensed as he stepped closer before moving around her on his way inside. She offered a weak smile as Livia took hold of her hands.

"Can you ride a horse?"

Neri hesitated. "I can a bit, if they're steady. I haven't had much chance though."

Not until recently. She shook the memories away.

"No matter. I shall teach you. But not now, there are things I need to explain."

Neri let herself be led as Livia secured her arm with possessive friendliness. Still wrapped up in the thought she might have to learn to ride a horse, Neri only noticed their destination when Livia opened the door to the library. Swallowing the sadness and squashing it beneath a deep, ragged breath, she moved into the room and sat on one of the long chairs as Livia fixed her with a serious stare.

"Now let me fill you in a bit. I explained before that the land is in turmoil and war could spill out at any moment. I didn't elaborate on what caused it though. The Lord of the Borderlands doesn't believe that we should be enthralled to the laws of nature. We in turn do not agree that he enslaves animals with pain to do his bidding and manipulates his folk into destitution to fund his lust for conquering as much land as he can."

"The Lord of the Borderlands? I think I've heard someone mention him before."

Livia frowned. "You've not heard of him in the east? The borderlands are the only route through the cursed forest, and it has been closed to us westlanders for a long time now."

"There's a way east?" Neri stood. "Why didn't anyone say?"

"Oh, you won't be able to go through that way. The borderlands are our enemy. They won't take anyone from the west not known to them, and from what Niall tells us, you're known to those in the east as an enemy already."

"Well, yes, but-"

"They'd have you in chains and with your Governance before you could reach the east gate. No, best we find you a safer route."

"So, he's the one you're at war with?"

Livia nodded. "We managed to keep him in the borderlands through diplomacy for a while, but now he sees a chance to take the west too. We are strong but there are no certainties. *Ama* and Viljo will fight but apparently I'm not allowed. I train every day and I will be there when the time comes, even if I have to fight my way out onto the field."

Neri listened with growing admiration to the strength in Livia's voice. The woman paced back and forth in front of the long chair, her face set in determination.

"I think it best that I train you for combat," Livia added. "We have another five days or so before we're due to leave the settlement. In that time I can at least teach you good defence."

Neri leaned back against the over-stuffed back of the chair, surprised at how much she enjoyed lounging on it and perturbed by Livia's use of 'we'.

"I can defend myself fine," she insisted. "It's holding back from attacking I usually find difficult."

"Good, so you can wield a blade?"

Neri shrugged, but that brought a renewed smile of determination to Livia's face.

"I will teach you. If you check inside the dark blue dress in your room, you'll find attire for fighting. Go change and I'll meet you outside. Behind the dwelling there is a smaller space where we won't be seen."

She grinned and swept from the room with an overwhelming aura of purpose about her. Shaking her head in amusement bordering on fondness, Neri groaned her way off the chair and went to change.

The outfit Livia had mentioned was perfect, better than any dress. Thick fabric trousers in muted brown fitted with an adjustable belt at the waist, and Neri delighted in the abundance of pockets. She also had a firm waistcoat with thin filmy sleeves that she could roll up to the elbow if needed.

With her old shoes on, she hurried over the balcony wall and dropped onto the grass below. She located the space that Livia had mentioned, just more grass filling the space between the rocky expanse of cliff and the back wall of the dwelling with some wooden logs embedded in the earth like makeshift seats.

A short while later, Neri goggled at the woman walking toward her. Livia's long sunny hair was pulled back from her face and tied in a tight high ponytail. Her regal robes were gone, replaced by burnished red shorts of the same fabric that Neri wore and a leathery waistcoat that left her arms bare. In each hand she held the hilt of a long blade.

Not a shred of the stereotypical lady remained and Neri knew then that the woman in front of her now was the real Livia.

"Surprising I know." Livia grinned.

She held one of the blades out point down for Neri to

take. Neri clasped the hilt and grimaced at the idea of handling such a weapon, but Livia stepped back and raised her blade. Neri copied her.

"Never let your opponent distract you," Livia began. "The blade is going to kill you but if you get tripped up while you're focused on it you can't avoid it. We're not going to disarm, only pretend. When I swing, try to block me."

Livia swung her blade in a slow, purposeful arc and Neri raised her arms to catch it with a dull clatter. At first she felt silly as she swung the blade about, but soon she became used to the weight in her hands. After a while, Livia insisted she practice attacking one of the tall, wooden posts set into the ground.

"I put this up for my own practice and now it should serve for you too."

Neri nodded and started to close her eyes as she attacked, trying to learn to sense things around her, a long while before she remembered that Livia watched her. She stopped, lowering the blade, and turned around.

"It's much better to train with real folk. You need to learn to target movement." Livia faced her once more. "Try to attack me."

Neri raised her blade and swung reluctantly, gritting her teeth with frustration. Livia parried the blow with practiced ease, ever patient while issuing constant instruction.

"Focus on the target rather than their blade."

Neri tried again and again, getting used to the weight distribution of the blade and Livia's swift movements.

The sun had long since risen and they worked on despite the dazzle in their eyes and the wind whipping their cheeks. By the time they were worn out completely, Neri had blocked several of Livia's best attempts and nearly succeeded in cleaving her in half. It was an accident, but she was counting it as a win all the same. She collapsed onto the grass, still panting from the exertion.

"You should practice with Viljo too." Livia huffed out a breath. "He's quicker than me and more agile so he could give you a more advanced fight."

She slumped down next to Neri, who doubted she'd want to face Viljo for a conversation let alone a fight given his constant staring earlier. She sought for a diplomatic answer.

"He doesn't seem the type to pull a blade on a girl."

Livia laughed beside her. "He has his moments. I'm so glad you came, for whatever purpose. I'm going to have so much more fun with you here, I can feel it."

Neri uttered a wry chuckle and let her entire body drop into the grass. She hadn't exactly been a bundle of laughs. Even the last few days with Niall before the summing ceremony and all the drama had been frenzied and tense. At least then she knew, or thought, that he loved her. Forcing the thoughts of him away, she sat up in one swift move.

"I don't know what this information is though that I'm supposed to know. Hamlin never told me anything of relevance."

Livia hoisted herself up on her elbows and frowned. Her brow wiggled in contemplation and then she glanced around, leaning closer with the heavy air of conspiracy.

"I'll tell you what Niall told me and see if it helps jog anything. He said, *where the two maids weep at the turning of the tides, the sorceress waits where the fountain springs. Beneath the land where trees dare not grow, the firebird will rest 'til the flame-walker sings.*"

Her voice echoed through the otherwise silent clearing

and Neri scrambled over the words, searching for some kind of clue or enlightenment and finding only more confusion.

"I have absolutely no idea," she admitted. "All Hamlin left me was a hollowed out book, a pocket watch and a letter, but none of them hold a clue or anything. I think he also left me Dog and boy, do I miss him now."

Her desolate tone brought Livia to her knees and she put a gentle arm around Neri's shoulders. When Livia whispered she would leave her alone, Neri couldn't stem the tide of relief. She waited for Livia to disappear and got to her feet.

Walking back along the edge of the dwelling she passed the library arches and saw Viljo seated on one of the wooden chairs. Even engrossed in a dusty tome he sat with a stiff, straight back, and Neri fought the rising temptation to giggle as she crept by.

She scaled the balcony into her room and settled onto her bed. Delving behind the headboard, she drew out her pack and emptied the contents onto her bed. There were two blankets that belonged back in the sanctuary and the blade Ma Kath had given her. Next to that was another blade and both of them, still stained with dried blood, set revulsion boiling in her stomach.

The memory of the summing ceremony came back to her, the smell of burning tallow and the sound of screaming filling the air.

She slid off the bed with a blade in each hand and dropped them into the bathing pool. Not caring whether they rusted or not, she left them there to soak and returned to the bed.

Finally she had all that was left of her previous life in the east. Hamlin's letter lay tattered at the edges from the journey and she opened it. She scanned the words in the hope some previously missed clue might jump out at her.

My dearest Neri,

I apologise for the journey I am about to send you on, but please trust me when I say Niall will see you safe and well. Trust the safe house, and keep Dog with you. He will show you the way when it seems hidden from you. If you believe in nothing else, follow his lead. I am glad to have known you, even at the end of my time. Carry on carving, you have a true gift.

Yours,

Hamlin.

She sighed and stroked a fingertip over the paper. Niall had kept her safe but not exactly well. She missed Dog and wondered whether the palace would give her wax and equipment to begin carving again if she asked. Livia might organise it for her.

The thought of having a task to occupy her, a purpose to make her feel useful, filled her with a gentle surge of hope. It might not be the brief dream she'd had of a future with Niall, but she had to occupy herself somehow.

Unable to find any clues on the page, she picked up Hamlin's pocket watch. She wound it for several moments and held it up to her ear to hear the gentle tick.

I need to get myself together. She dropped her hand and eyed the pocket watch. *I'll have to admit Hamlin didn't have time to tell me anything.*

Fears that they would go on their search without her

reared up, and she realised she would have to be very careful. These folk were being kind but that could easily change. They could lie to her, refuse to accommodate her or even ask her to leave if she wasn't useful.

Settling down with her head on the pillows, she let her eyelids close. She wouldn't nap long, but she wanted to rest and think things through without Livia hovering or Viljo staring or Niall being awful.

He hasn't come back for me.

The thought circled in her head, accompanied by the scent of cake-spice and *liliam*. As if Niall was right beside her, she could smell him and the flower she'd gifted to him.

With laboured breaths, she tried to force thoughts of him deep back inside, but the scent persisted. She sat up again to find the day had waned already and night reigned outside. Every shadow cast by the flickering torches on the walls caught her attention. Each one she searched in case Niall had returned, but there was only stillness.

The pocket watch lay on her pillow, glinting in the firelight. She'd disturbed the catch somehow in her brief rest and now the front was open.

With a startled gasp, she brought it right under her nose to see the inside better. Around the inside of the cover someone had etched crude markings.

"*Sirena Carahdyl.*"

Neri whispered the words aloud but nothing happened. No sudden gusts of wind or dancing of flames or unexpected gurgles from the bathing pool.

The words, probably a name, might have belonged to Hamlin's sweetheart or someone special to him.

She needed a walk and no doubt Livia would be wanting to spend the rest of the evening with her, so she pocketed the watch and left her room. Her walk took her around the other side of the dwelling until she happened on the waterfall.

The soft roar of the falling water gave her enough sound to calm the rushing in her mind, and she sat down by the water's edge with her bare feet submerged up to the ankles.

Steady footsteps echoed behind her, each one a copy of the previous. She guessed that if she turned round it would be Viljo standing there.

She said nothing in greeting as he sat beside her with his long legs crossed, wondering what he might want with her.

The lights from the dwelling gave them a soft light by which to see and a swift whirling smell of *liliam* filled the air that only served to bring Niall to the forefront of her mind. She glanced around, searching for some sign of the fragrant blooms nearby, but only saw empty shadows.

"Is there a *liliam* bush around here?" she asked.

Viljo startled at her question. Strange, to sit beside her without a word and be comfortable enough to stay in silence. His eyes still had remnants of faraway glaze in them when he turned to look at her.

"Magic flowers don't grow here. You mostly find them in the forests although Forlaith is the nearest for charms."

Neri's head still jarred over the subject of magic and she decided to imagine the man beside her as a normal person rather than an awkward product of some otherworldly nobility.

"When you say magic..."

She started but couldn't bring herself to finish. She wasn't entirely sure she wanted the answer. He might have guessed as he smiled.

"*Liliam* is used to seal two souls together, I'm not quite sure how. In ancient days when we had the last great wars, women used to give their partners *liliam* so that they would be able to follow it back home. If you can smell it without being near any, it means the person is thinking of you."

Viljo explained it all in his low and lyrical voice, not noticing the horror stealing across her face. She lowered her gaze from his and wondered if her waking to the scent of Niall around her was a product of flower sorcery. If she smelt *liliam*, did it really mean that he was still thinking of her?

She looked down at her knee and recalled Niall's dismissiveness on their journey to Jakiris. The waft of *liliam* filled her head so strongly in that instant and she wondered if he would smell it too.

"I should find Livia," she said.

Viljo nodded as she stood and left him sitting beside the pool, but she could feel the attention he set on her back as she walked away.

Instead of going inside to hunt for Livia, she walked around the edge of the dwelling until she came across Orin on a stool outside the kitchen doorway peeling fruits into a bucket. All the kitchen staff ever seemed to do when Neri was around was peel things but the food that came out to the table in the main hall had unknown seasoning and warmth. Then her eyes stuck on the small basket of candles by Orin's feet.

"You're out for a wander," Orin announced. "Come and sit a while."

While Neri deliberated, not because she didn't like Orin's company but because she didn't want to intrude, Orin rolled her eyes and threw a blade onto the grass beside her.

"Make yourself useful. *Ridag*. Sit!"

Neri sat. She thumped down onto the grass beside

Orin's stool and picked up the knife. Instead of leaning toward the basket of *calideh* in front of them, she leaned back and plucked a candle from the wooden basket. If they gave her wax and let her work, she could replace the candle and more besides. As she began to carve the silence stretched on between them. Neri sought for a way to fill it.

"How's the little girl doing?" she asked.

Orin grinned and raised her hands skywards, her animated expression implying faux exasperation.

"Somebody got her to speak and now she won't be silent. She has caused no end to uproar with her questions. Speaking of questions, you have a true skill with your hands."

Neri followed Orin's gaze to the candle in her fingers that now showed a geometric print of carvings. She shrugged. The thought of her wax setup at home, of Dog and her friends, and she was instantly homesick again.

"I carved candles in a previous life and made them. I'd like to do it again someday."

She focused on the wax in her hands not wishing to see the sympathy in Orin's eyes. Orin groaned as she leaned forward and took another vegetable to peel. Above the blanket of stars danced a comforting twinkle through the darkness, but they worked on.

"You remember past lives so you have past lives in your world," Orin said after a while. "If not, there seems to be something Kirelonian inside you."

The words jarred and Neri shook her head, half to disagree and half to shake off the feeling. Orin didn't notice.

"Each person has life flowing through them," she continued. "We cannot imagine how little each part of our body is, the little workers inside blood we bleed keeping it all together, the chain of events that allow our muscles to move us and our heads to make our thoughts. The land has life flowing through it. When an entity dies and the land reclaims the body, it becomes once more a part of the natural essences that birthed it. That land allows others to become part of life and, in that we all travel in the land's *heprica, tshh,* I do not know the English for it, the part of folk that lives on."

Neri thought for a moment, on her third candle and beginning to enjoy Orin's litany.

"You mean soul?"

Orin nodded and sighed her relief. Neri hadn't wanted to give too much thought to death, especially not after her mama and gramma were gone. As far as she understood it, folk died and got swallowed by the earth, then the earth gave nourishment for new folk to be born.

"You have a man in your life."

The question came out of nowhere and Neri wondered the same question. Niall had disappeared without any goodbye. Whether he intended to return and, whether she would still be waiting if he did, all lay uncertain.

"I did. He brought me here and then left me here. I'm hoping to find a way back to my home, but I don't even know where to start looking."

Neri jumped as Orin patted her shoulder. It surprised her further when Orin used the contact to press down and heave to her feet.

"Look at what is behind, beside and before you. Do not look at what might be. Trust *heprica* to give you honourable answers and do not ever lie with a man for less than a vow."

The last statement Orin said with a grin and a twinkle in her eye. She picked up her stool and disappeared into the gentle glow of the kitchen, the fire-pit finally simmering low.

Neri sighed. A promise and a vow were two different things. Niall had made promises but he'd never vowed to remain with her. She got up and went back to scuffing her feet along the grass in the direction of the dwelling front.

Orin had one thing to answer for at least, that Neri couldn't go more than a handful of hours before the thought of mouth-watering food had her stomach rumbling again. The hunger went some way to taking her mind off of Niall and her situation. She almost felt able to tolerate the Jakida's stiff company for the evening meal, if she absolutely had to.

CHAPTER SIX

Sliding down a rubble-strewn hillside, Niall steadied himself as he reached level ground and bent low behind a rock. He glanced down at the shadowed outlines of his hands. The steady buzz of his shade infliction almost masked the dull ache, the sensation like rough wool on tender, enflamed skin, except for the subtle balm around his chest where the wax charm Neri had once given him was nestled.

He surveyed the settlement gates, marking out the route he needed to take. Nobody would stop him passing through, not this close to the borderlands. They might well stare and then scurry about their business, but even an unknown shade could be doing the bidding of the Lord of the Borderlands. He had one purpose for visiting the settlement he'd been raised in, and he hoped the man he needed to see would provide answers.

The thought of the reason he'd had the strength to leave Neri's side in the first place spurred him on, and he straightened up to walk toward the gates.

The walls were nothing more than rough-hewn wooden stakes and barely high enough to keep an errant child in or out. The gates hung open, well entrenched in the dusty ground to show they'd not been moved since the last winter or longer.

Despite growing up in the settlement, he'd always known his differences to the other folk. They had tolerated him, always with one eye open or one hand free in case his shade side went bad. He learned more about shades in the whispered conversations he overheard as he grew older, even left to seek out others of his kind once, but his guardian always brought him back with a quiet word of warning and those stern blue eyes that reminded him so much of Hamlin. Now instead of escaping the settlement and his guardian, he was seeking entry for advice.

He ignored the fleeting, worried glances folk gave him and walked along the rutted dirt lanes, past wooden huts and small stone dwellings.

Soon he sensed a pair of eyes that weren't fleeting. Looking left he saw a woman standing in her small garden where little vegetation grew. She held a stiff bristled broom and swept with hypnotic strokes. Her eyes narrowed when he stared back. He half-expected her to startle and attempt a quick dash into her hut as he approached but she stood firm, still sweeping in the same, steady manner.

"I'm looking for Caden," he said.

Now he caught the subtle widening of the woman's eyes. She couldn't have been any younger than fifty winters and had no air of a traveller about her. He didn't remember her but a shade of his age showing up and asking for Caden, she would no doubt know who he was, which gave her an advantage.

"The crazy old man is gone."

Her voice carried loud across the silent lane and he glanced around, but they were alone.

If he hadn't paused, he might have missed the two white pinpricks in the hut doorway behind her. He focused on those dots until they grew larger and a child appeared. A boy of no more than eight or nine winters young hurried out with mischief in his smile and wickedness in his eyes.

"You mean the man in the mountain's mouth?" the boy

asked. "He's a gift-spinner I heard, and he can turn the whole land to night!"

Niall pushed aside the boy's jabbering and latched onto the only thing that mattered.

The man in the mountain's mouth.

So Caden had found reason to retreat to the caverns in the hills high above the settlement.

As Niall's childhood guardian, Caden had often said he would flee to the sanctuary of nature one day. Niall turned his head up and scoured the craggy cliffs that towered over the settlement. Caden had taken him to the caves only once before, but the way up was still etched in his mind.

The woman cuffed the boy around the ear but he ran off with a gleeful laugh. Niall nodded at the woman out of mocking courtesy and headed back toward the settlement gates and the path that would lead him upward.

With an arduous climb ahead of him, he succumbed to the crash of his thoughts. Neri loved him, he knew that much, with a fire so strong that he might have ruined every chance at being part of her life. She wasn't any good at hiding her emotions and she'd made them more than clear, but he couldn't stay by her side as half a person. His feelings ebbed and raged in fits and starts, and that meant that his shade-self had started taking control.

Caden had warned him once with all the gentleness of a stung horse kicking that it could happen. In a shade half-breed, the two sides would likely wage war until one triumphed and engulfed the other, leaving only whispers in the mind of what once existed. He refused to put Neri through that. But it didn't mean he had to give up while there was still a chance to fix himself.

He ignored the scoring of theoretical cuts on his hands as he began his steep climb. Not quite a rock-face but the assent of the mountain rose too steep to walk up. The cuts would not appear on his shadow-skin, but he still felt the pain of each scrape and scratch.

Other shades wouldn't have to feel pain or suffer emotions, but then they wouldn't know what it felt like to love someone with such ferocity that it gave life meaning.

Even the memory of his muscles ached from alternating walking and jogging, but he didn't want to hang around if he had a shot at becoming whole again.

After leaving Jakiris he headed east toward the borderlands, which sat near the northern part of the cursed forest on the western side. He wanted to lie down and sleep, and his mind wouldn't be as sharp as he needed it to be, but Caden wouldn't harm him. He was almost sure about that.

Neri stayed in his mind as he climbed on, his thoughts flickering to her whenever his train of thought lulled. He could almost recall the smell of her despite the *liliam* masking her natural scent. He knew every time it swirled in his nose, present more often than absent, that she was thinking of him, and it gave him the dogged determination to push on.

He reached the lip of the rock-face and hauled himself over. With the suns almost fully sunken in the sky, their brilliant white dazzle now casting a soft glow over the horizon, the borderlands showed a hint of prior beauty. Even the vast lake glimmered with the firelights of the wealthy, hiding the lords and ladies that dwelt and plotted within.

Niall groaned and heaved his aching body to stand up. It was a mockery that he was formed of shadow yet still carried the memories of aches and pains, but he only had a short way left to go. He followed the path that wound along the edge of the mountain and tried to remember some of what Caden had told him long ago.

The ancient *aerie*, the folk of old that all Kirelonians were said to descend from, had long since disappeared. Some said they hid in the woods or other corners of the realm, while others insisted their blood only remained in tiny drips through their Kirelonian descendants. But the caves Niall sought had once been full of *aerie*-folk, and he needed some of their grace and magic now more than ever.

The night drew in fast as Niall searched the mountainside, the dancing flickers of the stars above giving him little light as he blundered along the path, stubbing toes he didn't physically have and scraping non-existent skin cells on the jagged rock.

He almost wept with relief when he finally found the small gap in the rock and stepped into the darkness. The only thing his shade-self did have was the ability to see through the shadows, so he took a deep breath and prepared to face his past.

Caden would have no idea whether he had succeeded in reaching the east. Respects would also have to be paid to Hamlin and those that remained behind. Caden would want information and stories, and he would want to sit and to talk.

All Niall wanted was a solution to his dilemma so he could return to Neri's side.

The darkness began to concede to the faint glow of light ahead, brown at first as it showed on the walls of rock all around and lightening with each step Niall took despite the fact night had only recently fallen outside the caverns.

When the sound of bubbling water over rocks reached his ears, Niall took the last steps and slipped into the first cave ready for anything. A blade from the Jakirian palace armoury was steady in his hand, tucked close to his chest and cloaked by the dark shadows he swirled around it.

Brilliant sunlight streamed in through a hole in the roof of the cave and flowers grew all around, winding their way through the grass and over the roots of a tree.

Niall looked toward a corner and succumbed to the huff of relief when he saw a large turtle watching him with sleepy, unbothered eyes. The turtle's shell acted as a footstool for a very grubby pair of adult feet and Niall stared at the owner of those feet in amazement.

Caden had aged a lot. Despite the white hair that had once been a bluish shade of black and the streaks of white in a once dark beard, Caden still had an air of self-satisfied calm about him. He noted Niall's arrival as his fingers flew over a wooden pipe that emitted soft noises. Then he put the pipe down and pressed his hands together.

Niall stood by the mouth of the cave, an adolescent boy once more in the face of his old guardian. It was easy to see how Caden and Hamlin were related; one look at the eyes would give it away.

"Sit down boy, you're making the shellback uneasy."

Niall blinked at the sound of Caden's voice, the command no less powerful for the time that had passed. He dropped to sit in the grass, the feel of it under his hands reminding him of many nights lying outside with Neri, just talking to her and learning about her.

"You are different, I'll give you that." Caden nodded at him. "Taller and what's that light in your chest? You smell different too."

Niall tried to think of a sensible way to explain the events since he and Caden had last seen each other and failed.

"I need to know how to be whole in this realm," he said.

"A way to not be a shade anymore, even if I have to go back east again. I crossed over to the east and whatever sorcery you did worked, but since I've come back through it's been worse than it ever was before. I'm losing emotions that I had, ones that I can't exist without."

It came out as one long stream in the tone of a wounded child. He heaved a breath and then remembered his resolutions to respect the meeting by letting Caden discuss things first, and also that he'd to give him news that Hamlin was dead.

Caden's laughter rang through the cavern as he lifted his feet off of the shellback and sat up straight.

"How I have missed company. Do not worry yourself about Hamlin either. I have the news already and I've been aware of you crossing east, and of your return. I thought you might come to seek me out sooner rather than later, although this is sooner than even I expected."

He stood up with a groan and ambled to the tree. Placing his hand on the trunk, he reached behind and pulled out a wooden wicker basket.

Niall stared, his bottom lip dropping as he contemplated the possibilities. The wicker basket looked exactly like Hamlin's, although he could easily believe that there were more than one, either in the west or east or both.

Inside lay a small box of *gurbrys,* a root which Niall was sure folk of the west wouldn't recognise. They grew near spice mines in the furthest tips of the eastern plains, too salty and spiced for the fertile, moisture-rich land further west.

He opened his mouth to ask how Caden had something he couldn't possibly have had access to, unless he had a way east at will or had been around before the growth of the cursed forest itself, but Caden winked and pressed his finger to his lips. Niall knew better than to disobey if he wanted Caden's help.

He wanted to ask about the sunslight that radiated through the cavern as well, but Caden would tell him if he needed to know.

Niall caught the scent of *liliam* once more as it wafted with unbelievable potency and he clenched his eyes shut. Even his toes scrunched to stave off the overwhelming desire to run from the cave and dash back to Jakiris, solution or no solution.

"You want to get rid of your condition," Caden announced. "The east wasn't enough for you, although perhaps this has never really been home for you either. But maybe if this woman who has you so frantic to change loves you, then your condition will not matter to her?"

Caden's words roiled around in Niall's head. He knew the answer to Caden's question but it wouldn't help him. Neri would love him either way but if he remained in shade form then he might lose the emotional parts of himself that she loved. The parts that were able to love her the way she deserved.

Niall sat with an all-encompassing wave of sulkiness clouding his terror at the idea of help not being possible. After so many years trying to survive on his wit and his strength alone, fear clawed its way to the surface.

Caden rolled his eyes.

"Still dramatic. I would hazard a guess at your response considering you don't want to provide one, but perhaps if this lady does not have the staying power to accept you as you are, she's not worth the trouble?"

Niall took deep breaths to calm the surge of anger and He hauled himself to his feet, tensed to fight.

"The firebird came east for her. It *chose* her, left her a

kyne, and she's unfailingly noble. How am I supposed to care for her if I have no feeling left, if I lose what little emotion I have? How am I supposed to keep her safe this way?"

His voice boomed around the sanctuary of the cavern, his head ringing from it. Caden stuck a finger into his ear and wiggled it about. Clinging to the tattered strands of his self-control, Niall huffed out a sigh and forced himself to calm, to allow the shade numbness to leak in just a little.

"As soon as the bird arrived and we stepped into the fire, I sensed the change," he explained. "Whatever you did to make my shade-self go away, her fire burned right through it. Now I'm a lightness that needs to be kept together with concentrated effort. My old instincts are hemming in the shadow again."

Even when Neri insisted she didn't care about his infliction, Niall knew he should feel glad for that, but the yawning emptiness was snapping at him. Each day as a shade, he would become less like the person she loved, and each day the shadow would grow stronger until it consumed him. She would fight herself to death under the misguided notion that they could save him, when half-breed shades couldn't be saved once their emotional half was lost to the shadow.

"There is perhaps something that may give you what you desire," Caden said. "The pain is said to be worse than dying and more dire than anything else imaginable though. It is both mentally and physically unbearable and there is no guarantee that it will even work."

Niall heard the placating tone, an adult talking to an errant child, and his indignation bristled.

Caden broke open the *gurbry* box and held it out. Niall leaned forward to take one, recognising even in his anguished state that he couldn't refuse an offer of hospitality when he sat there exhausted, famished and ready to break. He managed a grudging thank you and chewed on the peppery root with no sense of propriety or manners. He barely even tasted it but the fullness it gave his stomach lightened his dark mood a little.

"Rest here." Caden waved his hand to indicate the cave. "You need sleep and more food when you wake. Then I will help you. Perhaps until then you can entertain an old friend with tales of another land."

Niall caught the exchange in Caden's words. If he remained in the cavern for a while, then Caden would help him toward becoming whole. He saw the old glimmer of attachment in his guardian's eyes, a man who wanted to help a lost soul, but something else twinkled deep beneath the surface.

Reluctant to waste even a moment, Niall settled back into the warm, tickling grass and took a deep breath of the sweet air. He could rest here just for a while. A day would make no difference to Neri because she was safe in Jakiris, and she would still be as furious in the coming days as she had been when he left. He allowed his curiosities to rise and distract him from the thought of her.

"Why is the hole letting in sunslight when I know that it's night outside?" he asked.

Caden smiled. He showed chipped teeth and fine wrinkled skin that no doubt meant he still smoked his pipe on occasion. Niall turned his head to watch the shellback make a slow, steady bid for the large hole in the wall that acted as a doorway to more inner caverns. Niall had never stepped past the one he now sat in, but he guessed that Caden had done a fair bit of exploring.

"Shellbacks are wonderful creatures." Caden's voice

sounded soft, far away. "They live extraordinarily long lives and yet they move through it so slowly. Nothing rushes a shellback, a wonderful mentality for life in general."

Niall rolled his eyes as irritability resurfaced. Since reaching the west his emotions had seesawed. Sometimes they didn't appear at all when he expected or needed them and at other times they swelled with blade drawn trying to strike him down.

"You mean you're not going to tell me."

In truth, he cared very little. He saw the light as it was and the origin, assuming it wasn't hazardous or threatening, had no bearing on him. As apathy swamped his tired limbs, he almost missed Caden's rambling litany.

"Well imagine one of these is true. Perhaps I have fire *aerie* in a large bottle over the gap or it might be *ai-tan* cast to bring this place into perpetual daylight. Perhaps if you step through the door over there, you'll find winter on the other side, or night, or forest. Maybe you'll just find another cave. It could be a different realm altogether. What matters is that it is warm and light is shining here."

Niall wandered mentally through the silence that dropped over them. Neri would love the cavern just as she revelled in the garden back at the sanctuary. He wondered whether she missed him, despite her inevitable pain and anger at his desertion, and if she would have him back when he returned. He had promised he wouldn't leave her again but he'd also hoped that crossing the cursed forest wouldn't bring his shade form back. That hadn't worked and she deserved so much.

His eyes fluttered closed as Caden began to play a soft reel on his wooden flute, and he slept without dreams. Caden played on, pausing only to murmur to the shellback and to fill a small wooden cup with water from the thin fall of water bubbling from the rock.

When Niall woke again with the infernal buzzing of his shadow around him, he opened his eyes to find another pair staring down at him, but while they were brown, they weren't Neri's.

The shellback blinked slowly at him as he shot up onto all fours, recollection of where he was and why he was there crashing around him. Caden sat watching him, a disconcerting habit from their past that Niall hated. He rolled into a seated position and glared, first at the shellback, then at Caden. He didn't say a word while food was distributed and he ate moodily, unable to explain his rumbling sense of mutiny to his host or to understand the exact cause of it.

"Now I did say I would help you," Caden announced. "Although I will advise once more against it. If you insist on this then you will need to remain here for a while. The process takes time and if I can stop you from the worst of it, I will."

As Caden stood and walked toward the tree, Niall wondered whether he'd find anything if he also looked behind it. Caden pulled out a sacking pouch of animal skin, its wooden stopper weathered with age and much use. He turned to face Niall with a dark frown on his face.

"I never hoped this would be needed. It's awful stuff but potent and gives you a nightmare ride. As they say however, the wine of one folk is the water of another."

Caden held out the bottle. With his shaking hands invisible beneath the shadows, Niall took the bottle and looked up, his thumb on the stopper.

"Do I drink all of it?" he asked.

The unnerving twinkle in Caden's eyes that Niall had

glimpsed the night before was back as he nodded. Niall unstoppered the bottle and thought of Neri, the glow he felt right to his toes when she smiled and the happy contentedness that curled in his chest when she laughed. He took a deep breath and threw the entire contents of the pouch down his throat.

The tingle started after he took a gulp of air, warming to a soft burning. Then it began to prickle. The sensation turned to scratching that rolled through his mouth, across his face and down along the memory of his skin.

Sinking to his knees, he gasped for air but felt no release. Something hammered through the shadow of his shoulder and Niall looked up through teary eyes to see Caden staring down at him with sad resignation.

"I would go for a walk if I were you. It should wear off but the discomfort will continue and pain will come in waves. Just remember that you wanted this. Come back when it's dark once more and we will talk again."

Niall blinked and stumbled away with his desire to get air rising as he choked and gurgled heaving gasps. The tunnels rambled forever and his consciousness almost failed him.

He burst out of the tunnel to find the night sky above and the dancing stars sparkling down at him. He had no clue how long he'd been in the caverns but as he gulped a lungful of air that began to rush into him all at once, he realised he was going to faint. He sagged to his knees with one hand on the rock and curled into a painful ball.

Caden had told him to come back when night fell again. He had time.

CHAPTER SEVEN

Neri woke to a knock at her door. The suns cast bright light into her room and she guessed the first portion of the morning must have passed her by.

She thought about pretending to be asleep still but apparently Livia didn't want to wait for an invitation. She burst into the room and flopped onto the edge of Neri's bed with a lively grin.

"We are soon at the hour of action. *Ama* says we must leave today instead and she needs your clue. I tried to put her off but she insists you're hiding something."

She looked half hopeful but with apology in her eyes. Neri sighed as she pulled out the pocket watch and flipped it open.

"That is all that Hamlin left me. There's a book too, but I've gone through the bits of the pages that are left and there's nothing. If you can make sea out of sand then please feel free."

Her bad temper, fuelled by a rough night's sleep, bounced around the room and settled back around her shoulders. She flinched as Livia gasped.

"Sirena, that's supposed to be Serena, the siren. She's said to rule the vast bodies of water that surround the land. Carahdyl is down to the south of the westlands on the border of the cursed forest. This must be leading us to the right place, then Niall's instruction should take us on to some way through the cursed forest. It's so exciting!"

Neri shook her head to dispel the sense of woolly

fantasy that edged in next to her bad mood. She couldn't exactly refuse to go with them. If a way through the forest had brought her here, then it stood to reason that she might find another to take her back again. Thinking of it more as a wide-reaching door rather than the magic of a flaming bird helped a bit.

"I'll take this information to *Ama* and we'll leave very soon." Livia grinned. "Pack what you need to bring and come outside. I'll make sure you have a suitable horse to ride."

She handed the pocket watch back and scooted off the bed, dashing from the room with no ladylike propriety whatsoever. Neri shook her head again and groaned her way out of bed to get dressed. She pulled her pack out from behind the headboard and folded her spare clothes and blankets into it. Then she remembered the blades at the bottom of the bathing pool. Unwilling to get undressed again, she settled on the edge and reached down. Her arm didn't cover enough distance so she ducked her shoulder and half of her head under until her fingers snared what she bobbed for.

Neither had rusted, a testament to their crafter's choice of blade-metal, so she dried and packed them. Once her hair had been roughly dried too, she took one last look around the room and left it behind. She likely wouldn't be seeing it again. Even if they had to search for winterspans, she wouldn't stop hunting for her way home.

The thought of seeing Dog, of speaking to Emelyn and the others at the sanctuary, being able to earn her keep with her candle-making and carving, filled her with a renewed sense of determination. She didn't need the westlands or the Jakida to save her home from the Governance. She just had to get back to it, formulate a plan and fight.

She stomped down the palace steps toward the lane, ignoring her urge to swing by the kitchens first, and assessed the assembled few readying themselves to leave.

Viljo stood beside a stocky brown horse with the reins in one hand as he surveyed the altercation happening in front of him. The thick-set, sturdy animal mirrored his owner as a solid, dependable carbon copy. This thought alone distracted Neri for a few moments before she noticed Livia standing, hands on hips, her face a picture of pure fury. The Jakida opposed her with arms folded, her face resolute to hide her irritation.

"I'll refuse to tell you! Niall told me what Hamlin told him and nobody else knows. You can't keep me locked up like my home is a prison forever and I can defend myself as good as Viljo can!"

After a long moment of silence, the Jakida turned away. Livia grinned and victory splayed across her delicate features. She turned to see Neri watching the show and waved.

"Come on down, we're ready to ride on out."

Neri caught the disapproval emanating from the Jakida as she mounted a chestnut mare with all the elegance of a noble. Viljo shook his head with resigned disbelief but Livia merely pulled a face at him. He sprang onto his own horse but it didn't even twitch at the sudden weight. If anything the horse closed its eyelids in dozy slumber, desperate to catch a few more moments of tranquillity before being urged forward.

Neri tried not to giggle at the comical thought of Viljo urging the horse on and the horse turning its head with complete refusal to lift so much as a hoof.

As Livia grabbed her hand and dragged her toward a white horse waiting for them, she tried to stop smirking.

"Neri this is your horse for this journey. She will keep you safe."

Livia pointed to the white horse, unharnessed with no saddle, and its large brown eyes fixed on Neri with dedicated focus.

"Is this the horse that brought me here?" she asked.

Livia nodded. "She's unfailingly loyal and steady, don't worry."

Neri approached the horse's side, but with no reins, bridle or saddle she had no way to mount. She squeaked as Livia grabbed her ankle and attempted to hoist her by the leg onto the horse's back. They failed, and she tensed at the sound of boots hitting the ground. Strong hands gripped her waist moments later and she rose into the air. She didn't even have time to argue as her leg swung automatically to clear the horse's side.

Her cheeks flushed, her face burning as she avoided Viljo's gaze. His fingers lingered on the top of her thigh for a brief moment, the gesture awkwardly telling, before he stepped away to remount his horse.

Neri stroked her hand down the iridescent white neck in front of her. With no reins to hold she had no control, but as the others set off the horse followed all by itself.

"She'll follow us, don't worry," Livia called back.

Neri didn't bother answering as they rode past the settlement's dwellings and approached the gates that led to the land beyond. She had no idea what to expect or what to look out for, but her horse moved alongside Livia's without any intervention from her the moment they were through the gates. The Jakida took the lead ahead of them and Viljo slowed to take a defensive position behind.

Neri glanced at Livia.

"Doesn't your *ama* need guards to escort her? I thought

she's like a vast ruler or something."

Livia glanced over, totally at ease on horseback with her hands relaxed and her reins slack against her horse's neck.

"The westlands are still civilised. Folk love *Ama* and if we visit any settlements along the way they will welcome us as we ride by. If they cause trouble, she has her own ways of protecting herself. I wouldn't worry yourself about safety whilst travelling with her. Even then you have me and Viljo. We're both handy with a blade."

Neri let that thought calm her, even though she could defend herself fine without their help. She focused instead on the movement of the horse beneath her as the Jakida set their pace at a trot. She bounced and pitched with uneven momentum, gritting her teeth and using her hands on the horse's neck to steady her seat, which only made the bouncing worse. Almost as though it knew her predicament, the horse changed pace to a leisurely, lolloping gait which settled her balance.

"Where exactly are we going?" she asked.

Livia hesitated. "How well do you know the westlands?"

"Not at all."

"You've never heard of Carahdyl?"

"Nope."

"Oh. Well, we're going there." Livia rolled her eyes and leaned closer, utterly at ease on horseback. "Ama has forbidden me from 'incessant babbling', but I don't agree with it."

Neri read between the lines well enough. If the Jakida wanted to keep her in the dark, for whatever reason, she had to keep her wits about her.

Their paced increased again as the suns beamed dazzling rays down, and Neri squinted against the glare.

She wondered if they would stop somewhere to rest at night, or even to rest the horses, but the day passed with steady speed and little chance for more than the odd word thrown into the wind.

They passed occasional outcrops of rock amid the dips and hills, but aside from the odd settlement which they always avoided, the land was all grassy plains with odd swathes of white-trunked forests.

"How long will we be on horseback for?" she asked.

Livia squinted against the glare of the suns as her horse stumbled over a stone.

"Tomorrow we should reach Carahdyl. There we can rest and make daily trips to the shore. Hopefully we can follow the clues locked safe in my head."

She tapped her temple with an impish grin and Neri couldn't help but smirk at her new friend's deviousness.

Neri shifted her seat and winced at the ache from being on horseback all day. As they joined a dirt track winding through one of the woods, the Jakida slowed their pace to a walk and Livia urged her horse forward.

Neri almost didn't notice Viljo arriving alongside her until his presence was a stoic outline fixed in the corner of her eye. Silence swilled between them and Neri scrambled for some kind of conversation to fill the void.

Viljo cleared his throat.

"How are you finding your stay with us?"

Neri hesitated, stuck between honesty and manners.

"I know nothing about this place or its history, but it's a beautiful place so far. I am a complete stranger to the rules and customs though. It's addle-minded when I think I grew up somewhere entirely other."

"It is interesting to think we have lived in entirely separate parts of the land all our lives." Viljo looked at her.

"Is the east an affluent place?"

Neri shrugged. "It's not as affluent as it seems to be here. The Governance rule the east and they don't tend to treat folk nicely unless it benefits them. They rule by taking away everything they can from us."

Viljo nodded as he scanned the woodland around them, still alert to their surroundings.

"Control of an entire group of folk can be complicated," he agreed. "*Ama* has always taught us to rule with fairness. Most end up tying far too much emotion to their desire to rule. Emotion can make a simple thing hard."

Neri shook her head. His words sounded too accurate for her to admit to and the denial that followed Niall's departure rose.

"Emotion makes the land flourish," she argued.

"In terms of gifts, perhaps. But many of us have seen all too often how emotion can make folk volatile."

Frustration swelled and but her resolution to be polite buzzed with irritating persistence. She forced a tight smile.

"Without emotion, we wouldn't have folk to care for those with no family. Without emotion, folk might not have taken me in when I needed help. My family might not have taught me everything they did. I wouldn't have found a family among friends after that."

She winced, thoughts of Emelyn, Ma, Moonshine, Hamlin and her family rising sharply.

Viljo hesitated, his lips parted as though he wanted to respond, but his gaze drifted ahead and he rode forward without another look in her direction.

Well that went well.

Neri looked ahead as the Jakida came to a halt. The suns were sinking fast and the wind whipped around them in intermittent gusts. Their destination for the evening appeared to be no more than an outcrop of rock, small enough to clamber to the top but still a good size for both seeing far toward the horizon and hiding behind.

She slid from her horses back before Viljo could offer any assistance and watched in bemusement as the horse wandered off once again. Nobody seemed to notice let alone care that the horse was loose, but she wanted to find out.

"Why do you allow my horse to just wander off?" she asked.

Livia's lips twitched as they stared at the horse heading for a small cluster of trees.

"She is a stray, and relatively wild. There seems to be an understanding between us that we will not try to own her and she will hang around."

Neri nodded. Livia hadn't told her anything real but it didn't rankle her as much as it might have done. She settled her blanket on the hard ground while Livia did the same, and they settled down together.

"Livia will attend me while I search for firewood," the Jakida announced. "Viljo will watch the camp."

She seemed happiest when issuing directives. Livia rolled her eyes as she followed the Jakida away from the rocks, leaving Neri with Viljo. Given their unsuccessful attempt at conversation before, she focused on stretching and loosening her seized muscles while he stood a short distance away, stiff-shouldered with his hands clasped behind his back.

She considered asking him if he planned to keep a standing vigil all evening, but the sound of brittle twigs under foot echoed behind her. She twisted around, hands braced ready to push to her feet. In the palpable silence that followed the noise, she heard the faint scrape of metal on leather as Viljo unsheathed his blade.

The crackling noise came again, louder and this time from some way off toward the trees. Breathing a sigh of relief, Neri settled again.

"It's just my horse I think," she said.

Viljo shook his head. In one fluid movement he was on horseback.

"Stay here." He eyed her with stern insistence. "If anyone comes, take one of the horses and be ready to follow me."

Neri caught the unyielding command in his tone. In that instant, he became a man bred to rule empires.

She watched his retreating back as the crackling noise grew louder behind the rocks. She grabbed the borrowed blade Livia had given her and crept closer. Muscles tensed in preparation, she rounded the rocks.

Her hands fell to her sides and her jaw dropped. Determination to defend herself ebbed into concern as she stared at the miserable heap on the ground near her feet.

The bird lay on the grass, naked but for hints of downy brown fluff that might have grown into feathers one day. The skin beneath the fluff was charred grey and smoking faintly, and Neri almost choked out a sob when she realised someone must have tried to cook the bird alive. It was bigger than the *watellows* she'd seen with Niall on her journey to Jakiris, more like one of the kitchen hounds that tended to hang around begging for scraps, but there was something fragile in the hunched wings and the scrawny legs.

She dropped to her knees and murmured pointless words of soothing nonsense as she reached her hand out.

"Ouch!"

She pulled back when a spike of heat radiated from the

bird's skin. She would have to light a fire to keep it warm and give it a shred of her blanket if she couldn't cool its skin with water.

She darted back to the camp and scoured the horizon for anyone returning. Nobody had returned yet so she grabbed her water pouch and took it back to the bird. The bird shivered as she opened the pouch, but the moment she dabbed the tiniest bit of water onto the wrinkled skin the bird snapped its beak at her.

"Sorry," she whispered. "I'm trying to help, I promise."

Unable to cool it with water and not sure giving it her blanket would make any difference, she placed the open pouch right against the bird's head in the hope it would encourage the injured fowl to drink. At the sound of hooves nearby, she stood up and forced herself to leave the bird.

Viljo was the first to return as she settled on her blanket, hoping he wouldn't ask so she wouldn't have to use relieving herself as a lie. The scant stops they'd made during the day seemed to be split into a matter of taking turns in the bushes at routine intervals before hurrying on.

Despite worrying about the bird, the nighttime darkness was welcome. She wanted to sleep and to rest her weary limbs, to have time for her thoughts to stop colliding and start making themselves useful. She still had no real idea what they were headed towards either.

When the Jakida returned with Livia a short while later, food was doled out and Neri ate with one eye trained on her companions. Viljo monitored her with constant dedication, his vigilance never faltering, and even the Jakida deigned to cast the odd glance at her, but very little was said by anyone. Neri kept her attention on the rocks behind her, waiting to hear any sign the bird might be in pain, but none came.

Livia was to be trusted with the first watch, then Viljo would relieve her. The Jakida would go last and Neri realised that she wasn't going to be trusted with the task. Instead of feeling aggrieved about it, she watched the stars dancing like icy flames of different hues caressing the inky sky.

The Jakida settled down on a blanket in the dirt with her back to them all, and as Viljo also took the form of sleep, Neri kept her ears keen for sounds of bird and her gaze fixed on the stars.

"Do you know what *ai-tan* is?" Livia's gentle whisper echoed nearby.

Neri shrugged. "Not exactly. It's gifts, but we don't see them as anything other than skills at home. At least, I don't know anyone who has remarkable abilities."

She sighed and kicked her feet idly across the ground as she flopped back on her blanket.

"*Ai-tan* is the essence of life," Livia explained. "It's the energy that runs through nature and through us. It bestows gifts and allows you to access the power of the natural elements. When we pass Forlaith tomorrow you'll see charms but they are just that. The world still leaves a fingerprint of *ai-tan* on all of us."

Neri allowed the words to wash over her. Forlaith was where she'd found the *liliam* that she gave to Niall. She would need to ensure she didn't make the same mistake.

"Orin in your dwelling kitchens said much the same thing. She called it, herico?"

"*Heprica*." Livia chuckled. "You don't have to be a wise woman to be wise. Orin has her own learned wisdom and she rarely shares it."

Neri let her mind slide away in the silence. She couldn't

think about what lay ahead because being so close to the forest she'd passed with Niall reminded her of him, and that he'd left her behind. She pressed a hand to her chest as if that could ease the sudden ache settling there. The scent of *liliam* echoed around her as though she'd summoned it into being simply by thinking of him, so fragrant and sweet that she had to quell a swoop of sickness boiling in her throat. They'd both made promises, but he'd been the one to break them.

"You really miss him, don't you?" Livia said.

Neri nodded and turned her head away in case Livia might be able to see the stinging tears through the darkness.

"I wish I could forget him," she admitted. "Or that I could remember and feel nothing, but I don't know how."

Her voice broke and caught on the lies. Even in pain she didn't want to forget him. The raw ache felt as much a part of her as breathing did. She wiped tears away with her arm and sought to cement her frail emotions.

"Do shades have this *ai-tan* thing?" she asked.

Livia's shook her head and wistful pity passed across her face as she looked out into the distance.

"They don't feel so they can't have a relationship with the land. Niall is unusual because his *ama* wasn't a shade, but usually shades don't have emotions and therefore they can't host *ai-tan* in their souls. It sounds like folk in the east do have it but maybe it's been diluted somehow."

Neri sighed. It would explain a lot. Although everyone else seemed to think Niall had emotions, he had discarded her and behaved so unlike the man she knew.

"In that first meeting where Niall mentioned a way home," she said. "Viljo said it was a myth, a legend that didn't exist. Do you think that's true?"

For Niall to abandon her had left it's scars, but to lose the only route left that might take her back to Emelyn and Dog and her home, it was unbearable to even consider.

"I think it exists," Livia said, her tone soothing. "Even myths have to originate somewhere. There are those that say the three brothers who were the original ancients of this land are a myth, but the lines of the elements are something folk rarely mention. If they do, they never deny the existence of it. But if your way home isn't around anymore then you can stay with me forever."

Neri managed a weak smile at that. She had no idea what would be happen but in a few days she might find out. As Livia fell silent, Neri drifted into fractured sleep with the plaguing scent of *liliam* settling around her.

CHAPTER EIGHT

Niall woke with a harsh breathlessness in his throat and an aching throb all over his body. He struggled to push himself to his feet and cast a wary glance around, the settlement still deep below him as he recalled his trip to Caden in the caverns.

With the suns high in the sky and preparing to make their descent once more, Niall started the long stumble back down the mountainside.

Each time a rock scored at him or his feet faltered he drew his mind back to the pain of not being able to breathe fully and tried to conjure the scent of *liliam* or a vision of Neri. When nothing came, he promised himself she was probably resting or preoccupied. He refused to believe that the lack of that connective scent between them meant something more permanent.

On reaching level ground and turning toward the settlement once more, he forced himself to head for some old haunts until he could begin the climb back up to be with Caden in time for nightfall.

The settlement gates fluttered and it took him a moment to recall why the scene was different yet familiar. Little strips of coloured cloth, worn and faded with age, were tied to the gateposts to announce the market. There would be shades of the East keeping watch which could cause him some hassle as an outsider, but his desire to go back in and slip amongst the stalls grew too strong.

He trudged along the rutted dirt track that led to the

main square and amused himself with the ridiculous idea that he could buy Neri a present as an apology. Once his mission was over he would remain near her for good whether she wanted it or not.

If he couldn't remove his shade-self then they would find a way back east together. The Governance would be a problem again but he would keep her safe. They could go and stay with Mik, or not leave the sanctuary, or try travelling so far north or south that the Governance wouldn't consider searching there.

The folk winding in and out of the market stalls paid little attention to him. He browsed a few of the wooden tables selling wares and practical items, but never stepped close enough to give a stall holder cause to worry about him.

Nostalgia keened inside his chest, too powerfully raw for a place he used to dream of escaping from. Then a conversation going on at a stall to his left captured his attention and chased the emotions away.

"I hear the west woman is on the move. She travels with her kin and a brown-haired stranger, a girl. They say the White Spirit rides with them so it must be of importance."

Niall turned his head and tried to get a look at the emotionless voice explaining information to the stallholder. The shade leaned over the table with rigid stiffness, the tone perfect for imparting secrets without any audibility issues that could misconstrue the message.

He couldn't see the stallholder but knew his time to disappear had arrived. If that message needed to be whispered rather than gossiped about loudly, it would be for the ears of someone who could reach the Lord of the Borderlands. Niall wound through the crowd and took a longer route back to the settlement gates.

Out in the dust plains, he stood at the foot of the mountain. He would have a better chance of solitude and safety from folk if he climbed the mountain now and waited by the tunnel entrance for nightfall, but he had one more part of his past he wanted to see. He wandered toward a craggy collection of rocks nearby and found the gnarled grey branches of an old friend.

The dead tree in front of him had always been dead, even when he was still a child. The rocks provided shelter from some of the suns' glare and the tree gave him a comfortable place to sit. For old times' sake he settled his back against the tree and slid down onto the dirt.

If the Jakida was on the move it meant they had figured out the location of the way through the cursed forest. The day he'd first seen Neri seemed so long ago, and that night Niall had climbed into Hamlin's bedroom at the candle shop for Hamlin to give him his last task.

Niall closed his eyes and allowed the memory to swamp him and drag him down.

"I trust nobody with this, but I know I have your loyalty."

Hamlin's blue eyes held Niall still where he perched on the windowsill. His shadow swilled around him, a by-product of his previous life in the west. When he wasn't concentrating on it his shadow still had a habit of creeping up unbidden. The occurrence had become rarer and more controllable, but now Niall could sense a shift in his future path that might drag him back to his past.

It had to do with that girl downstairs, the one who glimmered in the light and threw out warmth when she thought nobody was looking. Any idiot could see her natural temperament had been hampered by something sinister and her guarded eyes reminded Niall of his own defensiveness.

Realising he hadn't replied to Hamlin, he nodded.

"Neri will have a part in our land and our future," Hamlin added. "I need you to vow you will get her to the sanctuary unharmed."

Niall blinked in surprise. He suspected trickery but had no idea what it could be.

"That's it?" he asked. "My last great quest is to get her to the sanctuary? Is she unbelievable trouble or something? Also, is a vow necessary?"

Hamlin chuckled and mumbled something. Niall didn't catch it but guessed he wasn't meant to. Irritable at the turn of events, expecting to be given some kind of intense secret or perilous voyage, he relaxed his grip on the window frame a little.

"She will be vital. The entire land will be turned on its head soon and Neri will play a part, I can feel it. If you make back through to the westlands you will see Caden again at some point. You must convince him to help you as you are vital too. You must remember that if nothing else."

Niall opened his eyes and sighed. Like Caden, Hamlin had a taste for the dramatic. It had been those very words that drove Niall from Neri's side days ago in the hope that Caden could fix him, and it had been those words that had forced Niall's hand into searching for the way through the cursed forest. If Hamlin predicted he'd see Caden again then that time would inevitably come, and he wanted to get it over and done with.

He sensed the spasm before it hit, the ache rolling over skin and exploding with shards of pain through his head. He doubled over into a curled ball and heard himself whimper. His eyes saw red even though his lids were tightly clamped together and the thought of his brain bleeding through his eye sockets, nose, mouth and any skin pore it could find sent his heart skittering into a panic.

The vision of a *liliam* flower bloomed in his mind's eye but the scent of it made him violently sick. The flower grew and withered, turning to swarms of insects that attacked his face.

Niall guessed he would faint again and grabbed onto the only thought he could. Anchoring as many flashing, fleeting images of Neri to his mind as he could dredge up, he opened his eyes. The light of the suns already sinking below the horizon burned his eyes. Again he thought of bleeding but forced his weak limbs to push him upright.

He stumbled around the rocks and misjudged the distance with his blurred vision, smacking straight into the cliff face. Undeterred he hauled himself up and began to climb.

Every limb could have crumbled with each agonising movement and soon the light disappeared, leaving him climbing blind. Still he forced himself upward, afraid he wouldn't make it before morning.

When the level ground appeared under his fingertips he cried, assuming it would be a mirage created by his ruined brain, but he followed it all the same.

When he found the entrance to the tunnel he knew he was hallucinating. All he could do was stumble further, deeper, into the dream.

And when the light began to glow ahead, he followed it because instead of paining him, it soothed some of the torment.

He welcomed death now and yearned for its oblivion with the soft embrace of nothingness that would soothe his agony at Neri's absence, a disaster entirely of his own making.

The soothing trickle of water wrapped around him as he fell to his hands and knees, thanking the soft grass that cushioned his fall. He managed to open his eyes, and found the blurry outline of Caden standing near him alongside a blur of light that flickered gold. Heat emanated from the light, ready to either warm or burn him.

A chirping noise filled the cavern, as if Neri's firebird had appeared to him now that he lay on the brink of dying. He struggled to open his lips, to force the words out, because he needed the bird to know.

Croaking the first attempt, he swallowed against the feeling of thistles in his throat and tried again.

"She has to know I love her, that I did this for her."

The bird crooned a soft note and tender heat kindled some of Niall's pain. Niall stared into large, glimmering eyes, the colours swirling around each other in an infinite dance, older than time, until he realised the colours were contained in a droplet that grew until it splashed onto his forehead in a sear of blinding heat.

Niall closed his eyes. He didn't need sight to sense the warmth of the firebird leaving the cave. If Neri had any connection with the bird at all she would get his message somehow and she would know.

As his consciousness wavered, Niall heard Caden's voice strong and clear. It didn't hurt his ears or jar his mind so he allowed it to draw him away from the cosiness of oblivion and into the darkness of his body once more.

"You're not dying. It's the effect of the stuff you drank earlier. Sleep now and we will talk when you wake. There is much to discuss and to mend."

Niall let that thought soothe him into the natural nothingness of dreamless sleep. He would live to see her again. It had to be enough.

He didn't wake when Caden shook his head sadly, pushed Niall with one grubby toe to make sure he didn't wake, but the echo of words filled his dreams.

"He won't understand you know and I can't tell him," Caden grumbled. *"No patience that boy, never had any. Now I'm going to send him into the fray of life once more without a guiding light to hold onto because I made him believe in a dream long ago. I can only hope love will hold strong enough to keep him from doing anything ridiculous."*

Niall fought the visions those words brought forward, his dreams laced with memories. Caden had trained him to remain calm at all times, to think logically and use sense over emotion. In training the shade side, the emotions would remain at bay, for if the emotions rose too high the shade would grow to fight them.

He twisted and ducked through the carousel of pain and humiliation, of shame and loneliness, until a softness and a familiar scent guided him away. He followed it, clung to it, awareness sparking until he opened his eyes.

The cavern was still filled with light, and the water was still trickling on the rock while Caden played his flute. Niall pushed himself to a seated position and immediately wished he hadn't. He had no way of knowing if what he'd experienced was real without asking, but Caden would counsel patience and probably make him wait longer for the sheer torment of it.

"Its three days' ride to Carahdyl," Caden announced.

Niall looked up, confused. Carahdyl as a town held no worries for him, if anything he missed it, but why Caden should bring it up at all baffled him.

Caden sighed, groaned to his feet and walked to the tree. He brought out food for both of them which Niall bolted down in moments. He accepted more feeling like his hunger would never end. He could taste the food, revel in it, and he wondered then if that meant his shade-self had already begun to recede.

Thinking back, Niall recalled the conversation between the shade and the stallholder. If Neri was on the move then he had to find her before she found the way back through to the east. He pushed the food aside and remembered a mumbled thank you before turning his full attention to the matter at hand. He'd started feeling better already, stronger and more powerfully in control of his emotions.

"The process didn't work," Caden said.

Niall stared at him for a moment and flexed his hands and arms. He did sense his shade self, still fully in his shadow form, but something had changed, he was sure of it.

"The firebird came and healed you of the liquid but the process did not happen. It won't be attempted again. There's higher power than even the ancients at work among us now, and you'll need your shadow. It's your *ai-tan,* whether you believe that rot about shades or not."

Niall heard the words and knew not to contradict Caden. But in saving him, the firebird had damned him. A wave of numbness that should have frightened him to the core swept through his mind.

Neri, he had to focus on Neri.

He shook his head and stared back at Caden.

"The Jakida is on the move and Neri is with her," he insisted. "I think they've found a way east. I came through because it was requested of me and I vowed I would, but now I've done all that has been asked of me. I want to join them and walk through with her. Otherwise I have nothing."

The resolute, emotionless tone should have scared him but there was only determination. His shade-self had one purpose, to get back into the east with Neri and live a long life loving her. Now he would begin the final journey to rid himself of it.

"There's no guarantee your shade-self will dissipate even if you do venture east again." Caden put down his flute. "I often hear rumours, stories if you will. The cursed forest was grown from the four elements. We all know that air has never played by the same rules and it doesn't pay to spend your life chasing the wind or to wager on the air's shimmers."

Niall knew the rambling story would have some kernel of knowledge tucked amid the foliage, so he listened even though everything part of him itched to get moving.

"The earth tracks through the forest were long ago destroyed," Caden continued. "If what you believe of your girl is true, then the route of fire lies solely with your recent visitor. Only someone with *ai-tan* born of fire can journey through flames. That leaves one final element, that of water. It will be this that the Jakida seeks and that Hamlin's clues would have pointed to."

Caden paused, his blue eyes storming.

"The Siren will play. She has that of her element, a mistress that flows and never obeys. She will not give up any route through the cursed forest or around it, but the Jakida also has her own motivations. They're heading into a situation they might not walk free from. If the east is where you want to be, I urge you to seek another way by fire again."

Niall jumped to his feet as panic spiked in his chest.

"I can't let her get hurt. Carahdyl is three days' ride and they'll have an advantage over me, but they will go to

Mary first. Thank you."

"Wait, there's more-"

Niall ignored the sight of Caden shaking his head. He didn't have time to waste chatting over pointless riddles and whirled out of the cavern as a billow of thundering shadow.

If Neri was on her way to a route back to the east, he had to hope he wasn't too late to go with her.

<u>CHAPTER NINE</u>

Neri lay awake throughout the night, her mind stuck on the bird. She didn't dare try and sneak away from the others, conscious of Viljo standing on vigilant guard like a statue nearby. Even as the suns tipped their first shining white rays over the horizon, his gaze never wavered.

The Jakida had left them a while ago, perhaps to scout the area, and Livia lay in the deepest throes of slumber. The moment it was acceptable for her to get up, she rose to her feet and gave Viljo an awkward grimace of recognition. With his eyes on her, she tiptoed around the rocks to where she'd left the bird.

No bird, no blanket and no water canteen.

The only thing to indicate the bird had ever been there was a touch of charred grass in the correct shape and size of the creature. She wondered whether someone had snuck by during the night to relieve her of her items and found the bird. Another more worrying thought was that the Jakida had gone for an early morning stroll and found them strewn on the ground.

If the bird was gone, there was nothing she could do. She had to hope it had recovered and flown off rather than been carried away by some kind of predator.

She hastened back to her blanket and packed it, ignoring Viljo's disapproving stare. She nudged Livia with her foot instead and grinned when Livia groaned a plea for a few more moments.

Viljo distributed food and Neri ate hers quickly, her

attention fixed on the Jakida approaching with the white horse at her side. The horse made a beeline for her and she stroked its neck until the others made signs of mounting up. Before she could even look around for a suitable rock to mount from, embarrassed at the ease at which the Jakida and Livia vaulted onto their horses, hands gripped her hips.

Viljo lifted her easily onto the horse's back and smiled for a brief moment before leaving to mount his own. Neri bit her lip and fell in beside Livia. Still in a mood at the early hour, Livia didn't venture any conversation and Neri respected the silence. She kept an eye out for the borders of Forlaith instead as the outline of mountains grew on the horizon.

"Those are the Morlan mountains." Livia pointed to them. "I've never ventured that far before, but I'd love to one day.

Neri nodded, her heart sinking. That was where Cori had said she lived, and she couldn't exactly ask if they could detour that way to see if Niall had gone seeking Hareili out there.

Her mood sank further into darkness as the day dragged on. The lines of Forlaith forest passed on their right and sank back into the distance behind them. Her thoughts drifted so far away that she almost missed a blaze of light arcing through the sky. Livia gasped beside her as the glow landed in a copse of trees up ahead.

"Did you see that?" she asked.

The Jakida spurred her horse into a canter with Viljo and Livia right behind her. Neri wound her fingers in her horse's mane and sat tense as they set off in pursuit. As they reached the edge of the trees in a stampede of hooves, the Jakida's horse reared and backed up.

A melee of panicked horses ensued until Neri's snorted

a loud noise that seemed to steady them, but there was no steadying her pounding heart as she stared at the creature in front of them.

A dull thud echoed as a sacking pouch, tied with one of Livia's dark blue hair ribbons so they'd know which pouch belonged to who, dropped onto the grass by Neri's horse's hooves.

Neri slid down from her horse's back and took a few cautious steps until she stood in front of the large bird. The once-charred skin was covered in an unnatural level of deep brown plumage, so lustrous that this couldn't be the same injured animal she'd seen the night before, even though it was the same size. In the bright beam of sunslight, she noticed the odd quick shine of red and orange amongst the brown.

"Perhaps you will explain why a bird is dropping pouches at your feet?" the Jakida asked. "Pouches that clearly belong to us?"

Neri knelt down on one knee and stretched her fingers out to the bird. It's teardrop head butted against her hand, warm to the touch with the hint of charred skin still visible under the beak. The red glimmers on its feathers had caught the light from the suns and made it look like a flicker of fire.

Why it had decided to steal her water pouch and then return it, she couldn't know. She picked up the pouch to find it heavy and once again full of water. Deciding not to concentrate on how a bird could have flown with a heavy water container or how its feathers had bloomed so quickly, assuming it definitely was the same one, she focused on the relief that the bird hadn't suffered any lasting damage.

She still hadn't answered the Jakida's question. Her

unwilling host would be used to total compliance when she commanded information, so Neri turned to her now.

"This bird landed behind the rocks where we camped last night. At least, I'm assuming it's this one. It was injured so I left it my water. I didn't expect the bird to bring it back though."

The Jakida gave her a lingering, critical look before urging her horse onward at a fast walk. Before Viljo could make a point of dismounting to help her, Neri used a nearby tree to climb up onto her horse's back again.

She followed the group, excruciatingly aware that the bird had decided to plod along beside her and hopped with a shiver of its wings when the horses got too far in front. Neri made a few shooing motions with her hand but it didn't make any difference, and her cheeks flushed when she noticed Viljo laughing at her efforts despite the disapproving look the Jakida shot his way.

They'd wasted little time but rode on without further breaks until the suns were dipping and Livia pointed out a settlement ahead.

"There lies Carahdyl. We can expect a royal welcome there. Oh, your bird's leaving."

Neri glanced up in time to see the bird taking flight and veering away from the direction of the settlement, soon nothing more than a dark line against the evening glow of the sky.

"Maybe it just wanted some company," she said.

She turned her attention to the settlement, its flickers of firelight already glowing from within the low walls. Far beyond, a line of silver touched the horizon. She'd heard many a tale from passing travellers in the east about the great water, said to be vast enough for ships to sail for days without seeing land and stretching further than east or west could possibly imagine.

Their pace increased and they passed through high wooden gates of Carahdyl shortly before nightfall.

Livia reached over and poked Neri's thigh with a grin.

"Watch the welcome we get," she whispered.

Neri glanced around at the neat dwellings built from various shades of stone as they passed through the outskirts, amazed by as folk came out of their houses, smiling and waving.

Even the Jakida seemed cheered to see them. She waved with a fetching smile as folk threw small branches or favours in front of her horse while others clapped as she passed. The welcome continued as they approached a settlement square and rode right up to a sprawling dwelling with a wooden frame and worn stone walls. It dominated an entire corner of the square, and stablehands rushed out of barn doors nearby to take the horses. Neri dismounted and watched her horse amble behind the others, but even the stablehands refrained from approaching her.

Bemused and feeling very far from anywhere she could remotely consider as 'home', she fell into step with Livia as they moved toward the burnished black door of the inn.

Neri stepped inside, the instant hum of chatter swaddling her in a familiarity she hadn't known in a long time. She hadn't frequented any inns growing up, but her gramma had known everyone and often stopped by the local one to chat.

A ruddy-faced woman approached, with tumbling brown curls and a broad smile that could insinuate innuendos in the most innocent of glances. She bowed low and swept her apron free of her waist.

"Be welcome my lady," she said. "Your guests too. I have your rooms reserved as always of course."

The Jakida nodded and bestowed a smile full of warmth on the woman. Neri huddled behind Livia as the woman's shrewd blue eyes pierced into her own.

The Jakida swept through a door beside the bar and into the inn without another word, but Viljo settled his stiff form at the counter. Livia slumped on one of the wooden stools with her arms sprawled across the wood and grinned at the woman who took station behind the counter.

"What's been going on that we don't know about Mary?" she asked.

Neri hovered until Livia turned and pulled out the stool next to her, indicating she should take a seat between her and Viljo's ever present form. Neri edged her way onto the seat, the space barely big enough, her face flaming when the woman's roguish grin widened at her discomfort.

"*Ama* will not like you drinking this early Livia," Viljo said.

Livia rolled her eyes and took the wooden cup Mary slid across the bar to her. One appeared in front of Neri, full of dark liquid that sent a familiar aroma of spices and richness. Nostalgia swirled around her mind as the scent, so similar to the one she associated with Niall, hit her. She dipped her little finger into the cool amber liquid and brought it to her lips.

Closing her eyes as the wine coated her tongue, she sighed and pushed the ghosts of the past away, the bittersweet taste making her mind ache with memories.

She knew Viljo and Livia would be watching her so she turned her attentions to the woman standing before her.

"You're not from around here," Mary announced.

Neri took another gulp of the wine, glad when the memories remained at bay.

"I'm not, but I can drink as good as any."

Mary laughed and her gaze softened as she moved away to bring a glass bottle of the amber liquid closer.

"I imagine you can. I'm not from around here either, but this is as good a home as any to live out my days. Perhaps we'll talk a little later."

Neri nodded. Mary could be the woman to give her proper information if she asked for it.

Sinking the remainder of her cup, she smiled as Mary refilled it with prompt attentiveness and turned her attention to the siblings on either side of her. Livia struggled to finish her drink as quick as Neri had done but after one cup her pale cheeks flushed a pink so light the skin almost shone lilac.

Mary glanced with a wicked smirk at her, and Neri understood then that her friend had no head for drink as their cups were once again refilled. Viljo stayed at their side the whole while with his disapproving glance becoming less and less effective to them both.

The bar filled up even more to bursting with various townsfolk as the evening wore on. The Jakida might not have any intention of consorting with her folk directly, but Livia made enough friendly chatter at the bar to random folk that Neri forgot the Jakida was even travelling with them. By the time they retired for the night, Neri to share a room with Livia and Viljo off to his own quarters, Livia could only walk up the stairs with assistance.

With only a small candle on the edge of the warped wooden bathing stand to light their way into their narrow beds, Neri focused her drink-addled mind to the task of getting her head onto the pillow, rather than in a fruitless search of the shadows that skulked in the corners of the room.

She burrowed down in the blankets and delighted in

simple joys such as the crisp bite of the wind that whirled into the room through the glass-less window and nipped at her cheeks, heralding the imminent arrival of winter.

Even then, the last thought as she slipped into dreams was of shadow and the familiar scent of *liliam* wrapping around her.

CHAPTER TEN

Neri danced through dreams so deeply that her intention to wake early slipped away with them. She awoke to bright light and a gentle groaning coming from across the room. She sat up with a swimming head, hoping the groans weren't serious enough to force her into action too quickly.

She glanced over at Livia's bed and grinned with weary sympathy at her friend's limp form. Livia's hangover would no doubt plague her throughout the day and Neri eased to her feet, various muscles and bones creaking and complaining as she stretched and tiptoed across the room.

Livia cursed the half-hearted attempts to rouse her so Neri left the room and followed the corridor until she found the stairs. The inn, empty of folk, gave her space to gather her scattered thoughts.

She might soon find a way home again, if one even existed. The idea had sustained her during the journey but now she needed to think in terms of reality. She sat down at one of the wooden tables near the window, her gaze settling on the hustle and bustle of townsfolk setting up tables in the square.

If she found the way home there would probably be no way back to the west once she'd crossed back. She would have her home and her friends and she would see Dog again. Even though she hated to admit it, in the secret confines of her own mind, her heart still pulled her thoughts back to Niall. If they crossed through together and he got his previous form back somehow, would he see fit to rekindle their relationship?

Would he even want to if he was given the chance?

A dull clonk came from behind the bar and she turned to see Mary coming toward her with a plate in her hands.

"I take it our young lady isn't feeling too light on her feet this morning?"

Neri smiled and nodded her agreement. Mary placed the plate before her and sat down opposite, fixing Neri with a frank stare.

"The Jakida tells me you're searching for a way east." She frowned. "I won't pretend I'd want to go there because I don't, but you need to make sure this is the right choice for you. There's no power in the land, that side or this, that can hide heartbreak, but you don't want that to be your only reason for crossing the boundary."

Neri's cheeks flushed at the thought of being so transparent. Mary smiled.

"It's one thing to run into the unknown for love," she added. "But to do the same to run away from it might come back to bite you."

Mary voiced exactly what Neri was afraid to admit to herself, but even then the pain of being rejected sent her stumbling on with her crusade to find the way home.

"Livia mentioned *ai-tan* as we travelled." She changed the subject. "Do folk really believe it gives them actual special gifts?"

Mary chuckled and indicated that she should eat. Neri tore off a chunk of bread and smeared it in the pot of pale pink goop in the hope it would encourage Mary to talk at length.

"It took me a long time and many undeniable experiences before I believed it too," Mary said. "I would advise you to find your way east but then consider exploring our land instead of being so quick to leave it behind. You might find gifts of your own here."

"I doubt I have any gifts waiting for me."

I don't even have Niall waiting for me anymore.

Mary shrugged. "*Ai-tan* graces the folk that embrace it. I have learnt many interesting tricks but never has the land thought to give me a gift. I suppose it feels I'm blessed enough simply to be here and that I'll concede. Sometimes it will be an affinity with animals or the ability to read folk's emotions and feelings. I've seen folk control water with naught but their minds or hands, although elementarians are rare."

"Good for those that get it then," Neri conceded.

"You may well come upon *ai-tan* one day and I'll only warn you not to take it for granted. Everything has entirety; nothing is ever only good or only bad."

Mary sighed as Neri finished her final bite. The goop turned out to be some kind of egg whipped with a sweet, tart berry, utterly delicious with the pot all but licked clean.

It sounded unlikely, fanciful even, but Mary had no reason to lie to her. Neri had learnt at a young age the importance of being unimportant, and she was as unimportant as anyone could be.

Mary stood and picked up the empty plate.

"Viljo and the Jakida are currently about on business dealing with the important things," she said. "It will be up to you and me to entertain Livia until they return. I have strict instructions not to let her leave the settlement walls."

A rueful knowing glimmered in Mary's eyes and a smile crinkled across her lips. Neri couldn't help joining in. She guessed that Livia's first thought upon clearing her hangover would be to roam as widely as possible.

"Need any help?" she asked, nodding to the plate.

Mary hesitated. "I wouldn't say no."

Neri followed her to a big wooden tub behind the counter and set to work. They discussed the east briefly, then Mary detailed her experiences travelling the west. She spoke of places that Neri couldn't even imagine.

"The mines in the borderlands are grim in some ways but when you see the few left in their original state then you truly see a wonder of this land. It's just a shame that so many shades are used for the works there. Those that aren't buried in faults or cascades sometimes go mad, locked down there until harsh quotas are filled." Mary's face set in dark lines of foreboding. "Thought without emotion is easily swayed by the wrong logic sometimes. I don't hold a shred of goodwill to those that run the borderlands."

Neri snagged onto the one word that meant anything to her. Shades, folk like Niall, forced to mine for goods because they were considered lesser than folk. Heaviness settled over her chest as Livia arrived beside her, and she struggled to smile.

"My head is vile," Livia muttered.

Mary grinned. "I'll fix you a plate. Eat and you'll feel better."

"I am never drinking again."

"Said the archer to the farmer." Mary whisked a plate in front of Livia and ignored the queasy groan. "Perhaps after that a nice walk would do you good. I wouldn't want you to go too far though. The Jakida would not approve."

Mary bustled away and Neri caught the immediate mask of determination settling on Livia's face. Mere moments later, Livia had inhaled a wedge of bread and grabbed Neri by the arm. Neri let herself be dragged in the wake of Livia's intention to disobey her *ama*'s rules with as much flair as possible.

They entered the square and her skin shivered as the chill of the wind hit them. They made it halfway across before she heard Livia's frustrated sigh.

Viljo strode toward them, a smile of politeness for her and a look of determination for Livia.

"We are to go to the stables," he said.

Livia sighed. "Urgh, fine. If we ride fast enough maybe nobody will notice me being sick over the side."

Viljo merely lifted a supercilious eyebrow in her direction and set off toward the stable-barn.

Stable-hands led their horses out into the square for them, and Neri used a hay bale to swing up onto her horse's back. The Jakida was already off toward the settlement gates, and Neri's horse walked alongside Livia's with Viljo riding behind them. The locals seemed less inclined to make a big deal of their leaving, but Neri glanced over her shoulder to get one last glimpse of the market and the square. Viljo caught her eye and smiled. She grimaced a passable reply at him and faced forward again, her cheeks heating.

She expected a fast pace the moment they cleared the settlement walls and turned onto the plains, but the Jakida slowed to a halt instead.

"We go to the shore and we scout the area." Her tone encouraged no discussion. "No matter what we find we do not act. You follow my lead at all times. The shore is not a safe place these days."

Her gaze lingered on Neri for a moment, the glare of caution and potential threat clear. Neri caught herself just in time and forced the nod to stop. Despite the Jakida's considerate treatment so far, she wasn't a subject of the woman's lands. After a momentary stand-off, the Jakida reined her horse in the direction of the glimmering slip of silver on the horizon and set a smart pace.

"Well, she's in a great mood," Livia muttered.

Neri sighed as her horse picked up the pace, Livia riding alongside her looking suspiciously pale.

The rough grassland beneath their horses' hooves began to slope as the line of silver became a vast expanse that glimmered and swirled under the sunslight. Soon a strip of gold appeared beneath the silver, a dazzle of glimmering colours.

"We came here once as children," Livia called above the whistle of the wind. "The sand stretches on forever, as does the water."

The Jakida slowed her horse to a walk up ahead and Viljo appeared on Neri's other side, hemming her in. Neri glanced down the shining white legs of her horse to the sand, brown with red base tones. The grasslands ran down to the shore beside them but further ahead she could see crops of rock that eventually towered up into jagged cliff-faces.

As they moved onward her lips broke into a wry smile. The cliffs seemed to be forming a shape, their rough outlines showing something she couldn't quite make out.

"Ooh, there!"

Livia's horse side-stepped out of line and charged forward. The Jakida called after her with iron and stone set in her tone, Viljo's warning call echoing alongside it, but Livia made no attempt to slow or turn her horse.

Stuck between obedience and curiosity, Neri made her first attempt at riding since she'd first gotten on horseback. At the gentle touch of her heels the white horse lurched forward, the movement almost unseating her. Then the speed became fluid and their gait rolled with a flowing smoothness to rival the waves they left behind.

The rocks began to take formation, one crag appearing almost carved to look like a downcast face. The other jut of cliff formed a similar spectacle and she clutched at the horse's neck as it danced to a halt next to Livia's.

"Where the two maids weep at the turning of the tides," Livia recited. "The sorceress waits where the fountain springs."

"Is this it then?" she asked.

Livia nodded. "Must be. Those were the first lines of what Niall told us, and here are two maids in the rock weeping."

Neri stared up at the rock, the rough outlines of two faces visible if she tilted her head and squinted. She had no hope that Niall had somehow attempted to go on ahead of them. He wouldn't have known where to start without the clue in Hamlin's watch, but the thought of him captured her mind all the same.

Hooves beat a thunderous echo of incoming trouble behind them, so Neri dismounted and crept into the narrow inlet between the two rock faces.

A trail of water had carved a groove in the sand, bubbling down to the vast water. She followed the trail up the rock until she came to a stop in front of a small gap. Water flowed out from it, hardly a fountain but still a sign that they were in the right place.

Viljo glanced behind them, always on guard, and the Jakida's eyes were wide with suspicion. Livia stepped forward first, ducking the Jakida's arm as it shot out to hold her back.

"Can you see any larger openings?" Livia asked.

Neri shook her head and trailed her fingers around the rock.

"We'll go back now." The Jakida said. "We can decide what to do back at Carahdyl. If there is something here, we will need to plan accordingly."

It was the sensible thing to do, but it didn't stop Neri searching the rock for something, anything that might give her some sign.

A subtle shiver caught her eye. The ripple, gone in an instant, made the rock look like it had moved. She clenched her eyes tight shut and opened them again, convinced she was seeing things.

The rock shimmered again.

She pressed her fingertips to it and gulped down a startled squeak as her hand disappeared.

She yanked her fingers free and looked over her shoulder. The Jakida was already on horseback, glaring impatiently, and Viljo's face was stern as he held his horse's reins and Livia's.

Neri stepped away from the shimmer, loathe to leave it even for a second.

"What's the rest of the riddle?" she asked.

Livia frowned. "Where the two maids weep at the turning of the tides, the sorceress waits where the fountain springs. At rest where trees dare not grow, the firebird waits the fire-walker's wings."

Neri mouthed over the words as she committed them to memory. The softness in the rock was some kind of entrance, and she had to find out for sure if it was her way home or not.

She inhaled a sharp breath. "Well then, to where trees dare not grow I go."

She pushed her hand back into the softness and ignored Livia's startled gasp.

With morbid fascination she watched her arm

disappear, then she stepped forward. Instead of hard rock, a silken sensation brushed at her face, clinging to her hair. She held her breath as she stumbled forward, until the need for air welled up and clawed at her chest. Several steps and an aching chest later, the sensation disappeared and she leaned over her knees to catch her breath.

With no artificial light to see by, she had to rely on a dim glow coming from ahead. She shuffled forward and seethed through her teeth as pain slashed through her forearm. She cursed softly and touched where her arm had grazed against the rock. Pressing her fingers to her lips was the only way she could check whether she was bleeding, and the coppery taste on her fingers set her nerves on edge.

She glanced over her shoulder but couldn't see any sign of the others following her through. Even as her heart sank, determination rose.

It's probably safest they stay outside arguing. Livia would want to follow but the others wouldn't let her. *If there's a way home, I'm better off finding it on my own.*

She crept forward, her boots hardly making a sound, until the faint blue light shimmering against the rock around her grew stronger. The smell of salt and seaweed, the muggy cling of cold damp in the air and the gentle lull of lapping water against rock gave no encouragement to rush. As she turned a corner the light changed in colour, blue becoming turquoise then ebbing into an ominous green glow reflected off the moss growing on the walls.

Neri followed the tunnel as it sloped down, occasionally stumbling over the rocks and stones underfoot until the passage widened into a vast cavern with a shimmering blue lagoon.

Rising from the centre of the water, an island of rock glittering with stalagmites dazzled the humid air around her.

"Who're you?"

The rumbling growl echoed to her left, the voice of a burly man with a rugged black beard and arms like tree trunks. He glowered at her and her mind dropped to the blade at her hip that she hadn't even thought to hold ready.

"She is the saviour of the westlands."

The answering voice rang out, soft yet taunting. Neri looked to the island and the slender woman languishing on a throne hewn into the stalagmites hanging from the cavern ceiling.

The woman radiated a sense of beauty, but Neri recognised weathered lines and great age behind the flawless face. Like a rare book, the woman looked striking still but the age had worn her underneath.

"I'm here to find a way east," she announced, wincing as her voice shook. "I was told you might know where to find one."

The woman laughed, the sound like the tinkling of raindrops over rocks. As she leaned forward on her throne, Neri saw the statue behind her.

Detailed outlines had been cut into a slab of thick, pearlescent white glass. The kyne stood double her size and she yearned to dodge the huge guard inching closer to her so she could run her fingers over the firebird etched into the glass.

"You are bold to come here asking me for favours, young one. What else would you have me do?"

Neri heard the derision thinly veiled and sized up her opponent. The woman wouldn't be letting her try out the kyne, not without some kind of trade. Neri had nothing to trade, which left her with distraction and escape as her only option. She would need to explain to the Jakida and have some kind of deal struck on her behalf, or at least time to figure out if she could even call the firebird to the kyne again like before.

"I come to ask you to help fight in our war," she fibbed. "It was prophesised that you would help unite the two halves of the land and I ask you to fulfil your duty."

She shuffled a step backward as she fought to keep her voice calm.

"I don't hold with prophecies," the woman scoffed. "The wars of the upperworld are nothing to me. The Lord of the Borderlands may try to gain dominion over your realm but he will never think to conquer mine, and neither will those massing in the east. Your wars are of no concern to me."

Neri shrugged and took another step toward the exit. The guard was closing in on her with steady movements, as though she was prey to be trapped, but she could run fast and fight using his size against him if she had to.

"I've delivered the message. It'll be down to you to deal with your conscience."

She took another step but a swift movement across her only exit route sent her backward. Another guard even bulkier than the first blocked her way out and cackling laughter echoed behind her.

"Perhaps I shall not let you leave," the siren said, her tone viciously playful. "There is no purpose for you here but it has been long since I have had someone to toy with."

Neri slid her blade free and took her stance ready. She was ill-equipped for a fight but she turned to face the siren while keeping both guards in sight. As she inched back into the cavern and framed her back to the wall, the guard blocking the exit followed her.

Misdirection. She assessed the distance. *I just need to*

get between them and the tunnel.

"Oh, and now we have the hero, how fun!"

Neri groaned quietly as the siren dragged everyone's attention to the tunnel, and the man stepping out of it with his blade aloft.

Viljo's face was a picture of resolution but Neri mentally cursed him for spoiling it. She couldn't leave him alone to fight two men and whatever power the woman might possess, which meant they would be fighting, unless he had some secret super-plan up his sleeve. Somehow she doubted that.

"I think this will be fun," the siren announced. She lifted a finger, crooking it in Viljo's direction as her tone turned to honey. "Come to me."

A wave of power swept through the cavern, a fierce tug that almost brought Neri to her knees. Beside her, Viljo stood with his blade hand slack, his eyes glazed over. He tilted his head to one side, confusion scrawled across his face.

The siren laughed and Neri knew then that she would lose this fight. Viljo wouldn't best that kind of power. Her chest crunched with panic and her mind raced over the possibilities, all of them dire. If she ran Viljo might die, but if she stayed she might not be able to save either of them anyway.

A feral noise echoed from the tunnel before she could make any decision, a war cry of pure anger as the Jakida strode into the cavern.

Viljo shook his head as if waking from a dream, his awareness returning. He looked around and found her as she started forward, but the arm he swept out an arm in front of her caught her in the gut. She stumbled as he whisked her behind him in one swift move and raised his blade.

"I will not let you hurt her," he boomed.

The Jakida's eyes narrowed at that but she took her stance at her son's side.

The siren sighed theatrically and threw her hands up in the air.

"Well this will be fun at any rate."

Neri peered around Viljo's arm and swallowed hard as she realised two more guards, all as menacing as the first two, joined their companions.

Weapons were raised and she readied her own as adrenalin kicked through her system. The monster of mindless violence that had plagued her and nestled inside her for so long, coming out on rare occasions when she thought she was finally in control of herself, stretched its talons. They were evenly matched in numbers if the Siren intended not to fight but Neri doubted she would be much of an opponent.

She fixed her gaze on kyne and its breathtaking imagery of the firebird with its wings outstretched. The beak was open as if in song, or lament, and she would do whatever it took to get to it. She had hidden a tiny flint-stick in her pocket, one that she'd cobbled together from the hearth in her room at the palace, and that would be enough to light the kyne.

The guards advanced. One held a thick blade and the other two hefted large wooden clubs. The first clash of fighting came from Viljo's side and she dodged sideways as one of the men with a club came for her. He swung the club toward her and she leapt sideways, the wood thudding into the rock face.

Fear clawed at her insides, memories of swinging clubs bubbling up, but it sharpened her instincts. She swung her blade and the man grunted as it scraped his arm. He grunted and raised his club, giving chase as she darted away.

The haunting cackle of the siren followed her, bouncing off the rocks and echoing around the cavern as she tried to get closer to the kyne.

A dash of whirling water cut her off and Neri choked over a scream of frustration. She dodged the man attacking from behind and lifted her blade.

The man grinned, eying her then the weapon as though it were a toy and she a child, but he wasn't her target.

She swept her arm across her body and twisted. The hilt flew from her fingers, the blade spinning through the air. It sliced through the water and the tip caught the siren's shoulder. Spatters of blood appeared on her skin as the water-wall thundered to the ground.

Neri took her chance and ran. Her boots slithered over the wet rock but she used her arms to balance. The Jakida was almost level with her on the other side and she dug into her pocket.

A spasm of pain slammed through her shoulder, enough to bring her to her knees. She flattened against the ground and rolled toward the wall. Her blade clattered once and she lunged for it, her fingers scraping the hilt as it splashed into the water and the club thudded into the rock where she'd just been.

She pushed to her feet and faced the man without a weapon. She kept his eye contact, each step back being one closer to the kyne. There would never be any guarantee it would open for her, but she had no other option.

One of the guards folded quickly under the Jakida's blade, his body slain and staining the edge of the water. Given the weary sigh, the siren wasn't planning on mourning him much but Neri choked over a whimper of panic as she realised the Jakida would not come to her aid over her children's. Viljo stood with Livia fighting beside him, mid-battle against three guards, their blades whirling like a symphony of lethal precision.

Another guard arrived with another club, and Neri's hope guttered as she realised the siren might have hundreds at her disposal waiting to be called upon.

He lifted his weapon even though Neri had none, and she turned to make her last attempt at reaching the kyne.

A shattering sound tore through the air.

A moment of confusion echoed, the man's club suspended above her head, while Neri hovered with one foot raised to take another step back.

Then realisation dawned.

The Jakida stood with shards of the kyne still fracturing and raining down, her blade still halfway through the aberration she had committed.

Neri didn't hear her own cry of pain as the man's club felled her to the floor. She crashed against some jagged rocks, not noticing as they scored against her arms. She shuffled forward, a thud landing behind her as her opponent tried to hit her again.

All she wanted was a piece of the glass, a sign that there was a way to salvage the last doorway to take her back home. Her fingers snagged on a jagged edge but the sharpness cut her fingertips as she pulled it toward her.

The size of the piece she held was only that of a small looking-glass, and she blinked hard to clear the tears that sprang free. The large, expressive eye of the glass firebird stared back at her. The head had remained intact despite missing its plume and she used the last of her strength to lift her arms over her head.

She fumbled the remainder of the glass kyne into her pack. If by some miracle she escaped, she would use the shard to build a new shimmer back to the east. Her fingers burned from the cuts as she tried to pull the drawstring sacking closed again. Rolling onto her back, her vision blurred, her determination wavering.

Death with such fear about it had, when all things were considered, such a seductive pull about it. In her exhausted, grief-stricken state, she no longer cared nor felt. She could see the distant haze of blue still shimmering around her, and make out the pale waves that made the Siren's hair.

She heard a roar somewhere nearby, a battle cry, but she had no need to focus on it. Whoever it was wouldn't reach her in time as the Siren brought the bitter taste of saltwater waving out of the pool. It swirled around her, choking and smothering, but the need to hold her breath was no longer necessary.

Niall's here safe. Emelyn and Ma and the others are safe at the sanctuary. The Jakida is ruler of an entire land, so she'll take Viljo away once I'm gone.

Salt burned her nose but the sensation disappeared with abrupt finality, leaving only a weightless nothingness.

Her final thought would be for Niall. The scent of cake-spice and *liliam* swirled around her, and even though he'd betrayed her in the end, her heart still lifted through the fog of death. Her life had been worth it for the short time of bliss she'd had with him.

Her eyelids fluttered, one last spasm, and she imagined the familiar shadows clustering around her.

They were a comfort, she decided, as she descended with them into the void.

CHAPTER ELEVEN

Niall had to admit his strengthening shade-self did have positive sides. He had no remorse about stealing horse after horse on his way down to Carahdyl. Even the sight of the Morlan mountains, somewhere he now considered one of his memories of Neri despite all his previous memories there without her, didn't give him any flicker of emotion.

He arrived in Carahdyl just as their market wound down and let the stable boy take his weary horse into the barns.

Niall wiped a hand over his face, even though his shade-self wouldn't have collected grit or grime from the travel. The weariness was an automatic memory rather than an actual physical symptom, but it bothered him all the same. He had some trepidation at the thought of running into Neri as he scoured the market square for some sign of her, but found none and walked toward the inn. It would soon be packed but for that moment only one woman stood within that could help him. Mary took one look at him and dropped the cup she was wiping.

"Well this is a surprise! Niall back to darken my doors again."

The twinkle in her eyes proved her quip about his shade form had no malice in it, and Niall allowed himself a remnant of contentment at being in good company again.

"It's been a while," he admitted.

"A long while. I remember you in your more rebellious youth, staying for almost a season. You met that young woman here, what was her name?"

Niall grimaced. "Hareili. I've seen her since on the road, but that's not why I'm here."

"I'd ask if you want a drink, but it seems peculiar that an entourage of the Jakida passes through then here you are. They barely stay long enough to accept my hospitality, when usually they'd stay a full span of days, and now you turn up like a charging carthorse. All this talk of heading to the shores to find something. Strange, yes?"

Niall caught the mischievous grin but he also succumbed to the wave of aching gratitude. She'd told him what she guessed he needed to know without making him swim through social chatter first.

"Mary, you're a gem. I will visit again when there's time."

He darted away from the bar with Mary's laughter ringing in his ears. In the blissfully empty stables he took pity on his stolen horse and leapt onto one of the inn horses instead. The clatter of her steady, obedient hooves caused uproar in the market as he almost ploughed through a stall in his rush to leave.

He bent low the moment they left the settlement and raced the horse through the dimming light toward the darkening line of the horizon as the suns splayed blazing pinks and golds across the sky. The horse surged along the sands shifting underfoot but Niall slowed their pace as the words of Hamlin's riddle whirled in his mind.

The sight of several horses up ahead quickened his pulse and they snorted in alarm as his horse plunged to a halt beside them. All except one. The white horse stared at him, shining black eyes piercing into his own and he paused by her, knowing that she couldn't help him until night fell.

He ran his fingers over the rock until part of it gave way.

This would be his final chance. If the powers of the land saw fit to reward him for valour, they might let him have his old form back, his half-breed life. If not, as a shade he would end it himself.

Niall took a deep breath and pushed through the veil until he emerged in a dank underground tunnel. It took a moment for his eyes to adjust to the dull shimmer of luminescent light on the walls, then his ears caught the clash and clang of fighting.

He broke into a run and followed the sounds until he emerged into an underground cavern.

A hag on a stone throne wielded water while the Jakida stood near a towering kyne statue, her intent to move toward it clear. Viljo battled one burly man who seemed to find humour in keeping himself between Livia and Viljo, although Livia seemed to be faring fine defending herself, her attacks swift and accurate. Another man had emerged to fight for his mistress, from where Niall couldn't tell.

He caught sight of Neri standing apart from the others, and the man twice her size beating her to the floor.

Emotion spiked and Niall surged forward.

A loud shattering filled the cavern.

Niall lifted his head, horror slicing through him as the Jakida felled the kyne with a swipe of her blade, and with it the last hope Niall had of returning east with Neri.

One last spasm of emotion and a raw ache of uncontrollable rage burst in his chest, rippling throughout every part of him. He lifted his blade and moved, whirling it into the man who battled Viljo and Livia before grabbing Viljo's blade clean from his hands.

The hag, Siren, whatever she was, lifted a swirl of water toward Neri and attempted to drown her in a maelstrom, but Niall had grabbed her attention. The water she used as a weapon retreated and became a fort she wound around herself as Neri crashed to the ground.

The Jakida lunged forward and sliced at the nearest guard, leaving one towering over Neri with uncertainty scrawled across his face. Niall sheathed his blade while moving and let Viljo's drop to the floor with a clatter.

The final guard's eyes were glazed over as if he was stuck in some kind of enthralment, but he'd shown no hesitation in beating Neri to the floor. Niall wrapped his shadow around the man and willed it to suck the very life from someone who'd tried to harm her.

The man crumpled unconscious and Niall kneeled over Neri.

"Neri, look at me," he begged. "Please, open your eyes."

He pressed his hands to her chest and his ear to her face, but she was barely breathing. The promise of bruises and abrasions would soon blossom over her body but something held her to life still, her heartbeat a faint flicker.

"Come on, curse me, hit me, anything."

Not caring about the yawning silence behind him or who might be watching, he lowered his torso over hers and let soft kisses rain over her forehead, her hair and her lips. Using his shade self to keep the threatening emotions at bay, he gathered her in his arms and faced the siren.

"Try to stop me taking her and I will kill you. I will burn every drop of water from your body and delight in doing it."

She blinked back at him from behind her fortress of water, but he didn't wait for a response. He stormed past the Jakida, who was already grabbing Livia and hustling her toward the tunnel with Viljo in tow, and through the tunnel. There was only one person who would be able to help him now.

As he stepped through the veil and onto the sand outside, the stars were just done fading across the nighttime sky, the suns already showing over the horizon. Four horses still stood waiting, but the fifth was nowhere to be seen. In place of the white horse that had been there on his arrival, Zel stood waiting. Niall had known of the sorceress for a long time and she had many secrets, but he knew more than folk thought.

He faced her with Neri close to his chest, wrapping them both in swathes of shadow.

"I need you to take me to the great tree." He glanced around for any re-emerging dangers. "I don't care what the repercussions are."

He caught the low growl in his voice and guessed that soon the shade self would take over. The more his emotion spiked, the more his shade-self would fight it. But if it helped give Neri the life she deserved, he would make this his last journey.

Livia's quiet sobs echoed as she appeared beside him, her gaze on Neri in his arms. Even Viljo looked downcast. Niall didn't dare look at the Jakida for fear of killing her. She had destroyed any hope he had of a future and Neri's last chance of happiness with her friends.

"I fear it won't make a difference," Zel said gently. "Neri has no *ai-tan* so the tree will not recognise her."

Niall saw sadness in her eyes, no insidious intentions lying there, but he hated all of them for wasting time.

"I'll give whatever I have to her," he insisted. "We need to go now."

Zel shook her head. "There are no guarantees and the potential hazards are unknown. Perhaps your guardian would be a better path to follow. If you attempt this you could face-"

"Don't tell me I could face a fate worse than death. I already drank in the *aerie* caves and a friend of hers came to heal me. This is what I am supposed to do, to save her. Now stop stalling and take us where we need to go."

He glared at Zel until she bowed her head with a slow nod.

"This is inadvisable." The Jakida stepped in front of him. "Neri's loss is unfortunate but we cannot be running about the land for one person."

He clutched Neri tighter. "I don't care much what you or your family does from here on. Zel will be coming with me, three on horseback if we have to."

Livia stepped forward, her eyes red and face scrunched with determination.

"Zel can take my horse. I'll walk if I have to or she can ride with me until nightfall. I'm going with you."

The Jakida opened her mouth to forbid it but Livia was already turning toward her. As she spoke, an uncharacteristic rumble of thunder boomed overheard, rolling on deep and long to drown out Livia's words.

Niall glanced upward, wondering if he should find a cloak or get a blanket for Neri in case it rained, but the thunder settled and Livia gave him a nod.

"Zel will ride with me until nightfall," she said. "Niall, follow us. We'll need to ride fast."

Niall placed Neri on top of his horse and Livia held her steady whilst he mounted. Not entirely sure where he had to go to find the great tree, he had to wait for the others to ready themselves. Then Livia set off with Zel seated behind her and he realised that the Jakida and Viljo, both silent and looking mutinous, were coming with them.

He focused on keeping Neri steady in front of him with

one arm tight around her waist to keep her anchored and his other hand holding the reins. It would be difficult to steer but he trusted his horse to follow Livia's.

Neri's face was caught in a frown and he smoothed his fingertips over her brow, earning himself a slight puff of breath and a twitch of her lips.

Nobody spoke as they rode a smart pace across the plains, heading west instead of north back to Carahdyl. They would need to turn north eventually to get to the Morlan mountains, but by the time nightfall came with only a brief break for the horses and for Zel to regain her equine form, on they went still heading west, following the line of the great water. Soon a forest swallowed them, and Niall's orientation was skewed by the thick cover of leaves overhead. He clung to Neri as the night wore on, reassuring himself that this was for her.

Eventually the dirt track they followed turned to a mere footpath, lit only by the scant snatches of moon and stars above, and the firebrands everyone else carried around him. Then their horses were stumbling and hacking through vines and undergrowth and his only thought was keeping Neri steady.

"We will need to leave the horses here." Livia called back. "They won't go where we need to."

Niall frowned, reluctant to get rid of his option of speed.

"They will go where we tell them to. Are you telling me there's some kind of sorcery that forbids animals or something?"

His emotion flickered and ebbed, wavering between the all-encompassing ache that Neri might not survive and numb acknowledgement that he had to keep going so she did.

Livia reined her horse to a halt and shot a prim glare his

way.

"Not at all. It's a ravine path and the horses won't fit."

She dismounted beside a narrow gap in the rock and gave her horse a pat before tethering its reins. Niall swung to the ground and gathered Neri to him again.

The suns started to rise again as they squeezed into the rocky ravine, and the tops of the cliffs were already conceding their shadows to the light. He'd roamed the Morlan mountains previously, but never this far south.

If I'd known…

He shook the sombre thoughts away as Livia's pace increased up ahead. He soldiered on after her, conscious not to let any part of Neri flop toward the rocks on either side.

As the cliffs fell away, even he had to stop and stare. Two rolling hills rose on either side, leaving a wide green valley sloping down in front of them. Plants, trees and flowers grew wild and free, like the dawning of the world before folk and *aerie*, a riot of colours and intoxicating scents.

The suns were framed between the hills as they continued to rise, the horizon a riotous glow of gold, but dominating the colour was a towering tree, its gargantuan trunk and winding branches climbing up toward the skies.

Niall knew the fables of the great tree, all children heard it as one of the founding stories of the land itself. The great tree had grown first from the spark of some great ethereal mind, long before grass or plants, flowers or animals. Some said a tiny seed fell from the dawning of the land itself and the tree was borne into the fertile earth, until the land grew and from that spread *ai-tan* to nourish it.

The sunslight grew fierce and fast, tempered only by the bitter wind squalling around, and Niall had no idea how long he'd been standing there.

"Time to go."

Livia stood beside him.

"If you're determined to do this, you need to go up," she explained. "Zel said as much on the way here."

Niall hadn't heard that, but he'd been too preoccupied to pay attention to the others.

"Take the steps around the trunk," Livia continued. "Keep going even if it seems never-ending. Then place her in the hollow at the top and stay with her. Zel said that the land would decide and you will know when it does."

Niall nodded his thanks and set off down the grassy slope toward the base of the great tree with Neri nestled against him. He waded through a stream that ran across his path, not bothering to wait for the others, and forced himself to focus on the idyll around him. Neri would have a chance to see beautiful flowers again, and she'd feel the gentle sway of long blades of grass under her feet. It had to be enough.

He reached the base of the tree and glanced back, startled to see Livia pink-cheeked but still right behind him. She didn't say a word but the sheer determination on her face gave him strength. Even if Neri couldn't get back to Emelyn and the others, Livia would make sure nothing awful happened to her.

He wanted to ask if she would tell Neri the truth about whatever happened next, but before he could voice it her deep brown eyes sparkled and she nodded.

"I'll tell her you came for her if it goes wrong for you. The others won't be far behind. Let's go."

Reassured by her presence, Niall approached the rough steps hewn into the enormous tree. The trunk was wide enough to contain an enormous dwelling inside, possibly several dwellings, and he steeled himself as he put his foot on the first step. His shadow made no noise but the steady tap of Livia's boots behind him softened the silence as he began to climb, focusing on each step until the circular repetition lulled him into thought.

He only ever wanted a place where he and Neri could be safe and happy together. The east had been plagued by the Governance hunting them, but at least there they fought together. In the west he'd goaded her into fighting against him out of sheer anguish and habit and he regretted it now.

He hitched Neri closer and kissed her hair. Her skin was still cold to the touch but she was alive. He would give whatever he needed to for her.

After a while the view and their height stopped changing, the meadow below them a mere splash of colour and the white sky above rolling on forever. Niall soldiered on. He noticed on one look down below that Viljo and the Jakida were a few rotations behind but Livia's footfalls never stopped tapping solidly behind him.

Until he took another step and his foot thudded down. The stairs had ended and he stared at the wide circular platform at the very top of the great tree. Livia uttered a low gasp of astonishment as he took a cautious step toward a second, smaller tree growing out of the top of the first. A tangle of pale brown branches reached outward and upward from a squat trunk, with petals of the palest pinks, greens, blues and yellows shivering in a breeze of air and of life that none of them could feel.

"You told me to place her in the tree," he murmured.

Livia pointed to a gnarled hollow in the trunk, her mouth hanging open as Viljo and the Jakida appeared behind her. Niall ignored them and walked forward to place Neri's body gently into the husk of the tree.

He reached out to take her hand, but as his fingertips grazed her knuckles a firm weight wrapped around the shadow of his arm, pulling him back. Niall looked down to see Livia's hand holding firm.

"There's time." She kept her voice hushed. "I need you to listen to me and then I'll step back. Neri wouldn't want your sacrifice. She may never trust you again but I don't think she wants a life without you. I know you're affected by what you are but think of her pain if she does survive and realises you're completely lost to her. It will destroy her. Maybe the tree will save her on her own merit. It's worth it to at least try."

She bit her lip and let him go. She only wanted to help but Neri needed *ai-tan* for the tree to work on her, to fix her, and he would be the only one willing to donate it.

He took Neri's cold fingers in his own, his free hand stroking hair back from her face.

He waited to see what would happen, whether his *ai-tan* would slowly leak from his shadow or if it would happen as a sharp severing, but he didn't expect a sudden flow of breathtaking noise. The melody sounded like autumn, like leaves crackling under foot and children laughing, all embodied in one harmonious note that filled the air with the scent of berries and woodsmoke.

A fierce heat hit his face, burning as if it had swept his shadow clean away. He lifted his head to welcome it, to will it on with everything he had, but a searing ball of flame caught his gaze instead. It swooped, the shimmer of fire and feathers arcing up and shooting down, angling its flight path right into the hollow of the tree.

Niall's heart lifted in the moment he thought the firebird had come to save her. But the image wavered and shattered as the tree burst into flame. Fire raged over the branches, licking and caressing them into charred black limbs as they started to crumble.

Niall stared, horror clawing at him until a burst of pain split his arm. His shadow self wouldn't burn but the flames didn't gutter and die as he grit his teeth and clung on to Neri's hand.

He stayed hunched over as the fire grew, not knowing if he had to trust the flames or protect her from it. Distant shouts from Viljo and the Jakida for Livia to get back echoed, and the Jakida even shouted warnings to him, but he stayed with Neri.

The flaming petals whirled on an angry gust of air and turned an unmistakeable shade of red as they tumbled down from their branches like bloodied snowflakes. Placing his hand on his chest, he ran his fingers over the place where the wax charm Neri had given him was settled. It had been a constant warmth in his chest even though he couldn't touch the wax itself, couldn't remove it. The familiar warmth of it flickered at his touch, but his emotions spiked and guttered as the charm went deathly cold.

Neri wasn't waking and the essence of her gift to him was gone.

Niall stared at her face, ignoring the uncomfortable burn of the fire as someone tried to beat it off him. The last ounce of fight that had been kindled by hope of saving Neri was gone, and any lingering remnant of emotion he might have clung to died with her.

When someone hauled him away, he focused on her cold fingers sliding free of his, and his humanity along with him.

He barely noticed Viljo creating vines from the top of the tree, or the Jakida manhandling him toward the edge.

He didn't comprehend the fierce look of derision that Viljo
shot at him as he was rolled up secure in vines to be
constrained, as though they thought there was any point to
him fighting them now.

By the time they scaled down the side of the great tree
on the vines, Niall being levered down by an awkward
combination of Viljo's arm around his legs and Livia's arm
around his neck, Niall had nothing left to feel at all.

CHAPTER TWELVE

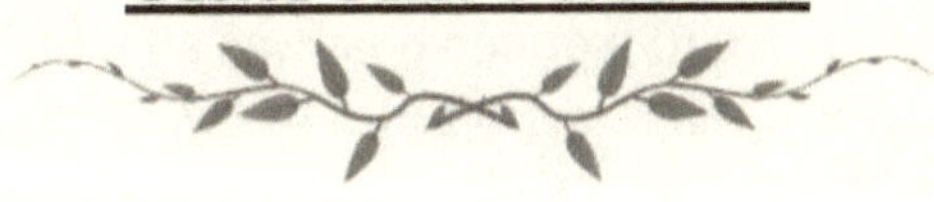

Neri's awareness sparked before she opened her eyes, quickly followed by the sensation of discomfort in her bones. She shifted and grunted at the feel of hard, pebbled lumps beneath her shoulders and back.

The sound of lapping water reached her as well as the smell of salt and weed, but she couldn't remember where she was supposed to be.

Neri opened her eyes and squinted against the bright whiteness of the sky. Sitting up slowly, she assessed the dull ache between her shoulders. No injuries, but she couldn't remember what had happened the night before or why it felt like she'd been fighting. She was at least in familiar short trousers and a short-sleeved shirt. Although both were grey when she didn't own anything grey, which was something of a confusion.

She eyed the long stretch of sand she was sitting on, running all the way from one side of the horizon to the other. She hadn't seen much sand in her life, not in such a natural setting, and she hadn't expected the sand to be grey either. She glanced over her shoulder and saw the mouth of a cave with the backdrop of shadowy dark trees behind it. The sight of it tugged on a memory, of caverns and the sound of water, and she frowned for several moments before an entire cascade of memories came rushing back to her. The sanctuary, the cursed forest, the firebird, then the west with its settlement and the white horse that didn't need to be bridled.

She began to laugh, hysteria twisting inside her head. She had no idea where she was or how she got there, but it didn't matter. A small wooden boat was attached to a small wooden platform reaching out into the water further down the grey beach, so Neri clambered to her feet to investigate.

As she drew closer, the towering figure of a man in a dark grey cloak appeared beside the boat. He had his hood pulled up and she stumbled to a halt as he turned to face her.

The slip of skin visible underneath his hood and above his high collar was gnarled and grey. She took a tentative step back.

"Where am I?" she asked.

The man leaned closer.

"Payment."

The low voice tugged at the very foundation of fear in her bones, her mind screaming at her to run away. She glanced over her shoulder but there was nothing except more sand and trees, no sign of civilisation among the endless landscape of grey. She frantically patted her pockets. All she could find were two grey coins made of wood and coated with hardened with a coat of *gar*.

A trickle of realisation filtered into her head, the coins horrifically familiar as she held them out.

"All I have are these."

All folk knew to carry two coins in case they met with upon death. Some folk hid their coins and trusted their family to coin their bodies, while others insisted on hiding theirs on them at all times. Neri had coined her mamma's body before the Governance came knocking, and had to hope someone had done the same for her gramma, but since then she'd carried hers in her pocket.

The man eyed the coins for a moment before swiping

them from her with a gloved hand. She inched back as he held his arm out to indicate she should get into the boat.

"No way off this beach but by sea."

The rumble of his voice echoed not just in her ears but all around them.

"Where am I?" she asked. "Where are you heading to?"

He paused long enough for her panic to escalate. She folded her arms across her chest, but where could she run to in a land she didn't know?

"You are in my domain," he rumbled. "Get into the boat and I may return you to yours."

It wasn't exactly a reassurance but she didn't have much option on the beach either from what little she could see. The endless expanse of grey frightened her and she clambered into the boat, sitting on a small ledge at the far end. If the stranger tried anything, she would jump overboard and swim back to the beach.

He showed no signs of untying the boat from the platform, but when it started moving by itself she clutched the sides with desperate hands.

"You want to go home," he said. "No home where this boat goes. I'll play a game with you. You win and I'll take you back to where you belong. You lose, I throw you overboard and claim you for my own."

Neri shrank as far back as the boat would allow, looking over her shoulder. The shore was nowhere to be seen. She twisted back and forth but the only sight to see was the vast expanse of still, grey water in every direction.

"I'm not yours to claim!"

Thoughts of Niall filled her head and she tensed, ready to throw her body into the water or to fight him, even though she had no blade and the unshakeable knowledge he wouldn't even need to try to best her.

"You're on the boat to the land of the dead, all souls are mine to claim. You chose to get into my boat and we only goes one way. Two coins to the dwelling of the dead."

The boat stopped moving and Neri clung to the sides of it, frozen in terror as he pulled a grubby pack of *chekana* cards from the depths of his cloak and held it out to her.

"Pick a card. If yours is more than mine, you win."

Neri had no skill at *chekana* as she'd only seen folk play a handful of times. She had a vague memory that most cards had images of different roles and folk on, so she had no idea which would be higher than the other.

With shaking hands that almost dislodged the whole deck, she picked up a pile from the top and looked at the card on the bottom.

"The maiden? Is that high or low?"

The man leaned forward and a soft cry of horror escaped her lips.

"Whichever one helps me win."

He grabbed hold of the pile and turned it over. She couldn't see his card but the small slip of face she could see beneath his hood contorted. Her heart thudded, the stillness dragging on for eternal moments.

"The forger. You have much to do."

Neri veered back as his arm swung forward and caught her off balance. Flailing her limbs against the sides of the boat, she struggled against the strong hands that landed on her back. She sucked a sharp breath as he kicked her legs out from under her and pushed her again, sending her flying into the water. She twisted, reaching up for the boat, her fingers grasping at air.

His hooded face was the last thing she knew as she was dragged under the water, surrounded by the choke of the water and the haunting scent of *liliam*.

Her mind wavered, awareness fracturing until the smell of *liliam* faded, replaced by the earthiness of nature and the unexpected ability to breathe.

She had no recollection of when she shut her eyes so she opened them again, surprised to see the hint of green and the faint glow from the dancing stars in the sky framed by darkness of wood in front of her. She reached out and ran her palms over the enormous knot of wood in front of her. It gave under her fingertips and crumbled, like a doorway to the land outside.

Neri grabbed the edges of the wood, her cocoon seemingly set into the husk of a tree, although why she'd woken up inside a tree she couldn't remember. She shook her head to clear the fuzziness in her mind, piecing together the chaos of memories.

She'd woken in a land of grey with a beach and a man in a boat. He had played a game of cards with her before trying to drown her, yet here she was inside a tree with an abundance of breathtakingly beautiful colour waiting for her outside of it.

With her legs shaking beneath her, she eased herself out of the tree and looked up. The trunk towered up to the night sky, but she still had no idea how she got there.

Further ahead past a bubbling stream was a grassy hill full of flowers, and beyond that a length of high grey cliffs.

She took a couple of steps forward but something restrained her. She twisted and winced as a sharp tug pulled between her shoulder blades, the sensation like peeling excess *gar* from her fingers. She watched a long length of vibrant reddish-brown root as it retreated back into the husk of the tree.

That was attached to me? She shook her head. *Strange, but better than the land of grey before.*

With a quick glance down at her utter lack of clothing, Neri turned away from the tree and began to walk. She waded through the stream, icy cold enough to reassure her this wasn't part of some dream. She shivered as she clambered onto the bank and continued walking through the flowers.

Up ahead she could see folk waiting for her, surrounded by a small glow of firelight. The closer she got, the easier it was to see the horrified faces of two women and one blushing man who quickly turned around to avert his gaze from her naked form.

She recognised them as the scant memories filtered back to her. The older lady, the Jakida, was frowning at her, intrigued but wary. Her red hair was curling around itself, a sign of her *ai-tan* perhaps, but there was a definite air of practiced confidence in the narrowed eyes.

Livia had no similar reservations, silvery tears streaming down her cheeks as she hurried forward with a pack of brown sacking that Neri recognised as her own.

"We thought you were gone!" Livia gasped.

Neri pulled some clothes out of her pack, her fingers tingling against the fabric. A bolt of amusement flickered as she glanced Viljo's way, his back firmly turned to her.

Then memories swarmed. The cavern and the shimmering rock, the hag drowning her in a whirlwind of water. And Niall, the scent of him being the last thing she remembered.

A whirl of *liliam* danced around her and she lifted her head, staring past the others to a cleft in the rock. Her breath caught in her throat.

A shadow swirled there for brief moments, a faint movement against the otherwise still cliff.

It wavered down as if bowing low. Then it disappeared.

She started forward, wild thoughts that maybe Niall truly had come for her as she lay dying in the siren's cavern, after even he'd abandoned her. But even if he had been there, he wasn't hanging around.

He made a vow to Hamlin to keep me safe. She sucked in a sharp, burning breath. *Maybe that's what's kept him coming back all along.*

She glanced at the others, her memories solidifying as she saw the Jakida, the vision of shattering glass filling her head.

She sank to her knees, a pain growing in her chest. It burned her; she could feel the lick of flames inside, charring as she remembered the kyne shattered into unusable pieces on the cavern floor. That had been her only way back to the east, assuming she could even get it to work. Her mouth dropped open and a scream wrenched from her gut as the smell of burning and smoke swirled around her, the grass singeing under her legs.

"Get her up," the Jakida snapped. "We can't linger here."

Livia inched forward but Neri shook off her anguish and struggled to her feet.

"I'm fine."

She wasn't. Her skin prickled as though it was burnt, her mind needled with anxious thoughts, and she had several gaps in the timeline that needed filling in. She had no way home to the east, and very little use to the Jakida now that would give her a measure of safety when they returned to Jakiris.

"We will see if there are any horses still waiting for us on the other side," the Jakida said. "Then there is much to be discussed."

Neri nodded. "I have no idea what has happened since

entering the siren's cavern, so yes, there is."

The Jakida's lips thinned at the subtle accusation there, but she turned away and started walking toward the cliffs without a word. Viljo set off after her with another lingering look in Neri's direction. Neri ignored him and let Livia set the pace.

"I made them wait," Livia murmured. "They insisted on leaving, but I made them wait for you."

They reached a cut in the rock and Neri shivered at the thought of the siren's cavern, but Livia gave her shoulder a pat.

"We're far away from there," she insisted. "I would normally babble the whole affair to you, but I've been told not to under threat of being locked in the Jakirian kitchens for the rest of my life. Are you hurting anywhere?"

"Confused. Everything else will mend soon enough. Is… was… Never mind."

She couldn't bring herself to ask about Niall. He might have come for her but he hadn't stayed. Up ahead, the ravine path trailed on.

"It isn't far," Livia promised. "Once we're back in the woods, we should be able to make camp."

Even as she said it, the cliffs ended abruptly and gave way to a jungle of trees and vines. A collection of horses were tethered in front of them, all except one and Neri's heart lifted to see the white horse watching them.

As the last first of sunlight began to filter through the treetops, the horse lowered its head and shivered. The front legs began to shorten and the powerful shoulders sank until the horse stood on hind legs, the long nose shrinking and the mane unravelling into coils of iridescent silver hair.

Neri stared at the woman in front of her and waited for Zel to cloak herself in a robe.

“Wow.”

“That’s one way of putting it.”

“What even is... how...” Neri shook her head, bewildered. “You’re a horse.”

Zel laughed. “I tell you no lies but not entire truths either. I must ask for your trust on that.”

The Jakida set off for water with Livia begrudgingly in tow, which left Viljo in charge of the camp and building a small fire. The moment Zel had composed herself, Neri folded her arms across her chest and stared her down.

“Tell me everything,” she demanded.

Zel eyed her for a moment. Then she groaned and slid down to sit on the grass. She smiled and indicated the grass beside her, so Neri conceded and sank onto the ground, weary and wanting nothing more than to ride fast and reach Jakiris so she could sink into the pool in her room and sleep off her pains.

“I know nothing of what transpired in the siren’s cavern but what the others have told me,” Zel began. “You almost died and the only option they had to save you was bring you to the tree of life.”

“The... what?”

Zel smiled. “The tree of life. Perhaps it is not often talked of in the east. I’ve never heard of it being used to save lives before though. By all accounts, you were placed inside the tree, then that bird of yours flew into it and the entire thing burst into flame.”

Zel paused as Neri immediately looked down to check her skin, unmarked by tingling in the presence of the fire nearby.

“That’s... impossible.”

“Improbable,” Zel chided. “There’s something about you, and clearly the land thinks so too. The firebird brought you west, then came to save you."

"The bird didn't save me, it was the game."

She frowned as Zel's head tilted in query.

"Game?"

Before Neri answer, even though she wasn't sure what part of her ordeal was real and what was mind-addled dreaming, Livia and the Jakida returned.

Viljo passed around food and sat with them, but the Jakida remained standing on watch nearby.

"It was the scariest thing I've ever seen," Viljo admitted. "The fire stretched to the skies, but then the flames died down and the tree was entirely unscathed. Of course it does have the life force of *ai-tan* flowing inside it, but we knew you were gone. Then we reached the ground and you stepped out of it."

"It's unthinkable," Livia added, unable to curb the excitement in her voice. "Unless that bird can only be one thing."

Viljo sighed. "Which would be a wonder indeed. Nobody has reported seeing one for a long time but then you turn up talking about kynes, and a firebird always comes to protect its own."

Neri pressed a hand to her forehead and yelped. Her skin, so hot from being near the fire, or possibly from being burnt alive, had burned her. She scrabbled to her feet and stumbled away from the group. The burning over her skin worsened until she had to stop and kneel in the grass.

She wanted oblivion, to sleep and not to think or feel. Niall's face swam into her mind and she whimpered. Niall had been born a shade, but for once she could understand how folk desired nothing more than to be emotionless.

She huffed frantic breaths until they steadied, until her mind had calmed enough for the burning to dim to a mere prickling. With a weary huff, she got to her feet and turned to find Viljo behind her, his hands clasped behind his back.

"I didn't mean to upset you," he said softly.

Neri waved her hand at him, trying and failing to show him that it didn't matter.

"I'm just realising everything I thought about who and what I am is probably a lie," she admitted. "Plus my skin keeps burning, probably an after effect but it hurts and I really need to just sleep and eat and get clean."

Viljo didn't reply. Instead he simply angled his body ninety degrees with his arm held out to indicate she should come back to the group with him. She conceded and let him fall into step beside her.

The Jakida was already lying on a bedroll some paces away from the fire and Zel stood nearby, but Livia jumped up to guide Neri to a blanket.

"Rest for the morning," she insisted. "We'll ride straight back to Jakiris after, then we can start to mend things from there."

Neri slumped on the provided blankets, torn between sorting a plan in her head and passing out. Her jaw almost cracked when she yawned wide, but the moment she closed her eyes, the vision of the shadow bowing by the cliffs filled her head.

He's out there somewhere, and knowing him he's probably safe.

It was enough, she decided. He was safe and she was alive. One day, she would find a way east even if she had to burn her way through the cursed forest one warped tree at a time.

It's enough, for now.

CHAPTER THIRTEEN

The speck of blood was tiny, but it was there. Niall stared in awe at the tiniest tinge of red glimmering through the swathes of shadow that made up his forearm.

He'd broken free of Viljo's control at the bottom of the great tree, his emotions bursting in a cacophony of static that deafened him as the cliff-lined valley around the great tree rushed past. He had no idea how fast he was running but something sharp had pierced the agony. He stood at the edge of the ravine between the cliffs to take one look back and utter joy and panic mingled with rising hope spasmed through him.

Neri was naked and he had the irksome thought that Viljo was between them, but another look down at his shadow kept him welded in place. His sacrifice had worked, but she would fight to get back to her friends after this, he knew her well enough to be sure of that. Rumours of the borderlands attacking raised another spike of terror, that she might get caught in the fighting.

Neri lifted her head and the bittersweet scent of liliam swirled around him. She was looking right at him and the hope made his mind up for him.

He bowed in recognition, idiocy when he should be running back to her, begging forgiveness.

Caden. Niall stepped into the ravine and started running. Caden can send us both back east like he did last time. We'll take our chances, get everyone to travel really far south.

He ran until he couldn't run anymore and sat overlooking the deserted plains, the suns sinking above him. In shadow form he didn't get aches in his legs or pains in his side, not physically anyway. He felt the pain of it in his mind, but his body could keep going and he'd trained himself in younger years to mentally sever the two sides so he could keep endurance.

Now the subtle sting on his forearm wouldn't go away and he dabbed a fingertip against it, eying the droplet of red hanging from the swirl of shadow.

His shade-self didn't bleed. It didn't even suffer being run through with a blade, or at least it never had before.

"It can't be," he muttered, heaving to his feet and beginning to pace. "Unless the fire burned my shade away again."

He glanced around to make sure nobody had managed to sneak up on him somehow, but his voice in the evening silence was a small comfort so he kept talking.

"It burned away whatever protection Caden put on me to go east. What if my sacrifice burned the shade away this time?"

He took a deep breath. It could be a random speck from somewhere else, someone else, Neri even. But that wouldn't explain the stinging.

With hope firing in the region of his chest, he started running again. If by some miracle his shade-self was fading, or failing, he would lose the ability to cover vast ground.

He marked landscapes as he ran, slowing only to check himself over for any more signs of his shadow receding. He found none but kept pace, running through the night until the suns rose. He grabbed some berries and a few stalks of grain to crumble as he passed through forests and the odd boundary field of a settlement, determined to have fuel ready if his body did reappear. He kept an eye out for a suitable horse to 'borrow' but found none, not wanting to veer to close to the larger settlements and conscious that smaller ones might not be able to spare one without consequence.

Such inner growth. He grinned. Neri will be impressed, if she ever forgives me.

She would forgive him. He would spend his entire life earning it.

A long while later he reached the edge of the borderlands and veered toward the edge of the settlement at the base of the caverns.

He reached a hand up to starting climb with his mind screaming pain, determined to get the worst of the effort over with. His stomach had growled a short while back, a sure sign something at least was 're-forming'. His hope grew along with it and he grit his teeth against the aches, forging on.

He paused as a soft thud hit his chest. Dropping his chin, he stared down at a beautifully carved lump of pale wax dotted with lilac. The delicate scent of liliam hit him, faint enough to know it was from the charm and not his link with Neri.

But the charm was there, not sucked inside his shadow self but swinging against a dark blue shirt covered with a thin veil of shadow.

Niall's cheeks almost split from beaming, and he focused the last reserves of effort on the rest of the climb. Rocks scored his fingertips and he blessed each and every sting, until finally he struggled over the lip onto the ledge.

Taking a break and calming his mind before facing Caden to ask for a huge favour would have been the sensible option, but he crawled to the cliff wall and used it to clamber to his feet, limping toward the cavern entrance. His boots scuffed up loose stones and his toes throbbed, but he didn't care. He stepped into the aerie cavern and sagged with his back against the wall, his chest heaving.

Caden lifted his head, eyed Niall over and scoffed.

"No sense," Caden said by way of greeting. "No patience. I never managed to teach you patience."

Niall bit his lip and nodded. Caden was in one of his brisk moods and that meant the only thing that worked was meek obedience, not his strong point.

"I-"

"I know, boy. The last thing I need is your blathering. You raced off to save her before I could tell you that sacrifice is often a balancing act."

Niall slid down the wall and sat against it, his arms resting on his knees. He turned his hands palms up and grinned at the scratches and hint of bruising there.

"You did sacrifice something, didn't you?" Caden asked.

Niall nodded. "I found them at the siren caves. Neri was half-dead so I made Zel take me to the great tree. I placed Neri there myself, held onto her until the firebird came to claim her. I saw her step out of the tree, then realised my shade-self seems to be fading."

"Zel, hmm." Caden rubbed his whiskery chin. "There is no knowing what will happen in the days to come. The west is about to face the might of the borderlands and they have dragons by all accounts, chained to their will with freirer ice."

Niall spat and Caden nodded.

"Exactly. The cursed woods are withering too, so soon the might in the east will be spreading their poison here too."

"What do you know of the might in the east?" Niall asked.

He contained his suspicion, his tone entirely neutral, but his mind drifted back to the gurbrys Caden had given him, not a thing to be found in the west. If Caden had some way of reaching the east easily, Niall could bring back news of Emelyn and the others for Neri.

"What does anyone know of the east? The Jakida is the one with her spies twitching in all the dark corners. Ask her. Why don't you focus on going back to your girlfriend. Make amends and leave an old man be with your questions."

Niall rolled his eyes. Caden was facetious when he wanted to be, but he was also the kind of hermit who found social interactions irritating. Niall's novelty had worn itself thin and now the best thing Niall could do for his old guardian was disappear until he was interesting again.

He got to his feet, amazed to find he actually had feet, fully formed inside extremely grubby boots. He stopped in the mouth of the tunnel, knowing he had to ask, had to beg for that reassurance.

"Will the shadow come back?" he asked. "Should I worry about it?"

Caden huffed but his face softened the smallest amount around the eyes.

"No. You burned that bridge, literally."

Niall nodded his thanks and put his hand on the wall, knowing the journey home to Neri and Jakiris would be even more painful than the run from the great tree.

"But Niall." Caden's unyielding tone stopped him dead. "You should thank your fortune every day that you picked the path of sacrifice. It saved you and Neri both."

Niall let that sink in for several moments before setting off down the tunnel. Caden wouldn't be bothered by gratitude if he gave it, but his only motivation now was to find Neri. If she wanted to go east, he would bring her to charm Caden into getting them there. If she wanted to stay in the westlands, he would find some way to support them and build a suitable life for her.

Assuming she forgives me.

He grinned as he exited the tunnels and stared at the long climb down.

Time to grovel.

CHAPTER FOURTEEN

Neri sank onto the bed in her room at the Jakirian palace with a weary sigh. Arriving back that morning had been bittersweet, the relief at being somewhere she could rest mixing with the continual stab of sadness that she was stuck there.

She flinched as a knock came at the door. After saying farewell to Livia some moments before, she guessed it would be Viljo finding some reason to talk to her.

"Hang on."

She'd only just climbed out of her grimy clothing so she pulled on a thick robe to open the door in, clutching the neck tightly so it didn't gape.

The Jakida stood on the other side of the door and flicked a disapproving frown at her. Given the high track of the suns across the afternoon sky, she wasn't impressed by Neri's lack of clothing despite only returning recently.

"The time has come to discuss the war effort," she announced. "Zel suggested it would be prudent to include you."

Neri hesitated. "I'm not sure what help I can be, but sure."

"In our absence we have received word that the East country is planning to send an army to engage us in battle. We anticipated this but it has come sooner than expected. We are sending runners to all corners of our land asking them to stand and fight alongside us."

The Jakida paused when she noted the confused look on

Neri's face and then continued regardless.

"The west and the borderlands will meet in battle when the time comes and we need all those able to wield weapons to aid our cause. You will be allowed to choose your station when the war comes but I would choose early for you will need guided practice."

Neri felt like it was a big ask before she'd even had breakfast, especially from the woman who had destroyed her only chance of getting home, but she didn't interrupt.

The Jakida might have seen a flicker of it on her face, as she sighed heavily.

"I am sorry at what occurred in the cavern but I cannot let those on the other side gain entry at such a fragile time. I believe those on your side of the cursed woods call themselves the Governance?"

Neri nodded. "Among worse things."

"Well, there are few that can travel far, but it is possible. We get scant reports and while the Governance is a product of the east, they share the same views as the borderlands do. I will not risk them uniting against us."

"How could they?"

Regret shimmered in the Jakida's eyes for a moment, her shoulders tensing.

"It seems when you were taken to the great tree, a bird of fire came for you. The great tree was born of the elements as the cursed woods was."

Neri frowned. "I'm not understanding."

"Reports have reached us in the past day that the woods are withering and it is a sudden thing. Whether it has to do with what happened at the great tree or there's some other cause, we can't be sure."

"The cursed forest is withering?" Neri clutched the edge of the door tight as hope leapt. "So folk can pass through it now?"

"No, it will take a long time for a curse like that to be undone, but that's not to say your Governance or the lord of the borderlands won't find a way. They say he has dragons at his call, and airborne is the only way to pass the cursed forest."

Neri inhaled, froze, and tried again.

"I'm sorry, dragons? Dragons. The winged beasts from myth? Dragons?"

The Jakida's lips twitched.

"Yes, dragons. Winged beasts that are rare but most definitely not a myth. I have no idea how sheltered or uneducated folk are in the east, but dragons would be a way to fly over the cursed forest."

Neri tensed, determined not to let the Jakida guess her instant thought process. The knowing look the Jakida sent her way suggested she'd already considered exactly what Neri was thinking, but Neri could only focus on a potential way to get her back into the east, to Emelyn and Dog and the others.

The Governance would be an instant problem, as would finding and being able to ride an actual dragon, but it was still a way home.

The Jakida regarded her for a moment with the glimmer of pity crossing her face.

"You will always be welcome here to call it home. Perhaps in time you will find skills to settle here with but that is all I can offer. Now, we will see you in the main hall the moment you are dressed."

She walked away but Neri had no words of gratitude or even politeness to offer anyway. She shut her bedroom door and leaned against it.

There was no avoiding the summons, not without

causing needless hostilities, but as she scanned the rail of fancy dresses, she decided to wear her travelling clothes instead.

With her stomach rumbling, she left the room and wound her way to the main hall. Livia stood the moment she entered, her face alight with relief.

"I'm so glad you're here," she muttered. "I promised Viljo I wouldn't bother you until you surfaced, but I've been *dying* of boredom."

Neri skated over the reference to dying, still queasy at the thought of what had apparently happened to her. She'd avoided all thought of it, belligerently focusing instead on idle plans of finding ways east again.

She let Livia guide her to a seat, but in doing so she saw two familiar faces across the table. Cori grinned at her and waved a leg of meat she was halfway through eating.

"Hello again, glad to see you made it okay," Cori said.

Neri nodded weakly, her gaze fixed on Hareili sitting in the next seat. Hareili sent her such a venomous glare that even Livia's sunny smile dimmed.

"She really doesn't like you," Livia whispered as more folk cascaded into the hall with loud chatter around them. "What did you do?"

Fell in love. Got screwed over.

She shrugged. "Couldn't say."

Everyone fell silent as the Jakida strode to the head of the table, but Neri grabbed a huge chunk of bread as her stomach threatened to growl loudly.

"We must all discuss the situation at length and now is the time for conference," the Jakida announced. "The borderlands will soon make their first move against us, so those who are willing to fight will need to join training. We will also need a team of healers, so anyone with significant skill should report to our head healer."

Neri missed the next few words as a whiff of *liliam* passed her, but was gone in an instant. She glanced toward the door, half expecting and half hoping Niall would be there to smirk at her through the shadow, but the doorway and the corners of the room were empty.

"We have drafted as many folk to fight as we can and should be expecting more to arrive over the next few days," one man said.

"I'll be healing on the battlefield if allowed," Cori offered. "I can fight and heal equally well. My sister will fight."

Hareili nodded. "My unit are on their way as we speak, and they're the best we have from the Morlan mountains."

"Good." The Jakida's gaze swept around the table. "The rest of us I think are spoken for and know our roles well."

Neri tensed as Hareili's fierce gaze turned to her, but she kept her mouth shut. She had no idea what the Jakida thought she would do, if anything. Perhaps the plan was for her to keep Livia entertained so she wouldn't insist on fighting.

She'll have us out to fight before the enemy even arrives.

She fought a smile but it froze on her lips as Viljo appeared beside her chair.

"May I speak with you?" he asked.

She almost winced at the formal tone, but she had no excuse to refuse. Livia huffed but didn't argue, so Neri had to ease to her feet and follow him out of the room.

"The time will soon be upon us," Viljo said as they set off down the hall. "I believe *ama* intends for you to keep Livia out of trouble."

Neri groaned. "I figured as much, but I don't see how

anyone will manage that."

Viljo laughed as he led them out of the palace and down the steps.

"You won't, but I think the hope is that in having you with her, Livia will be less likely to get into proper danger on the battlefield. You shouldn't need to fight."

Neri bit her lip. "I'd rather fight that sit around waiting. I may not have immaculate blade skills, but I can look after myself fine."

Viljo halted beside the waterfall next to the palace and shoved his hands in his pockets, the action so casual and unlike him that Neri had the urge to laugh.

"I'm sure you can, but this doesn't have to be your battle," he said. "You've already been through a lot, and the last thing we want is anything happening to you."

"Would you refuse to fight if someone asked you to?" she asked.

"No I wouldn't but it is my duty to protect my home and those that I am fond of."

Neri couldn't help but smile then, thinking of Livia and the possibility of not finding a way east any time soon. She had to be practical, and if Livia saw her as a friend then perhaps Jakiris wouldn't be the worst place in the land to be stuck.

"Then there is no rhyme or reason for me to back out either," she decided. "Livia's been so kind to me, and now there isn't a way east I'll have to settle somewhere. There are still so many questions."

The scent of *liliam* burst around her, so strong she had to force herself not to whirl around looking for shadows.

Viljo glanced at her with a soft frown.

"Perhaps if you do have questions in the future you may come to me. Zel can sometimes be sparing with the truth and my sister always dramatizes things."

Neri nodded. "Perhaps I will, thank you. I won't keep you, but if I could beg a favour?"

"Of course, anything you need."

He turned toward her and her stomach lurched when it looked like he might reach for her hand.

"I want to have a walk around, see the place for myself, a tiny bit of peace. Could you distract Livia if she's looking for me?"

His lips lifted. "For you, I'll try. Don't be too long though. There's much to be done."

"I won't."

She set off toward the lane, conscious that he was most likely watching her leave. The *liliam* followed her as she walked past dwellings, but it seemed to fade as she reached the halfway point between the palace and the settlement gates. The square was further down, but she slowed as she passed charming path on her right.

A couple of stone cottages stood on either side of the path with a larger one at the end that looked neglected. She walked toward the overgrown garden, following a scent similar to the inside of the *calideh* she was now addicted to.

She inched through the briars and riot of bushes between the path and the cottage, determined to see inside. The wooden door hung open and through the gloom beyond she could make out a large room. The space was empty, but amid the bare earth underfoot there was a large slab of stone in a far corner. She noticed a candle stub on a wooden shelf nearby and went to pick it up.

A small kitchen stood at the other end with a wooden counter and a sink for filling with water, and there was even a grimy old tub of clay which could hold a stoked fire.

Plenty of space for a bed as well, but set above head height was a wooden ledge that ran beneath the arched roof, big enough to keep a bed with possibly a small bookshelf and a trunk for clothes.

Neri dropped her head to stare at the wax stub in her hands, suddenly warm and pliable. The prickle and burn that seemed lodged inside her bones now warmed her fingertips, and she used the heat to press grooves into the wax. That, along with the grass burning underneath her after she emerged from the tree, proved something had happened to her.

She allowed the thoughts to roam free as all the heat in her hands channelled into keeping the candle soft enough to mould. She formed a large round ball, smoothing it with her fingertips, and then took a deep breath and allowed the heat to leave the wax.

Hamlin had taken her in and taught her the tricks of candle-making. Had he known then what she would become?

Setting the misshapen lump of wax on the floor, she backed out of the cottage. The stone slab in the corner would be perfect for candle-making. She wouldn't want to step on anyone's toes but if nobody owned the cottage perhaps the Jakida would let her trade for it with candles and sculptures. She perched on the uneven, jagged stones of the garden wall, unwilling to go back to the palace until her thoughts were organised.

Despite shivering in the late afternoon air with her bare arms and legs on show, she didn't get up as Zel approached. She had nothing to lose by asking some questions, and there was something about Zel that screamed 'I know more than anyone could ever guess'.

"I have *ai-tan* now, don't I?"

Zel nodded. "That was the gift you were given for Niall's sacrifice."

Neri grimaced at his name.

"What did he sacrifice?" Fear bubbled up. "He's not… nobody will tell me but I could have sworn I saw him leave."

Zel sighed and sank onto the wall beside her.

"Niall is alive, if that's what you're asking. I know no more than that. He took you up to that tree, insisted on it, and stayed with you even when it burst into flame. Livia's told me as much, and I believe her."

Neri settled, her shoulders sagging.

"What exactly did he sacrifice?" she asked.

"I have no idea. Sometimes the willingness for it is all that is needed. By all accounts, well, Livia's anyway, he would have gone to his death for you."

Neri forced the rising hope firmly down.

"He made a vow to protect me once, so that's probably it."

"Ah. He has some strange ideas about nobility from what I've heard. His time in the east will have changed little of that."

"How much do you know of his time in the east?"

Zel smiled. "How much do you know of his time in the west?"

Neri heard the subtle re-direction in Zel's amused tone, but she had more questions about other things.

"Did you ever know Hamlin?" she tried.

"I have known many folk in my long life."

It wasn't a no, so Neri decided to keep going with some information of her own.

"He taught me candle-making, and he's how Niall and I met." She hesitated. "Do you think the Jakida would let me take this cottage, if it's not occupied, and I can trade for it with anything I make?"

Zel chuckled. "I doubt she will see a problem with that. This cottage used to belong to a candle-maker long before he died. But come, Livia will be looking for you."

Neri nodded. "Do you think I can avoid the inevitable for a bit longer? I could do with a long soak."

It was an excuse and they both knew it, but as she walked with Zel back up toward the palace, she needed just that little bit longer to get her mind settled.

"I will tell Livia you will find her in the library when you're done," Zel offered the moment they reached the hall to Neri's room. "Don't be too long about it though."

"I won't, thank you."

She escaped down the hall and hurried into her room. The bathing that morning had been purely indulgent, but she still could do with washing her hair properly.

She slid into the pool and dunked her hair under, floating on her back to swish the last remnants of dirt out. Even with the scents of the bathing oils from the bottles nearby, *liliam* dodged between them, invading her senses.

Niall was out there somewhere and even though he'd been the one to save her life, he wasn't willing to come and see her, not even to close whatever had happened between them.

It has to be the vow he made to Hamlin. She pressed a hand to her chest to ease the growing ache.

Her skin flushed hot and her face, the only part not submerged in the water, burned. She sucked in a breath, dizzy as bubbles fizzled against her skin, the water too hot against her. It stung and pinched, burning as she flailed to get out.

Something hard gripped her arm.

She pulled away and choked as her head dipped beneath the water. A sudden rush of cold air scraped her skin as someone hauled her out of the water and onto the floor, which carved against her skin like ice.

She gasped, panic grabbing at her chest, and lifted her head to find Livia in front of her with a red face, her cheeks stained with silvery tears. She had her hands held out in front of her and the palms were marked with red, angry blistering.

Neri looked back at the water, at the steam curling up from it, the tiny bubbles frothing on the surface. Unable to stand, she crawled toward Livia, who scrambled back away from her.

"Don't touch me! Calm down first!"

She stopped moving and anchored herself to the cold bite of the floor. Her skin still tingled like it was embedded with tiny little shards of ice, scratches she couldn't see that stung her, but her calm returned in full force at the sight of her friend's pain.

"I'm calm. Tell me what I need to get for you."

Livia glanced at the door then back to her.

"You're not wearing any clothing. I found you in the pool and I think you let your ai-tan run wild because the water was boiling you alive yet there's not a mark on you."

. Neri stared in anguish and wished she could somehow take Livia's burns into herself. She grabbed her robe and pulled it on, focusing on the physical feeling of softness rather than the emotion inside that would spike the heat again.

"Stay here and I'll find someone to help."

She slipped out onto the stone deck before Livia could argue, and over the wall onto the grass below.

The archways were shrouded in lengthening shadows as

night fell around the palace, all except for a glow coming from library. She peeked inside to find Viljo sitting alone. He seemed to sense her presence and glanced up, a wide smile breaking across her face before he reined it back to something less intense.

"I need your help," she begged. "Livia… there was an accident. She's alright, but her hands are hurt."

Viljo stood and slid the book he'd been reading onto his chair, instantly ready for action.

"Tell me how. I will need to know what to bring."

Neri hesitated, but she couldn't leave Livia unattended.

"I was bathing and she came in. Somehow I managed to burn her hands. I didn't mean to, honestly, but she was helping me out of the water. It was burning."

Viljo frowned, a dark shadow falling across his face that carried an echo of familiarity with it, although in her frantic panic she couldn't place where from.

"Go back to her. I'll fetch something to help."

He strode out of the room without another word and Neri hurried back to Livia to find her sitting on the bed.

"I'm sorry I shouted." Livia bit her lip. "I know you don't have full control over your *ai-tan* yet but we can help you. Viljo and I will help you channel it and it will work for you instead of at you."

Neri nodded despite knowing she would never put anyone in that situation again. The heat linked to her emotions and if she had to retire into solitude then she would do. She managed a weak smile for Livia as her door opened and Viljo came in without knocking.

He knelt down by Livia and instructed her to hold out her hands. Neri caught the subtle wince as he saw the angry weals there but he took out some blue gunk that she had seen used many times before.

"We don't need to bandage them but please stay out of *Ama*'s way until the pain subsides." Viljo sighed. "She won't expect you for a day or two and by then the worst should be past."

Livia nodded, her attention fixed on him, and Neri took the opportunity to slip from the room. She'd need to return for her pack with her things in but her main focus was to find the Jakida and put her offer forward.

She asked various maids who all insisted that the Jakida had retired for the evening and would not be disturbed, so Neri found a quiet corner and asked for some parchment and a stub of lead.

Her letter to the Jakida explained what had happened with several apologies, then she issued her request for the cottage. She promised that with enough wax supplied to her from the stubs of old candles, and some equipment which she listed, she would provide new ones as a trade.

She handed the letter to another maid and insisted the letter must reach the Jakida as soon as possible, then left the palace in nothing but her bathing robe.

Torches lit her way down the lane through the night, and she walked up the lane to what was hopefully her new home. The cottage was still empty, so she stepped inside and heaved the front door shut behind her.

She found a candle in the kitchen with enough wick to last her the night and lit it. The glow danced through the shadows, but even Niall wouldn't know to find her here.

Not that he's even going to bother looking.

She sighed and set the candle on a clay holder in the middle of the floor to illuminate the room.

The platform hovering over the room had a ladder leading up to it, but although there was a bed already up there, it was made with wooden slats and had no mattress.

She considered creeping back up to the palace to get her pack and the blankets in it, but instead she squashed herself into a corner of the platform and crunched down to sit on the floor.

I've survived worse than this. She closed her eyes, exhausted. *I'll wait a short while until the palace is asleep and creep back in for my things.*

She had to hope the Jakida wouldn't be too angry about Livia's injuries, and that she agreed to the trade for the cottage.

With enough trades, she would be able to earn herself supplies for the next part of her plan.

CHAPTER FIFTEEN

Neri woke and wished she hadn't. Sleep had claimed her before she could go back to the palace for her things and now a night of slumber wedged against a wall set her muscles screaming.

She managed to climb down the ladder but with the sunslight streaming in through the open window, it didn't need much of a critical eye to see all the work she would need to do to make the cottage any kind of liveable home.

Still dredged with excess sleep, she shoved the door aside and walked into the short stretch of garden to see if there were any recognisable berries or anything to stave off immediate hunger.

She hid a yawn behind her hand, her mouth stuck open as she recognised the woman striding toward her. Because of course, she hadn't mentioned which cottage she wanted in her letter but Zel would have blabbed everything immediately.

"I have come to discuss what has transpired," the Jakida announced.

Neri tensed under the stern gaze and held her tongue.

"I give you this cottage with goodwill," the Jakida continued. "We will talk no more of Livia's injury. I've instructed that all the used candles will be brought to you here, as well as the equipment you listed. You will need to supply a set to the dwelling each day, but any extra wax is yours to do with as you will."

Neri fought the burn of excitement that fired in her

chest. She clenched her hands behind her back to control it and nodded to show she had heard.

"Training begins today," the Jakida added. "The enemy have left the borderlands and are marching across Orlain as we speak. It will take them a number of days yet, but training will still be brief. No doubt Livia will want to train you herself."

She turned to leave but Neri realised her entire reason for running away from the palace had been overturned.

"I can't go back," she insisted. "I don't want to risk hurting someone again."

She caught the stiffness in the Jakida's shoulders, the rigid set of her back so like Viljo's when he was doing his duty. The Jakida didn't turn around but Neri heard the words with crystal clarity.

"Zel will tutor you in controlling your *ai-tan* and you will work hard. There will be no more accidents for as long as you decide to remain in my lands. Take the morning to settle yourself, but this afternoon your training must begin. Oh, these may be needed too."

Neri reached out to catch the bundle of clothing the Jakida threw at her. The clothes alone were far more luck and kindness than she felt she deserved, especially as she was still in her bathing robe. She watched the Jakida disappear into the main lane and then she decided she would gift herself one morning to forget about the war and Niall and everything else.

Her stomach growled in protest but she ignored it as she changed her clothes and set about cleaning. She found old rags in the trunk at the end of the bed and searched about for some water until she found a small stream behind the cottage. The water bubbled down along the rock toward the edge of the settlement, clear with a rocky bed devoid of sand.

She dug out an old wooden bucket and filled the clay sink full of water to wash the rags in, then refilled the sink over and over, becoming bolder as she used the warmth of her excitement to heat the water and purge the dirt from the stone and the wooden shelves and counters.

When she couldn't risk any more effort without collapsing from hunger, she stood back and stared. She would soon have enough spare wax to trade candles for various wares. Perhaps she could find a warm rug for the floor, some wood to make a bookcase and eventually books to fill it. She wanted warmer blankets for when the winter inevitably drew in and she would need to shift for herself when it came to finding food. The garden could be razed of weeds and filled with bushes that produced fruits. She would set up a screen also opposite the stone slab she would use for candle-making. That would be the place to build a bath.

I won't be able to do any of that if I'm late for training and the Jakida takes the cottage away again.

She grimaced at the thought, uneasy about having to face Livia after running away. With a deep breath, she steeled herself for a lot of loud questioning and left her new home. As she pulled the door shut, she added a mental note to find some way to fix the hinge.

The wind whirled around her as she walked up the lane to the palace, and it masked the sounds of activity until they were right in front of her.

Droves of folk had turned out sporting various weapons, and there were several training rings roped off in the valley beside the palace. Neri walked through the crowd until she reached a small table where the Jakida stood with the captain of the guard.

"There are more to come but we cannot force folk to fight when they'd rather hide and flee," she muttered.

Neri glanced around, but it seemed the Jakida was talking to her as the captain was looking elsewhere.

"What exactly are we expecting to face?" she asked.

The Jakida stared out over the training rings.

"We have reports coming in now and he has many folk marching with him in large numbers. We must come to either an agreement or to death, but the laws of the land must be upheld. Each person must be free to practise their *ai-tan* without fear, and the lands cannot be ravaged for their materials."

"Do his numbers outmatch our own?"

The Jakida grimaced. "Slightly, but he also has terrible contraptions ripping through the earth to find materials that will subdue more dragons and enslave them to fight against their will."

Neri didn't have any words of comfort, or any words of any use at all, but her attention snagged on one of the nearby training rings.

Viljo stood with a long blade in hand. Given the slow, controlled movements he made against his opponent, he was the one doing the training.

"He fights well," she admitted.

The Jakida nodded. "He does, and trains others well too. But war will not be slow or practiced like training often is."

As if he'd heard them, Viljo lifted his head to look in their direction. A moment later, he swept his blades with lethal precision to rob his opponent of their weapon. the man fell to his knees in concession, and Viljo stood above him with both blades to the man's chest. He hovered a moment before turning them to face the floor, but Neri couldn't help the traitorous thought running through her mind.

The only person I've seen fight that well is Niall.

She shook the thought away and looked around for some sign of Livia. It was unlike her to be absent when all the activity was happening outside. She noticed the white horse nearby, still untethered with her head turned as if to watch the fighting. Perhaps if Neri hadn't caught the horse's head shooting upright she never would have noticed the subtle tremor in the ground.

The earth pulsed beneath her feet and the Jakida stormed past as someone ran up from the lane.

"Folk approaching, hundreds coming fast on horseback," the woman panted. "They are coming to attack."

The Jakida didn't hesitate. She cleared her voice and stepped in one smooth leap onto a nearby chair and then onto a table.

"Guards from the East are about to perform an ambush." Her voice rang across the crowd, silencing it. "I want everybody ready and willing to fight down to the gates. We will face them head on. Archers into the trees and gain any vantage point you can find."

The sheer commanding power in her voice flew through the air and folk hurried to collect weapons. Cori and Hareili were among them, but didn't spare them more than a glance as Livia dashed toward her.

"I heard it, we've got to go!"

Livia was dressed in her fighting clothes, waistcoat and sturdy trousers with her hair tied back, but she didn't manage to evade the hand landing on her shoulder.

"Not you," the Jakida insisted. "Back inside."

"I'm fighting!"

"You are not. Someone needs to guard the settlement, and that is your role."

Neri took the opportunity to slip away, promising herself she would make it up to Livia when she returned. If she returned. She shuddered and approached the white horse's side. She used a nearby chair to mount from and joined the reams of folk filing down toward the main gates, her blade hanging from her hip.

She didn't say a word as Viljo appeared at her side, his blade already drawn. So many folk wound their way down to the gates that they couldn't progress faster than a walk, but nerves carried through the almost silent crowd and it seemed like an entire age before they rode through the gate and onto the vast grassland.

A mass of riders clothed in red and blue filtered down the sides of the hills in front of them, while more arrived through the trees to take their places.

"I meant it when I said you don't have to do this," Viljo said.

Neri tensed as he leaned close to her, but the white horse sidestepped slightly to gain them more space.

"And I meant it when I said I can look after myself."

She fought to keep the snap out of her tone as the Jakida brought her horse to the front of the battle. Even without a word, her mere presence and energy surrounded the crowd in a strange bubble of courage. It coursed through Neri's chest and the desire to fight and win seemed to come forward from some unknown part of her mind. The strange heady sense of bravado filled her head and intoxicated her stronger than *liliam*, stronger than the anger she felt kindling inside her at those coming to try and take the land from them, so much so that she almost couldn't hear the distant sound of a horn.

She couldn't imagine having the strength or steeled resolve to plunge a blade right into a human's body, to sever flesh from bone, but the power the Jakida was pushing through everyone calmed her fears and she knew in that moment that she could burn anyone in her path.

The enemy's horn answered the call as the front of their defences surged forward. Neri tensed as folk in front of her moved and she realised her horse would likely follow the rest without any reins.

Everyone roared, perhaps a side effect of the Jakida's power, but as soon as a spare space opened the horse set off at a gallop, zigzagging through the crowd.

Neri leaned low over the horse's neck to avoid the wind, the sound of hooves close behind her. Blades clashed which meant the two sides had met in battle but she resisted looking in case she saw the worst. Blurs of red and blue dashed toward her, six or seven on horseback, but gritted her teeth and swung her blade out to meet the chest of the enemy. Her fear banked as her fingertips burned against the hilt of her blade, but someone fought beside her with feral strength.

Two of the enemy fell from their horses under Viljo's blade, and Neri managed to injure one enough for them to back off. Her horse skittered around and she saw Livia charging toward them on horseback with a small pack of riders following.

"Your *ama* is going to be furious," Neri called out.

Livia rolled her eyes as their side moved around them as a solid unit of protection.

"Yes, and it's tiresome. Can you light these? I soaked them in wine."

She held out a bunch of arrows, and Neri saw a bow hanging from her shoulder. She hesitated, but Livia urged her horse right alongside.

"It's okay. Your *ai-tan* will respond to your will. Stay calm, let it fill you and light the arrows."

Around them the battle waged on, but Neri was secure inside a circle of guards, no doubt there to protect both Viljo and Livia. If Livia wanted to shoot flaming arrows, she wouldn't be the one to stop her.

"Can you shoot straight?" she asked.

Livia scoffed. "Of course I can. Here, light the arrows and you can have a go."

Neri choked over a horrified laugh at the thought of the battle being like some market stall game, but she did as she was asked. With her eyes closed, she focused on the tingle of warmth inside her. It leapt forward into her fingertips at the mere thought, and her skin seared with heat moments later.

"That is amazing."

She opened her eyes in time to see Livia nock the now flaming arrow and take aim. It fired through the air into the melee below them and Viljo seethed through his teeth.

"Your aim's off," he muttered.

"Is not."

"It is, look, he's still limping."

"I was aiming for the leg actually."

Neri bit her lip, torn between their bickering and the quelling sickness as she thought about all the pain and death the battle would bring.

Then Livia handed the bow to her.

She shook her head.

"Go on, give it a go. Worst you can do is hit the ground."

"No. I'll light them but that's it."

She held firm, the thought of shooting some nameless,

faceless person dead turning her stomach.

Livia sighed. "Fine."

Neri passed her hand over the arrow Livia held out, but nothing happened. A loud thundering of hooves approached them from behind, all the horses swinging around.

"We need to go," Viljo shouted.

Livia scrunched up her face in protest. "No, not yet. We can handle these. Light the arrow quick!"

Given the sheer number of enemy riders racing toward them, Neri doubted it, but Livia had an arrow in her face. She passed her hand over the soaked tip of the arrow again willed the wine to catch aflame. Her gift struggled, the roil of it curling fitfully through her limbs.

"Quick!" Livia's panicked voice filled her head. "I need to start thinning them!"

Neri bit her lip and thought of Niall. She called up every shard of pain that had dug deep and nestled inside to stay with her and her fingers seared. She snatched her hand away from the flames that flared, roaring high enough in one frenetic spike to singe the tops of the trees.

Livia aimed the bow and shot, but the fire was still raging from Neri's palm, licking up her arm as her mind reached out to follow the band of her fire. She closed her eyes and felt the flames as extended fingers, so far away yet still a part of her. She flexed those fingers along the ground away from her side and toward the enemy. She urged the flame to find sticks and leaves on the ground, anything it could kindle on, stretching the length of her gift across the grass until it reared in front of the enemy and brought them to a stampeding halt.

"Neri, stop." Viljo's voice echoed nearby. "Call your gift back now."

There was innate command there, overriding the wave of exhaustion that was building inside her. The fire didn't want to retreat. It wanted to fight and to burn, but she fought it until it yielded.

She sagged, ready to fall off her horse's back, but through bleary eyes she could see Viljo's horse beside her, his hands steady as he took control and her consciousness finally conceded.

CHAPTER SIXTEEN

The scent of *liliam* woke Neri enough to summon her back to her body. She tingled with warmth and felt her fingers and toes again without opening her eyes. She wanted to cling to the serene feeling but the scent of *liliam* grew and entwined with the swirls of frost and cinnamon.

She struggled to fight it, to put Niall out of her mind, but the scent of him strengthened until she could feel the softness of a bed beneath her. The scent reached a peak and brought an ache inside her body, but when she felt the burn of pain on her skin and opened her eyes she recognised her room at the dwelling.

The room stood empty except for Livia sitting on her bed. Neri realised that her cheeks were wet and she began to sob. Shocked by the sudden display of emotion, Livia couldn't do anything as Neri threw shaking arms around her. Neri wept so hard that her body shook and the anguish came out in her whimpers.

Livia held her, disturbed, and made soothing noises that had no basis in sense. Neri sniffled and pulled away, realising that if she had waited any longer Livia might get hurt. She shuffled away and stepped out of the bed, moving toward the balcony. Scents lingered, real around her, and she knew Livia would be the only person she could ask.

"Was Niall here?"

She heard the silence engulfing the space behind her as though Livia were deciding what to say with the utmost care.

"Viljo caught you just before you fell out in the trees. He bought you back here and he left only a while ago."

Neri sighed, unable to be cross with Livia's diversions.

"So even if he had been you wouldn't tell me?"

"I saw shadow as I walked into the room but only for a moment and it either disappeared out of the window or out of my mind. I can't be sure which is why I didn't want to say a thing."

Neri nodded. If Livia had seen Niall rushing away then he obviously didn't want to see her. Perhaps the vow he made to Hamlin still had hold of him. Perhaps he was bound to her and she had become a duty and a burden he had to undertake. Even so, the idea that he might have been spotted nearby brought a traitorous thrill of relief to her soul.

"What of the battle?" she asked.

Livia approached her side and stared out at the remains of the deserted training rings.

"We have minimal injuries and the settlement is safe. Your *ai-tan* sort of burned a huge edge of the trees though, and that sent a lot of the enemy fleeing. It brought us more time in which to prepare."

Neri nodded and there was a long moment of silence before there was a knock at the door and a young man poked his head in.

"How's the wounded?" he asked.

Livia smiled. "Awake and demanding answers, so I think she's fine."

Neri grumbled under her breath at that as the man approached with a large hide bag in hand.

"I'm Gyphur," he said. "You know my sisters, I believe."

Neri frowned. "Your sisters?"

"Yes, Cori's spoken of you. Hareili, well she ground her teeth a lot when your name was mentioned, so I'm guessing you're not the best of friends."

Neri sat up and winced at the weary ache in her arms.

Gyphur chuckled. "I'm a healer, and have absolutely no interest in my sister's squabbles. You're safe with me. I'm going to listen to your chest first, okay?"

Neri held herself tense as he dropped his ear to her chest.

"It's amazing," he murmured while pulling at the skin around her eyes. "There's a light pulsing inside you, and you're strong too. Most would still be unconscious after using such volatile *ai-tan*."

Neri didn't feel strong at all, especially when she noticed Viljo standing in the open doorway. She thought of her cottage and yearned to leave everyone around her in exchange for solitude.

"I thought you might want to avoid the main hall," he announced.

She eyed the plate he flourished from behind his back, full of food. In his other hand was a cup, and she managed a proper smile for him.

"I'll leave you be a while," Livia said. "You two will have things to talk about."

She rushed from the room with Gyphur trailing behind her, but Neri couldn't think of a single thing she and Viljo would need to talk about beyond basic gratitude on her part. She kept her eyes fixed to the plate in his hands as he approached and handed it over. He even moved to stand on the deck outside while she ate so he wouldn't hovering over her, and she smiled to herself at the thought.

"I want to thank you for protecting me." She called him over the moment the plate was empty and the cup dry. "I wouldn't have made it if it wasn't for you catching me."

Viljo moved inside and approached the bed.

"Will you take a walk with me?" he asked. When she hesitated, he smiled. "Consider it a tiny debt paid if you must."

She couldn't exactly say no. Swinging her legs out of bed with a groan, she found her boots, glad nobody had bothered to remove her clothes as well when putting her into bed.

They walked together through the halls and he led her out to the waterfall, which seemed to be his favourite place.

"Do you regret having to stay here?" he asked. "You must miss your home."

Neri sat on the edge of the water and trailed her hand through it.

"I don't mind being here and everyone has been very kind. The east wasn't that great a place to be in the end, not for many folk but especially not for me. I do miss my friends though."

"What's wrong with the east exactly?"

Neri hesitated. It was a fair question, and one they should have insisted on asking her before now.

They've asked me very little, which means they either know everything, perhaps from Niall, or they haven't trusted me to tell them the truth.

"It's a long story," she tried.

Viljo slid to sit beside her, his knee brushing her thigh.

"We have time."

She shrugged. "Fair enough. It wasn't so bad when I was little. Everywhere had problems but they were manageable. Folk travelled to different settlements, trade was everywhere and nothing was hard to get if you needed it. Then the fields dried up and crops failed. Folk continued to use more than they needed and fights broke out. Soon the Governance insisted on taking control."

The memory of the first curfew leapt back to her mind, and the fear and whispers that came with it. Folk had disappeared around that time too, then the grey-cloaks started arriving to do checks. They blamed it on safety of course, but often they took more than they saved.

As her memories threatened to drag her down away from conversation and into misery, so she rolled her tense shoulders and focused on Viljo instead.

"We had to turn in a lot of our things and the healers were the first to leave for bigger settlements, better trades. Normal folk had to make do. Soon the Governance controlled everything. Many don't have gifts over there either, not like you do here. If they did, they'd get accused of all sorts and carted off, never to be seen again."

The hatred cascaded off of her tongue and she almost pitied Viljo as he shifted awkwardly beside her.

"It sounds like the current state of the borderlands," he admitted. "The lord there controls with fear, and now he has supposedly chained dragons to his will. The scant rumours we've heard from folk that escaped tell us he is also rationing supplies, much like you say has happened in the east. It wouldn't surprise me if they were working together now."

She nodded. "It's definitely possible. Trouble comes fast for anyone stepping out of line, or even outside during the night without permission. Then there are those folk that specialise in doing bad things in the shadows, and somehow they get given all the allowances."

The mention of shadows sent Neri's mind fluttering to thoughts of Niall. She waved her hand through the water and watched the delicate petals of a lily shiver on its pad.

"Do you think flowers feel pain when you pick them?" she asked.

Viljo leaned forward and extended a solid hand toward hers.

"No, plants don't feel pain like we do. But they like to grow. They need the space and chance to grow strong and tall."

Neri flinched as his hand skated close to hers, but he only plucked the lily off of its pad and held it in his hands. One of the roots stretched out to curl around his index finger and Neri gasped.

Viljo chuckled, holding the flower closer so that she could lift her own finger to be ensnared. The flower grew and the petals plumped as the blushed a more vibrant green. The shoots spread over Viljo's hand and down the short distance to the water.

"It's considered rude to ask what a person's *ai-tan* is," Viljo said. "I'll tell you for nothing though that mine is of the earth and the root."

Neri couldn't stem the thrill of wonder as the tiny tendril of life hugged her finger. Viljo smiled at her expression, all his dark brooding and silence blown away momentarily as he began to laugh. The light caught his mossy green hair and she smiled to see him so animated.

Before she could ask him to show her something else, a shadow of doubt crept through her mind. She extracted herself gently from the flower and pushed to her feet.

"I should make myself useful," she said. "Candles don't make themselves."

He nodded, but a hint of the smile remained on his face, as if he found her obvious hesitation amusing, endearing even.

"I've enjoy discussing our different lands, and I'd very

much enjoy doing it again sometime."

Neri nodded and took a step backwards.

"Okay. Sometime."

She turned before he could see the awkward grimace brewing on her face and hurried down the lane to her cottage. She hadn't secured any plans with Livia either so nobody could chastise her for being absent.

As she pushed her door aside, she saw the state of her home and her mouth dropped open.

The stone slab was partially covered with a thick tapestry for a rug in swirling dark blues and forest greens. Thin, gossamer curtains in a deep, dusky pink covered her windows and a pock-marked, dark table stood near the kitchen, which shone with utensils and large wooden containers.

Someone benevolent had decided to pay her a visit at some point, even to the point of providing the candle-making equipment she'd asked for. A deep vat stood in the corner on a pivoting stand with various tongs and carving knives laid out for her. Lumps of used wax were piled on the stone and a wooden settle held a pile of chopped logs to make a fire with.

Neri headed toward the table with her mouth still open and grabbed a scrap of the thin parchment that sat beneath a slender wooden vase full of colourful flowers.

'Please accept this for what it is in the hope you will wake to come back to it: an offer of eternal friendship from your closest friend. Viljo did all the heavy lifting.'

Livia had signed it and Neri pressed the paper to her chest. Heat bubbled through her bones and ignited a heady rush of kinship that set her skin a-jitter. She assumed it had been Viljo who fixed the hinge on her door and she went to open and shut it a few times in happy awe.

Well I can't skulk around in here now after she's done all this.

She closed the door behind her and stood in the garden. She liked it wild but the unrulier growth would need cutting back. One particular vine with dark blue stems and thorns took over the more delicate plants. She bent low to see the tiny green oblong berries growing on it and smiled through the thorny branches to see a vision of bright purple flying down the lane.

"You're not escaping me any longer," Livia insisted. "Viljo has had his turn, and there aren't any signs of the enemy approaching. I checked."

Neri grinned. "I bet you did. I'm all yours." She glanced over her shoulder. "The cottage is beautiful now. I can never thank you enough."

"It's a small thing for me to do to keep you happy here." Livia leaned closer. "I am going to ask for your help though in return. I teach the young ones occasionally and I want you to come with me."

Neri grimaced. "I don't know much about them, but if you want me to. Is it now?"

"No, this evening, and after lessons there will be a party in the square. Until then, I'm going to finish helping you fix your dwelling."

Neri bit her lip as Livia marched past her through the garden and gained several new tears in her fancy purple cloak as it billowed out behind her.

"I was going to get started on the candles," she said.

Livia waved a dismissive hand in her direction.

"You do that. I can entertain myself."

Bewildered, Neri did as she was told. She stoked a small

fire on the stone in the corner and dumped wax in the vat over it. Once melted and free of old wick, Neri ladled the wax into the waiting moulds and set new lengths of thin rope. With water from the stream outside, she doused the fire and waited for the embers to go cold.

Livia watched with surprising patience as Neri grabbed a stiff broom and swept the ashes out, but the moment Neri was done Livia chivvied her onto a long cushion beside the table. With plump feathers and fine stitching on the material, Neri wondered whether the entire contents of her cottage had been stolen from the vaults of the palace storage.

"Oh, I brought you another present," Livia announced.

Neri opened her mouth to protest but a thick bundle of fabric dropped onto her lap. She spread it out over her legs with a frown.

"It's a cloak."

"It's a flight cloak," Livia corrected. "Thickest you can get to keep out the weather, but good for fighting and riding in too."

"Flight cloak? As in birds?"

Livia rolled her eyes. "Of course not. Our elders used to ride dragons before they all fled north. The dragons I mean, not our elders."

"Dragons? Really?" She still couldn't believe it.

Livia hustled over and dragged her to her feet, forcing her into the cloak like an errant child.

"Yes, really. Look, it has these buttons across the chest like a waistcoat, and the tails at the back have straps for the legs."

Neri took a couple of steps once the straps were fastened, the cloak finer than anything she'd ever been close to, let alone worn.

"Is it valuable? Won't someone be missing something like this?"

Livia grinned. "I don't imagine so. I unearthed it from the storage."

"That's where you hide is it?" Neri guessed.

"Absolutely. Sometimes I can even hear them arguing. *Ama* asks Viljo where I am and folk are sent searching. They assure me it gives them a break or an excuse to take out their pipes, so nobody tells her where I am."

Neri laughed. "You have everything as you want it."

"Not everything. I have to escape if I want to fight. One day she'll hire someone who I can't sway to guard me, or worse, unite with me. Then my life will be over."

Neri's mind drifted east instantly, memories surfacing.

Niall had asked her to unite with him, and she'd told him to ask again when they weren't in trouble.

Why ask if he wasn't serious, at least back then? Or did he know I'd deflect so there was no danger in it?

She refused to dwell on it, on him, not now she was finally making a home for herself. The urge to find a way east still burned, but she had the tiny shard of kyne buried in her pack. One day she might find a use for it, but training in Jakiris until she was strong enough to fight whatever came couldn't hurt, and the others would be safe at the sanctuary until then.

"Right, time for lessons," Livia announced.

Neri looked down at the fine cloak, yet another debt she owed even though Livia refused to see it as such, and nodded. Time for lessons.

Livia chatted animatedly about the plan for the lessons as they walked up to the palace, and Neri let herself be hauled along to the library with a smile pasted on her face. Viljo sat at a table in the corner and gave her a wry smile, as if he knew exactly how unwilling she was to get dragged into the whole thing.

Before she could ask Livia where she wanted her, there was a soft knocking and a bunch of young children trickled in.

"Come in! Gather around and sit."

Neri watched Livia, amazed at how easily she charmed and settled the children. Viljo came to her side and tilted his head close enough to whisper.

"I pity you," he teased. "I can usually find some excuse when she's in one of her determined moods."

Amused, Neri stuck her tongue out at him.

"I owe her many things," she admitted. "This is the least I can do to repay her."

Livia clapped her hands and gained everyone's attention, but Viljo pulled a face and Neri had to smother a snort of laughter.

"Today we're going to talk about friendship," Livia announced. "I know most of you already have your friends but sometimes new folk come into your life and you have to make room for them. What did we say about folk last time?"

Livia's prompting led into a lesson that subtly touched on sharing, accepting all different kinds of folk and eventually she turned a wicked grin toward Neri and Viljo's corner.

"Now my friends and I are going to show you a demonstration."

Although Neri had counted about thirty children of varying ages, their collective gazes bore into her like a crowd of thousands.

"Neri here can wield fire," Livia announced. "She's not done it for very long yet but she's going to show us something cool. How do we welcome folk that are going to show us things?"

The children descended into polite clapping which grew to a violent crescendo as each tried to outdo the other..

Neri hesitated as Viljo shifted beside her and she caught the wary look on his face.

"Be careful," he warned.

Neri approached the group and took the unlit candle Livia held out to her. There was no harm in just melting the wax and moulding it, that she could do without too much danger.

She sat on the floor, cross-legged and facing the children, and took a deep breath.

"When I was little, I hated the dark," she explained. "I refused to sleep without a candle glowing. Then I got older-"

"How old are you?" someone piped up.

She grinned. "How old do you think I am?"

The children looked between each other, a rustle of voices passing around.

"OLD," they chorused.

Neri shot Viljo a glare as he choked over a laugh, but she let it slide.

"Okay, so I'm old, but that means I've had lots of time to get used to the dark. It became a friend sometimes when I wanted to hide away, but light and dark both exist together. Everyone put your hands tight over your eyes, no peeking."

Despite several spread fingers with telltale eyes poking through, the children had obeyed her.

"Can anyone tell me what you see now?"

She heard a few mumbled shouts of 'darkness' and 'nothing', before they all fell silent.

"Okay, imagine you've never seen anything else. It's all darkness." She focused on the candle and pinched the wick between finger and thumb. "Without light we wouldn't know what darkness is. Hands down and open your eyes."

Her *ai-tan* flared and pulsed through her fingertips as the wick caught alight. Gasps of awe ran around the children and she allowed the hushed whispers. Her fingers zinged, possibly from her tight pinch on the candle.

"Nothing is dark forever," she added. "Even in the darkest parts of the land, when we have no idea which way to go, there is always light somewhere."

She stood up and set the candle on a spare holder on one of the spindly legged wooden tables.

"Don't think though that light has to come from something special. It can come from the most unlikely places."

She grabbed a nearby flint stick and ran it across the block provided, the tip catching alight. With it she lit the remaining candles.

"You don't need *ai-tan* to create light, just like you don't need to be anything noble or lucky to be kind." She tensed as she remembered that she was dealing with young children. "But of course fire and flint are for when you're really old. Like Livia."

She dodged the cushion Livia threw at her and grinned when it hit Viljo's disapproving frown instead. As the children descended into excitable chatter, even Livia had to try several times to get them calm enough to leave.

CHAPTER SEVENTEEN

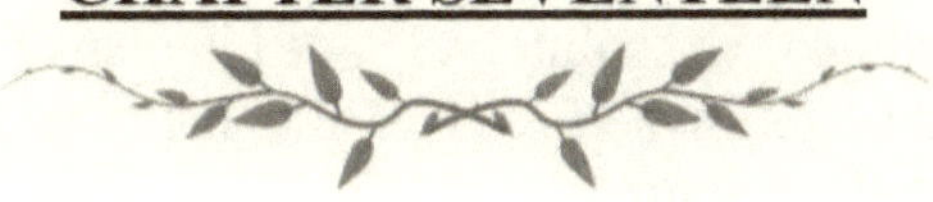

Neri waved as the children left the library, Livia rushing after them.

"Your gift is improving quickly," Viljo said.

Neri shrugged, her cheeks flushing at the compliment.

"It was only a candle. I still need to be extremely careful."

She sidestepped his attentive gaze and fixed hers on the nearest bookshelf until Livia hurried back in.

"They really liked you!" she insisted. "I'm going to take you out for bow and arrow practice tomorrow if the weather is good and then we'll have to practice on moving targets and also from horseback."

"Sounds fun, but I'm exhausted," Neri admitted. "Is there any expectation for dinner this evening?"

She took the cup Viljo handed to her, the spiced wine inside swirling thoughts of Niall through her head.

Stop thinking about him. Stop it. That's been and done.

Livia gasped. "You can't disappear yet, we still have the party in the square!"

"She didn't ask about that, Liv," Viljo reminded her. "She asked about food. If you want, I can ask the kitchens to send some food to your room while you get ready?"

Neri shook her head. "I can do that myself, it's fine."

"It's no problem," he insisted. "I'm heading there anyway."

She lifted a hand to rub the back of her neck, her determination ailing in the face of his intense smile.

"Alright, thank you." She turned to Livia. "Any particular dress I'm supposed to wear?"

Livia grinned. "Absolutely. I have big plans for you, but first I need to get myself ready. I'll come to your room in a while to help you prepare."

Neri held in the groan with valiant effort as Livia hurried from the room.

"She means well," Viljo said. "Go, I'll sort out the kitchens."

In that moment, it was scarily easy to nod and let him handle it, but the moment she was alone in the hall, she fought the urge to run down to the cottage. She had time yet to stake her authority and her freedom. For now she would behave herself and follow the whims of the others.

She bathed in her old room, and by the time the knock came at her door, she sat combing her fingers through her hair and was weighing up the option of eating the wood at the end of her bed, she was so famished.

She swung the door open, her hopeful smile getting stuck on her face.

"Food as requested," Viljo announced.

Neri froze. "I… you didn't need to bring it yourself. I could have gone and gotten it, or requested it."

"I have no doubt, but it's no hardship. When Orin heard it was for you, she shovelled some extra bits on so she must like you."

Neri took the plate from him. Not only was it a big enough portion for two, but she also had the vague notion the polite thing was to invite him in to share it.

When she hesitated, he took a step forward.

"I also have something I think might be of use to you."

He reached for something out of sight beside the doorway and held it out with a flourish.

Neri stared at the fine wooden archer's bow laid across his palms like an offering, as well as the strap of a quiver hanging from one wrist. He pushed the offerings closer when she didn't reach out immediately to take them.

"I can't accept these, they must be so valuable," she murmured.

There's no way this is a simple gift between friends, and I can't offer him anything more than that, not while I'm still addle-minded over Niall.

"I hope you will accept it," Viljo insisted. "The finest woodsman carved this for me, the arrows too. Their balance is perfect and they'll serve you well. If not for yourself or me then accept it for the happiness it will bring Livia when she can teach you to use it."

Neri struggled to find some kind of response that didn't sound ungrateful, but she simply couldn't refuse without offending him.

With a deep breath, she allowed her fingers to slide forward and snagged the bow and quiver.

"Thank you. I'll take good care of them."

Viljo nodded, a broad smile of satisfaction breaking across his face.

"Good. I hope you'll save me a dance tonight."

He headed down the corridor with his usual steady gait before she could answer him, leaving a swirl of mortification brewing behind.

Neri shut the door with her knee and clambered onto the bed with the gift. She couldn't reject it or give it back, but she would have to take great pains to show him that all she could offer was friendship. Even as she promised herself that it wasn't because of Niall, that Viljo was to be Jakid one day and therefore deserving of a high-born lady worthy of him, her gaze scanned the shadows dancing in the corners of the room.

I will not let him get to me. She made it her mantra. *I will not let Niall get to me anymore.*

She waited for Livia, the thought of wearing her boots and going down to the square alone filling her head, but Livia banged into her room moments later and dashed the idea to pieces.

"Right, let's begin."

Neri sat obediently as Livia fussed around with various unnameable implements that looked more like torture devices, and she giggled at Livia's horrified face when she refused to wear any enhancement around her eyes.

"They'll just have to take me as I am," she insisted. "I'm going to observe and meet a few folk."

I most definitely am not going to dance.

Livia accepted that with a weary sigh and linked arms with her to walk down to the square.

In that moment, Neri could almost imagine she was back in the sanctuary with Emelyn and the others, about to attend a party in the oasis of a garden they had. She'd only been to one, and Niall had turned up eventually to wrap her in his arms and whisper things in her ear to make her blush.

"Ouch."

Neri's emotion spiked and heat rushed to her skin so strongly that Livia had to tug her arm free.

"Sorry, my mind got the better of me." She pulled a face. "It won't happen again."

Livia patted her shoulder but made no attempt to regain contact.

"That's okay. Don't think about him tonight."

Easier said than done but Neri managed a weary smile. "Is it that obvious?"

Livia grinned. "Kind of. Don't worry, there's my

brother waiting to escort us."

Sure enough, Viljo stood at the bottom of the palace steps, his head tilted up to them. Neri caught the admiration in his eyes and squared her shoulders as they approached.

He didn't make any move to offer her his arm thankfully, although Livia joked about it on the way down, but Neri picked their pace and hurried them down to the square as quickly as she could in the slippers Livia had insisted on.

"Wow, this is beautiful."

She stared up at the lights floating over the square, with long wooden tables set out and benches running on either side. Livia's arm slipped cautiously through her own once more, squeezing when Neri kept her heat resolutely in check.

"All we do is enjoy the fruits of the harvest, drink a lot and then there's dancing," Livia explained. "But look, we donate the tablecloths and this year I got to choose!"

Neri dutifully admired the nearest tablecloth, a dark and rich purple with golden vines stitched on, and allowed Livia to guide her onto a bench. Viljo claimed the seat next to her with rapid speed and insisted on pouring wine from a large cup for her. She flinched as his warm fingers brushed hers, but he showed no sign that he'd noticed.

She took a swig of the sweet, syrupy tang, although which berry it was made from she couldn't tell, and watched the locals sweeping in.

There were no speeches and no sense of order prevailed. Folk moved seats, joked with others and ate whenever they felt like it. Neri stuck close to Livia but she waved to Orin who turned up with the small kitchen girl hanging off of her hand. She intended to go and say hello, not having seen them for a while, but she got waylaid by the settlement children who ran up and begged her to light their candles.

Amused, she lit one then insisted they had to share the flame between them. As they grabbed it and ran off squealing, she looked for Livia, but Livia stood with her head turned toward the lane, her eyes wide and her mouth hanging open.

Neri followed her gaze, wondering what could have caused such a reaction, as a sudden hit of *liliam* choked the breath from her lungs.

Her *ai-tan* roared and her feet carried her forward even though her mind was screaming at her to run, to set fire to something. She passed through the growing crowd without a single shred of attention for anything else and stepped into the dim shadows of the lane.

She allowed her burning eyes to rake up the legs and torso of the man in front of her, his arms covered by fabric and his pale fingers hooked into torn pockets. The *liliam* dimmed, but that left the natural smell of cake-spice swirling around her, making her dizzy.

Neri finally settled her gaze on Niall's face, now devoid of any shadow besides tiredness and his dark copper hair hanging loose around his ears. She eyed the familiar quirk of his sheepish smile, like he thought this was something they could argue their way through easily enough, and the pure dark circles of emotion that made up his eyes.

He thinks he can walk back in here and smile at me like that? After everything he said?

Her insides seared, the emotion close to bursting. Any moment tears of relief, pain and confusion would fall and possibly burn her skin clean off.

She pivoted away from him, her foot sliding in the ridiculous slipper, and ignored the sound of Livia calling after her.

Even more embarrassingly after his dramatic reappearance, Niall didn't say a word to her at all.

She broke into a run and hooked into her lane. Her feet slid and slithered on the path, and her fingers scorched the door as she banged into it.

He's here and in his normal skin. She shook her head, the burn of her *ai-tan* clawing at her. *I need to calm down.*

Still in her dress and caked in drying mud, she kneeled on the stone in front of the vat and took as much wax in her hands as she could hold. If Niall intended to make a dramatic entrance in the hope of tormenting her a little further just when she'd finally gained control over her heartbreak, she would calm herself so much that he no longer had any sway over her.

Within mere moments wax dribbled in her fingers and she threw the gloop into the cauldron. She worked until all the candles were simmering over a fire lit with her anger.

She cleaned the moulds as she waited for the wax to cool and then set the wax in the moulds ready for the morning. A sizeable lump of wax lay in the bottom of the cauldron, still warm, and Neri scooped it out with her hands.

The wax balled between her fingers and she focused on Livia. She needed a gift for her friend, a simple token of goodwill that would keep her mind calm. Reluctant to go to sleep in case bad dreams set her covers ablaze, she rolled the wax into a cylinder and then sculpted a circle at one end. She narrowed the middle and squared off the remaining end. Finally she set it down and got to her feet.

Neri moved outside and grabbed her trusty wooden bucket to gather water from the stream behind the cottage, her mind calm enough to sort through the reality before her.

Niall had no shadow left, unless he could now transform at will, but even so she'd never been that good at sensing his arrivals. She wouldn't put it past him to spy on her and hurried back inside.

With the fire properly doused Neri noticed the first tinge of light through her open windows. She should be exhausted but the sensation felt far away. She set about breaking her candles free, then she picked up the lump of wax she'd started forming as a gift for Livia. The desire to finish what she started tugged at her and she sat to whittle the charm.

As she whittled her thoughts slowed and the irritating tingle of her heat finally ebbed away.

She had no reason to skulk and hide. Livia would be missing her and she needed all the training she could get. There was no guarantee Niall was even here for her, although she couldn't think why he'd bother coming back.

Hareili's still here though. With her *ai-tan* all but exhausted, she barely felt a flicker at the thought. *Good. I can face him. Women have faced men endless times over far worse.*

She changed her dress for her spare pare of fighting clothes and threw her fancy flight cloak over her shoulders. With her blade ready at her hip, she stepped out into the garden and pulled the door shut behind her. The wind whipped her hair around her face and she hurried along the still muddy lane with leaves whizzing past her legs.

Thoughts of creeping through the palace to her room with the excuse of retrieving her bow filled her head. If she could manage that, then she could use her deck as a vantage point to make sure the coast was clear.

Livia and Viljo stood by the training rings folk practised their bladesmanship in the training rings, but she didn't get a chance to tiptoe past.

"There you are!" Livia hurried toward her. "I made myself promise not to bother you, but I'm glad you're not moping about."

"Inside thoughts, Liv," Viljo muttered.

Neri glanced his way and noted his unusually stiff smile as he nodded a greeting to her. Livia spared a withering look for her brother before her expression brightened again.

"I think we should practice your archery," she insisted. "I took the liberty of fetching your new bow from your room."

Neri had no reason to refuse. She'd already filled her candle quota for the day and now she wanted to let out some aggression without the risk of her *ai-tan* flaring.

"Is there somewhere a bit more discreet we can practice?" she asked.

Livia shook her head. "For blade-play yes, but there's no sense shooting in such a small space. You'll be fine."

Neri succumbed as Livia started teaching her how to hold the bow. The moment she was firm in her stance, Livia marched her across to the nearest available targets. With all of Livia's instructions circling in her head, Neri raised her bow, focused and let go.

The arrow thudded into the target to the bottom left but she couldn't help grinning.

"I hit it!"

Livia nodded. "Yes, but only just. Try again."

Neri drew out another arrow and changed her angle.

"A bit higher," Livia called out.

"Any higher she'll be shooting past it," Viljo argued.

Livia huffed. "Who exactly is teaching who here?"

Neri turned her head toward them to ask for some quiet,

but her gaze snagged on someone standing a short distance behind them. They hadn't noticed Niall, and he'd always had that skill of walking without attracting attention. But she could see him clearly enough and her *ai-tan* woke.

Sliding her hand to the tip of the arrow she allowed the spike of energy to transfer as the head of the arrow flamed.

"That's a bit ambitious-"

Livia gasped as Neri squinted at the target and sent the arrow on its way. This time she almost made the outermost circle. Her fire, still a part of her, remained flickering until she called with her mind to extinguish it.

The heady rush from her gift gave her the strength to turn around, but given the brooding expression on Viljo's face, he knew Niall was behind him and what had triggered her rashness.

Neri pulled the quiver free of her back and shouldered the bow awkwardly.

"I need better aim, I know," she said. "Just give me a short break to practice on my own and I'll be back."

Niall didn't show any signs of leaving or approaching and she couldn't bring herself to look directly at him. She dug her thumbnail into her index finger to focus on the physical bite as opposed to the emotional one.

When Livia looked like she was about to argue, Neri sent her pleading look.

"I won't use *ai-tan* I promise. I just need to focus on accuracy."

Livia nodded. "Okay, but no flaming ones. Practice where we did with the blades before."

Neri left them giving each other wary looks and walked along the side of the palace past the training rings. It was the only way she could go that didn't take her anywhere near Niall, but she would take the time to calm her mind.

She laid her bow on the ground by the wooden posts at the back of the palace and slumped onto the nearest one. She pressed the heel of each hand to her eyes and bent over her knees.

It's normal to be affected by seeing him again. A couple more times like that and I'll be able to ignore him.

"You're not going to talk to me then?"

She didn't need to remove her hands to know it was him. Even with her sight extinguished, even if she didn't have his voice hammered into her memory, she could still smell him, just a hint on the wind.

I'm not speaking to him. It was childish, but in some small way it helped.

"You look different," he added.

She scowled behind her hands. "Being abandoned then dragged halfway across the land to be slaughtered will do that to you."

"No, I'm sure that's a new cloak you're wearing. You look like a fabled huntress of old."

She risked lifting her head. If they were going to do this, she would do it with her dignity somewhat intact. The mere sight of him hurt but she stood and faced him down with her arms folded and her pulse racing.

"You left."

He grimaced. "Yes, but I came back."

"But you left."

"I know, but I'm here now. I did sort of say some things I didn't mean-"

"Don't lie," she snapped. "I know that vows are binding and you made one to Hamlin that you'd keep me safe. That's why you dragged me here, and that's why you abandoned me. Well congratulations, I'm safe, vow over. There's no need for you to hang around anymore."

She stood and turned toward the tiny gap between the palace and the rocks. From there she could move toward the waterfall and run down the lane.

She managed all of two steps before Niall's hands landed on her arms to hold her back.

"Is that really what you think?" His breath wisped against her ear and she shivered. "I made a vow its true but that only included getting you to the sanctuary unharmed. I told you that before. Everything since then has been all me."

"You mean the dragging me here, abandoning me, dismissing everything else and disappearing? Wow, aren't you wonderful."

Her *ai-tan* took over her weakness of will and she let herself burn just a little. Niall snatched his fingers away and cold winds swirled behind her, the freshness exactly what she needed to keep her mind clear. Even then, she couldn't bring herself to turn around and see his face.

"You saw a good chance and took it while it lasted, I get that," she added. "I expected as much deep down. One day I might even thank you for bringing me here. I've made good friends and found a home for myself. They've been very welcoming and *affectionate*."

"Don't."

She made it two more steps when a low rumble brought her to a halt. She turned instinctively in time to see Niall's eyes turn darkly feral as he reached out and pulled her to him, his lips only centimetres from hers.

His closeness squished any hope of retort, but instead of bending his head to kiss her as she thought he would, his lips ghosted by her ear.

"Don't pretend you feel anything for him," he warned. "If you're trying to make me jealous, then you've forgotten that you're already mine. You'll only hurt him by encouraging him."

She stared back at him, mesmerised, her entire body warming gently. It wasn't the sear and sizzle she was used to either and without her gift, her strength was nothing compared to his vicelike grip around her.

He left me.

The thought surfaced and she blinked away the sting of tears. This time, when she pushed at him gently, he stepped back.

"You're not mine anymore though," she reminded him sadly. "You didn't want to be."

CHAPTER EIGHTEEN

Niall rubbed a hand over his face and forced himself to stand there and let Neri walk away.

Okay yeah, I've utterly screwed up.

He'd have known her anywhere, and it hadn't been the lights and merriment of the market square that had drawn him to it. She glowed now, no doubt the side-effect of whatever ai-tan had literally burned him moments ago.

But unlike the flimsy dress she'd been wearing the night before, today she was dressed like a warrior from old paintings and he had no idea how to face her anger now it was between them.

I don't deserve her.

Protecting her from a distance didn't appeal to him though. He wasn't fooled by her temper, but the fact he'd been the one to hurt her had him rubbing a hand over his chest. The pain didn't fade, but he could push the awareness of it aside as Viljo stormed toward him with Livia chasing at his heels.

"You're not welcome here," Viljo spat.

Livia's worried gaze darted between them and she reached both hands forward to grip Viljo's arm. His entire being was vibrating with defensive anger, radiating through to the ground beneath him, but Niall didn't care.

"When she truly wants me gone, I'll go." He faked a grin despite the exhaustion tugging at his eyelids. "As it is, she's got every right to be angry with me. Next time I leave, she'll be leaving with me."

"She disowned you," Viljo insisted. "That should tell you enough."

Niall ignored the stab in his chest. She had, but she didn't mean it. He was still mostly confident about that.

"And you believed her?" he scoffed. "She's hurt and I get it, but I'm not going anywhere."

Viljo locked eyes with him, shoulders squaring and his hand dropping to the hilt of his blade. Niall forced his body to stay relaxed with great effort.

How long as he been eying her up? Have I even been gone that long?

"Well she isn't going to give either of you a second glance if you're going to behave like squabbling children," Livia snapped. "She's not a toy to fight over. When she decides, you'll both have to be content with her decision. Until then, no fighting. No arguing. *Vahda,* no looking at each other if that's what it takes."

Viljo flicked a fierce glance at his sister and Niall took the brief reprieve as a chance to draw a weary breath and let his confident mask slip momentarily. Before he could play the gallant and be the first to agree, to concede and promise at least a vague attempt at maturity, Viljo turned on his heel and stalked away. Niall watched him go, torn between chasing after him in case he was going to seek Neri out straight away and making good with Livia, who might possibly put a good word in for him with Neri.

"I'm in a very difficult position." Livia announced.

Niall shrugged and wrapped his hands around the back of his neck with a groan.

"Aren't we all."

Her expression softened and broke into a devious grin.

"I have allegiances to my family," she continued. "And I do mean all of them, no matter what has happened in the past, but then I have a fierce need to protect my dearest friend. I believe what's expected of me but it goes against what I feel is right. What would you do?"

Niall turned his head and assessed her fully for the first time. Her sunny not-so-innocent smile reminded him strongly of Emelyn. He also wondered from the shrewd gaze she fixed on him how much of the vast, complicated truth she actually knew.

"Those in the east have a saying," he said carefully. "You can choose your kin but you can't choose your blood. She comes first for me, above everything, but I imagine her friends would come first for her."

Livia's grin widened. "Assuming she forgives you."

"I may need a bit of help with that."

"A bit?" Her laughter peeled through the air. "You need an entire battalion to help with getting her to forgive you. You need to be on your knees begging for the next six winterspans at least."

Niall chuckled. "I will, happily. She'll probably kick me in the face."

"She might. I hope by now she respects my opinion, so I'll make my own decision on who I think deserves her. But I like you, so I'll do what little I can."

Her eyes bored into his with sudden intensity, the sunny grin slipping, and he had to steel himself to avoid flinching away. A strong wind gusted through the clearing, dark clouds rolling overhead with remarkable speed.

"I don't expect she'll take my advice," Livia added. "If she chooses you, then so will I. Somehow I doubt we'll all be the best of friends, at least not when it comes to *ama* or Viljo, but as you said you can't choose your family. Although I suppose in a fight you can choose between them."

Her words whirled around the clearing, the sound moving on the wind rather than directly from her lips. Niall wondered again how much truth she knew. He could tell her, or ask her, but then she might not know. Even if she did know, she might not tell him. Theirs was a fragile link and one he wanted to pace with caution.

Either way, he definitely wasn't in awe of Livia's social standing or her family, but he did recognise a potential adversary or ally depending on his future actions.

"What happened to you?" she asked. "Forgive my bluntness, but you seemed dead inside when we got you to the bottom of the tree. There was nothing but a shade left."

Niall shrugged. Livia was his quickest route back into Neri's life and she was offering him a hand of friendship. He didn't care who knew the truth now.

"I left to die. Neri gave me *liliam* when we first arrived here and I smelled it at the ravine path. I turned back and saw her stepping out of the tree, but I was willing to let her go if I couldn't be worthy of her."

He sighed and rubbed his fingertips over his chin, still revelling in the rough stubble that had disappeared during his short period stuck in shadow.

"That's thrilling!"

He grimaced. "If you say so. The moment I was on the move the shadows started to fade. I scraped my arm and it bled. Now my shade-side is under complete control and by all accounts the shadow is my *ai-tan*. I can still call it if I need it, but the emotion won. I don't know it was her bird that granted me a second chance, or maybe the great tree did, but I won't let her go again."

If Viljo thought himself a contender for Neri's affections then it would be a bonus to let him know Niall still had power. He turned his attentions to Livia next, a suspicion already formed in his mind.

"Nobody really knows what your *ai-tan* is," he said. "But the weather has been… odd of late."

He hoped to distract her from thoughts of Neri for a moment but he also wanted his question answered, no matter how cryptically.

Livia's eyes danced with playful scheming as her lips curved wide.

"Clever boy. I find secrecy is the key to my freedom. I wouldn't like to think anything will undermine that until I'm ready."

Niall smirked and played along, splaying his arms out wide in a mocking gesture of obedience.

"What do I know?"

Livia smiled. She turned away but rotated back again as her face fell into anticipative worry.

"All I ask is make sure you're worthy for her before you go after her. If you hurt her again she may never recover."

Her words staked him like blades, the plea in them no less powerful for the submissiveness of her request.

"I have no intention of hurting her ever."

Livia nodded. "Good. Try not to kill Viljo either if you can help it. It would be extremely tiresome to have to train new brothers to take over the westlands so I can escape to freedom one day."

"I promise nothing, but I will try."

"You're trouble." She grinned. "I happen to like trouble though. I knew you and Neri would make life more interesting."

She disappeared and Niall wiped a hand over his face with a rueful laugh. He had such a long way to go to redeem himself, but Livia's approval was a good start.

He took a step forward, thoughts of finding Neri and

professing abject apologies filling his head. Then he sniffed his shirt and pulled a face.

Perhaps bathing first wouldn't hurt, especially if he was putting all his effort into going courting.

CHAPTER NINETEEN

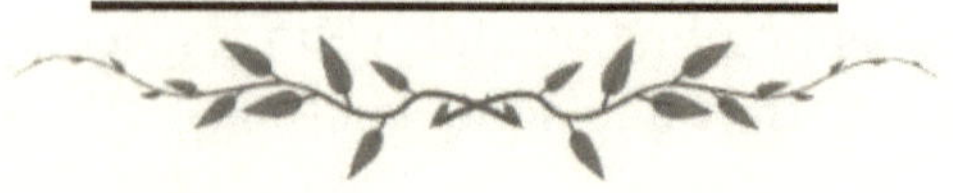

Neri woke to a banging noise. It rolled over and over until she regained full consciousness and realised someone was hammering on her door. She'd managed to hide and avoid Niall for the rest of the previous day, and even Livia insisted they could practice archery around the short space of grass behind her cottage.

As the hammering increased, she struggled out of bed and hurried to the front door. Livia almost fell on her as she opened it.

"Enough moping," she demanded. "Today we train properly, no excuses."

Neri blinked at the sharp admonishment in Livia's voice and glanced outside the door before closing it. She assumed there had to be a reason for Livia's arrival so soon after the first tinges of the suns' dawn had fallen across the lane.

"Does the Jakida know you're out this early?" she asked.

Livia wrinkled her nose and stuck her tongue out.

"I don't need minding. Ooh, this bread is still good."

Neri watched as Livia ferreted around in the kitchen and whipped up a breakfast of slightly hardened bread, still moist on the inside, some wedges of the crumbly cheese-like round that actually tasted similar to the mushrooms growing outside, and a bunch of unnameable herbs.

"I have my candles to make first," she said.

Livia shrugged. "Fine. Are you worried about seeing

him again?"

Neri stomped to the stone and started breaking the previous set of candles out of the moulds.

"Wouldn't you be?" She hesitated. "I'll be fine as long as he leaves me alone."

Livia muttered something under her breath but Neri guessed she wasn't meant to catch it. She focused on channelling her *ai-tan* instead, warming the old wax into the moulds and setting new wicks.

She waited for a thousand questions to burst out of Livia's mouth about Niall, but to her surprise Livia never uttered a word. Instead, seeing Neri had finished, Livia clapped her hands.

"Right, training."

Neri grabbed her blade and her bow with a groan. She owed Livia still and with the enemy bearing down upon them, she needed all the training she could get. The tempting thought that she might one day be able to pass through the borderlands to the east to find her friends if the Jakida's side triumphed filled her head, but she mentioned nothing of it as they left the cottage.

"Do you lot have feastmas?" she asked.

Livia grinned and waved her hand down the hill as they rounded the end of the lane and joined the main path up toward the palace.

"We do have feastmas to celebrate the turning of the seasons," Livia said. "We have our longest night and then we'll hold a party in the settlement to celebrate that the winter has turned. It's a beautiful event, and you'll be here to see the next one."

Neri nodded. She could take comfort in the fact that east or west, nature would always be constant. It would snow, it would rain and the sun or suns would shine. The waves would ebb back and forth and plants would grow, wither and regrow from new seeds.

The training rings were filling up already, but Neri recognised the man fighting in the nearest one with a falling of her heart.

"Niall fights really well, doesn't he?" Livia asked slyly.

Neri rolled her eyes. "For a vagrant who doesn't keep promises, sure."

She glanced toward the palace and her heart sank as Viljo strode toward them, his long-blade already in hand. He pulled a tight smile of recognition in their direction, but his focus was already turning to the training rings.

To one ring in particular.

Niall moved with inhuman speed, his blade whirling around him in precise, artful strokes.

"It's easy to see his *ai-tan* is of air," Livia muttered. "Look how fast and easily he moves, although how his gift works I can't even begin to guess."

Viljo grunted in answer and removed his cloak. Neri grimaced as he left them and walked toward the ring where Niall fought against a man and a woman. Neri knew him well enough to recognise the slight linger of his movements. His parries and strikes were growing jagged with less of his usual grace. She wondered where he slept at night. Worry for him fizzled and she inched away from Livia as her emotion burned.

A waft of *liliam* surrounded her, fast and potent. A moment later Niall lifted his head, a mere glance thrown in her direction before he disarmed the last opponent standing against him. He took a step in their direction, but even as he lowered his blade Viljo stepped into the ring to face him.

Niall's shoulders hunched, darkness and a hint of the

shadow flicking over his shoulders. Whatever challenge he saw in on Viljo's face, it renewed his waning vigour.

"I can't watch this," Neri muttered.

She shrugged Livia's hand off her shoulder muttering about not wanting to burn her. Viljo and Niall were probably close to evenly matched in a blade fight but her only thought was for Niall's tiredness.

"I don't particularly want to see this either," Livia said.

Neri couldn't bear the knowing, pitiful compassion on Livia's face and squared her shoulders, steeling her resolve.

"We're meant to be training, right? Let them do what they want."

Livia eyed her for several moments, until a wicked grin flickered across her face.

"I need to practice. Let's go."

Livia followed her across to one of the empty rings, both of them drawing blades and taking their stance. Neri made the first swing and stumbled when Livia dodged.

"You think this alters anything?" Viljo's voice blasted through the air. "I will not have my heritage, my right, undermined by an outsider, a mere shade!"

They turned together to find Viljo shaking with anger and Niall utterly relaxed with a look of triumph on his face. He stood with one leg loosely bent, his hip cocked and his fingers hooked into the pockets of his trousers.

"Oh, this is bad," Livia muttered.

Neri shrugged. "Let them argue it out. At least they're not fighting."

She shouldn't care, she knew that, but denying it wouldn't make any difference. She still has as many irritating feelings for Niall as she'd always had, and while she couldn't risk trusting him again, she didn't want him getting hurt.

"I don't want your crown or your title." Niall cast a lightning quick glance their way and started grinning. "I came back for one reason only and that is one thing you have no right to."

Neri flinched as Livia grabbed her arm.

"I don't have much time and its better you hear it from me," Livia insisted.

Neri opened her mouth to interrupt and almost bit her tongue when Livia's fingers dug into her arm.

"*Ama* had a child before Viljo and me. I'll leave the details for later when you start talking to me again, but she doesn't know I know. That child would still be first in line to inherit the Jakiris. *Ama* didn't keep the child because the man it came from was a shade. Do you get what I'm saying?"

Livia's words struck like a flaming arrow.

Neri stared at her, then at Niall and Viljo about to circle each other, as clarity slammed through her head in one large hit.

"You mean Niall's the rightful heir to the entire stretch of the westlands?"

Her chest crunched. She wiped a hand over her face, a hysterical laugh bubbling out.

Of course he wanted to get back here any way he could. Of course he used me to do it.

She turned away, assessing whether she should escape into the palace or risk dashing past them toward the lane as the Jakida swept toward them.

She abandoned him because of who his father was.

"This is a private affair," the Jakida warned.

Viljo turned obediently to face her but Niall folded his arms across his chest as he deigned to angle his head in her direction. Neri doubted he'd be so easily obedient.

"He started it," Niall retorted, wickedness curling at the corner of his mouth.

"I don't care who started it, I'm ending it. I will not take part in the petty quarrels of men when I have a land to govern and a war to prepare for. If you refuse to get along, take it inside and fight it out between you there where folk won't see."

Neri clenched her fists, but as the Jakida swept back inside, Niall wasn't done.

"Run back inside," he mocked. "Do as you're told, but I'll warn you now, I'm not here for any of this except Neri. You might impress her with gallantry but she was mine long ago before we even came here and she will be mine if and when we leave."

His languid posture never faltered but Neri caught the raw bite in his voice and the slight tension of his shoulders. As Viljo raised his blade again, fully prepared to strike, Niall laughed.

"Try it and see what happens. I don't want to bother fighting you, brother, and I definitely don't want your role in this world but you won't get between Neri and I."

Brother. Neri shuddered. *And he's so confident I'm just going to run to his side again.*

His arrogance infuriated her beyond all sensible reason and she lifted a hand, letting her *ai-tan* spike freely. A flicker of flame curled over her palm and she grabbed one of the fluttering pieces of cloth from the edge of the training ring, letting it feed the fire until it engulfed her hand.

Viljo lowered his blade as she walked toward them, worry dancing in his eyes, but Niall had shuttered his expression entirely.

"I don't belong to *either of you*. Fight each other for power but leave me out of it."

"You haven't had your *ai-tan* long," Viljo insisted. "Let it rest."

"Don't tell her what to do," Niall snapped.

Viljo ignored him. "That rag is almost burned to cinders. You've made your point, and I apologise, but you need to call your gift back before it rebounds."

Neri blinked. She hadn't heard a word, her gaze fixed on the seductive dance of the fire over her skin.

"*Ej-va*, Neri, let it rest." Niall's worried voice pierced the haze.

She looked up at him, not sure when he'd managed to get so close.

"Let it settle back down," he pleaded. "Then you can yell at me some more."

She did need to yell at him, but so entranced by the pull of her gift, she couldn't quite remember why. Her arm was tired though. She could barely hold it up any longer, and she focused on cooling the fire until it dissipated and the glow retreated into her skin.

Oh. Right. Her mind re-surfaced. *That's why I'm supposed to be yelling at him.*

She sucked in a breath and started forward, but it didn't entirely surprise her when strong arms wrapped around her waist. She twisted to make sure it was definitely Niall heaving her against him, then she settled for struggling as hard as she could.

"What are you doing?" she shrieked.

Her cheeks burned with humiliation as he lifted her clean off her feet and swung her into his arms. The land twisted and she gulped down the urge to throw up, but he only uttered a low scoffing noise and carried her off toward the lane.

"Technically, I'm kidnapping you."

He was, and she guessed Viljo and Livia wouldn't do a single thing to stop it either, not unless she screamed. In Livia's case, probably not even then.

Traitor.

"This is inappropriate," she muttered. "Seriously, I think you should just let me down and go away."

Niall sighed. "We'll call a truce for today. You need rest. You've been using your gift too much too fast."

"You don't know that."

"Zel said as much. Livia did too."

"When did you speak to them about me?" She saw the turning to her lane and realised they were heading down it. "Where are you going?"

He settled a soft kiss against her temple before she could dodge it.

"I'm going to look after you until you're feeling better. When you're ready to try and burn me to death, I'll let you make the decisions, but until then you're only wearing yourself out."

She scowled as Niall headed straight for her cottage without one single sign of hesitation.

"You're kidnapping me to my own dwelling?"

He nodded. "I want you to be comfortable."

There was some mad Niallesque logic in that, but she had to stand her ground now or he'd be walking all over her.

"How do you know where I live anyway? No, don't tell me, Livia told you."

He said nothing, only settled her closer against his chest as they fought through the tangle of her garden. She banged a half-hearted fist against his shoulder, but it made no difference.

"Let me down," she insisted. "I will concede to being dragged through the settlement but I'll be damned if I'm letting you walk into my home like you belong there."

After several agonising moments where she rolled and writhed in his arms to get free, Niall tightened his grip. The moment she fell still, he lowered her to her feet with all the chivalry of a gentleman, his devilish smile never fading.

"I'm supposed to be polite and leave you here alone I take it?" he asked.

She bit her lip, aware he intended nothing of the sort, and nodded. Niall's face marred with a momentary frown. If he expected her to swoon or even invite him in, he really was addle-headed.

When she didn't give in, he took a step back and resignation settled over his features. It tore at her heart, so she hardened it.

Not going there again.

Niall shrugged one shoulder, hurt shining in his dark eyes as he turned away and Neri opened her door.

A lightning quick bang echoed above her head. She glanced up in time to see the door rebound from the force with which Niall had hit it. As it swung wide, he bent low and grabbed around the tops of her legs to lift her flailing body against him.

She fought as he kicked the door shut, but then he dropped her back to her feet, grinning as she glowered at him.

Always a game. She sighed. *I can't even bring myself to play anymore. What's the point?*

She moved toward the kitchen and the remnants of the meal Livia had fixed them earlier.

"I don't have much here at the moment," she said,

keeping her tone wooden. "There's wine if you want it and some bread, and what I think is flavoured cheese."

Silence gathered behind her.

She tensed as he stood behind her, but for once he didn't move to touch her. Her insides fired and her skin tingled, every part of her dying to give in, to rage at him or jump on him, but she pushed it aside.

"Neri?" he asked, his tone almost fearful. "Where have you gone?"

She forced the burning tears to remain inside her and shrugged.

"I haven't gone anywhere. You're the one that left. You think this is all some game. We'll dance around arguing for a while and it'll be fine, but I can't trust you anymore."

She breathed through the instinctive thundering panic as she heard his footsteps retreating. She waited countless moments but, in the absence of her door swinging shut, she turned.

Niall sat on her table with his arms crossed against his chest and his dark eyes fixed on her. He looked pained, his face scrunched, but he was silently refusing to leave.

She didn't know what to do with that.

"Do you need to eat?" she asked.

He shook his head.

"Aren't you going to at least leave me to rest?" She tried again.

He shook his head.

Ire sparked but she kept it in check. Niall might be stubborn and pig-headed but she couldn't back down now. Even though it was barely afternoon, she climbed up to her bed and peered down at him.

"I can't see why you're insistent on remaining here but I'm taking a nap. You can sort yourself out."

She heaped onto the bed, glad that at least from the ground he couldn't see her.

She waited for the telltale sound of her door shutting, but there was only a quick round of shuffling below.

He really did intend to wait it out. Unnerved, Neri forced her mind to go through the scant memories of Livia's archery training, mainly in the hope that Niall wouldn't smell the *liliam* the same as she could and take it as an invitation to invade her bed.

A soft snuffling noise echoed through the silence. The urge to giggle bubbled up but she choked it back down and sat up. She could make out Niall's form on the large cushion and couldn't stop the grin that crept over her lips as another soft snore left his partly open mouth.

He's exhausted.

She tried not to let that sway her, but Niall had evidently had a tough time of late if he was falling asleep so easily.

It took her an age to creep down the ladder, and she winced every time her boots made a noise on the wood, but halfway to the door she glanced back at him. Even in sleep, his brow was wrinkled in a slight frown.

He needs his sleep, and I need my space. She eased the door open and crept outside. *This is best for both of us.*

She wandered up to the palace and hoped to find Livia without causing a scene, but she had mixed feelings as Viljo approached her from the waterfall. Determined to stop any awkward conversations, Neri made the first move.

"I've only come looking for Livia," she said.

Viljo halted and his shoulders bunched. She gazed at him with renewed realisation. The dark look she sometimes saw crossing his features was familiar because it mirrored Niall's.

"Livia has been missing since you left," Viljo announced. "She ran off."

Neri stilled as her warmth left her at the thought of possibilities. Perhaps Viljo sensed this because he hastened to reassure her without stepping closer.

"She disappeared into the palace and nobody knows where she went. It's unfathomable that she can always hide from us here."

A glimmer of memory returned and Neri stifled a smile. She had a vague idea where Livia would be but shaking off Viljo had to come first.

"I think I know where to find her, but she'll never forgive me if I say where. I'll spend the rest of the day with her, and might use the room here tonight too."

Viljo's eyebrows raised and his mouth quivered. Neri hated herself in that moment for giving the suggestion she was running from Niall, however true. Viljo indicated with a sweep of his arm that she was welcome and turned away, walking back toward the waterfall.

She hurried up the steps and tore through the palace until she reached the kitchens. Despite the door being shut, she hoped to find either Orin or Livia inside, or both. She swept through the door and stopped short on top of the kitchen steps.

Livia sat on the long bench that often held the prepared food, her eyes wide with playfulness and fixed upon a young man who wore the purple clothes of a servant. It didn't take a genius to realise the cause of Livia's happiness to hide out in the kitchens. Neri smirked to see her admiring what appeared to be one of the cooks. Smiling at the flush in Livia's cheeks, Neri leapt up to sit on the counter beside her. Orin possibly made herself scarce during Livia's visits, but Neri guessed that would be out of kindness rather than necessity.

"I'm sorry I went rotten again." She pulled a face. "I am trying."

Livia shrugged. "You should be practicing your *ai-tan* anyway."

Aware that the cook had immediately hastened to go about his business, Neri lowered her voice to a whisper.

"Is that why you like hanging out down here then?" She asked.

Livia flushed deeper but her natural good nature surfaced and she nudged Neri hard in the ribs. Neri accepted wine from the young man who, whilst evidently easy in Livia's presence, wasn't willing to be so relaxed around her.

"I need to learn more about this place," Neri announced. "Folk tell me things that mean nothing to me, names and descriptions I don't know. Mary told me that the buildings are held together with tree sap which is mad in itself and then I have no idea how the land actually functions. What's the currency? How far does the land really go?"

Livia's expression brightened.

"I can answer all of that. The bit about the tree, sac you called it? We call it gar. The properties of it mean that it sets as hard as rock and the real trouble hutteers have is to protect the wood from warping or getting water-rot."

Neri nodded as Livia's explanations calmed her disgruntled feelings. She had time to study and she recalled that the dwelling had a whole library full of books she could learn from if she chose. Livia glanced around as she tried to think of more things to explain.

"Hutteers are dwelling-fixers by the way just in case you didn't know."

Livia leaned sideways away and her fingers snaked

along the counter inch by inch. She attempted to balance and snare the bottle of wine that had been left in a conveniently unguarded position. Neri grabbed Livia's other arm as she lost her balance. Livia's fingers snared the bottle and Neri dragged her upright. Grinning, Livia re-filled their glasses.

"What about currency?" Neri pressed. "Trades, or do you use coin?"

"We use tokens, but that's mostly for folk who earn a living off the palace. It's not the main part of how trade works here. Folk who don't have tokens will provide services instead."

Neri smiled. The fond memory of helping her mamma and gramma with chores in exchange for things swelled up. The more she learnt, the easier it became to recognise how the place had started to feel like home.

"Tomorrow we'll go and I'll introduce you to some of the local folk," Livia decided. "I should have done it long before now but things have been hectic and I didn't exactly get a chance at the party what with Niall showing up."

Neri's mind drifted out of the kitchens, through the dwelling and down the lanes to the man currently asleep in her cottage. She drained her wine and noticed the easy slump of Livia's shoulders. One more glass, which Livia had already started pouring, and she would be explaining Livia's state to a less than impressed Jakida. The suns were barely sinking outside yet, but still she couldn't help but press on with her questions.

"So the flower I had, the *liliam*, how exactly is it magic? How does it work?"

Livia grinned with her eyes half-closed. If Neri focused on it her own head now seemed to be swamped in softness and haze. The drink tasted similar to the drink she had at

Mary's, lethal in any more than small quantities.

"I don't know, ask Zel."

Neri sighed and slid off the counter. She grabbed a cup of water and insisted Livia drink it.

"I'm fine," Livia argued.

The kitchen door opened and Neri tried to shush her, but Livia responded by joining in with loud hisses that morphed into honking and hooting laughter as Orin strode in. She took one look at the situation and grinned.

"Someone needs her bed," she announced. "No point pulling a face at me, Lady. If the Jakida sees you like this, she won't let you out of the palace, let alone the settlement."

Livia scowled. "She's no fun."

"Not her job to be fun. Up we get."

Neri hovered as Orin bodily slung one of Livia's arms over her shoulder and got her to her feet.

"I can take her from here," Orin insisted. "Come along and bring that bucket."

Neri grabbed the bucket and trailed them through the halls. Livia's room was much deeper inside the palace and up a wide set of stairs. Orin threw open a door and dumped Livia on Neri before she could protest.

"Here we are. She's half asleep already."

Neri had her doubts, but she watched Orin disappear down the hall again before lugging Livia into her room. The drapes were a vast array of bright colours, and several pieces of furniture decorated the space.

The moment Livia's head tumbled onto the pillow, she rumbled a tiny snore. Neri pushed the slippers off Livia's feet and tucked one of the many blankets around her, uneasy at how similar the noble siblings were turning out to be.

She shut the door behind her and faced the hall. With no idea how to get back to the main thoroughfare of the palace, she set off down the stairs and through the winding corridors until she found her old room.

With the beginnings of a headache brewing, she shut herself in her room and shed her cloak, trousers and her shirt. The only person bursting in would likely be Livia, who was in no position to be bursting in anywhere.

Neri closed her eyes and snuggled into the bedding.

With all the upheaval, I deserve a rest.

CHAPTER TWENTY

Neri wrinkled her nose as something wisped against her cheek. As her awareness emerged from the deepest pits of slumber, she scrunched her eyes tight shut to ward off the offending item. The same tickle happened again and she groaned as she slapped a hand to her cheek. The sensation disappeared only to reappear as soon as she lowered her hand.

She snapped her eyes open and screamed. The sound rang short and high-pitched, hardly loud enough to call any attention, but it brought a frown of irritation to Niall's face all the same.

Her hand flew to her chest as she laboured over her breathing, shocked beyond belief as she scrambled through the recent memories. She'd escaped her cottage the moment he fell asleep, but she never gave him the impression that he should expect her to be there when he got up. Livia had passed out too and Neri had come for a nap of her own, but none of that explained why Niall was in her room and kneeling over her on her bed.

She turned her head toward the door and flushed to see the trail of her clothing on the floor.

At least I still my undershorts and top on.

Niall watched her inner torment with the lazy smirk spreading over his lips. Unable to scramble away from him, Neri pressed herself into the bed. She stared at him and willed her *ai-tan* to rear up, but it didn't respond.

Something flicked past her eyes. As the familiar tickle kissed her cheek, she realised that Niall had woken her with strands of her own hair. She cinched her arms tighter around her chest, securing the top edge of the blanket and then hooking the bottom edge beneath her heels so he couldn't remove it without a struggle as he smirked down at her.

"I don't like to wake up and find you not there."

His voice purred with teasing but Neri's long sleep had equipped her mind well. She frowned at him and turned her gaze away.

"I'd say the same but you were the one that left." She shrugged. "That was enough to deaden the deal for me."

His tension increased above her and the stiffness of his muscles transmitted to her, making her nervous. She could easily scream and somehow she knew either Viljo or Livia would be nearby, but she couldn't bring herself to do it. The pain in his eyes was enough to hurt her too as he sighed.

"I left you I know, but I wish you could understand why. The person you wanted suddenly becomes half a person and I couldn't live with that. I had an idea of how to fix it and I went for it even though I couldn't be sure. I didn't want to put you in danger if the worst happened to me so I left you here in safety."

The raw emotion sent a spark of burn across her skin, and she kept her head turned away.

"I can't leave you alone," he insisted. "If that's what you want, I can't do it. My life is tied to yours and I'm nothing now if I'm not near you. I felt it on my way there and my way back. When you almost died in that cave I nearly died with you. I barely got you out in time."

He was there.

Neri scrambled to sit up, surprising him enough to knock him back. He crashed against the edge of the bed and then over it as he thudded to the floor. No longer caring that she was unclothed, she clambered to the edge of the bed on her knees and gripped the wooden post for support.

"You were there? I thought I imagined it."

Niall frowned, still settling from her sudden movement. He knelt too but refrained from reaching out to her.

"I never really left for long, and I was always hoping I'd be back."

The feeble smile faded from his face in an instant when he saw her expression.

"I went through all that, thinking you'd left me, and you were there?" She swiped angrily at her cheeks. "All the time I could smell you and thought I was going mad, you were following me?"

She eyed the bath. She could boil herself alive, or him, or both of them. She could set the entire dwelling on fire and walk out of the ashes and into the wilderness beyond.

Possibly a slight overreaction.

She bit her lip and pulled the blankets around her body, more as a distraction than from a need for modesty. Intending to lay some kind of ultimatum at his feet, Neri squeaked and scrambled to cover herself fully as the door swung open. There were no curtains she could hide behind, no screen or safe place. She had to stand there half-clothed, in full view of Viljo's shock and Livia's suggestive grinning. She dragged the blanket firmer around her waist to hide her legs.

Flushing bright red, her *ai-tan* giggling its way through her system, she realised in that moment that Viljo could have rivalled Niall in temper, his eyes narrowed and his clenched fists almost quaking at his sides. He turned with methodical preciseness and left the room as quickly as he'd entered it, but Neri focused on gripping the blanket as one corner escaped her little finger and left part of her thigh on show. She knew it was visible because Niall's eyes immediately locked onto it.

"Doesn't anyone knock around here?" she muttered.

She dropped her free hand and tugged with delicate fingers to cover herself once more, giving up when she realised she stood on the wrong parts.

"I only came to tell you that tomorrow we will be on the brink of war." Livia's grin could have put a fiend to shame. "I suppose it's fitting that you get all the fun in before the gritty stuff."

Her giggles could be heard all the way down the hall. Neri barely refrained from balling up the offending blanket she barely wore and throwing it at her friend in a fireball of ire. Crossing her arms, she tried not to focus on the edges of it gradually slipping open behind her.

Niall sighed and his shoulders sagged. His eyes were still shadowed and there was a weary stiffness as he rolled his shoulders.

"I've no right to expect anything from you, I know," he said. "I went about the whole thing wrong and now you can't trust me. I'll live with that but please don't expect me to disappear. There's nothing if I'm not with you."

It was everything she had wanted to hear since arriving in the westlands, but too late.

"Words are easy," she muttered.

He shrugged. "True, but I'm not going anywhere now."

She knew he would give her answers about what had happened, both in the siren's cavern and after it, but that involved conceding enough to talk to him.

His lips lifted before she could figure out how to steady

the uneasiness between them.

"I won't take too kindly to other men around you either," he warned. "I see how Viljo's been looking at you, and I can't help it."

Never mind. Her tiny flicker of hope burned away. *This is still about his pride.*

"You need to leave," she insisted.

"No." He hesitated. "Why do I need to leave?"

"I need to get dressed for a start. Then I need to find Livia and- explain."

She stopped herself short of saying Viljo's name as well, knowing that would only incite Niall to hang around.

He grinned. "Why? I've seen you naked before."

She clenched her fists and the scent of burning cloth filled the air.

"Once and never again, I promise you that."

"Okay, I'm going." He backed to the door, smirking the whole time. "Never is a long time though, and you know I'm not a patient man, especially not where you're concerned."

He shut the door behind him before she could find a suitable curse to throw his way, so she threw the smoking blanket instead.

Insufferable, arrogant, addle-headed.

She growled and took advantage of her lack of clothing to bathe, needing the soothing warmth of the water to wash her irritation at bay.

Do I owe it to him to at least hear him out?

She bathed for a long time and dressed in her fighting clothes, but as she pulled her top over her head, her fingers snagged on the cord around her neck.

The stone token her mamma had given her long ago nestled warm against her skin.

Niall brought me this far and kept me safe, mostly. She sighed. *Maybe hearing him out isn't the worst idea.*

She left the palace by vaulting over the wall of the deck and stopped to watch bands of folk carting the training rings toward the lane.

Livia's words about the war being imminent swirled in her head, but Livia was walking toward her with Viljo in tow and Neri could stop the heat burning her cheeks. Viljo's gaze never fixed upon her and the odd fleeing glance he did throw her way remained resolute on her forehead.

"We're going down to the plains outside the gates to train today," Livia announced. "More space and it will give us a better vantage point for anyone approaching."

Neri nodded. "I need to stop at the cottage and grab my bow and blade on the way down."

She grimaced as they started walking toward the lane in stilted silence and her stomach growled irritably.

"Out on your own?" Viljo asked, his tone flat. He frowned as Livia shoved a not-so-discreet elbow into his ribs. "What? It's a simple question."

Neri shrugged. "Should I not be? Oh for the love of-"

She trailed off as Niall appeared beside her. His sleeve brushed her bare arm, already chilly from the wind, but it was the enormous pastry in his hands that had her full attention.

"I'm fine," she muttered.

He grinned. "No you're not. You didn't have time to pass me in the halls and you didn't go via the kitchens. Besides, you get grouchy when you're hungry."

"I do not!"

He waved the pastry in front of her, weakening her determination to ashes.

"See? Grouchy. Go on, I won't read anything into it."

He would and she knew it, but she needed strength for fighting. Viljo stalked on ahead without a word, and a lightning quick glance at Livia showed exactly how amusing she thought the whole thing was.

Neri finished the pastry in several furious chomps and stopped at the entrance to her lane.

"I need to get my weapons, wait here."

Niall dodged around her so he was standing in her way.

"I'll fetch them, hold on."

He was off before she could argue, so she turned her ire sideways instead.

"What?" Livia asked, her face a picture of innocence. "He is trying."

"He doesn't need to try, that's the problem. How easy it would be to forgive him, then what happens when he does it again?"

"He left because he didn't want to hurt you."

"He failed."

"Well, yes, but he had a good reason." Livia frowned. "He's in control of his *ai-tan* now, and he was ready to sacrifice his life for yours."

Neri folded her arms, her gaze fixed on Niall already striding back toward them with her bow on his shoulder and her blade in hand.

"As it turns out, you're his sister," she retorted. "You would defend him."

Livia slid her hand through Neri's arm, holding firm.

"I am, but you're my friend first. I really do think he means well."

Niall held her blade out hilt first, then her bow and quiver. Neri secured them around her waist and shoulders, then faced the lane.

"Let's get on with it then."

"I'm due at the armoury," Niall announced. "I'm sure I'll find you after."

He bowed low, a wicked smile on his face. Neri tensed as he passed by her on his way back up to the palace but he was wise enough at least to not touch her.

Nobody said a word as they joined the folk filtering down toward the gates, and Neri settled into the unexpected excitement at the thought of being outside the settlement again.

"We'll practice together still I think." Livia looked around for an empty space. "You're not too bad with the bow but you'll need to defend against blades too. After practice we'll take a walk to the square."

Neri drew her blade and eyed the groups of folk battling around them. Several were as un-practiced as she was, but others moved with finesse and experience. She caught sight of Hareili in one of the rings further afield, her back straight as she marched along the lines.

No avoiding her. Neri scowled. *I wonder if Niall has already cosied up to her.*

"Ready?" Livia asked.

Neri nodded, and forced thoughts of Hareili, Niall and all of it from her mind. As they began, Livia's controlled movements were for her benefit but when Neri improved, she could feel the odd feint in her friend's attacks and reacted with instinctive grace.

Livia dropped her blade a lot later and held up her hands, grinning as Neri panted with exhilaration. Viljo had arrived to watch them but he stepped forward when Livia beckoned to him.

"Viljo will take over, I need a rest," Livia insisted.

Neri bit the fleshy inside of her lip as awkwardness

spread through her. She doubted Viljo considered her worth sparring with but he raised his blade in preparation and she had no reason to refuse.

She gripped her own blade, using the stepping feint that Livia had taught her, and Viljo moved fast with his blade swinging high as though he intended to slice her at the neck. She doubted he would ever bring himself close enough to cause harm at such speed, but the clash of metal above her head brought a squeak flying from her throat.

She dropped to the ground and rolled, her heart thudding in her ears as Viljo's blade locked in a struggle of strength against Niall's. Both glared at the other with aggressive fury, Niall's lip curling and Viljo's jaw clenched.

Standing with no thought other than to stop them, Neri turned to Livia. Before she could say anything to distract them she heard Niall's low growl.

"If anyone's going to fight her it'll be me. We've had plenty of practice."

Unsure if the taunt was meant for her ears or Viljo's, she stared in surprise as Viljo drew his blade away and bowed with a mocking smile. He stepped back several paces until he drew level with Livia.

Tension leapt as Neri turned to face Niall, her body warming instantly. He grinned, the savage, feral glint appearing in his eyes and playing with the corners of his mouth. He raised his blade and began to step a circle around her. She rotated, calming herself, waiting for her moment. If he wanted to fight her he'd be in for a shock.

He moved and she dodged, bringing her body into a twist so she faced him just as her blade came to clash against his. Grinning with the adrenaline pumping through her, she parried another blow and faked one of her own.

When he came at her once more she pitched to the side and hooked one leg around his. With an almighty effort, she grunted and pulled his foot out from under him. He crashed to his knees and she couldn't help the playful buzz of their old teasing running through her as she brought the tip of her blade to his neck.

"It seems I've had more recent practice than you."

Relaxing her guard, she missed Niall's hand sneaking up to catch the flat edge of her blade. He yanked it with effortless fingers from her grasp and threw it onto the floor.

She darted backwards, knowing she couldn't outrun him and that he must have let her win. All their previous anxieties seemed to pale into insignificance when he turned and she caught sight of the shine of predatory intent in his dark eyes. He stood, holding his hands out to the sides.

"I'm unarmed and you're making girly eyes at me. If that's the kind of fighting you've got in mind then I'm right here."

The words were low, a whisper meant only for the two of them, but she flushed and looked around to make sure nobody had heard. Her adrenaline began to ebb and frustration welled in its place. She turned away and almost groaned when she caught the gentle breath of crisp, cinnamon air. His arms wound around her waist and pulled her tight against him.

"I know you're thinking about me when you blush." He murmured against her ear. "Even when you hate me I can still irritate you. That's how I know you still care."

Neri growled and the frustration threatened to spill out as heat. As quickly as he'd captured her, Niall's embrace disappeared and left her skin rippling with sudden chills. She rotated to see him stepping back, his face once more a picture of modest gallantry.

With the blur of Livia standing alone out of the corner of her eye, she knew only one thing would comfort her now. She folded her arms across her chest, each hand gripping an elbow in the hope it would keep her steady.

"I have stuff to do. You may think this is all a game, but it's not to me. It never has been."

She kept her voice level and walked toward Livia, who stood with untold emotion splaying over her face. Her eyes seemed concerned but her lips quirked. She forced a smile for her friend, then recalled the gift she had made.

"I'm going to do some candle making but that reminds me, I made you something."

She drew out the tiny little wax charm she'd made for her friend and opened her fingers. The tiny, thumb-sized key looked so delicate against her palm and she noticed Livia's speechless awe with growing mortification.

"It's just a token of friendship to prove nobody can stop you opening doors or wandering free if you don't let them. Hurry up or I'll end up melting it down again by accident."

Livia took the charm, her green eyes shining as she smiled. No words were necessary as she linked arms and propelled them away from Niall and those still practicing behind them.

"Just take a quick walk around the square first."

CHAPTER TWENTY ONE

Livia's cajoling made Neri concede, but she didn't put up much argument because it was a fair trade to escape Niall's unerring determination for a while. Only at the gate did she allow herself a quick glance back. Niall sat on the grass with his gaze still fixed on her, his shadow flicking lazily over his shoulders and arms.

Neri shook him from her mind as she followed Livia up the main lane and into the settlement square. Several wooden tables filled the space, all covered by colourful table clothes and various wares. Folk bustled about, selling and trading, and Neri smiled to see it as Livia pulled her from table to table.

One stall sold the moist dark bread and large rounds of mushroom-tasting cheese. She wished she could stock up but knew she couldn't ask Livia for coin or influence when she owed her friend so much already. One stall sold fabrics and she stared at the fingers of the woman running it, so gnarled and calloused that she wanted to ask if the craft was painful.

She admired the clothes on offer but shook her head when the woman made offers, vowing to herself that she would find a way to barter for things or earn something to pay with. She passed a large stall of different fruits, the *calideh* amongst them making her mouth water, when Livia gasped and halted, her hand clamped against her forehead.

"I completely forgot," she groaned. "This is one of the

horrible side-effects of living in a big palace. I haven't given you any coin."

She delved into her cloak and brought out a dark pouch of thick grey fabric.

"Hold your hands out," she demanded.

Neri obeyed and Livia tipped several wooden discs into her cupped palms. Several small wooden squares had various nicks and chips carved into the edges, a tally of their worth, and each one shone with a lacquer of tree *gar*.

"I can't, I haven't earned them. I already pay for my cottage with candles."

She took a hesitant step back as Livia's face twisted with weary frustration.

"Yes but you also get coin for the candles we use. I'm sure I mentioned it or if I didn't then *Ama* might have. She refused to let this be a favour and said she'd have to pay you like anyone else. Folk don't owe us for their homes here."

Neri decided to let it slide and find someone else to ask to be sure. Zel would know. She didn't really want a reason to bring Viljo into the conversation, although he'd probably be the most honest in his response.

Niall might even know. She bit her lip. *Assuming I ever forgive him.*

"So, I can spend these?" she asked.

"You can." Livia grinned and waved a hand toward the market. "What are you going to buy first?"

Neri glanced around the busy square. Several folk were shaking hands instead of parting with any coin, and she had no idea if the west kept any of the same trading customs as the east.

"Is there some kind of expectation here?" she asked. "Is this considered a lot of coin? How many of these do I make and how often? How much are things around here?"

Livia laughed. "You get one eight, two fours and five twos for each set of candles you make. I promise I'll get someone to take over giving it to you but usually folk just make deliveries and collect. I didn't sort it out. Generally bread is a couple of twos, cheese is about four I think."

Neri blinked and looked down at the coins in her hands.

"So each day I can buy more bread and cheese and fruits."

Livia's patience waned and Neri allowed herself to be tugged back to the stall with the cloth and the smiling woman behind it.

"Do you have a coin pouch?" she asked.

The woman produced an array in a small wooden basket from under her table and Neri leaned forward.

"For you, I think this one would be best," the woman suggested. "See the dark green of nature here but the tiny strands of autumn and flame woven in."

Neri looked at the pouch in the woman's fingers. It was beautifully made, each tiny stitch painstakingly in line with the next, the green shimmering in the sunslight.

"How much is it?" she asked.

"For this, one eighter."

Neri noticed the almost imperceptible flick of the woman's eyes in Livia's direction. She had no idea if the woman had asked for more coin because Livia had lots, or if the pouch had been under-priced because of who her friend was.

Bewildered, she paid up and shoved the handfuls of coins into the pouch. She pushed it deep into the pocket of her trousers and thanked the woman, setting off with a determined stride toward the stall that sold wood.

The man running the stall smiled at her. He looked

harassed and tired, with a teenage girl and a young boy zipping around his legs. He put a small bristle brush into a pot of shining brown goop and clapped his hands.

"What will it be?" he asked.

He noticed Livia then and bowed low over his table. Neri raised her eyebrows and watched as Livia frowned in reluctant anguish.

"Hi, Silu. I hear you've asked to take on guard duty."

The man, Silu, nodded and grinned. He moved with speed to rival Niall's as his hand darted out and caught the young boy by the collar.

"It'll give me some peace and quiet, lady. You trust me, I could do with it."

He smiled as he shook the boy, extracting giggles before the boy dropped to the ground, leaving his shirt in Silu's hands as he ran off into the crowd.

Neri smiled and ran her fingers over a wooden bowl. She asked how many he had, thinking she might one day have company, and bought three from him. Wooden cups came next and then she asked if he did commissions.

"I do indeed. Do you?"

Surprised, Neri stared at him. He smiled and scratched the back of his head.

"It's my united's birthday. He asked me to get him a meaningful centrepiece for his birthday dinner. I haven't the faintest idea what he wants but he likes books, and I hear you can carve more than just candles?"

Neri nodded slowly. The idea of this being an initiation test into the settlement and its local craftsfolk entered her mind, but she couldn't shy away from the challenge.

"I can whip something up if you tell me when you need it. If she has a favourite book perhaps I can do something on that or I can make her a book or a bookshelf?"

Silu grinned and asked for a candle in the shape of a book. Neri matched his smile with a fiendish one of her own and asked for a bookcase. When Silu extended his hand, she shook it.

After buying a wicker basket, several rounds of cheese and loaves of bread, plus another basket full of *calideh* that got thrown into Livia's arms, Neri's pouch clacked a lot less.

She paused to get another set of practical clothing similar to the ones Cori had given her, in an identical green to her pouch, then insisted she needed to work.

"I'm so glad you're finding your way here," Livia said.

Neri nodded. "It's a lovely place."

"Lovely enough to stay?"

She couldn't answer. The settlement didn't feel unusual to her any longer, but hadn't known a home for a long while, not since her family died. Not until the sanctuary.

But as she walked up the lane to her cottage, through the gate and onto her path, it was starting to feel scarily like home. The briars and strange creeping vines of blue and dusky orange waved in the wind like friends greeting her arrival. Her nostalgia for those she'd left behind panged in her chest.

I'm sure they're fine. The thought didn't settle her anxiety any. *They have the sanctuary to stay safe in.*

Once inside, Livia unpacked the new items and settled down on the big blue cushion to watch Neri work. It seemed the only time Livia could sit still or remain calm.

Neri heaped down onto the stone slab and took the basket of wax she'd brought in from the doorstep. With her mind settled, she took the first two stubs with one in each hand and closed her eyes. Her *ai-tan* set to work and focused on the temperatures, cautiously moving her hands to the moulds. She set the wick in each and took the next two stubs from the basket before the remains could cool on her hands.

By the time all the moulds were full, she'd gathered enough wax to form into crude rectangles for the book candle she intended to make for Silu. Then she slumped onto the stone slab with her back aching.

She looked up as someone knocked on the door, and smiled as Livia hurried to open it. The thought it might be Niall filled her head but when she eased to her feet, Viljo swept in.

"The time for battle has come," he announced. "They've made camp but the lines are forming. The lord of the borderlands is said to be in attendance this time also."

"*Vahda*," Livia muttered. "*Ama* is going to insist on seeing me to make sure I haven't crept off."

Viljo nodded. "Why do you think I'm here? I'm to escort you. What you do after I've delivered you at the gates however, and she's seen you, is entirely up to you."

"Perfect." Livia grinned.

Neri's mind flitted straight to Niall as she grabbed her blade, bow and quiver. She hadn't even had time to talk to him properly, let alone ask if he planned to fight. In the face of a war, an actual battle, refusing to speak to him seemed childish.

The entire settlement was a hive of activity the moment they stepped outside. The suns had only just fallen to night but folk were getting astride horses in the lane and banding into groups to defend each other, while others were arguing about the merits of blades against archers as they filed down toward the gates.

"Zel has offered you to ride with her, Neri," Viljo said.

"If not, I've found a suitable horse for you. She'll do for the daytime rides as well, sturdy and steadfast."

Neri nodded. "I can trust Zel, but if need be I can sit on a normal horse well enough."

"I'll stay with you too, don't worry," he added.

"Niall won't like that," Livia said merrily. "The last thing we need is you two fighting each other instead of the enemy."

Neri shrugged. "He doesn't own me, and I don't need anyone minding me either."

She strode ahead toward the gates where the Jakida was waiting, Zel in horse-form by her side. The moment they reached the gates, the Jakida had Livia in hushed conversation and Neri scrambled to find a place to mount. The last thing she needed was Viljo offering to help and Niall, who was probably lingering somewhere nearby, to appear and start a war over her instead.

The image that conjured brought an ill-timed smile to her lips and she hastened to pin it back down.

"Fine," Livia snapped. "Although why you think it's okay for you and Viljo to defend our land but I have to sit behind, I don't know."

The Jakida sighed. "You defend the settlement if they break our defences."

"But you're not planning on letting them break the defences."

"Of course not. Help the healers instead."

She strode off and Livia's mutinous frown lifted instantly as she swept off her robe to reveal fighting clothes underneath.

"I stashed spare weapons," she announced. "Go on ahead and I'll find you in the crush."

From Zel's back, Neri watched her jog off in the

direction of the square.

"You're not going to dissuade her?" she asked.

Viljo gave her a weary look. "Have you ever tried? She'll fight with or without our blessing. *Ama* even tied her up once. She still got out somehow."

Neri choked over a snort of laughter as they filtered through the gates and followed the moving crowd toward the field of firelight beyond.

Just once Neri thought she heard a familiar voice calling her name and telling her to wait. She ignored it and pressed forward as part of the horde. As the mass spilled out onto the plains she got a proper look at the army they opposed.

The front lines extended as far as the eye could see, a swathe of red and blue that lit up the night with their fire torches. The Jakirian force was significant in number but her heart sank that it was probably not significant enough to win an easy fight.

At the very front of their lines, the Jakida sat regal on a large black horse, issuing directions to various folk. Neri allowed their leader's glamour to sweep over her as it roiled the crowd into anticipation.

Warm weight snared around her hand.

"You're going to hate me, but I have to say it," Niall announced.

Neri tensed as he tightened his grip on her fingers.

"Don't you dare," she warned.

"Go back inside, I mean it. This isn't just practice and I won't let you get hurt."

Her skin warmed as her ire spiked, and she wondered if he really cared enough to try and force her back to safety, in which case he didn't know her well at all, or if he was sparking a fight to get them both mentally prepared. Either way she wrenched her fingers free.

He leaned to grab her again and Zel skittered sideways. Neri smiled lips despite the dire circumstances ahead of them and, with complete disregard for the seriousness of the situation around her, she stared spirited fire into Niall's hooded, angry eyes.

Then she stuck her tongue out at him.

She half expected a speech from the Jakida for morale, but there was no word spoken as the attention of the crowd fell toward the enemy. They still filed in large hordes toward the waiting front lines and a wave of anticipation quivered through the ranks.

Someone blew a horn as the Jakida raised her blade and the enemy answered with their own war-cry.

The front lines surged forward and Neri tensed as Zel charged forward. Before the two sides could meet, clouds rolled overhead with a feral crack of thunder and a fierce onslaught of rain fell.

The enemy's horses got mired in the mud that formed quickly under the pounding of countless hooves. The horses and their riders slid and slithered toward them in a muddy landslide, some falling while their companions now riding over them in a hope to return home alive. Arrows flew from behind the Jakirian front lines, passing far over her head as the two sides clashed.

Neri closed her eyes and her *ai-tan* flew. Flames licked at the ground between the two armies and the arrows that still came from the ranks behind caught the fire, dragging it into the enemy's midst. Screams and yells tore through the air. As she opened her eyes again, the two sides clashed.

Blades clanged and chaos roared through the air, while Neri's insides burned with adrenalin and thoughts of those she loved beside her. The enemy would reach them any moment and she would have to fight.

The first came at her, a faceless body in its enemy uniform. She managed to parry a good blow and tried not to think about the enemy as folk with families when she sank her blade through someone else's shoulder.

Niall's presence slipped from her sight and she waved her blade with wild abandon toward the next flash of red and blue. She gritted her teeth as the blades clashed overheard and she fought again and again, trying to disarm the woman opposite rather than kill her. Zel plunged back and forth, holding her out of harm's way, but it meant she couldn't get a clear shot either. She pushed her heels into Zel's sides to urge her forward and snapped her shoulders forward just as someone else swiped his blade through the air at her.

His blade clattered to the ground and she gulped down a fiery wave of sickness, her own blade nowhere near him. He fell from his horse with blood dribbling from his abdomen, and she twisted to see Niall pulling his blade free from a skilful curve that cleaved another enemy's head from its shoulders.

There was blood on Niall's cheek, whether his or someone else's she couldn't tell, but a line sheen of shadow cloaked his body. The physical form of him hadn't disappeared but it seemed as though he could draw shadow still whenever he chose. Despite the veil of darkness he wore, his face was flushed with rage. Neri leaned low and shouted to Zel over the shout of the battle that she had to find Livia.

Zel surged forward, veering from side to side to avoid confrontations, and Neri caught sight of Viljo up ahead. She used her hands to redirect Zel's path, her attention caught as Viljo speared one man with his blade and disarmed another without even flinching.

So stuck by the emotionless mask of duty on his face, Neri didn't see the woman come flying out of the crowd with a long, thin wooden fighting pike and drive it into Zel's chest. Zel crumpled to her knees with a deep grunt and Neri sailed off her back.

She curled on instinct as she hit the ground with a jarring thud, but managed to stand and lift her blade ready as the woman swung a savage blow with her pike. Her blade carved the pike in two, but the woman was too quick for her to get another blow in. She dodged to the side as the splintered end of the wood slid narrowly past her ribs and lifted her blade again, her arms screaming from the effort and the fall.

The woman magically folded in front of her before she could strike or defend. Viljo retracted his blade, and Neri had no time to fight or argue as he reached down and hauled her onto his horse in front of him.

She struggled against the strength of his arm as it anchored her back against his chest, like he owned her.

Neri saw Zel still down, head sagging and eyes lidded, and her *ai-tan* roared. She let it spike until Viljo hissed through his teeth and withdrew his arm, then she swung herself back to the ground.

"Neri!" he shouted. "There's nothing you can do."

She dropped to one knee beside Zel, eying the ugly wound.

"I can defend you enough for you to walk to safety," she insisted. "But you have to get up."

Zel raised her delicate head, giving Neri a better look at the deep, bloody wound on her chest. The first attempt to stand came to nothing, Zel's front legs shuddering too much to hold her weight.

Panic tore at Neri's chest, but she could feel her heat bubbling inside her. She closed her eyes and placed her hands on the unharmed stretch of Zel's shoulder, hoping for it to warm some of Zel's pain enough to help her stand. She could feel her gift drying the blood at the edge of the wound too, enough for it to clot over some. Whatever magic she now bore sang through her until Zel's chest bore a slightly smaller hole caked in oozing blood.

"If you can stand now, I'll protect you to the settlement gates."

There was no time to be exhausted from using her gift, even though her inner well was all but depleted and her knees were close to knocking from effort. Zel struggled to stand on all four legs, the pain deep in her dark brown eyes. Neri walked at her head and tried to use her blade to create a path for Zel to follow through. Most were too busy now defending in groups or holding their own fights elsewhere, so it was as much dodging the carnage as it was defending from errant attacks.

The gates were so close, enough to see the worried faces of those still left to guard it, but Neri's gaze drifted sideways.

Hareili battled a tall woman who wove so quickly that Hareili hadn't noticed a second person making a beeline for her back. Neri had no time to reach them, and Hareili she felt the need to defend only because of the sullen woman's relation to Cori, but she still had her bow and quiver.

She took the bow and fed her flame onto the *gar* covered wood of the arrowhead, then took aim and fired. Hareili turned a fraction too late to defend herself from the second attack, and Neri was already reloading the bow in case her first shot missed, but the enemy folded to the ground with an arrow in her neck.

Neri sucked in a sharp breath to quell the guilt bubbling up her throat and forced herself to focus on the gates. Zel had almost reached them, a big blessing, but now Neri stood alone in the mud with the clash of blades and the yells of the dying all around, waiting for the enemy to find her. She blocked out the disgust at defending herself to the point of death, of taking lives and endangering folk.

But they seemed to be winning. Jakirian purple covered the landscape in larger number than the blue and red of the enemy. Neri barely had time to lift her blade when a loud horn split the air and the enemy retreated.

The Jakida led the remaining crowds in a cheer of victory, but Neri's only thought was to find Niall and make sure Livia was safe.

She took a couple of steps toward the gates but couldn't go any further as folk swept out of them, healers carrying blankets and large pouches that clacked.

Neri couldn't see anyone she recognised, but if Livia and Niall were on the field they would have to pass her to get back into the settlement. If they were already inside, they were likely safe.

She lagged behind to help wounded onto horseback and to coin the eyes of the dead. The devastating process took ages and she nodded to Orin in passing as she returned through the settlement gates in the midst of the villagers.

She fit herself to the side of the lane as the sound of hooves filled the air, and lifted her head until she saw Livia riding at the head of the returning troops with Viljo at her side. Livia's eyes darted over the crowd until her gaze settled on Neri. The folk parted for her horse but Neri walked forward with slow steps, waiting for Livia to reach her.

"We have not much time," Viljo insisted. "We must regroup and send word across the land that another attack has come and we need everyone beside us on the plains. They will give us a few days."

Livia shrugged and swung off her horse to hug Neri tight. The comforting gesture was for both of them and Neri held her friend just as secure.

"You have less scratches and knocks than I do," Neri mumbled, because it was either that or cry.

Livia let go, her eyes shining with unspent emotion.

"You're alive and upright, mostly. We'll train more the moment you've had some rest."

Neri looked past Livia to where Viljo stood. She thought she should probably apologise for burning him, but then she would do it again if she had to, and they both knew it. Before she could find some weary words of truce, Viljo stumbled as Niall pushed roughly past him.

Neri tried to tense but her limbs were like melted wax. She couldn't be in a fight with Niall now, not after all the folk that died, but she forced her aching back to straighten and planted her feet steady all the same.

CHAPTER TWENTY TWO

Niall had told her not to fight and she hadn't listened. She expected at least a verbal beating for disobeying him and prepared for another argument, but the moment he reached her, he folded his arms around her shoulders and pulled her tight to him.

Sandwiched against his chest with her hands losing all their ability to pull him off, Neri took a deep breath of him and settled. His lips roved over her hair as murmured words got lost on the top of her head.

She choked over the sudden emotion and tried to extricate herself from his grasp but he held on tighter. Just as it threatened to turn into a full-on wrestle, she sagged and he found the right angle to sweep her clear off the floor and into his arms.

"Everyone's watching."

Her mumble got lost in his shoulder but the sudden shaking from his laughter suggested he'd heard anyway.

"Do you think I care about other folk? I'm furious with you to the point of insanity, but you're in no fit state to hear it so I'm going to take care of you instead."

Neri didn't bother to struggle as he walked toward her lane, but she fought herself for the strength to stand her ground. Somehow, fighting Niall gave her strength instead of stealing it.

"You might be in line to inherit the throne of the west or whatever this place counts as, but you don't own me."

"I won't ever inherit, don't worry," Niall scoffed. "My

dearly boring brother will take that role, so if it's a title you're after I know he'd be more than happy to oblige."

There was a bite to his tone that brought a flush to her cheeks, both of them knowing it was true. But she wasn't letting him off that easily.

"Apparently so."

The inevitable strength of Niall's vicelike grip carried her down her lane toward her front door but she folded her arms to make her weight more difficult to hold. She couldn't get herself free and likely wouldn't be able to run far, or at all, but she could try baiting him with enough sass to ward him off.

"Are you going to let me stay here?" he asked, his tone not in the least bit polite. "I could do with not having an argument about it, at least not until tomorrow."

He dropped her to her feet at her front door, but his hands lingered firmly on her hips to keep her upright.

"We haven't had a chance to talk about any of it yet," she reminded him. "Let alone argue."

"Who's decision was that?"

He grimaced the moment the words left his mouth, but Neri's anger flared instantly.

"Mine, and you can hardly blame me! All I'm good for apparently is getting you here, then a toy for you to challenge your brother over."

It was a cheap shot, but his closeness was throwing her senses into an absolute frenzy.

"I can think of plenty that you're good for but aside from the smart mouth, do you really think I'm that easy to brush off?"

She moved her hand to the latch on the door, ready to swing it open and dart inside.

"What exactly do you think is going to happen?" she

demanded. "We dance back and forth over insults and taunts and then what?"

Her challenge kindled a familiar darkness in his eyes and his lips curled at one corner. Sensing a tremor in the air around them, tension rising in the short space that lay between, she forced herself to stare up into that darkness as he glowered down at her.

"Do you realise that in some parts of the land I could kidnap you, and nobody would bat an eyelid if you screamed? We're at war and all I want is to know you're safe! None of this is a game."

His voice, animalistic and gravelly in his throat, brought the necessary fury firing through her veins. She flipped the latch on the door and whirled in.

"Screw you."

She hammered the palm of her hand into the door to slam it shut, but it rebounded back into her as Niall did the same thing. She sensed his capture of her before she actually felt his fingers grip her arms.

He kicked the door shut behind him without looking, the feral glint in his eyes fixed on her as his hands branded against her hips.

"You only have to ask," he murmured. "I didn't use you to get past the cursed forest, and Viljo can take the west and the east and the whole land for all I care. All I need is you."

The confession startled her into silence. He was so close, too close, to the point she could see the tiny nick of a scar beneath his left eye. The first thing that came to her head shot from her mouth before she could catch it.

"What about Hareili then?"

He froze. "I- what? What about her?"

"You and her."

"Oh, no, Neri." His short bark of laughter echoed through the otherwise silent room. "You definitely don't need to worry about her."

She hesitated. He'd told her everything she'd wanted to hear, and there was still so much they had to talk about, but talking involved thinking about feelings and all she had left was the irrational desire to feel instead.

But even then, a strain of vulnerability leaked through. "Promise?"

His lips landed hard on hers and he lifted her until she had to wrap her legs around him.

"Is this the behaviour of a man who wants someone else right now?" he demanded.

The 'right now' wasn't lost on her. The last shred of her feminine indignity rose and she pulled away to free her arm. The slap echoed through the cottage as her palm landed against his cheek without much force or any serious intent.

Niall laughed as he walked with her clasped against him, until the slanted lines of the wooden ladder thudded between her shoulder blades. With her hands free, trusting his hold on her completely, she settled her fingers over both of his cheeks.

Her *ai-tan* flared with her emotions and Niall's grip loosened. With a careless hand she focused on the set of newly made candles in the corner of the room and sent her gift flaring until the wicks caught and light danced a seductive tango with the shadows.

Feeling the burn and tingle of magic leave her, Neri focused her attention on Niall as he watched her with disturbing stillness in return, his gaze roving hungrily over her face.

"I need you to admit that you're mine," he whispered.

"We can fight all you want, about anything you choose, but give me that and I'll give you everything I have, and everything I ever will have. Say you're mine."

"'You're mine'," she echoed with a smile.

He grinned, wicked and dark. "That'll do for now."

She smiled as he backed her up the ladder and onto the bed. His shadows curled over his arms and chest, soft flickers that moved in time with the dance of the candle flames. He crawled over her until all she could do was blink back up at him, although the thought of moving even an inch away was the furthest thing from her mind.

"Say no," he muttered. "Say you don't want me to chase all the doubts away."

He couldn't, she knew that, but to distract herself from everything even for a night, it was enough. She trailed her foot up the inside of his thigh.

"No."

He groaned, eyes closing as he tilted his head back in torment. She scanned the column of his throat, the urge to lean up and nip there filling her head.

"No." She repeated it before he could misunderstand her. "I won't say it. Distract me. Make me forget."

His eyes snapped open, barely distinguishable from the darkness as his shadows flickered over his skin. Then he bowed lower to cage her body in, his nose inches from hers.

"Forgetting is the one thing I'm going to make sure you never do."

His lips landed on hers, a blessed familiarity that chased away all protest. She tangled both hands in his hair and pulled him closer, whimpering as his leg slid between hers.

"I'm going to make sure you remember this." He dropped a kiss to her jaw. "And this." Her neck. "This."

Her collarbone. "And especially this, so you never doubt again that you're mine."

Desire curled in the pit of her stomach and rippled down, her skin tingling with a wholly different kind of fire as his mouth trailed downward. His hands tore at laces and fabric, and she was just as rough with his clothes, wanting to feel his skin bare against hers.

"Niall," she gasped.

He reached up a hand to find hers, his fingers curling tight around hers as his tongue curled in other places. Spasms of pleasure coiled and exploded, but she had no clue why he was laughing. She opened her eyes and lifted her head to find her other hand still snared in his hair with a lethal grip, some strands singed at the ends.

"I think I'd look extremely dangerous with no hair, it's fine," he teased as she let go.

She laughed, too boneless to do more than drop back against the cushions as he kissed his way back up. Each soft movement reignited sensations and she reached for him before he made it past her ribs. His lips ghosted over hers and she grumbled as he held himself back.

"Are you sure?" he asked.

She nodded, echoes of their past swimming in her mind.

"I'm not made of glass, remember?"

His eyes narrowed, a smile of pure wickedness spreading over his lips.

"Oh, I remember. Louder than glass too."

He smothered her squeak of outrage with his mouth and silenced her moan as he entered her with one steady move.

She clung to his arms as he increased to a fierce pace, until she was too far gone for coordination. He clasped both her hands in his and lifted them above her head, baring her body to him. She gave the control willingly, welcomed it, her lips parting as he found the perfect angle to send her into ecstatic oblivion again and tumble over the edge with her.

A while later, he pressed a heated forehead to her sweaty one and hovered over her, a panting mess. She squeaked as he slid free and rolled to lie beside her.

"Can I stay?" he murmured. "Tonight I mean."

She nodded. "Please."

He smiled and kissed the top of her head, settling her against him. Neri rested her head on his shoulder, bewildered by how complete the simple act made her feel. Moments later, tears of exhaustion and relief leaked free and began to cascade down her cheeks. She gritted her teeth and kept her face buried in Niall's shoulder, trying with valiant failure to hold the shaking from her body.

His warm hands found her cheeks and he pulled her up to face him. The dopey brownness in his eyes glimmered with concern as he stared at her.

"What's wrong?"

Neri forced a weak smile. "It's happy tears. I'm relieved, that's all."

She pressed her hand to his chest, but flinched when he seethed through his teeth.

"What?" She sat up. "What is it?"

Before he could answer, she saw the marks beneath his shoulder.

"Oh, I burned you." She eyed the fingerprints with regret. "I'm sorry."

He pulled her against him, holding tight.

"Don't be, I'm glad. You've marked me now, and I'll do whatever it takes to keep them. I'll parade them through the settlement so everyone knows I belong to you."

She giggled. "You're addle-headed."

"For you? Always." He shifted so he could see her face. "Unite with me."

She sighed. "What, because of the war? In case we don't make it?"

He grabbed her hand and lifted it to his face so he could lay kisses on her palm.

"Of course not. I didn't let you die before, and I won't let you die if you insist on fighting on the battlefield either." He nestled her close again, his voice soft. "But I will keep asking until you're ready to say yes."

Neri kissed the first piece of bare skin she could reach, which turned out to be his arm. There would be time to talk in the morning.

"Zel said the Lord of the Borderlands would be at the battle but he wasn't," she murmured. "So it's only going to get more treacherous as the fight goes on."

"He'll be making an appearance tomorrow, if he's got any sense. His folk will need to see him leading after seeing our side today. He'll probably have held half of his force back, and we went in with most of ours."

Neri reached out a hand and extinguished the final flame beneath the platform. Whatever came next they would deal with it in the morning but for now she could pretend nothing else existed.

CHAPTER TWENTY THREE

Neri's slumber waxed and waned, and her consciousness surfaced occasionally to find Niall's limbs still entwined with hers. Only when the suns were high in the sky, casting bright, cold light in through the windows, did she wake properly to find emptiness beside her.

Panic filled her sleep-dredged mind and she bolted to sit upright. The flutters of anxiety quelled when she looked down to see Niall bare-chested as he moved with silent ease around her little kitchen. Smiling to see him so comfortable in her home already, she clambered out of the bed and tiptoed down the ladder.

Although he had the stealth of a jungle cat, Niall jumped as she wound her arms around his waist from behind. She chuckled and rested her cheek on his shoulder blade. He relaxed and continued an attempt at breakfast from her threadbare supplies.

Neri flinched as her front door banged open, and Niall hissed as he hit his hand.

"Sorry to barge in." Livia didn't sound sorry at all. "*Ama* has called everyone to meet in the library to discuss the next wave of fighting."

"And that's reason enough to storm in without knocking?" Niall asked irritably.

Livia grinned. "We're family, it's fine."

"That's no excuse."

"Is."

"Isn't."

Bewildered by the apparently easy and fast development of their kinship, Neri gave Livia a weary look.

"We'll be there soon," she said.

Livia giggled. "Make sure you do. I'd hate for *Ama* to have to come and haul you out halfway through. Or worse."

She didn't bother to close the door behind her as she left. Neri moved to go and close it, but Niall pulled her close and she settled her cheek against his chest instead.

"Come on, they'll have food up there," he grumbled. "As much as I want to keep you here forever, they really will send someone down if we don't go."

Neri dressed in fighting clothes, her attention happily diverted from worries by the sight of Niall pulling his shirt back on. She had no idea where he kept changes of clothing but guessed he had his own room at the palace, or had hidden some bits away. She thought of asking but as they grabbed weapons and he took her hand, she let the simple act be enough.

The lanes were deserted as they walked up to the palace, everyone no doubt inside their dwellings with their families or already up at the meeting.

"Do you think they'll start without us?" she asked.

Niall shrugged. "Probably not. The Jakida will want you front and centre."

"You mean you?"

"I mean the woman who she's shown considerable charity to since you've been here. The woman chosen to wield fire, which isn't an *ai-tan* usually gifted, not at the level you have it."

Neri slowed her pace but he towed her along, his shoulders rigid and his chin set down against the wind.

"What are you saying?" she asked.

"You didn't wonder how I found you on the battlefield so easily?"

She shrugged. "The *liliam*?"

"No. You were glowing. Literally a beacon of light. I never had to go more than two steps from you because I could always see where you were."

How many folk did he slaughter before they got to me? She shuddered. *How safe am I really without him?*

She wiped her free hand over her face as they approached the palace.

"So, you think she wants me because I'm some kind of battle night-light?"

Niall chuckled. He dropped her hand only to sweep an arm around her waist and pull her close.

"A beacon. The enemy already know the west have someone who can wield fire, because apparently you've been showing your new talents off to all around. She'll want to trade on that asset. It's what she does."

Neri bit her lip before the inevitable question could bubble out.

The Jakida was Niall's maman, and the woman who had discarded him because of what he was.

She must have known it was a risk to get him in the first place, yet it still happened and she still abandoned him.

He stopped at the bottom of the steps and tucked a finger under her chin, lifting her gaze to his.

"Do I still have you?" he asked. "Before we go in to face the wolves? I won't let her use you for anything, but it'll be easier if we're on the same page."

Neri's heart fluttered and her skin warmed against the chilly wind.

"We're on the same page, but we need to agree on what

book it's in when the time comes."

He nodded. "I'll take that. Come on then, this is going to be exhausting."

Neri didn't ask why as they ascended the steps and wound their way through the halls to the library, although the thought settled heavy in the pit of her stomach.

"There you are." the Jakida announced, drawing several murmured conversations to a close. "Let's begin."

Neri didn't comment on Niall clinging to her hand as he guided her onto a vacant long-chair, but she caught the dismissive glance Viljo sent their way as Niall edged himself right beside her.

"The Lord of the Borderlands is only a puppet for his advisor," the Jakida began. "He is a figurehead drenched in arrogance, but our spies tell us that his advisor has a link to someone in the east."

Zel nodded. "Their dragons are few but now grown enough to fly over the cursed woods. They're growing in number too by all accounts. Meanwhile, the cursed forest is withering from the edges, swathes of it rotting at the root. We need to act now."

"This is why the siren's kyne had to be destroyed," the Jakida insisted, her gaze flitting to Neri. "We must keep our folk safe above all else. The moment the cursed forest is traversable again, the east will want to firm their position, but by taking the borderlands now we can ensure that we control at least that route while the forest is still a boundary."

"The cursed forest is rotting?" Niall asked, his tone sharp.

"So they say," Zel replied. "It will take a while for the curse to fade enough for folk to pass through it, but you're right to be concerned. If we can ease the threat from the borderlands then we can face the threat from the east head on when it comes. There seems to be even more disturbance in the east than we've ever heard of before, settlements being searched and destroyed, folk being hunted."

Neri shuddered, thoughts of Emelyn and the others being targeted at the sanctuary. Even if they managed to get to Mik's, it was nearer the cursed woods where they would be in even more danger from the Governance.

If the firebird brought us through it by fire using a kyne, could the same thing happen the other way?

"We need to convene our forces, get any wounded able to fight fit again, and send out requests for aid from anyone within reach," the Jakida concluded. "Niall, a word?"

Niall frowned. "Me? Why?"

When she didn't answer, he pulled a face and swept a brief kiss over Neri's forehead. She wondered in that moment whether that kiss was for Viljo's benefit, as he followed the Jakida to the corner of the library with Niall slouching across to join them.

Neri thought of the shard of kyne she'd managed to hide in her pack. It had been there when she returned and on getting her cottage she'd buried it deep in the chest at the end of her bed with Hamlin's watch.

Unsure if she was wildly overestimating the depth of her *ai-tan,* she wondered if she could recreate a way east herself using the kyne and an effigy of wax.

Even if it doesn't work, I have to try. She bit her lip. *The forest might take winterspans to fade, but if the west does gain control of the borderlands then I can get everyone to sneak up there and pass through to the west.*

She wouldn't tell Niall her plan yet. He would likely forbid her from going, and they still had the war to win before she could risk going anywhere. The Governance would be watching the borderlands if the west took control of it, so she wouldn't be able to march out of their gates and across the east.

But by stealth I might be able to get Emelyn and everyone else through to the west from that side.

She eyed Niall as her plan set up camp in her mind. He stood with his arms folded, hip tilted and a moody scowl on his face. The Jakida seemed to be doing all the talking, but every now and then he'd mutter the odd word or two. The whole time, Viljo stood stiff-shouldered nearby like someone had thrown manure under his nose.

Neri stood as Niall stalked back to her, irritability scrawled across his face. He stopped in front of her and immediately wrapped his arms around her waist to pull her close.

"I'm going to have to leave the settlement for a couple of days but I will be coming back."

Neri tried to step back but he clung on.

"The war is coming any moment now!" she hissed. "Where could you possibly need to go other than here?"

She managed to get her shoulders back enough to fold her arms across her chest, but the previous night had left her weary despite the long sleep. Her *ai-tan* slumbered, evidently not willing to wake for something as trivial as a lover's spat, and her skin rippled with chills.

Niall covered the inches between them, one hand landing on her hip and the other cradling her cheek. Neri cast her eyes away, refusing despite her vulnerable state to back down.

"I have to go," he insisted. "She's asked me to find the shades and try to bring them to our side. It's a day's ride, so I'll be back in two days all being well. His wearisome lordship is apparently going with me as well, so I'll try not to drop him over a cliff on the way there."

Neri bit her lip and said nothing. The familiar ache she'd ignored for a long time and only hours ago shed crept back into her chest.

"I could go with you," she suggested.

He shook his head. "If you come with me, Livia will insist on going too. Besides, if you come with me, I'll insist on stopping so you can rest and eat. On my own I can push hard and be back quicker."

"You won't be on your own though."

"Ah but he's not my problem. All he has to do is keep up. If he doesn't manage it, oh well."

She sighed, even though his logic made some kind of sense, but she couldn't fight the voice in her head insisting something else must be going on behind her back.

"Do you believe me?" he asked. "This isn't me leaving you again. Nobody else will likely be able to get close to the shades without shadow."

She nodded, her fragile hope sliding away. She had no idea if he'd return and he'd broken promises to her before. Even if his intentions were good he could get harmed if the enemy were nearby.

When Niall guided her head around until she couldn't avoid his gaze, she took a deep breath. She could choose to believe he was off again or she could trust him. The sheer torment raging in his eyes told her he meant every word, but she couldn't resist needling him just a little.

"I might stay up here at the palace until you come back then. Livia wants to train me more."

He smiled. "If you like. Viljo's going with me, and I have nothing to worry about while he's not around you."

She bit back a small smile.

"I didn't realise you thought he was such a threat."

He shrugged. "I don't, but Hareili told me all about him slaving after you like a dog. If he wasn't coming with me, I'd insist you stayed in your cottage instead."

Neri's smile wavered. "Didn't realise you were busy having cosy chats with her. Either way, I think I can handle myself for a few days, even if there are men around."

The thought of Niall not trusting her tickled her *ai-tan* awake. The tingle erupted over her skin but Niall didn't let go, a sudden rueful smile breaking across his face. He took her fingers in his, a slight pained pinch appearing at the corners of his eyes as her hands flared with heat at the contact.

"I like it when you're jealous," he murmured.

Neri huffed a meaningless noise at him and took a deep breath to calm the tingling of her gift.

"I'm worried. It's not the same thing."

"If you say so. I should leave now, but I'll be back before the fighting begins."

Neri bit her lip and nodded. She raised her own hand and let it rest on the wax emblem lying against his bare chest.

"Stay safe and come home as quick as you can."

Niall smiled but wistfulness swarmed in his dark eyes. He held her one final time as his lips sought hers in a long, gentle kiss and then he strode away, the library door banging shut behind him. When she looked around, Viljo and the Jakida had already left the room, but Livia was still there, grinning wickedly at her.

CHAPTER TWENTY FOUR

The moment Livia was beside her, Neri bent her head low just in case anyone appeared.

"I need your help."

"Thrilling!" Livia whispered. "What with?"

"I need a lot of wax, as much as we can get away with, but we can't draw attention to it."

She expected some kind of hesitation, but Livia shrugged.

"Okay. There are a few maids I know who can be trusted to be discreet, and everyone is distracted with the battle anyway."

"Thank you. I'll also need a short length of rope."

Livia's eyebrows lifted. "It's not that bad, surely?"

"Of course not. I'll also need a flat square of stone if possible."

"I can have them brought to the cottage. Can I ask why?"

Neri hesitated. "I need to help get my friends back here. After the battle obviously, I won't leave until I know everyone here is safe, but the Governance will destroy everyone in the east unless I can get them over here."

Livia's brow crinkled.

"How will you get them through the cursed forest though?"

"Well, that's the thing." Neri took a deep breath, the plan still unfurling in front of her. "If the we win, and the west takes the borderlands, all I need to do is get them there. To do that, I need to get to them. For that, I need to try and recreate the kyne the Jakida destroyed."

Livia frowned. "I'm not sure I understand, but if you say you can do it then I believe you. It doesn't sound like the attacks will come today. *Ama* insisted everyone take the time to prepare and be with their families. You go down to the cottage now and I'll source everything I can."

Livia hurried out of the library, but Neri lingered a moment longer before following her and continuing out of the palace.

Leaves skittered around her feet and she glanced up into the cold, clear dazzle of the white winter sky. Soon the tree branches would be bare and eventually it might snow. She hoped the war would be over before the feastmas festival Livia had mentioned.

Maybe if all goes well, I can get through to the east and bring the others back in time to celebrate it together.

She almost didn't notice the woman approaching from the bottom of the lane. Her feet stumbled to a halt and she looked straight ahead into startling eyes of pale gold. She mumbled an apology as she side-stepped, but Hareili followed until she stood blocking Neri's way forward.

"Niall's left again I take it?" Hareili asked. "He never was one for longevity, I should know. But then you have plenty of options I see."

Neri caught the subtle acid in the question and her *ai-tan* hissed heated threats through her mind. Tempted to pretend she had no recollection of who Hareili was, she recognised the rivulet of bitterness veiled beneath the spite.

Maybe he didn't kiss her goodbye then. Unless he went her way after he left the library.

She resisted the urge to ask her own questions. Until Niall proved himself untrustworthy, she would give him the fairness of believing his word.

"Maybe that's true." She shrugged. "He's a wanderer by nature but then he always comes back to me."

Sounding more confident than the low-lying anxiety would allow her to feel inside, she side-stepped again.

"He said the same to me once," Hareili insisted. "He promised that no matter what stood between us, he would always be there for me."

Neri's *ai-tan* flared but she didn't let it free.

"Did he come back for you though?" she taunted. "Because he did for me. Saved my life too. He even asked me to unite with him twice already."

Hareili scoffed. "How do you know he hasn't asked the same of me?"

Neri's insides washed icy with revulsion, but she kept her expression impassive as she pushed past and set off toward her cottage, one foot in front of the other.

"Because you would have said yes by now if he had," she shouted back.

She powered through her garden before Hareili could find other insults to sling at her.

Hateful woman. What did that even achieve?

The idea that Niall could have made false promises in the past, however well-meaning, stabbed at her chest, but she wouldn't be able to demand answers for another day or so and dwelling on it wouldn't help. As she waited for Livia, she threw herself into filling the candle moulds from the collection of stubs that had been left for her over the recent days. Then she finished the commission of the book candle Silu had asked her to make.

After those tasks were done, she sat throwing all the wax she had left into the pot. Once the bubbling mess cooled enough to handle and mould, she would be able to make square tablets. Then they would be fused together and carved into an effigy with the kyne at the centre.

It's a fool's hope, but if a kyne got me here, maybe a part of it can get me back.

She sat in the silence after quenching the fire and waited for the wax to cool. Her thoughts ran to memories and the past. She hoped Ma Kath, Emelyn and the others were safe and then her mind moved onto the Governance. Amis was still out there creating chaos, and she vowed with silent determination to stop him somehow, even if it took her entire life and the whole might of the west to achieve it.

A loud, steady knock jolted her mind back into the moment and she scrambled to her feet. She swung the door open and balked at the sight on her doorstep. Livia stood with two large wooden crates, one under each arm and her cheeks decidedly red.

"There's also the square of stone in one of them somewhere," she gasped.

Neri grabbed one of the boxes and ferried it over to the stone on the floor.

"*Ama* is being tiresome, so I'm staying here," Livia announced. "I'll be ever so quiet. I even brought a book."

She extracted a small volume from her pocket, and Neri wearily pointed her toward the cushion. She didn't mind Livia's company. In some ways, she welcomed it. If she needed to distract her mind from querulous thoughts of Niall and Hareili in between her work, Livia would be more than ready to provide it.

She knelt on the stone and tested the wax in the vat. Just right for moulding. She used her fingers to savage and pummel it until she could press it to the corner of the stone floor. Her muscles ached but her thoughts were blessedly focused and clear. After a while, she heaved to her feet, surprised to find a plate of food beside her, along with the square of stone and length of rope she'd asked for.

There was even a large cup of wine and she downed that first before attacking the plate. Hunger sated, she returned to work. The stone square levelled the wax and created a perfect flat indentation, but she needed more firewood.

Groaning to her feet, she turned in time to see Livia traipsing back in with her arms full.

"You fetched firewood?" she asked.

Livia grinned and dumped the wood on the table.

"You looked like you were running low. I didn't take it from the palace or anything. There's a lot of bits behind the cottage."

As Neri passed to grab an armful, she paused to squeeze Livia's arm.

"Whatever happens, I'm so glad I met you."

Livia smiled. "As I am that I met you. Whatever you choose to do, east, west, Niall, no Niall, it doesn't matter. I'll love you like I would any sister I could have had. If all goes well, you will be my actual sister someday."

Neri blinked as the burn of tears prickled the corners of her eyes.

"We don't know if it'll work yet," she muttered, her tone gravelly. "It might come to nothing."

Livia shrugged and flopped onto the cushion.

"If it doesn't, then you can storm the borderlands and sneak into the east that way. Or steal a dragon, but I imagine we'll be setting them free once the war is over."

Neri nodded. "Well, that's something then."

She fed the fire fresh wood and set to warming more wax, which dragged her thoughts away from her emotions and into the methodical process of her task.

When she'd melted and cooled enough wax to cover the

whole large stone slab, levelling it with the square as she went, she sat back and stared at the blank canvas waiting for her carving blade.

If all else fails, I'll have something to trade afterwards.

CHAPTER TWENTY FIVE

The landscape stretched ahead with the greens of grass, tree and bush merging their variety to become one mass of endless colour.

Niall focused on keeping his pace fast and his mouth shut. He glanced sideways to his brooding companion, fully aware the dislike he felt for Viljo was entirely mutual.

"You won't succeed in taking over Jakiris, even if you are first-born." Viljo broke the silence first.

That again.

They'd managed almost a whole afternoon and a night with barely time to rest the horses. The shade camps were meant to be nearby, but Niall was irritable at being away from Neri, and Viljo opening his mouth only made it worse. He decided to take the high ground and not give an answer.

"Girls want security," Viljo added. "Even the ones that have wandering in their nature. Neri will see the merit in a stable future in the long run."

Niall's shadow leapt as his instinct clawed at him to let it go free. He clenched his fist over the reins and forced himself to remain whole. Viljo's interest in Neri didn't mean she reciprocated the attentions, but the idea of someone, anyone, trying to steal her made his insides icy. He took a deep breath and tried to control his anger.

"I don't want your kingdom or your title," he muttered. "I never have. You think Neri is like most other girls who will be swayed by fancy riches and palaces but she's special. She sees effort and merit in folk rather than what they have. If you haven't figured that out yet then you'll never understand who she is."

To distract himself from throttling his brother, he focused on their surroundings instead. He knew the land in theory from his more youthful travels, and they might find the entrance to the camps anytime soon.

The stilted silence continued as the grass began to slope up and their horses soldiered on. Niall smoothed his hand down his horse's neck. After stealing her from Mary's on the way to the siren's cavern, he'd formed a steady kinship with her that gave him some sense of humanity while stuck in shade form. Now he decided he would keep her, and had already sent word to Mary that he'd send or bring a replacement when he was able to.

Wiping his hand across his forehead, he revelled for a moment in the feel of coarse skin and the flick of perspiration. As a shade his mind had echoed the memory of the sensations but his empty form had mourned the loss of them. Even recalling the previous night and the simple act of Neri sleeping in his arms, skin against real skin, brought an urgent, restless happiness to him.

Maybe we don't need the shades, but maybe they could use a reason to be seen as more than everyone thinks they are.

It was that thought alone that stopped him whirling his horse around and going straight back to Neri.

"Why did you bring her here at all?" Viljo asked.

Niall sighed. He knew there would never be any brother-like affection between them. Even if Neri hadn't been in Viljo's mind at all and no inheritance stood between them, the man would have irritated him anyway. But the truth remained that Viljo's mind had fixated on

Neri with an unerring strength, a persistent fly battering on a closed shutter.

Just don't answer.

Viljo frowned, unable to let it lie.

"If I loved a lady I'd want to keep her safe, not throw her straight into a battlefield."

Niall's bitter laughter slipped free.

"I'm sure even you're not starry-eyed enough to miss that she has a knack for getting into trouble. There's a very powerful man in the east who wants her dead. In the end, the westlands seemed safer. He'd never have stopped hunting her."

Niall glanced down at his arm where it rested in front of him with his fingers holding the reins. He ran his free hand across the skin to reassure himself that the hairs still stood on end and flexed his fingers as his irritation grew.

He didn't have to explain a damn thing to Viljo, who had no idea of hardship or loss or real love. If anything Viljo's nature seemed more akin to a shade's than his own. This idea comforted him and he gathered the slightest hint of shadow against his skin before glaring his threat through the few feet between them. He hoped he could make his idiot of a brother understand once and for all.

"When I left you all at the old tree I saw Neri step out of the trunk." He tensed at the memory. "I went via Carahdyl and tried to go back to the guardian your family so kindly left me with. He had almost managed to rid me of my shade before we met in the siren's cave but Neri's firebird came to me and healed me. Then something else happened and I haven't a clue how. Perhaps the tree saw fit to help me or the bird gave me its blessing."

Niall paused and looked away from Viljo's unwavering, emotionless stare. The landscape dipped down and their destination came into view. He pushed his horse a little faster; the thought of Neri left behind with men slaving after her spurred him on.

"As I travelled I started to see progress. I bled again and I ached. By the time I reached where I intended to go I had no shade-self left. I reckon Neri is descended somehow from the line of fire and her bird chose me. Even your sister has chosen me for her and you know it. Neri is my ray of light and I will kill anyone who tries to take or hurt her."

Niall forced the shadow back down as the power gathered. He'd learnt the trickery and skill of calling it at will but like Neri with her fire, his shadow responded best to emotion. He couldn't see trepidation in Viljo's eyes but the slight white press of his lips showed Niall's words had had some effect.

Niall almost grunted as a spike of *liliam*, gone in an instant, hit his senses. He urged his horse on toward a cut in the trees without waiting to see if Viljo followed.

The Jakida had insisted the shades would be a turning point for their cause, but only when Zel echoed her agreement and Livia gave him a small nod did he consent to the journey. The shade dwelling had been rumoured, but on looking for the portal in his youth he'd never ventured close enough to risk seeing it. Now he would face it as a part of his past and return to Neri as his whole present and future.

The ground dropped and his horse's hooves skittered to a halt. He patted her brown neck, soothing her as he insisted she walk down on unsteady legs. The forest of trees that ran on either side of the path disappeared, rocky crags taking their place. Cold stole with icy fingers into his body and his limbs began to jitter as his horse seemed reluctant to plough on.

The rockfaces on either side opened out but where there should have been grass and trees, and fresh sweet air, there was only the unsettling quiet of decay.

Niall turned his head back and only now saw the difference between the lush greenery behind and the natural death in front of him.

He knew the layout of the west from maps and wandering. Before Neri had come into his life, his one method of calming his mind had been to memorise the locations over and over. The *rikler* mines, rumoured to be the final resting place of the bodies whose souls had gone the way of the Ferryman, had to be nearby. His shadow recognised it, that slip between the tangible and the ethereal, and it was close.

Sensing a trap Niall looked up and noticed Viljo at the head of the path. Viljo's oh-so-solid horse snorted its refusal to descend any further. Unable to turn back and yet afraid to push on, Niall decided he would let the goodness of his horse decide. He pushed with gentle heels and his horse stepped down into the ashen wastelands. They cleared the rocky path and this time he brought their progress to a halt.

Something deep inside of him pinged with remorse as he stared. All across the barren earth lay remnants of folk. Bodies, not full or whole but spectral, littered the rocky pit he stood in with their wisps of shade no longer curling. His own shadow seemed to shudder and pull away from him. A part of him seemed to be dying, his body weak and his breath rasping, as if whatever depraved violence that had taken the dead shades in front of him was still lingering to claim him too.

He watched the landscape blur as his horse whirled around and clattered out of the pit, leaving the graveyard of shades behind. The grey rock, the ash, the creep of decay, it all settled into his bones and echoed around him.

His horse almost ploughed through Viljo's and he noticed his brother's shocked face as they dashed past. The sudden explosion of nature as he reached the grass and trees and freshness breathed life back into him, and he dragged ragged breaths of strength from it.

He let his horse gallop on for a while until the anger got too strong. He had to know. Pulling his horse up short, he turned her to face Viljo, who was approaching at a steadier pace.

"*Mekhan*!" Niall spat. "Did she plan it? Did you?"

The acid his swearing caused, such foul language spewing from him, made the rage worse. He hadn't used the word before but he knew that language had some semblance of power. *Mekhan* wasn't a curse used lightly.

Viljo's eyes widened and his hand flew to the hilt of his blade. Niall sensed himself passing the point of being in control of his shadow and his temper.

You promised her you'd come back safe. You promised.
Even that couldn't stop him yelling more.

"Did you plan it together then?" he demanded. "You and your maman, to send me to the fields of dead shades in the hope the land would take me? You'd be free to chase after her and nobody would question me taking your pitiful little title."

His growl cut short as he mentioned Neri and his mind distracted him with a momentary thought of her. He needed to be near her, to see her again. She would calm him down.

"That is not true!" Viljo sounded horrified at least. "We had good advice that the shades still dwelt there. You jump to the assumption that we have arranged this rather than someone has thought of our same plan and removed the opportunity from us."

Niall shook his head, not believing a word of it. He couldn't. Instead, he wheeled his horse round and pushed on. The suns were fading already and his horse would need to rest, but the thought of Neri kept him pushing on. He would give the horse every kindness when he returned. Whether Viljo followed or not, he didn't care.

Once the stars shone above and the land slumbered, Niall settled his body against the cold onslaught of the wind and thought of the warm fires in Jakiris. Viljo called up to suggest they should stop and camp for the night but Niall growled and pulled his horse to a halt. He intended to set his ultimatum with utter clarity in the hope he wouldn't be driven to slicing his brother in two before they could reach the safety of the settlement.

"I don't care what you do," he announced. "I'm lucky enough to have someone back there waiting for me, and I'd be a fool to sit out here stargazing while she's there without me."

The wind whipped his words around but Viljo's silence suggested he'd heard.

Niall allowed his mind to dwell as his horse raced on. The essence of vitality that kept him pushing on and stoked his anger and his emotion, it all came from the knowledge that Neri loved him. Even when she was furious at him, she was still his. But everyone else loved her too. He couldn't blame Viljo for wanting her, even though he hated it.

How long before someone comes along that is worthy of her?

The thoughts hounded him until the sky began to lighten and Jakiris became a pale, glimmering speck on the horizon. Niall finally allowed his horse to slow down. She huffed, exhausted, but his gaze was stuck on the sight unfolding in the distance.

Red and blue tents with banners fluttering in the wind stood tall, others being set up to form a solid wall against the landscape. The tents alone indicated a group of countless fighters, and Niall swore again under his breath.

The enemy were numerous, possibly unbeatable. His glance flicked to his side as Viljo dashed past him. No doubt he would raise the alarm. Niall clenched his fingers around the reins. The thought of Neri hearing the news and readying herself for battle, perhaps slipping into the crowd and into the fray of the war before he could stop her, sent him racing after his brother.

CHAPTER TWENTY SIX

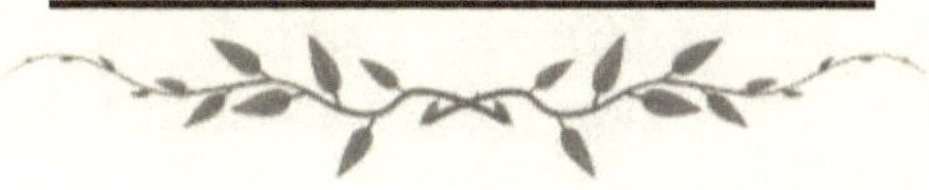

The darkness outside, halfway through lightening to morning, told Neri she'd worked not only all day but all night as well. Knowing she should sleep more in preparation for the coming battle, she almost sliced her finger when her door swung open and Livia swept in. The wooden basket over her arm clinked and Neri could just make out a large, fresh round of bread poking over the rim.

"I've returned to bring you friendship and food," she announced. "Also, I want to force you to rest, even though you won't listen."

Neri sighed. "I've been trying to imagine how far Niall's gotten but I don't know the land. He said two days but is that two days and then he'll be back after? Two days in total? He and Viljo aren't exactly the best of friends either. What if they end up fighting each other?"

"They're evenly matched." Livia shrugged. "I imagine Niall won't want to waste time fighting when he could be here with you."

Neri shrugged, petulance fuelled by exhaustion winning through. She struggled to push her body to stand up and groaned at the quivering muscles as she finally made it to her feet. Her bare arms and legs rippled with chills and Livia rushed up the ladder to bring her blankets down. She mumbled disagreement as Livia piloted her bodily onto the large blue cushion. When her back thudded against the wooden leg of the table memories of Niall's previous post in that position made the agony worse.

"Hareili said Niall had asked her to unite with him before," she mumbled. "Or insinuated it. I can't remember exactly now, but she definitely said it."

Livia frowned. "I don't know about that. From what I hear, and I hear a lot because her sister is in with the kitchen staff and loves to talk in whispers, Hareili was in love with him."

"Doesn't take a clear mind to work that out."

"True, but it sounds like he befriended them both on his travels. I truly do believe that Niall doesn't want anyone but you, and how can you hold something against him that happened before he even knew you, assuming it happened at all?"

Neri shrugged again. Unable to believe anyone with tiredness plaguing her mind, she said nothing whilst Livia set about warming broth and plating up bread with cheese and slices of *calideh*. Livia sat beside her as she ate and forced her to manage just one more mouthful, and another, until the plate was empty.

The snapping coldness outside, combated only by the blankets Livia had wrapped around her, reminded her that soon the winters would fall. If she managed to bring her friends back to safety, then she could consider the westlands her home after that. The thought of those she didn't know, strangers who suffered, filtered into her mind and she swallowed a wave of nausea that swelled.

"I also spoke to Viljo before he left," Livia admitted. "He seems to think you'd be better off at his side, and that your 'misguided addiction' to Niall is merely an obstacle. I'm only warning you, because I love you and I want you to be happy."

Neri sighed. "I did try not to give him any encouragement. I'd be content to be his friend."

"I'll tell him that then, when they return." Livia cleared her throat with a small smile. "Until then, I know you'll want to carve immediately but I have a present for you first. It won't take long."

Neri opened her mouth, intending to argue out of habit at being ordered around, but then she shut it again and nodded. Livia hauled her to her feet and hurried her toward the door.

"Close your eyes."

Neri did as she was told, aware of Livia pulling the blankets around her tighter and swinging open the door to the blast of freezing air and the disorientating scent of something else.

Frost?

Neri opened her eyes, then her mouth dropped in awe. The end of the lane looked hardly visible. Only the trees and the edges of the cottages poked out from the endless haze of dazzling white. Not thinking of her bare feet, she dropped the blanket and darted out into a world of snow. *Ai-tan* giggled through her blood and sent a rush of warmth to combat the freezing sting underfoot. The snow melted wherever she stepped with a disgruntled hiss, but she didn't care.

Even the wild growth of her garden was cloaked in white, with clear droplets of frost and ice hanging from every branch.

"It's beautiful! Will it last? How did I not even notice it snowing?"

Livia smiled. "It may, until the natural elements melt it. This isn't real as such, or it is, but orchestrated as a simple gift from me to you. You'll likely get real snow soon through no fault of mine."

"This is your *ai-tan*?"

Livia glanced around at the wonderland with a modest nod.

"Yes, but not many folk know of it. I find it's safer not to admit I can control something that could be used by so many. I do try to help the harvests where I can in secret if things are struggling though."

Neri's mind filled with the past, of the vast barren fields in the east, the dying crops, the endlessly dry summers.

Without thinking I'd ask her to do exactly what she's afraid of.

She smiled. "I only need the snow. Thank you."

"Good. Hopefully the weather won't turn entire until the war is won though."

Neri's mind skidded over the thought of the upcoming battles and onto the prospect of counting days. Niall had left her the previous day mid-morning, and soon it would be the second night. The war approached but if her luck held then so would Niall. She had questions for him, plenty of them, but if he returned then she could at least shed some of the worry stuck inside her before they went out to fight other folk.

She kicked up a steam of sizzling snow with her bare foot and danced in a circle until she reached the front door once more.

"If the war is soon here then I need to carve now." She frowned at the thought. "If I pull this plan off then I can do the same in the east and bring my friends back home, or take them through the borderlands. We may win the war here but there are still those over there wielding power and hurting folk."

Livia nodded and pressed a calming hand to Neri's bare arm. Neri took a deep breath and pushed her emotion further into her frozen feet. The first chattering of her teeth forced her inside but she turned in the doorway to get another look at the snow.

She took several long swigs of strong berry wine at Livia's insistence, then allowed Livia to settle on a thick blanket beside her as she knelt over her wax tablets.

Livia told her stories that were cornerstones of a westlander's childhood, and Neri smiled to realise she recognised some of them that were shared with ones she'd heard as a child in the east, although with several embellishments and alterations no doubt on both sides. As the top two tablets were gutted to fit around the glass head of the previous portal, Neri's mind drifted from Livia's lively voice and back to her past.

The stories her gramma had told her, some of which were still in the book packed safely in her trunk, sounded like westlander stories. She couldn't bring herself to think of her delicate, silver-haired gramma as one of them. Even when the hair remained a shining sheet of silver, rather than going grey or white, Neri couldn't recall it now without admitting that she had been destined for this side of the land all along.

Then again, what wonders might the east have once had before the cursed forest and the Governance?

The body of the firebird took rough shape in the wax, the wings spread out and the spindling legs routed down until she had the basic outline. The craft came from the detail and Livia's voice disappeared completely as Neri leaned over the effigy. She almost struck her nose due to its close proximity to the surface as her knife flicked over.

Her mind assessed the sound of candles breaking from moulds as Livia set them around the room. They danced light and shadow through the air as she lit the wicks and the last vestiges of day gave up their strength to the dark cloak of night.

Each individual feather had to be a perfect plume and each line of muscle and body exact. Neri felt her *ai-tan* soothing her. It warmed her jarred muscles and the locked pain of her knuckles and joints.

Sitting back on her heels, she bit her lip and struggled to her feet. She stepped back with frown, then scurried up the wooden ladder. Staring down at the wax firebird, she saw the multitude of inaccuracies and cursed. Sliding down again with no thought for her safety, she fell to her knees and smoothed *ai-tan* over the mistakes to start the tiny marks again.

Throughout the whole, painstaking process, Livia's presence comforted her. Even in the times Neri had no awareness of the air around her, she sensed deep down that almost familial calm as it wandered the room or sat silent on the big blue cushion.

Again she dashed up the wooden ladder to the platform and sagged with relief. Livia had extinguished the candles since and, despite her masterpiece being complete, Neri's only trill of happiness came from the hope that Niall would have to return soon.

"It feels real." Livia's voice startled her.

She turned, surprised by Livia's presence despite the comfort it had brought her.

"You rest for a few moments." Livia pointed to the balcony. "I'll pack the tablets in the boxes if you'll trust me. I'll be so careful."

Neri nodded and settled onto the bed. She could see Livia's movements and wondered where she would set the portal up. It had to be somewhere safe and hidden from others. She clambered back down the ladder with stumbling, weary steps, intending to ask Livia for a suitable hiding place. After that, she would see if any of the snow was left outside.

The front door slammed open and let in a burst of freezing air.

Neri missed her footing on the last few rungs of the ladder and winced as her feet slammed into the floor. She couldn't manage more than a startled squeak at the sight of Niall's face almost upon hers. His nose bumped against her forehead and he gathered her into his arms.

Relief bubbled and she managed to squeeze her arms around his ribs with as much force as he applied to her. She caught sight of Livia's tender smile around the edge of Niall's arm but had no time to process it as Niall pulled back enough to take her face in both hands.

"The war is here," he announced. "They've assembled tents and it looks like ranks are forming."

The gasp in his ragged voice told her that he'd ridden straight for her front door. Then the sudden reality of what lay before them all swelled in her mind. She was exhausted and probably little able to use her gift well but she steeled her resolve and drew strength from the instant spike of adrenalin in her veins. She pulled away from him.

"Run and tell everyone."

Her instruction to Livia caught the woman's back as she hurtled through the door. Neri moved with as much haste toward the door and caught up her bow and quiver over her shoulder. Her fingertips only managed to brush the hilt of her blade when something caught her free hand and pulled her back.

"You look half dead." Niall glared at her. "I don't know what you've been doing while I've been gone, but I don't want you out there getting yourself killed. You stay here. Help the healers if you like but you're not going out to fight.”

The hard flint in his voice sent a quick shot of tender love through her heart. Then tiredness-induced ire followed. Neri pulled her hand free.

“I’m going out there to protect my home and you can’t stop me.”

Livia had thoughtfully left the cottage door open so she caught the blade in hand and darted outside. Niall’s fingers drifted across her shoulders, quick but not enough to catch a firm hold of her. She couldn’t outrun him and she sought with a frantic mind for a way to evade him.

He won’t ever let me go east. The realisation swelled with bitter clarity. *He’d find some way to go alone maybe, but he won’t let me risk going back into Governance territory. He won’t even let me fight now.*

Thoughts of her friends filled her head, of the Governance hunting them. It was only a matter of time until they overtook the whole east and razed every inch of it to find their enemies.

She stared at Niall with her mind whirring.

“What happens after we win then?” she asked.

He frowned and pressed his hands to her arms.

“We’re safe. The borderlands will be under western control and the Jakida will turn her focus to securing the forces along the cursed forest.”

She had her answer and her heart sank.

“What about the others? Emelyn and Ma and Mik? The Governance will find the sanctuary one day. Eva might have given them the location-”

“They know what to do,” he cajoled. “Our place is here.”

Only the thought of what she’d heard would hold him back now, and she lifted her weary head to meet his gaze with every inch of fire she could dredge forward.

"Because of your birthright?"

He grimaced. "I don't care about that, but we belong here."

"Oh, so it's about your older friends rather than newer ones?"

She hated herself for saying it, but it was the only way she could think of to stun him into backing off.

"It's where you're happiest, where you're safe. What's going on? Why are you pushing me away?"

As he closed the distance between them, she forced herself to tear herself free and say the words.

"From what I hear either way it's not me you owe protection to. I've been hearing whispers that you were already promised to someone else. I expected you to have a least some shred of honour."

The words hurt. Even then, some deep part of her needed him to deny it. The shock that crossed his face made it worse. Guilt swam in his eyes and she choked over the sob that threatened to break free. He should have yelled at her, baited her and tried to deny it. Instead he stood there with a horrified look on his face.

She turned away before he could recover and found Zel in shining white horse form waiting for her by the gate. With agility she had no idea she could possess, Neri shot forward, vaulted onto the garden wall and then swung up onto Zel's back. She ignored Niall's angry roar behind her as he commanded her to come back.

A memory, inappropriate for the seriousness of the situation, came to her as Zel set off with a clatter through the melting snow on the lane. Her second encounter with Moonshine had been another time she'd witnessed Niall's fury. Moonshine's serene, knowing smile swam in front of her mind as Zel plunged into the fray of folk hurrying down toward the gate to the battle.

"They're marvellous when they're raging."

The words Moonshine had spoken long ago, before they'd even set off to seek the way through the cursed forest, leaked into her mind. She took a deep breath. The thought of Moonshine made her even more determined to create the effigy and rescue her friends. She could imagine Emelyn running a sunny riot through the Jakirian palace, or Ma and Moonshine coming to blows with Orin in the kitchens. She missed them so much, and that alone quelled some of her fear at having to fight again.

No doubt Niall would catch up with her and she'd be in for a host of trouble when he did, but she kept her attention focused forward as Zel trotted through the gates. They moved along the gathering crowd toward the Jakida, who sat astride her horse near the front lines. Although Neri had no place alongside the ruler of the westlands, aside from her friendship with Livia and the cottage, she broke through the crowds and steered Zel forward.

The Jakida glanced at her, an emotionless expression, but mad thoughts filled Neri's head of filling the silence.

"This probably isn't the best time but I wanted to thank you for your kindness to me. I'm proud to stand alongside your folk as if I were one of them."

Neri's words caused no rivulet of emotion in the Jakida's voice. The woman's posture never altered and only her lips parted.

"You are as much of our kin and our land as any standing to fight today. I welcome you to fight with my children beside me."

Gratitude guttered in Neri's chest and her breath heaved with appropriate surprise. Only the Jakida's next move shocked her further. The woman leaned close and broke her regal pose.

"I doubt Livia would forgive me otherwise."

Neri stared, catching a sudden quirk at the corners of the woman's mouth. The Jakida turned to face the battle, regal and impassive once more.

Is it because of Livia, or because of Niall?

The truth of his heritage thorned its way into her head, but Neri took strength from the leader's offer as Zel moved of her own accord to slot between Viljo and Livia's horses. The Jakida set off to ride the length of the front lines, her voice strident as it rose over the heads and through the ears of those that stood to fight for her.

"We love our land. We live here and we love here. Today we will fight here. Think of your friends, your children and your families. Today you don't fight for me. We all fight for our freedom and for each and every person in this realm."

A horn blew. The Jakida's raw power swept over the crowd and Neri's fire rose to answer it. She tightened her grip on her blade and spied a cropping of rock that rose to the left. If the battle went ill she would ride there and send flaming arrows into the enemy.

"You carve the earth and I'll fill it." Livia's voice echoed over the baying crowd noise. "We only need enough to stem their flow as they approach."

Neri's mind scrambled. Viljo's gift was of the rock and the earth, Livia's of the raw elements of the weather. A water pit or river would slow the enemy down.

Viljo grimaced. "We won't have much time."

"I'll keep watch and give you room to work," Neri insisted.

The enemy began to move. Tense with Zel beneath her,

Neri joined those charging forwards. She saw the earth crumble as Viljo rode resolute on horseback, his hands clenched on his thighs. The skies rumbled in the distance and clouds loomed, gathering to lash thunder and rain along the enemy and the crack growing in the already pitted ground.

The front lines crashed with the enemy, pikes and bladesmen on foot moving first, the riders weaving between immediately after. Neri met the crush with her heart pounding and swung her blade to meet the enemy. A man on a brown horse lunged as he passed her, his gloved hand moving toward her face.

She lifted her hands to fend him off, but even through the arch of her arms, she saw him crumple and his head sail away from his body as someone else took a swipe at him. His horse, free of the weight, bolted away into their crowd.

Niall retracted his blade from the man's body, one hand still on his reins as he wheeled around to ride alongside her.

Neri sent a feral noise his way, adrenalin and heady fury powering through her.

"I don't need saving!" she yelled.

He glared his own wrath back at her. She turned, a footman with a pike swinging for her, and her blade cleaved the brittle wood of the pike in two.

Niall's horse plunged around the front of Zel to bring her up short. His blade slammed into the enemy's back and she swore.

"Let me fight!"

Niall's sharp bark of laughter only fuelled her *ai-tan,* and she held back the temptation to start fighting him instead as the hordes of the enemy broke over Viljo and

Livia's banks, bottle-necking onto the wide stretch of plains in one massive swarm.

Neri had a feeling they were outnumbered but had no real experience to make a confirmed guess. Instead she took a brief lull in enemies to lean low over Zel's neck, aiming for her ear.

"Get me away from him or he'll get himself killed trying to 'save' me."

Her hiss was heeded instantly. Zel plunged forward and charged bodily through two of the enemy. Neri almost fell when Zel staggered to a halt. She pressed her hands hard to Zel's neck and lifted her head as a deep, ground-shaking roar filled the air.

Dark greens and browns dominated the landscape in front of them and even a flash of icy blue and one of fiery red, the scales glinting in the sunslight peeking through the clouds.

Doubt ran like disease through the ranks as the battles faltered and several turned to see the sight.

Dragons.

Neri heard a horn calling their side back into lines but she couldn't draw her attention away.

Some were enormous, snouts snapping and showing lethal teeth the size of branches. All were on foot but two were also winged, each one bigger than the largest of all horses, and some rivalling the lower levels of the palace.

Zel heeded the horn and plunged in the direction of the Jakida, who had gathered Viljo and Livia to her already.

"Six dragons," Livia said, her tone awed. "Only two winged. I'll bet they've tried to get at least one of each element too."

The dragons stood waiting on the banks of the sharp slope Viljo had carved between them.

"They'll be able to get down the bank easily enough, but the river might slow a few," Viljo said.

Livia squinted and a soft gasp puffed out of her mouth. "Look at their heads!"

Viljo swore. "They've chained them with *freirer* ice. Of all the wicked, depraved-"

"What's *freirer* ice?" Neri asked.

"It controls dragons." Niall appeared beside her, his expression grim. "They make a harness for the head out of it, and it reacts with the dragon's scales to cause them pain. Makes them easier to manage."

"How is it made?"

He frowned. "It comes in crystal form naturally, but if they crush it and melt it with blade-metal, it can be formed into all sorts."

Neri searched the skies and hoped for a sign. Even if her firebird flew far away, she needed to know if her *ai-tan* could do it. The bubbling of magic under her skin was screaming in her veins, promising her success, but she wanted a sign.

The skies were empty. She received none.

I can't do nothing.

Trusting only in herself, she cast her glance around those she loved.

"We need to fight the best we can," the Jakida announced. "We can't risk retreating back to the settlement and them invading. We tell everyone to avoid the dragons and press on."

Niall scoffed. "Of course, avoid six dragons, so easily done. Half our folk aren't even on horseback."

Neri made sure nobody was looking her way as she crouched low over Zel's neck.

"I'm going to try burn the ice," she whispered. "I only

ask that you get me close enough with all the speed you can summon."

She put the request in despite knowing that *ai-tan* always came with a price. She thought of those she loved and how the dragons would likely stampede the entire westlands. She chose to take whatever price would be asked.

Zel didn't charge forward through the crush like Neri expected she would. Instead, the land simply slipped away. Neri caught a flash of silver water moving beneath Zel's shining white legs as they leapt, then a rushing blur of colour.

A savage jolt whipped through Neri's limbs as Zel landed and she tumbled toward the ground. Muddy grass rushed up to meet her and pain jarred through her shoulder and her hip as she crashed.

Gasping in ragged breaths, she stumbled to her feet. Ranks stared at her, faceless folk with eyes that could only watch as she cast her gaze up to the dragons nearby.

Her *ai-tan* prickled and the source of her gift's ire came from the dragons' heads. Platelets of ice, shining clear like glass in the blaze of the two high suns, were welded on the left side of each scaly head. She could feel their discomfort and the idea of her firebird suffering the same fate brought anger to the surface.

Zel snorted to gain her attention, and bent her forelegs, her nose to the ground. Neri clambered back on as those around her gathered themselves.

Furious shouts rose up but Zel was off weaving through the crowd to avoid capture.

Neri clung to Zel's mane and focused on the nearest dragon. She could almost sense its pain and flames erupted over her lifted hand, her emotion firing through the air as a burst of licking fire. It lashed up like a whip and hit the side of the beast's head.

The dragon roared and Neri could sense the ice fighting, spiking against her fire, but each little shard conceded. How many of the magical bindings she could fight before her gift rebounded and brought her to death she didn't know, but she pushed on.

"If I don't make it, tell Niall to bring the others here," she mumbled to Zel. "Our friends. Tell him."

Unable to fight with methodical process as she did with her candle-making, she took the dangerous path. She shut her eyes tight and forced her worst and best memories to come forward.

Niall holding her and whispering sweet words, her mamma lying dead as she grabbed what she could before the Governance arrived, Emelyn and Moonshine laughing with her, finding her gramma missing and knowing without doubt that she wouldn't be coming back, her gramma reading stories, her mamma's laughter.

And Niall. He filled every other memory with smiles and laughter and that pain of rejection that had burrowed itself so deep she may never find the end of it.

She burned and boiled in her pain and emotion as the ice bubbled under her gift and the harness dribbled free from the first dragon's head.

She barely noticed the beast breathe a snort of smoke and dark flame as it took flight and headed away from the battle, the distant scream of riders falling from the deadly height of its back.

She turned her pain onto the next one as images swam through her mind again.

Amis killing Hamlin, the absence of her family, Emelyn's petrified eyes full of horrors when they faced

The second tie broke free.

Zel stumbled and Neri swung her blade out on instinct, unable to open her eyes but intent on getting closer to the third dragon. Blades clashed around her, but she couldn't sway from the task.

Another jolt and she tumbled to the ground, the sickening thud jarring every bone in her body. She couldn't get up, couldn't open her eyes, but even as the fight surged on around her, she forced her *ai-tan* to find the ice through feel alone.

The third and fourth bindings slid free as the agony grew inside, each moment passing with painful slowness until she felt someone lifting her. The gentle hands suggested the person meant her no immediate harm, which was all that mattered at that moment.

The fifth binding fell free and the ground shook as the dragon stampeded away.

She cried, unable to focus enough on her eyelids to open them.

One more dragon.

She pushed her gift onto the final binding but it strained and sputtered. Any moment it would fail and rebound on her. Doubt filtered through her dim consciousness. If it rebounded then it would hurt whoever held her. Her awareness cleared enough for her to judge the moment when her rescuer's blade met that of someone else, and she fell onto her side as she concentrated on the last remnants of her gift.

The final binding broke and the dragon's roar of release echoed frighteningly close overhead as it took off.

She pulled her *ai-tan* back, her mind fracturing even as she nursed it, kindling the tiny guttering flame that remained and feeding it's weakness from the scattered remnants of her half-conscious mind.

Firm hands took hold of her, whether male or female, familiar or foe she didn't know. Then a voice cursed at how cold she was. Her lips trembled toward a smile.

He knows some really filthy words.

Shines of white flickered against her eyelids and the recognition of softness appeared at the forefront of her mind. The dazzle was Zel's mane and the arms anchored tight around her were Niall's.

Her body changed hands, where or who to, she couldn't tell.

"Neri, wake up." The commanding voice wasn't Niall's but it had enough strength and power in it to lend her some. "Your *ai-tan* is strong enough to recover fast. Open your eyes."

CHAPTER TWENTY SEVEN

Neri's body shuddered back to life under the Jakida's will. She opened her eyes to light that burned them and struggled upright, every part of her screaming in pain.

"You must go and rest now," the Jakida insisted. "You've done so well."

Neri eyed the Jakida holding her upright, both of them standing in the mud of the battlefield. She looked toward the enemy, now over the bank of the hill but dragonless.

Her memories formed fast and she looked around for Niall. Not seeing him, she struggled to break free and fell to her knees, launching up with all the grace of a new-born horse.

The battle was raging around them and she was back on the Jakirian side of the riverbank, but up ahead the shining light of Zel's equine form was darting back and forth with Niall still aboard. He fought with shadow cloaking his figure and her chest squeezed in torment.

Before she could run toward him or shout any words of worry, Zel moved. Almost as though Zel's allegiance existed only for her, Niall had to cling on as Zel whirled away from the enemy and steamed toward her.

Neri sagged as a woman flew toward her with a blade raised ready, but she was barely able to lift her own. She dodged the first attack on sluggish feet but the next hit sent her flying.

"Touch her and you're dead," Niall roared.

Zel skidded to a graceful halt as Niall's blade swooped

overhead and sent the woman tumbling to the ground.

Neri stared at the life leaving the woman's eyes and the urge to be sick bubbled up. She didn't fight it, doubled over in the mud. She might have mumbled something about it when Niall's arms snared around her, but he either didn't hear or didn't want to. She winced as he threw her up onto Zel's back and vaulted up behind her.

A scream echoed nearby and she clung to Niall's arm with both hands as she searched the chaos, until she spied Livia racing toward them still on horseback.

"*Ama* and Viljo are going to pull back." Livia had blood on her neck and arms. "The enemy won't try to attack the settlement until nightfall at least. There will be a temporary cease until morning, which they will break of course, but we have a short while until we need to be ready for an ambush."

Neri choked down the whimper and coughed with the effort, her throat burning and her insides pulling tight. The battle would continue despite all the death lingering in the blood-streaked mud puddles. The dragons were gone but nobody could promise her there weren't any more on the horizon.

Livia pushed her horse closer to Zel and grasped Neri's hand.

"I can't believe you managed to free the dragons." Her smile was brief and grim. "They won't forget you. You can rest though and Niall too. He'll stay and look after you."

The arms around her tensed but Neri knew Niall didn't care about fighting as much as she did. He anticipated her desire to defend her home but he didn't understand it. The dead around her might have chosen to fight, or been forced, but their families hadn't asked for a war to come and tear their loved ones away.

As they passed through the heavily guarded gates to the settlement, Livia led the way up the lane toward the palace. Neri wanted her cottage but she didn't raise any protest as they reached the palace steps and Niall lifted her down from Zel's back. She didn't say a word when he heaved her into his arms and carried her inside. She settled her head against his shoulder instead and hoped as many folk as possible would have made it out alive.

Niall settled her down on the long-chair in the library and Livia flopped next to her with a huge sigh.

"The troops will soon be returning and we have little time. Nobody will distur-"

Livia's voice faltered as the library door slammed open. Neri tried to tense her muscles for a fight but couldn't. Viljo strode into the room with blood-spattered clothes and the Jakida right behind him.

"When the first of the suns are just visible we will regroup at the gates." The Jakida sagged against a table. "There are the few we have held back taking the path to the hilltops already, but until then we must make our peace."

Servants brought food in, some of them looking as though they'd been fighting with bandages or smaller cuts visible. Neri forced herself to stand on legs that almost failed her as she saw Orin in the mix, chivvying her flock with tired admonishments. Neri moved toward the food and stalled when Orin caught her arm.

"I saw you do well in the field," Orin said. "We stand a good chance now the dragons are gone, and you may not believe it but those who get to spend a few final moments with their families owe it to you."

Neri shook her head and Orin smiled. With a soft pat on her shoulder, Orin moved on but Neri stayed by the food.

She helped folk pull the food out and took a little for herself. As she glanced down at her plate, her vision swayed. Despite feeling fine inside her skin had all the hallmarks of burnt flesh. Ash crumbled off her clothes, tiny flakes of bare skin fell along with dry mud as she moved, and several scrapes and cuts began to sting as she acknowledged them.

She ate a few mouthfuls but her gut was still churning and she couldn't manage much. The moment everyone else was distracted with their own thoughts or each other, she slipped from the library and ambled to her room.

The water in the bathing pool was still warm, so she struggled out of her clothes and clambered in. She couldn't risk floating and balanced her arms on the edge instead, her cheek on her hands.

Even without the dragons, it's going to continue. She pulled herself out of the water before she fell asleep. *Even if the west wins, the cursed forest is dying away and the Governance will be attacking next.*

Some of the clothes the palace had provided for her were still hanging unused, so she pulled on fresh trousers and a shirt and settled down to rest.

Her mind flirted with sleep several times, each attempt wrecked by memories of the battle as the suns fell, until she sat up to the sound of a horn blowing in the distance.

The distant hum of fighting echoed through the open archway to the deck.

"Vahda!"

She scrambled off the bed, grabbed her blade and her bow, her quiver half-empty of arrows that had fallen on the field. The door slammed into the wall as she threw it open and she hurtled down the halls. She passed the healers and ran down the lane toward the gates, the enormity of Zel's absence clear.

Rain dashed down in torrents as the sound of clashing metal and screams of pain tore the air. On reaching the gate, a guard put out his arm to stop her but she cannoned through.

Blue and red stood some way from her yet but she couldn't see Niall or Livia or the Jakida in the chaos, and it was nighttime so Zel wouldn't be a horse anymore.

She reached out to catch the reins of a riderless horse dashing past, but it moved too quickly for her to stop it. She groaned and stared around, her vision wavering.

Atop the bank stood a man, his red fighting clothes and the crown atop his head setting him apart from the rest of the enemy. Neri clenched her fists as her *ai-tan* roared in her chest. The crown atop his pale hair was made of *freirer* ice given the way it glinted in the firelight, and she dodged a fighting couple as she drew an arrow.

With so many folk between them the shot was impossible, and she looked around until she found a young boy on horseback. His hands trembled around a blade and he didn't even manage to lift it in time as she approached and grabbed his horse's reins.

"Get down. I need you to run back to the settlement and help the healers. I need your horse too."

The boy slid down and dashed off without another look, and Neri struggled to mount the horse from a combination of jumping and swinging her legs up its side.

The horse fought her as she urged it forward, but the lines of the battle were closing in on them and the Lord of the borderlands came into view again.

She used the hatred for all she'd been told about him to keep her resolve strong and the horse snorted as her gift spiked and sent it charging forward.

The Jakida was riding toward her but she didn't wait, her gaze fixed on Niall fighting two men up ahead.

She hauled on the reins and brought the horse to a stumbling halt, unable to hold it steady and fire arrows at the same time as the Jakida reached her side.

"Lords girl, go back to the settlement. You can't be thinking of fighting him yourself!"

Neri ignored her and raised her bow. Her quiver had only two arrows left, but she only planned to need one. She threaded the arrow and froze.

Her heart squelched in her chest and sucked breath from her lungs as Niall caught her gaze and followed the line of the arrow. Before she could re-align and fire, he turned on foot and charged toward the Lord of the Borderlands.

Neri urged her horse forward.

The lord had mounted a horse and sat up high as Niall reached him.

Something was said and Niall's blade twirled through the air. Neri winced as the lord's foot severed from his leg and his mouth twisted open, the sound lost in the crash of the battle.

Her horse ploughed through the rising water at the bottom of the bank Viljo had made the day before, and she kicked out at someone before they could attack, her foot making contact with their face.

At the top of the bank, the lord had one hand on his horse's neck, his other resolute around the hilt of his blade as his lips moved. Neri slowed her horse to a ragged halt, ready to spring in and grab Niall if she had to, as the words filtered across loud and clear.

"Are you going to kill me, bastard?" The lord uttered a ragged laugh tinged with pain. "Fighting for a land that never wanted a shade like you as part of it?"

Niall grinned, the sight of it wicked and fearsome. A warning.

So focused on them, Neri didn't see the woman dashing toward her with a pike in hand. A savage blow caught her shoulder and she tumbled from the horse's back as it shied away.

She hit the ground and twisted to anchor the crook of her knee around the woman's leg. Even as the woman tumbled down beside her, Neri clambered to her feet and brought her foot swinging to knock the woman out cold.

Her insides crunched, the sickness rising at what she'd done, but she forced herself to look for Niall again, her anchor in the madness of war.

Niall's blade danced through the air, then all too quick the lord fell to his knees. His eyes rolled wide as he stared down, the tips of both Niall's blade and his own now held against his throat.

A thunder of hooves turned Neri's head, and she sagged with relief as Viljo approached. Niall's surprise almost brought Viljo down as well, but he stayed his blade and returned to holding the lord in his gaze.

She flinched as something gentle tugged at her shoulder.

"They'll finish it," Livia insisted, her tone dark. "Can you mount?"

She indicated to the spare horse she had walking alongside her own but Neri shook her head. She had no way of mounting and walked forward beside Livia's horse instead.

Niall's head bent low to Viljo's, the disgust at being so close clear on both their faces. An infinitesimal pause passed before Niall smirked and Viljo muttered something with a dark look in his eyes.

Niall backed away from the lord and his lowered his blades as Viljo stepped forward and raised his own.

His blade moved in one precise stroke, and Neri shuddered as Viljo stood with his blade held aloft and the body of the Lord of the Borderlands crumpled at his feet.

A loud roar filled the air. Neri barely had the energy tot turn, but she clung to Livia's leg as they pivoted together.

The Jakida's horse flew like an arrow through the crowds that still battled. Most of them hadn't realised that the Lord of the Borderlands now lay minus his head.

"Come on, I'll leg you up," Livia muttered.

Neri stood beside the spare horse and kicked her leg out, grunting with effort as Livia used a foot to shunt her up onto the horse's back.

Niall stood with his blade raised as the Jakida dismounted her horse and picked the lord's head up by his hair. She offered the head to Viljo and his face twisted with disgust.

"It is your birth-right and your duty." Her tone was set, unyielding. "You must show your victory and take up your place as the new Lord of the Borderlands. You are their leader now, and our sworn ally."

Her voice carried no overt threat but Neri heard the finality in it all the same. Niall said he didn't want to rule the west, she knew that much, but he had been the one to disarm the lord and given Viljo the kill. She had no doubt that Viljo would carry that as a private embarrassment for some time to come.

Viljo took the head and his usual mask of dutiful countenance fell. The Jakida uttered another victory roar and he held the head aloft, urging his horse forward to ride along the bank.

Down on the remnant of the battlefield blades fell,

enemies continued to fight, and folk tried to flee and chase in equal measure. The entire crowd descended from petrified chaos into absolute bedlam.

Neri looked to Niall and her adrenalin quelled. In her assessment of the madness erupting around her she hadn't noticed him leave the field. Whirling around and almost falling from her horse's back she could see him already on a horse and riding toward the settlement gates with the slightest flicker of shadow around his shoulders.

She had no idea if Livia saw Niall leave but her friend leaned close all the same and insisted they return to the settlement.

"They will fight and flee now. Once the dead and wounded have been mourned and seen to, there will be a raucous party. It will be an absolute mess, so if you're thinking of leaving for the east still, at least stay until after that."

Neri let Livia take over the decisions and let her horse follow Livia's toward the settlement at a hasty trot. Panic simmered low at the thought of her rash words to Niall when she'd left the cottage. He had honour, more so than any man she'd known, and she'd dismissed him out of panic and spite. For all his insistence about her safety, he hadn't stayed to talk to her after the danger was done.

As they rode through the gates and up toward the palace, she resolved her intention to go east. She would stay a bit longer for Livia's sake and try to talk to Niall. She would apologise and explain that he would always be hers in her mind, but if there was anything outstanding like promises to Hareili or other issues standing between them, then she would let him go. Whatever the outcome with him, she needed to find a way east and she would going alone.

They dismounted at the palace steps and someone arrived to take the horses away.

Neri watched them go back down the lane, her heart sinking.

There's so much I still don't know about this place, and I'm having to leave it behind.

She tensed as Livia clasped her hand.

"We will need to be seen," Livia said.

Neri sighed. "We do?"

"Yes. You're not planning on disappearing for a day or two yet, are you?"

She looked at Livia's face, the worry creasing her brow and the flecks of mud and blood still spattered over her skin. She had a torn shirt at the shoulder as well, but other than that she looked unharmed. Neri guessed she would need to rest a while as well before she left, and organise some travel supplies from the kitchens.

"I'll stay for a bit." She glanced around. "I'm going alone though. I want a chance to talk to Niall properly, but I don't want him to know I'm going. He can have the cottage if he wants though."

Livia's eyes widened and her mouth flapped in shock, but after a moment she nodded.

"If you insist. I'm good at sneaking away. I'll pack your things in a bag by your back door and move the wax slabs outside under a cover so it's all ready for you. I'll make sure you have food to take as well."

Neri couldn't choke the automatic sob down in time. When she reached out for a fierce hug, Livia held her just as tightly.

"Now, you need to bathe." Livia wiped her damp eyes with renewed determination. "I do too. I'll ask the kitchens to send food to your room as well. Sleep, Neri."

Neri nodded. Sleep sounded so good. She turned away but stopped again as Livia's voice followed her.

"No sneaking off until we've had our celebration either. Take a few days' rest, then I'll be coming to get you ready."

Neri grimaced. "Alright, I won't."

As she walked into the palace and through the halls, she let her footfalls become a mantra.

Another day or two won't make much difference. Another day or two and I can see if the effigy works.

Another day or two.

CHAPTER TWENTY EIGHT

The palace lay in silence but Niall couldn't stop the clamouring in his head after the battle. He'd lingered in the shadows after returning to the settlement, content to watch Neri return with Livia. He needed her to rest and she wasn't fit enough to have the kind of argument she would inevitably start when she next saw him.

Not wanting to dwell in his room upstairs, he'd sought solace in the kitchens instead. Orin had grudgingly agreed to let him stay there on his own after the kitchens settled for the night, but only under the promise he stayed on the steps near the door out of the way and touched nothing.

He lifted the illicitly touched cup of wine to his lips, his gaze stuck on the low embers of the fire pit across the room.

Neri was safe. The battle was over, and Neri was safe. He'd even escaped the wearisome possibility that he would be expected to take over as Lord of the Borderlands, because he'd given the kill to Viljo.

That'll haunt him for a while. His lips lifted and he let out a weary laugh. *She's safe, and he can't have her.*

No doubt the question would be raised in the coming days of who would inherit Jakiris when the time eventually came, but perhaps now the Jakida would use her dislike for him to see Livia as the heir like she always should have done.

He tensed as the kitchen door swung open at the top of the steps. Soft footsteps pattered in, then stopped abruptly.

"Oh." Livia frowned down at him. "Why are you-actually, never mind."

Niall lifted his cup.

"I'm under strict instructions to sit here and not touch anything."

Livia snorted. "Orin doesn't trust you yet."

"She's a good judge of character then."

He moved his legs aside as Livia swept down the steps and past him into the kitchen. She helped herself to a cup of wine from the decanter on one of the many tables, then dragged a stool across to sit with him.

"What's your plan now then?" she asked.

He shrugged. "Stay here, if that's what Neri wants. She seems to think of it as home, so it'll do."

"You're not thinking of going back east at any point?"

"Why would I?" Niall drained his cup and set it on the step beside him. "Neri's here now. The west is safe and the borderlands will be under the Jakida's control, at least in terms of allyship. The east isn't safe."

Livia trailed her fingertips over the stone step nearest her. She still had marks across her cheeks and the side of her neck from the battle, and Niall wondered if she'd scared off any potential lady's maids. He had a vague memory that ladies were meant to have maids, but couldn't remember where he got that from.

Neri won't need maids, not unless she wants me to take over this place. He shuddered. *Hopefully she won't. We can travel for a while soon. I can take her to the Morlan mountains properly, show her the plunging pools and the flower meadows.*

"What about your friends in the east though?" Livia pressed.

Niall sighed and let his head drop back against the wall

behind him.

"Neri's mentioned them, I take it?" He waited for Livia to nod. "They're not dim. Several measures are in place to keep them all safe, and trust me, the Governance won't want to come up against some of them in a dark alley. I have one friend who Neri hasn't met yet, and she's the kind of woman who stabs first and asks later, if she remembers to."

"She sounds delightful."

Niall smiled, amused that Livia sounded intrigued rather than disgusted.

"She has her moments. Neri saw the few folk that needed saving when she met me. She hasn't seen the ones that enjoy the dark corners and the brutal fights yet."

"Because you didn't bother to introduce her to those ones?"

He shrugged. "Never got the chance to. Now she's safe here, and I won't be dragging her back there either. When the cursed forest falls, we can find ways to get people through safely."

Livia got up and fetched the decanter, refilling his cup then her own.

"I'm glad she has you, and that you pulled your head out of your rear enough to prove yourself."

"Hold that thought." Niall ducked his head, unable to keep the smile off his face. "She might be a bit angry with me again."

Livia groaned. "I'm not sure I even want to know. Actually, yes I do. Drama soothes me."

"She wasn't at the beginning of the battle tonight," he hinted.

"No, but neither were you."

"I was, but in the crowd. She wasn't. Ever heard of

bluestone?"

Livia's jaw dropped, her mouth popping as wide open as her eyes.

"You didn't."

"I did. Bluestone's easy enough to get if you know where, and all it takes is a quick swipe over the forehead to induce sleep."

He flinched as Livia launched to her feet, the decanter still in her hand swaying perilously close to his head.

"That's awful!"

Her voice slammed off the walls, loud enough to wake the entire settlement.

"I had to," he grumbled.

Livia dumped the decanter on the table and marched back to him with her hands on her hips. A crack of thunder rumbled ominously overhead.

"She deserves the right to make those choices! You can't go drugging her every time she wants to make a stand. Vahda, you're no better than *Ama*."

Niall pushed to his feet, his shadow responding to the immaculately lethal taunt.

"That was uncalled for-"

He froze as Livia's hands landed on his chest to clench fingerfuls of shirt, her nose almost touching his.

"No, your behaviour is uncalled for. Do that to her again, to anyone, and I swear now I will make sure you have no extremities left."

Another crack of thunder shook the walls and all Niall could do was stare as the furious woman, his sister of all people, pushed roughly past him up the stairs and slammed the door behind her.

He wiped a hand over his face. Livia had a point, not one he wanted to pay attention to, not yet, but she did.

I'll face it in the morning. Maybe give Neri a day or two of peace. She can come find me if she wants me.

He bit his lip and swiped his cup from the step to drain the contents. His room upstairs wasn't home or in any way homely. Someone, Livia he guessed, had given Neri one of the fancy ground floor rooms, but he had one of the draughty ones with the dark corners and cold, unforgiving furniture. Neri's cottage was even better, cosy and full of signs of her.

Probably best I start getting on everyone's good side if we're staying here.

He crossed the kitchen and washed up his cup, dried it, then placed it exactly where he'd found it.

He couldn't bring himself to go back to Neri's cottage without her, but they would have all the time in the coming days to talk and mend.

CHAPTER TWENTY NINE

Neri found it surprisingly easy to do as she was told and rest. Nobody disturbed her for two whole days at the palace, no visitors to her room except for servants who brought a continuous stream of food and wine.

No Niall either, but she let the resignation settle.

I pushed him away and away he went. I can't blame him either.

It would make going east easier. Her various scrapes and wounds from the battle were healing well, and Livia had sent several small missives via the servants bringing food to reassure her the preparations for her big escape were being handled.

It was afternoon two days after the battle that Livia sent a threat along with the food, a small note that read:

'Tonight the settlement is gathering in the square to celebrate Viljo's victory and to honour those we've lost. I will be at your room to dress you and so had you better be.'

Neri smiled and folded the note inside the hollowed out book Hamlin had once given her. It had taken all her effort and stealth to sneak out of the palace the night before and fetch her personal effects from the cottage, and Niall clearly had no intention of using it in her absence.

She bathed as long as she could in preparation for the party, then sat detangling her hair until Livia arrived.

"I have a dress for you," Livia announced without greeting. "Go put it on."

Neri did as she was told, not wanting to mention that the dark green gown would likely be the last she'd wear for a long while. It bared her shoulders and flowed, opening and closing around her calves, and she forced her lingering thoughts of what would be waiting for her in the east aside for one night.

"Viljo will want to talk to you," Livia announced as they left the room. "Consider it a warning, because he has a thing for you."

Neri squelched a groan. "I'm spoken for. Maybe. I don't know. For my side, I'm not interested in him."

"I know that, but it won't stop him trying. He may even try to convince you to go to the borderlands with him."

Neri hesitated as they walked down the palace steps.

The borderlands might have an easy route into the east, whereas the effigy would be unreliable, if it even worked.

Unless I try the effigy tonight. I promised Livia a few days and technically she's had that.

She shrugged. "I have no interest in pretending with him."

She did have an interest in talking to Niall, if only to chase away the inner torments taunting her over whether he really did love her or not.

Assuming he even shows up. He could be halfway across the land by now, free to follow his own path without being burdened by vows he made about me or his heritage in need of saving.

Livia kept a firm hold of her arm as they made their way down the main lane. Candles adorned the trees and banners flew from every roof and open doorway. Neri smiled to see the happiness in the faces of folk they passed, glad that the others would be safe even if she had to leave before it really began.

She followed Livia into the square and the cold wind blowing soon ebbed away. Neri smiled as Livia grinned with imp-like knowing and nodded her head over her shoulder. Neri turned and failed to stem the disgruntled groan that crept out of her mouth.

Viljo came to stand in front of her and her life-support in the form of Livia's arm disappeared with rapid speed, accompanied by the fading sound of smothered giggles.

"I wanted to bid you farewell for now." Viljo's eyes raked up and down before settling on her face. "I'm to go and take charge of the borderlands in the hope we can bring peace. I will ask you now if you'd consider joining me at my side but I suppose you'll decline."

Neri caught the question hidden in his steady, even tone and frowned. She had hoped to avoid anything awkward but now faced with the situation she had no choice except bulldoze on with blunt honesty.

"Sorry, yes, I have to. I wish you all good things, and I hope you can make the borderlands safe again, but I'm already someone else's."

Viljo nodded, sad resignation flickering in his eyes. He bowed low, his hands never unclasping from behind his back, walked away.

One down.

Neri looked around to find Livia and saw Niall instead. He stood leaning against a tree, his eyes full of brooding darkness and fixed on her. She set off toward him but strong hand gripped her arm and her *ai-tan* flared in frustration.

Turning to apologise to her assailant as they released her with a timely yelp, her words faltered and dried to ash.

"You've won," Hareili muttered. "Niall and I were never promised to each other. I hoped, but it's not going to happen. I doubt, even if we were promised to each other, that he would love you any less."

Hareili glared deeper with each word and walked away the moment her voice had ceased.

Neri looked again for Niall.

He was still gazing her way as she sidestepped staggering celebrators and dodged folk trying to invite her into a dance. He straightened up as she approached, but his arms hung stiff by his sides and he glowered his intent to bait her.

Neri stormed into his personal space and without a thought for propriety, feelings or anyone else that might be watching, she leapt forward. Her fingers snared up through his hair and dragged his head downward, her other hand curled around his upper arm.

Before he could rage at her, or possibly throw her over his shoulder and cart her off somewhere, Neri passed her lips over his.

She felt the silent catch choking his throat as his shock at her actions stilled him into compliance. She pulled her mouth away and did the only remaining thing she could. She still intended to leave without him. His life would be safe here now and she wanted to return, but she had to go and find her friends. She couldn't tell him either, not without him finding a way to stop her.

"I know there was nothing between you, you and Hareili, I mean," she babbled. "She told me just now but I knew it before deep down. I was just angry and tired from carving and she said things, and it was easier to believe them. You're the most honourable person I know and I'm really sorry."

She tumbled over the words and her voice shook, thoughts of him simply walking away once more filling her head and gripping tight in her chest.

She stared hard at the lump beneath his sweatshirt, the wax charm she'd given him long ago, unable to risk looking at his face and seeing the rejection.

His arms wrapping around her waist, loose but still there, calmed a little of her hysteria but she couldn't bring herself look at his eyes.

"You are the daftest woman alive." He chuckled. "If you thought I had no honour you wouldn't care for me at all. I knew that then and I know it now."

His fingers pressed beneath her chin and lifted her head up until her eyes met his.

"I admit arguing with you is half the fun, but even when I saw Viljo asking you to go with him I know your heart still lies with me."

Neri caught the flash of naughty ruefulness pass across his face as he smiled down at her.

"Where have you been the past two days then?" she demanded.

His brow lifted. "Where have *you* been? Did you try to come and find me? No, I thought you needed some space so I did my best to be absent, and you know patience isn't my strong point. I thought you might be angry as well that I stopped you fighting."

"You didn't stop me fighting though."

"I sort of did." He lifted a hand and wiped a thumb over her forehead. "I gave you a little something to help you sleep."

"You did what!?"

"I gave you something to help you sleep. I was going to come right back and let you fight me instead after. Better you're safe and angry than in danger."

"That's… Don't *ever* do that again."

"Alright." He grinned. "I doubt I'd get away with it a second time. Livia actually threatened my extremities when she found out."

Neri choked over a snort, emotions bubbling up with gleeful heat.

"You're going to kill me probably," he added. "When I had the lord of the borderlands under blade I made a trade with Viljo. I said I didn't want the title so he would leave you alone and I'd let him have the honour."

Neri pulled back in horror. Niall's grip tightened around her and his lips curled up, his eyes shining with devilish mirth.

"He agreed without too much reluctance. Even then he tried to convince you to go with him just now and I knew you would be mine no matter what. I'll still be the one to choose you before anything else."

Neri smiled as relief clashed with doubt and mingled with the hot tears on her cheeks. Unable to contemplate leaving him now, she almost told him of the portal and her plan. Niall chuckled, wiped her tears away with his nose, then kissed her deep and sweet. She felt her resolve begin to fade as Niall broke the kiss and brought his tender thumbs up to stroke her cheeks with a sigh.

"Now that the west is safe, and with someone as boring as my dear brother running the boundary settlement it will be, you won't ever have to be in danger again. I can relax a little and never have to worry about you running into mayhem. I won't let you."

Doubt shivered through Neri's mind once more. She and Niall might be safe but the images of Emelyn and her other friends, who had all taken various risks previously to protect her, deserved her loyalty.

He won't take it well when I leave.

"What about the Governance though?" she asked. "What about everyone stuck in the east? Em, Mik, Ma and everyone else?"

He sighed. "They know where to hide if all goes wrong. In time the cursed forest will fall, the Jakida said as much. It might take years but when there's a way through we'll need to face the east. Until then, we can be safe here. Make a life together."

Her heart sank. Their friends might not have years, and all it would take was one trip from the sanctuary if it got invaded by the Governance to land them all in trouble.

"We can't just leave them there," she murmured.

"There's no way back," he insisted. "The siren's kyne was destroyed and the forest is still between us. Even if there were another way, the east is too perilous, especially for you."

She forced a weak smile, her heart breaking as she stepped back.

"I've got to get something from the cottage," she lied. "I'll be back. Remember then, I'm yours and you are mine, always."

Niall grinned the lazy, seductive smile that she had missed so much for so long and it brought another stab of pain to her chest. He held onto her hand for as long as possible as she stretched away from him. She forced herself to break the contact, her chest aching as though she'd left half of it behind.

She searched the celebrations and caught Livia's eye. Her friend was deep in heated conversation with Zel, who also turned and nodded at her. Zel obviously knew what she intended but she could trust Zel not to tell Niall until she'd gone.

Livia joined her and they walked side by side in tense silence up the main path. They turned into her lane and only when they approached the back of the cottage did Livia speak.

"I've set everything out. I figured you might try to sneak off tonight, but I'm going to miss you so much. I wish I could keep you here but I do understand. I'll move the wax to safety once you're gone and you may even be able to come back through with any luck."

Tears streaked Livia's face and Neri had to wipe her own from her cheeks as Livia pulled into a tight hug.

"Okay, I'll do my best. I need to forge the blocks together quickly, then I'll change my clothes."

Livia helped heave the wax blocks into place on the grass, then stood aside as Neri set about warming the edges until they fused together. By the time she was done, she couldn't help wondering why Niall hadn't come looking for her yet.

He would have started shouting by now if he had.

The mere thought of him, of what she intended to do alone, leaving him behind, had her stalling. He might never forgive her, and she might never find a way back.

It would be a dangerous road to the borderlands through the east, and while she knew Viljo would let her in once they reached his gates, she couldn't guarantee anyone's safety or her own.

Her *ai-tan* surged at the thought and she flinched as flame flickered out from her palm.

"No!"

The fire curled through the air and flicked at the length of wick looping out from around the kyne embedded in the wax effigy before she was ready. The pearlescent glass head of the firebird glowed as the makeshift wick caught alight. In moments the flames engulfed the effigy in dancing orange fire.

"No time to change."

Livia appeared beside her and threw her quiver strap over her head along with her bow and her pack. Neri tensed as Livia buckled the blade about her belt and both of them lifted their head to the nighttime sky and the dancing stars.

As if answering the call of the burning kyne, a sudden blaze darted across the horizon, a ball of fire that flew and swooped with ultimate grace. The firebird had honoured her call once again.

She only had one shot and ignored Livia's soft gasp behind her as the flames grew. The wavering image of something other than the trees behind her cottage appeared, it was blurry but didn't break. She could smell heat and see vast browning fields in the flames, and hoped for a settlement near to the sanctuary.

She stepped forward, lifting a hand to the shimmer in awe.

"You are my sister," Livia called after her. "By blood now as well as by choice. I'm so sorry."

Her voice sounded echoed and far away as Neri raised a hand to the flames and moved forward.

She flinched as a swirl of cake-spice scent wrapped around her and an unyielding embrace snared her waist. She stumbled toward the heat, her arms pinned to her sides by whoever held her as the familiar voice growled right against her ear.

"Did you really think I'd let you go without me that easy?"

Her body jerked forward and the weight of Niall's hold disappeared. His fingers slid desperately over her hand as a blinding flash of flame seared all hope of sight away.

"Niall?" Neri hit something hard and the scent of dust plumed around her. "Niall!"

The sear of the flames dissipated and she lifted her head, her limbs aching as remnants of ash danced into nothing, until only the dust remained to catch powerful rays of sunslight.

"Niall?"

No answer.

She looked around, nostalgia and disbelief choking a laboured breath from her lips.

The candle shop had been abandoned for a while by the look of it, the baskets long since ransacked and the dirt blown in through the windows layering every surface. A gust of arid heat wafted through the open window, and she recognised the lane outside with a sinking heart.

I'm in the east. She shook her head and wrapped her arms around her middle. *This is what I wanted.*

She had to hope Livia had pulled Niall back before he could follow her all the way through. He would be mad with fury, but he'd be safe.

Or he's here somewhere and likely to annihilate me when he next sees me.

She wasn't sure which option was worse. Niall knew his way around the east far better than she did, but she'd have to take her chances alone on the road if she was going to find him.

With her pack on one shoulder, her bow and quiver on the other, and her blade at her belt, she faced the shop door.

Next stop, the sanctuary. Then I'm taking everyone back home with me.

ACKNOWLEDGEMENTS

This book has been at least two decades in the rewriting, so thank you to everyone who encouraged me to keep writing, to my family and also my writing family as always, your support means everything to me – Anna Britton, Debbie Roxburgh, Samantha Williams, Sally Doherty, Marisa Noelle, Emma Finlayson-Palmer, Katina Wright, Alison Hunt, writing Twitter, everyone who joins #ukteenchat, the WriteMentor crew, libraries and shops who will take a chance on this series and give this indie author a chance to reach more readers, and to the readers who will find these books in the future.

THANK YOU!

ABOUT THE AUTHOR

While always convinced that there has to be something out there beyond the everyday, Emma focuses on weaving magic realms with words (the real world can wait a while). The idea of other worlds fascinates her and she's determined to find her own entrance to an alternate realm one day.

Raised in London, she now lives on the UK south coast with her husband and a very lazy black Labrador who occasionally condescends to take her out for a walk.

Aside from creative writing studies, an addiction to cake and spending far too much time procrastinating on social media, Emma is still waiting for the arrival of her unicorn. Or a tank, she's not fussy.

For the latest news and updates, check the website or come say hi on social media:

www.emmaebradley.com
@EmmaEBradley

www.ingramcontent.com/pod-product-compliance
Lightning Source LLC
Chambersburg PA
CBHW031310210726
48287CB00005B/1488